The
Relic

ALSO BY WILLIAM HENSHAW

The Doomsday Tablet
The Sentinel's Map

WILLIAM HENSHAW

The
Relic

ISBN 978-0-473-51084-8

A catalogue record for this book is available from the National Library of New Zealand.

www.williamhenshaw.com

For my family, without whose support
this story would not have been written.

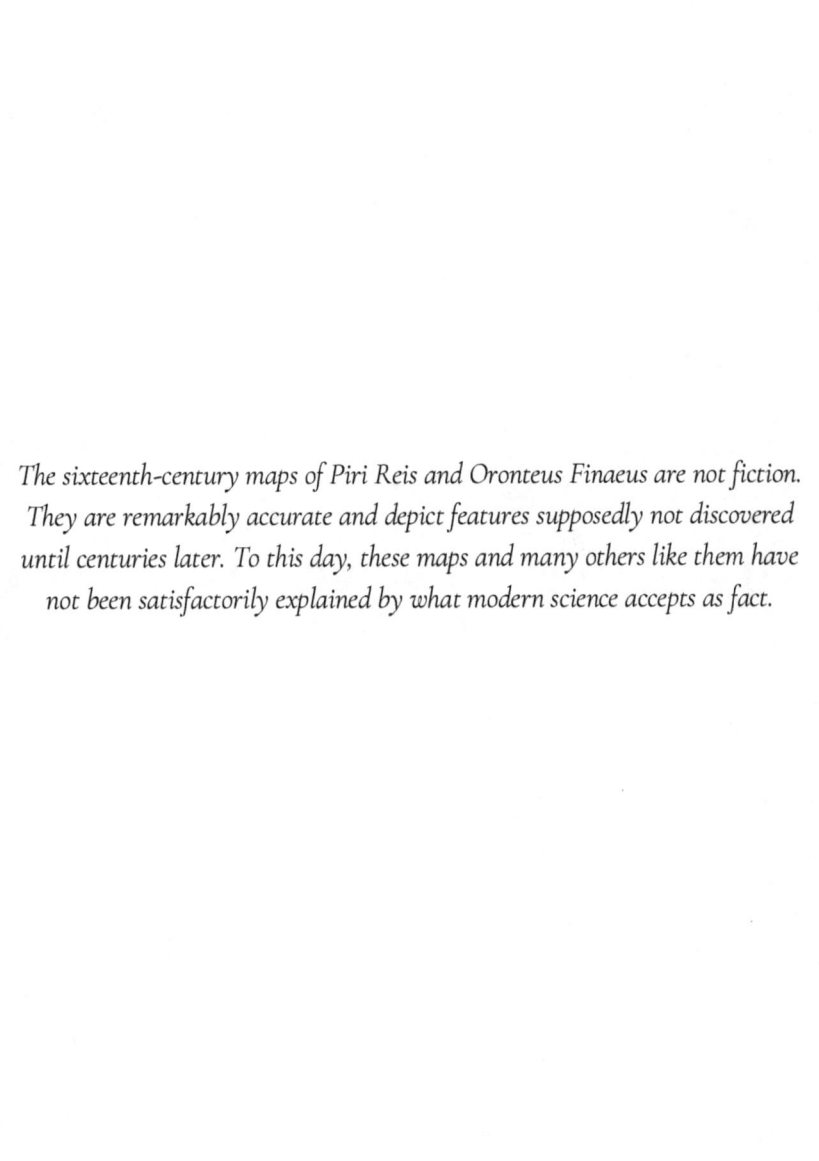

The sixteenth-century maps of Piri Reis and Oronteus Finaeus are not fiction. They are remarkably accurate and depict features supposedly not discovered until centuries later. To this day, these maps and many others like them have not been satisfactorily explained by what modern science accepts as fact.

I

Richard Summers was looking forward to getting back home to his family, and to the relative warmth of Melbourne in July. Although midwinter in Australia, it was warm compared to where he'd just picked up his two passengers. As he'd left Ross Station it was minus forty degrees Celsius, and locked in the endless darkness of the Antarctic winter.

After a six-month assignment at the station, the men were very pleased to see Richard. They had made much of his last name; rather ironic for a pilot whose job it was to ferry scientists and visitors from one of the coldest and bleakest outposts on the planet.

This particular flight, the Antarctic–Australia run, at this time of year, was not one Richard relished. It wasn't just the flight distance – many hundreds of kilometres of ice, followed by thousands of kilometres of frigid, blue-black ocean – but the arduous nature of it. The weather conditions were usually very poor and the wind furious.

The terrain of Ross Island also made it a very dangerous flight path, particularly in white-out conditions. The aptly named Mount Terror and its neighbour, Mount Erebus, both well over three thousand metres, whipped up the winds even more. Every pilot who flew to Antarctica remembered the Erebus crash of Flight 901.

Richard's plane carried cargo, scientific equipment and samples, and two passengers. One of the men had been on edge at the start of the flight, and Richard had initially just put it down to the man's strong desire to get back home. He knew that months of darkness and long periods of confinement, when the weather was simply too wild to venture outside, could deeply affect a person. Now, more than halfway to Melbourne, the man's behaviour had become problematic.

Richard had been absorbed with the weather conditions for the past few hours. Outside, a battle raged noisily, the hail and wind fighting to push inside the small cabin. They'd struck odd patches of vicious turbulence, and he knew there was the risk of a lightning strike. It had been a struggle to maintain a constant altitude safely above the Antarctic mountains, thousands of metres above the tops of the icebergs that rose starkly out of the sea far below.

The troubled man was now jumpy, constantly looking out the windows on both sides of the plane. He was muttering to himself and nervously shifting in his seat. His face was almost alabaster and had an unhealthy sheen of sweat, even though it was damn cold in the cabin. *Was the man ill?* They had all certainly seen weather conditions like this, in fact worse than this, many times before. *Something* had made this trip different.

"Please God, help me," the stricken man moaned to himself. *What the hell is the pilot trying to do? He must be crazy.* The man stared, open-mouthed and frozen with terror, through the cockpit glass as yet another iceberg seemed to hurtle towards them. It was a monstrous, jagged blue-white cliff and would be upon them in seconds. Then, just like the ones before it, it vanished as though it had never existed. *Something's terribly wrong.* The man could feel his breathing being constricted and the life being squeezed from him. He looked across at his colleague a few seats away and was astonished to see he was peacefully sleeping. *How can he sleep?*

It's obvious the pilot's insane, flying so close to the tops of these huge icebergs. Either that, or the plane's instruments have malfunctioned. The man couldn't see the dark water below, but he was sure they must be flying way too low. He was panicked, pinned to his seat with fear. Looking down at the strange souvenir he was clutching, his fingers white from his vice-like grip, he barely noticed that he'd emptied his bladder.

Maybe the pilot's delusional. Maybe he just can't see the icebergs. Yes, that must be it. They're only visible for a few moments, and then they somehow disappear from view. The pilot just hasn't seen them. We're going to crash if I can't make him understand the danger! This is such an important object, such a beautiful object; he needs to be brought to his senses. The others were wrong about this stone. It's 'just an ordinary stone,' they said. 'To be analysed and dated,' they said. 'So what if it happened to have been found under thousands of years of ice? So what if it's impossibly uniform and smooth?'

But they didn't understand. The man could *feel* it. There was something truly special about this beautiful stone. It was *too* smooth and so perfectly symmetrical. It simply had to be man-made. He gripped it tightly as he felt sweat running down the side of his face. Outside was an ominous, dark chaos, and he could see in his mind that something unimaginably horrifying was happening to them all. He was now sweating profusely. "Look out!" he screamed.

Richard Summers could see nothing out of the ordinary, but the man kept shouting and pointing wildly.

Then he stopped yelling as quickly as he'd started.

"It's gone," he muttered in confusion.

Is he drunk? Is he delusional? Is he sick? Richard was about to tell him to calm down and shut up, that it was hard enough flying the plane without someone shouting at him, but as he turned, something stopped him.

The little remaining colour drained out of the man's face, and his eyes bulged from sheer terror as he looked directly ahead. "*Iceberg!*" the man mouthed.

Richard quickly turned back but could see nothing, and the altimeter still read 5,000 metres. There was no iceberg ahead. *What the hell's going on?*

The other passenger had now woken up and was just staring dumbfoundedly at his friend.

The plane hit some fierce turbulence and lurched violently, all the instruments suddenly dying. Richard quickly tapped the altimeter, the oil pressure and fuel gauges, but they gave no response. He felt an awful sense of foreboding in the pit of his stomach, rising up into his throat. Without a functioning altimeter in this poor visibility, they were in trouble. *Big trouble.* Richard checked each of the instruments hurriedly, looking for electrical faults, magnetic interference, anything that might help. But he found nothing.

It didn't take long for the two passengers to see that something was now seriously wrong. The iceberg man panicked. He started screaming at the pilot to do something, and jumped out of his seat. Richard could see the man was carrying something. It looked like some kind of polished stone.

"Seat belt!" Richard shouted. This is crazy. *What the hell is this guy doing?* The man's eyes were still wide, holding a look of uncontrolled terror. With the stone firmly gripped in his right hand, he lurched toward the cockpit. Richard could see he had wet his pants. He glared at the other passenger, imploring him to help, but *he* seemed to be stunned. *What the hell is wrong with these people?*

Finally, the second passenger seemed to snap to his senses. He leapt up and charged at iceberg man.

Thank God. We have to get this maniac to calm down and stay seated.

Richard Summers turned back to the controls, and at that moment he sensed the plane was losing altitude. Before he had time to recheck all readings, they hit another patch of rough turbulence. The plane dived, plummeting a few hundred metres in just a few seconds, and wind shear pitched it sharply to one side as it plunged. The fall jolted Richard sideways, and he saw the iceberg man thrown violently against the fuselage. The other passenger was hanging on to his seat, half standing, half falling. He was clutching a small rucksack that had struck the back of his head a moment before; a thermos of coffee had smashed and dumped most of its contents on his clothing. Everything had gone crazy.

Richard wrestled with the joystick as the plane lurched sharply, thinking no one would believe this story, *if* he lived to tell it. In less than two seconds, these thoughts had passed through his mind. As the plane lurched again, a solid object struck his head forcefully. Instinctively, he put his hand to the back of his head and felt something warm and wet. Then the noise in the cabin gently faded out, and so did everything else ...

"*What have I done?*" iceberg man screamed. Just seconds before, it had suddenly become clear to him. His prize, the stone he had been clutching – his artefact from the deep past – was somehow linked to this insanity. Maybe it was the reason the pilot had been trying to kill them all. In a moment of madness, he had hurled the stone towards the cockpit and watched as it made sickening contact with the intended target. As soon as he had released his grip on the beautiful relic, an oppressive and suffocating fear had given way to a cold realisation of what he'd done.

His colleague was shouting something at him, but all he could hear was the roar of the engines as the plane started to dive.

2

At Ross Station, Peter Hennessy was preparing for the long flight back to Australia, and he wasn't looking forward to it. The trip over from Melbourne to Ross had been rough. The winds were unpredictable and strong, and convergence of the Pacific and Southern oceans played hell with the wind currents, causing bone-shaking, stomach-clenching turbulence. And, as if that wasn't enough, the old Hercules aircraft was cold, uncomfortable and very noisy. The Ross Station scientific base, he reflected, may well be one of the most uninviting places in the world. It was certainly the most hostile environment Peter had ever seen in his thirty-nine years. Not that he regretted going there. Actually, he was glad to have had the opportunity. *In fact*, he thought, *it's probably only a matter of time before tourism starts to take off* – the sort of adventure holiday that would appeal to people looking for that 'frontier experience'. Or middle-aged men who had decided their lives were too dull. *And at least it's not snowing today.*

He was looking out into the pale, moonlit ice shelf around him. Peter had only been at Ross for a few days so hadn't got used to the perpetual darkness; it was nearly eleven in the morning and it was black as night. It all served as a good reminder that Antarctica was the wildest, remotest

8

continent on the planet, and he looked forward to getting back home and seeing sunlight again.

He hadn't known what to expect at Ross Island, but he'd had some sort of vague notion that it would be a small, lonely place separated from the main land mass by an ice-cold, iceberg-littered ocean. Of course, it wasn't like that. Ross Island was indeed separate from the Antarctic mainland, but it was separated by the *frozen* Ross Sea. In the pale, eerie light of the new moon, it just looked like part of the rest of the Antarctic – you could walk from the mainland to the island, though Peter couldn't imagine anyone really wanting to do that, especially at this time of year.

During the winter months, there was no daylight at the Ross Island station; the sun's warmth did not reach inside the Antarctic Circle until early August, and not to Ross Island until September.

As an anthropologist, his particular skills weren't often called for in the Antarctic. Peter had never even thought of travelling there before – at least not until he'd been told by a friend at ANARE, the Australian National Antarctic Research Expeditions organisation, that the Ross people were excited about a strange new find. Ice cores they'd been drilling had brought up some plant matter from deep under the ice. The initial tests indicated that it was apparently a member of the *Vitis vinifera* family – more commonly known as the grape. There was nothing particularly extraordinary in that, except it didn't appear to be millions of years old. There was no way to reliably date the sample at Ross, but the scientists there thought it might only be thousands of years old. And the depth of the ice cores they were taking out suggested it should be about 6,000 to 8,000 years old. Quite remarkable, Peter had thought, because it was generally accepted that Antarctica had been frozen for millions, not thousands of years.

Of course, it probably *had* been frozen for millions of years – this wouldn't be the first time bored station personnel had devised an elaborate hoax. But what was also remarkable was that the ice cores were bringing up a fine-grained sediment from a depth of about 800 metres. Peter knew the kind of sediment they expected was known as 'coarse glacial till', meaning it had been scraped from the earth's surface by glacial movement. Fine sediment had to be carried by rivers before they froze into glaciers.

True, it wasn't really a job for an anthropologist, but he had always had a thirst for knowledge and adventure, and he'd never seen Antarctica so had asked to be included in the next flight over. He'd said he wanted to see 'a continent largely unaffected by the evolution of man'. But he knew, at least in his own mind, that if Antarctica had been more temperate a mere 6,000 years ago, then man *could* have lived there, and that thought intrigued and captivated him.

Before he had arrived, they'd brought up a couple of unusual stones in the ice and sediment, too. In fact, Peter was bringing back one of these as a kind of souvenir of the trip. They had sent the first one off with the last flight out, but that flight had been reported missing a few days ago. Peter had promised Kelly he would have this one analysed. 'There's something strangely interesting about these stones, Peter. I'm dead sure of it,' Kelly had said.

He took the oddly symmetrical rock out of his coat pocket. It was very smooth and black, about the size of a tennis ball, though elliptical in shape. He thought it looked too even, too smooth to have occurred naturally – it was *too* symmetrical and almost had a polished look. Then again, the natural erosive action of a river could have produced it. It very likely was a natural piece of rock and had probably been there since before the last ice age. But he was curious anyway.

As a scientist, when curious about something, he usually investigated until he was satisfied. Even as a small child he had always done that. He still carried a vague recollection of inserting his father's keys into an electrical outlet and turning the power on 'to see what happened'. Then he had dutifully reported to his father, 'Daddy, the house shook.'

Strapped into an old worn seat in the Hercules, he was still holding the beautiful stone. He wasn't sure exactly what sort of analysis he wanted done on it. It should be dated, of course, if that was even possible, and its composition analysed. Then maybe he could keep it on his desk as a souvenir or paperweight. There seemed to be something special about it. It would make a good conversation piece, at the least.

He slowly began to thaw out as he waited for take-off. Just walking across the ice to the landing strip in the darkness had been an ordeal. The outside temperature was minus thirty-five degrees Celsius, and the wind-chill factor made it a good deal worse. The air was so cold it hurt his face. He had stayed inside almost the whole time he'd been there, and when he'd been outside briefly, he had learned to breathe slowly. The frigid air was *so* cold it actually hurt to breathe. Some of the other men ventured out occasionally – those who had been there in summer said they used to go out regularly to kick the football around, the temperature getting up to around ten degrees on some sunny days. But in winter, they said, there weren't many days you could 'kick the footy'. For a start, you'd need a good moon and a clear sky. Peter didn't know whether they really did that, or if it was just talk to impress visitors.

He considered himself lucky the station was near the coast, for far inland he knew winter temperatures reached an unimaginable minus eighty degrees. Cold enough to kill a man in just minutes. And at the South Pole, it was dark for six months of the year, and daylight for the other six, the sun travelling around the horizon, never dipping out of sight.

The airfield itself was nothing more than a strip of ice they kept cleared with a small bulldozer called a Bobcat. A long, thin ice-skating rink, marked out with half-metre-wide lengths of bright-orange nylon, it didn't inspire a lot of confidence. It was difficult enough just walking across the ice, let alone trying to race an aircraft over it. Even the pilot had admitted that take-offs and landings were 'a bit dicey' on the ice.

During take-off, he was more nervous than he'd been before any other flight. Looking out the small window, out into the endless white and grey gloom that was their world down here at the bottom of the planet, he could see the volcanic Mount Erebus just out to the east. In the dull moonlight it looked bleak and menacing.

He thought again about the missing plane. There had been nothing: no word of a crash, no sightings of floating wreckage, no word at all of the pilot or the two contractors he was taking back home. They'd had some extremely bad weather the day of the flight, and by now everyone had assumed the worst. The plane had probably crashed into an iceberg and dropped into the freezing Southern Ocean. If the impact hadn't killed them, hypothermia would have quickly finished the job. He had heard some of Ross's people say they should never have used the small plane in that sort of weather. Everyone was an expert – *after* the fact.

Once in the air, he started to relax a bit. There were only a few passengers, and none of the others seemed the least bit nervous, although no one was talking – the plane was just too noisy. Soon his thoughts wandered to more familiar ground. At thirty-nine years of age, as a trained scientist, he was a little more careful with his experiments than as a child, but sometimes he was just as inquisitive, and his mind still occasionally led him into trouble. He had also found, almost immediately on arriving at Ross, that life was less complicated. It was tough enough just *living* down there, and it appealed to his sense of adventure. If he had any worries before he got there, they paled into insignificance compared with the wild battle the Antarctic winter raged against the station. The hostile environment outside helped him put things into perspective.

"Would you like a coffee, doctor?" Jack asked, bursting through Peter's thoughts. He was holding a rather dirty-looking thermos flask. Jack was one of the mechanics from Ross, returning to his family after an eighteen-month stretch. Jack always called the scientific staff 'doctor'; it got confusing sometimes. Most of the others had just called him Pete.

"No thanks, Jack," he said. Jack shrugged and took his seat. Peter closed his eyes and allowed his thoughts to wander back to the past again. He reflected that almost nobody ever saw the real Peter Hennessy. It had nearly always been that way.

"Somethin' on your mind, then?" Jack enquired.

"I was just thinking of my family," replied Peter, keeping it simple.

"Me too, mate. Haven't seen 'em in more than a year. I was s'posed to go back last summer, but my replacement was killed in a car accident, and they offered me more money to stick it out."

"Funny business about that other plane," Jack added. Peter looked over, raising his eyebrows and waiting for Jack to finish the thought. "That bloke guarding that stone we found like it were a jewel or somethin'. They were all a bit edgy, if you ask me. *And* he couldn't wait to get away. Then the plane disappearing like that. We'll probably never find out what happened, you know."

"Well, there's always hope ..." Peter's words drifted off.

Both he and Jack knew there was almost no chance of survival. There's very little land between the Ross Ice Shelf and Australia, and the Southern Ocean is cold enough to kill a man in minutes.

"If the plane went down, let's hope they find the wreckage, at least. The families of those men will need to know what happened." Peter thought again of his father.

"Yeah, true enough," said Jack.

"It was my father I was thinking of before. He died when I was young. Went out fishing and never came back." It had been twenty-five years since Michael Hennessy had died, but Peter had never forgotten, at fourteen years of age, the pain he had felt when his aunt told him his dad was gone. *Taken by the ocean, just like those other men,* Peter thought.

"He taught me how to fish when I was a boy, and we used to go out on the bay most summers," Peter said. Dr Michael Hennessy had been a keen fisherman and often said he couldn't get away from his practice as much as he would have liked.

"Must've been nice, though, havin' a dad," Jack said. "I never had much to do with me dad, with him and mum being divorced. But it must be kind of like havin' *me* for a dad," Jack added thoughtfully.

Peter wondered what it would be like to leave your wife and children for a year. He didn't think he could do it, even if he wanted to. Peter remembered going to the beach with his father, years before. Michael had taken him many times during the summers of his childhood, and they'd walked, kicked a football around and fished occasionally. Once Peter caught a shark. Well, it was only a young gummy shark, about a foot long, but a shark nonetheless, and he had been fiercely proud of it.

"Do you have kids, Jack?"

"Yep, two girls. And I miss 'em heaps. One's nine, and the other's eleven now." Jack pulled out his wallet and dug out a dog-eared photo of two little girls smiling cheekily at the camera. They were sitting one on each knee of a woman who would once have been attractive were it not for the obvious wear in her features. *All the same, she looks happy,* Peter thought.

"They'll be there to pick me up ... I hope," Jack said with a wink. The background of the photo looked to Peter like a serene, semi-rural setting. A lot of big trees and no houses in sight. "Only an hour's drive to our place, and then there'll be a list of chores the missus wants me to do," he said happily. Jack put the photo carefully back into his weather-beaten wallet and stuffed it back into his pocket.

"Maybe I'll take the girls fishin' this summer, but I don't reckon they'll take to it much. If it's horses, though, they're keen as mustard." Jack sat back in his seat, closing his eyes for a moment. "Poor buggers," he muttered.

"What's that?" Peter asked, not sure he heard correctly.

"Those blokes on the other plane," Jack explained, closing his eyes again.

Peter closed his eyes, too, and didn't really even try to stop the familiar thoughts of a night a long time ago.

Many times he had imagined his father out in the boat with his friends; it was always dark in his mind. He wasn't sure whether it *was* night when it happened, but they usually went out fishing before dawn. He imagined the wind whipping up the waves, the freak wave catching their boat awkwardly and overturning it so quickly they hardly knew what hit them. The other two men had managed to swim to safety – some six kilometres away – but Michael had a weak heart. The shock of the cold water and the blind panic of being thrown into a dark, violent sea must have brought on an attack. The others didn't even know he'd gone until they reached the safety of the shore – they were damn lucky to make it. The image of his father hopelessly fighting against the freezing waves filled his mind as Peter drifted off to sleep.

In what seemed like only an instant later, Peter knew something was wrong. His heart was racing, his stomach knotted and he was sweating. He quickly looked all around to see what had happened. Everything seemed okay, but something had set him on edge. The other passengers, those he could see from his seat, all looked relaxed. He took a deep breath to steady his nerves. *What is it?* Out the small window, he could see daylight. At last! The sky was still dirty and threatening, but it was light at least, and nothing seemed to be wrong. *Something* had woken him, though. Then the dream came flooding back into his mind's eye. He'd seen his father's face; Michael Hennessy was trying to warn him of a terrible disaster looming. But no matter how hard his father tried, no matter how loud he screamed the words, Peter just couldn't understand him.

Shaking off the oppressive feeling, Peter looked at his hands to see his stony souvenir, gripped so tight his knuckles were white. The picture in his mind was still vivid – his father's clear, green eyes, the look of grave concern and warning on his face.

The feelings it left unsettled him; he hardly ever remembered his dreams and couldn't think of the last time he'd had a nightmare. And he had no idea what his father was trying to tell him. The intensity of the dream, coupled with the fact that he remembered it so clearly, made him wonder ...

He put the stone back in his pocket, got to his feet somewhat unsteadily and went forward to try to find that coffee. Maybe he'd better stay awake for the rest of the flight. They would be landing in Melbourne in a few hours.

3

Jimmy Davis didn't feel very well. Yesterday he thought he'd caught a cold, but today he felt like he'd been hit by a train. He ached all over and could hardly move. He'd had the flu before, but never like this, and never so quickly. As he lay on his bed, he wondered what the temperature was inside his hut; it seemed cold but he was bathed in sweat. Macquarie Island's penguins would just have to wait; he wasn't going out today. Outside, the temperature would be about zero degrees. For all but three months of the year it was *about zero degrees*, and raining, in this godforsaken place. Occasionally, when the wind picked up, it was a couple of degrees colder, but never for long. As he lay there, he felt worse in each new moment of lucidity; just breathing hurt like hell. He couldn't even drag himself out of bed. *This fever has to break soon*, he thought, *and then I'll fix that damn aerial and call for the doctor ...* He half smiled to himself as he imagined Gary's reaction when he called for Doc.

Gary Masters was the Macquarie Research Station boss, and Jimmy knew Gary didn't like the fact that he lived so far away from everyone else. Twice this year he had lost contact because of bad weather, and that was more fuel for Gary's argument. Masters was a good project leader, Jimmy thought; he cared for his people as much as he cared for their results. The only reason he allowed Jimmy to be so isolated was Jimmy's irrefutable logic that, as an ornithologist, he had to be close to the birds he studied. His hut was close to colonies of many types of penguin, including the only known royal penguin rookery. Jimmy had spent many hours watching these uniquely beautiful birds marching some 150 metres up the rocks to their home, with their two bright-yellow plumes sticking straight up from the sides of their heads like antennae. It was a wonderful sight, and not many people could say they had seen it. Jimmy even had the privilege, once, of nursing an injured royal penguin back to health, and working with the rookery to ensure the bird was accepted back in. They were beautiful, noble birds, and for much of the past few months, they had been his only real company.

Even so, as Jimmy had pointed out to Gary, he was usually within quick radio contact of the station. They still used the old VHF radios, having found them very effective on the island, despite their use of satellite telephone communications to the rest of the world. No matter what Gary said, they both knew that generally communication was pretty good.

He lay there a little bit longer, then decided he had better make the supreme effort and force himself out of bed to get some more water – his profuse sweating was dehydrating his body rapidly. He struggled to sit up, but it was too much of a strain, and he slumped back on the bed. Lying there, he consoled himself that at least he was better off than those poor people in the plane.

Three days earlier, Jimmy had heard a plane flying close overhead. The storm was noisy but he could still tell the plane was too low and would be well short of the airstrip. Then he thought he heard a crash, but it was hard to be sure. After donning his thickest woollen jersey and his foul-weather gear, he stepped out into the hail and sleet. Visibility was barely five or six metres, and the gale-force winds were certainly not helping.

Jimmy knew he should stay inside, but he went to check anyway. He would be the first there – maybe the only one there if the others hadn't heard the plane or had radio contact. If there were any survivors, they would need immediate attention, and protection from the weather. He had found the wreck in twenty minutes; it was a small passenger aircraft, maybe privately owned, for he could see no government or corporate identification. His face was stinging from the freezing sleet, and the wind pushed the icy water into every tiny gap in his clothing.

"Hello!" he'd yelled into the storm. Shouting was pointless, the sound disappeared completely into the raging wind. Walking around the wreckage, he could see from outside that the pilot was dead; the awkward angle of his neck, the dried blood on his face and in his hair, and the cold, grey pallor of his skin; there was no mistaking the face of death. Even though he'd seen it before, it wasn't something he would ever get used to. The plane was a hell of a mess, both wings had been completely sheared off. The fuselage must have turned sideways as it slid forward, and it had rolled half onto its side.

Reluctantly, Jimmy squeezed his tall, lanky frame through a gaping hole in what remained of the cockpit and went aft, slowly and carefully edging past the pilot's body, picking his way through the debris. Inside was like a scene from a disaster movie. The seats were at odd angles, there were papers and equipment everywhere, and further back through the fuselage, he saw the twisted bodies of two other men. No survivors. A piece of metal fuselage or frame had dislodged and struck one of them. Jimmy could smell death. And there was something else in the air, too. Something ominous and foreboding that he could not quite put his finger on. He felt weak and physically ill. He steeled himself and went a little closer.

The piece of metal was like a spear with a square shaft. He couldn't see what or where it had originally been, but could see clearly enough that it had entered the lower left side of the man's chest with great force. It must have pierced his heart. There was so much blood. Jimmy looked away, trying to hold back the contents of his stomach.

He looked down and saw that he was standing in the man's blood, which had already started to freeze. His stomach knotted and convulsed, and he was violently ill. He leaned, almost fell forward and steadied himself. Instantly, he realised he had put his hand on the steel skewer, his weight opening the man's wound. Jimmy turned and ran through the wreckage, out of the opening in the cockpit. At that moment the penetrating cold didn't matter; he just stood looking up as the rain washed the blood and death away. Once outside, his panic quickly subsided. It must have been the awful reality of the crash and the confined space inside, Jimmy told himself. After a few quick gulps of freezing rainwater, he circled the wreckage a couple of times. As he looked, he had a feeling something was amiss but couldn't quite put his finger on it.

He thought he'd been there for about an hour, and now started to wonder where the others were. Surely they had heard something from the main station? He was frozen to the core, shivering uncontrollably, perhaps more due to what he'd seen inside the wreck and the eerie feeling he had, rather than from the storm outside. He took another twenty minutes to carefully pick his way back to the hut and didn't see anyone from the station. As he walked, he thought he would have to skip some of the gruesome details in the next telephone call to his sister. She worried about him enough, simply because he was isolated from the rest of the group. No need to remind her just how harsh this environment could be.

He would have reported the crash to the station right away, had his radio aerial been intact. He knew Gary would want to thoroughly check it out for himself, to try to work out what caused it. There would have to be an examination of the bodies, battered and twisted as they were. Jimmy decided he would fix the antenna as soon as the storm cleared and would fill Gary in then. Nothing was going to help those men on the plane now, so he didn't think it necessary to hike down to the station immediately. He was now attuned to life watching the birds, and time was something he had plenty of. He would at least wait until the wind died down some. But by the time the worst of the storm had cleared the previous afternoon, he wasn't feeling well enough.

And now, half sitting, half lying limply in bed, he felt much, much worse. Breathing was a hell of an effort, every part of his body ached terribly, and his mouth was sore and parched. He *had* to get some water.

He forced himself to sit up and slowly swung his feet off the bed. He felt dizzy and weaker than he'd ever felt before. Was that blood on his pillow? He didn't remember cutting himself. His sister Susie's firm voice filled his thoughts: 'You should be in a hospital!'

Carefully, he stood up, balancing himself with both hands on the bed, and slowly staggered across the floor to the plastic kitchen sink. He looked out the window to see a dull, grey, lonely day, a little drizzle, but no storm.

"At least the weather's back to normal," he muttered hoarsely to himself, meaning the doctor could come up fairly easily.

He had almost struggled over to the makeshift kitchen area when, rather suddenly, it came to him that it was time he got out of this place and flew home to Australia. He was starting to feel very much alone. He'd had enough of Macquarie Island, the 'Jewel of the South Pacific', as they somewhat facetiously called it, and he missed his sister badly. Anyway, at twenty-four years of age, he had plenty of time to return to the island one day if he wanted.

He was muttering to himself, but no sound was coming out. A violent cough racked his weak body and spattered his hand with blood. As he looked at it, wondering distantly where the blood was coming from, the window and door seemed to move. Before he had time to put his bloody hands out to stop it, his knees buckled and the floor flew up to his head. No sound, no pain, just blackness. As Jimmy floated into unconsciousness, his last waking thought was an odd one. Seat belts. That was what was wrong at the crash site. The passengers hadn't been wearing seat belts. They had obviously died quickly in the crash; surely they would have been wearing seat belts ...

Gary Masters was concerned about Jimmy; it had been four days since Jimmy's last contact, and they couldn't get him on the radio. Not that that alone was unusual – Jimmy was often out with the birds. But he always called in every two or three days, so Gary decided the best thing to do was to check it out. He went out in search of Doc, intent on walking to Jimmy's hut, just to make sure. He found Doc having a cup of tea in the recreation rooms. "Hey, Doc. Let's go up to Jimmy's and see how he's getting on."

Paul 'Doc' Holderay could see Gary needed to put his mind to rest, so readily agreed, though didn't want to make a big deal of it. He was slightly worried too. "Sure, Gary. Could use the exercise."

Jimmy's hut was about one and a half kilometres away, still close to the ocean, but it was built on a rocky plateau about eighty metres high. The track started out deceptively easy, then nearer the hut it turned fairly steep and in some places was an almost treacherous climb – well, it would have been to the uninitiated.

Gary expected to find Jimmy out at one of his hideaways, studying the local birdlife or other fauna. He'd probably forgotten the number of days since his last contact, because of the storm. When isolated in conditions like that, it was easy to lose track of time. Hell, it was easy to lose track of *reality*.

They walked down the dark volcanic gravel road, out past the station's numerous buildings and sheds, towards the lush, gentle green slopes. The air still smelt of the storm, just a hint of the delicate aroma of ionised air, tinged slightly with diesel and the sea.

"He'll be okay," Doc said. "He always is."

"I'm sure you're right. Just like to see for myself."

As they left 'Main Street', Gary turned and looked back to survey his station. He saw a kind of organised confusion. The buildings were arranged in seemingly no particular order, although Gary knew they were laid out according to the type of access they required, and other more fundamental considerations, such as natural drainage. He thought that, from a distance, it could have been anything from a kind of modern farm to a remote construction camp. What it didn't look like was a scientific research facility. Looking down, he reflected that life at the station was generally quite good. It was a civilised community in a very uncivilised place. Early pioneers must have felt like this, except that now, in the twenty-first century, they had reliable communication with the rest of the world, they had good food and comfortable sleeping quarters. There was an excellent recreation area, and they usually even had the latest (almost) video releases. And all of it was provided free, while they got paid to be there. Of course, the lifestyle didn't suit everyone, but then no one was forced to stay either.

"Come on, Gary, let's get moving," said Doc, briefly snapping Gary out of his thoughts.

Masters was a big bull of a man; at a hundred and ninety centimetres and a hundred and ten kilograms, most of which was muscle, he looked like a heavyweight boxer. Not many people would take him on in a fight. Fortunately for his crew, they liked him and he liked them. Gary was never one to back away from his share of the work, either. He had a lot of people to look after at the station, from scientists and doctors to diesel mechanics and a cook, and he helped them all get their jobs done one way or another. They were his family. Gary's parents were killed in a plane crash when he was fifteen, and he'd been looking after himself ever since, even as far as putting himself through university while working part time delivering pizzas.

It was sixteen years since his parents had died and even he himself admitted, somewhat reluctantly, that he had come a long way. From an orphaned kid to a research station manager, responsible for thirty-seven people. His science degree, majoring in geology, was the reason he had volunteered for Macquarie Island. Geologically speaking, it was an interesting place. A volcanic mass stuck out in the middle of the Southern Ocean, nearly a thousand kilometres south-west of New Zealand, lying on its own sub-marine ridge. It was at once rocky and desolate, and lush and green; it even had glacial lakes. It was an environment unlike any other he had ever seen before. There was no officially sanctioned geological survey of the island being undertaken, Gary just found it a fascinating place.

On the way to Jimmy's hut, Masters listened as Doc talked about the general morale of the station. Doc was worried that some of the team had been there for almost eighteen months, which was a long time in a place like this. Masters knew how the isolation could affect a person, and although he'd been there for nearly fourteen months without any apparent problem, he understood that not everyone was as independent. Gary understood that he was a product of his unusual upbringing.

Dr Holderay had been the station's doctor for the past seven months, and with his easy-going, likeable manner he had also become a sort of father confessor for some of the station personnel. Gary remembered when Doc arrived.

Like most of Gary's people, Doc had a sense of adventure, and that was what kept him taking postings like Macquarie. Before the island, Doc had spent a year in Australia's Northern Territory, he and his wife living in a small town in one of Australia's most desolate and isolated areas. He was interested in the effects tough climates had on people. When Doc had accepted the Macquarie station job and agreed to start early in the new year, Jenny Holderay had reluctantly accepted that she'd be without her husband for some time. He'd said, 'Jenny knows I've got to do this ...' But Dr Harry had bad flu four weeks before Christmas the previous year and had to be flown back to Hobart to recuperate, so Doc had been asked to start a month early. He had arrived cursing about missing Christmas with Jenny and the kids, but soon he'd made some good friends at the station and became an important part of Gary's team. He had a gift for keeping people's spirits up, keeping morale high, and he clearly cared about the people. For him, the stay on Macquarie was another adventure. And he was a damn good doctor, Gary thought.

"You've got about thirteen people on sleeping pills now," the doctor was saying, "thirty per cent. That's way too high, you know."

Gary stopped, turning back to face Doc, concerned.

"And I'm treating a few more cuts and abrasions from 'minor accidents'," Doc said, knowing Gary would understand; no one admitted to being involved in a fight because they knew Gary would ship troublemakers out.

"Should I be sending any of them back to the mainland, Doc?"

"Well, eight of them are due to fly back next month. I'll keep an eye on the others for you," Doc replied.

They reached Jimmy's hut a little after ten o'clock, and the temperature had reached three degrees – almost a heatwave in winter! Though there was rain coming, of course.

Gary knocked forcefully on the door but got no answer.

"Jimmy!" he yelled. "Jimmy, you in there?"

No answer.

"Must be out birdwatching," Doc said.

"Well, let's take a look anyway, maybe he's got a pot of coffee on," Gary said optimistically, opening the door.

Inside, the air temperature was as frigid as the outside.

"Shit," Gary said. "Something's wrong."

Doc knew it too. The gas heater had clearly died some time before and Jimmy hadn't switched over to a full propane bottle. The hut was well insulated, but without heating it took just an hour or two for almost all the warmth to dissipate. Even if Jimmy was out for the day, he wouldn't let that happen. Doc went through into the back room, which served as a kitchen, radio room and makeshift washroom, and saw Jimmy lying face down on the floor. "Gary!"

Gary was behind him in seconds. He found Doc kneeling at Jimmy's side, checking his temperature and feeling for a pulse. Gary started to turn him onto his side and saw blood around his mouth and nose, and on his clothes. The colour of Jimmy's face alone was enough to tell Doc all he needed to know. He touched Jimmy's neck; his lifeless body was as cold as the bitter, freezing air in the hut.

4

Peter Hennessy looked out of the tiny window. Far below was the almost treeless farmland of south-west Gippsland. In the distance, to the west, he could see the Dandenong Ranges, the outskirts of Melbourne. He imagined his own house, not too far north of the foothills. Below, much of the land had been cleared for farming earlier last century. From the air it looked as though the gods had decided to sweep the land clean, leaving only the grass. When the trees were all cut down, it was a great boon for industry in the area – not just logging. Everyone had acres of lush green farmland and firewood to last a generation, and no one thought about soil erosion, salt and other problems now faced by the farmers of the area. In some states, the problem had become so serious that previously fertile land was no longer arable due to salt leaching up to the surface.

Peter had argued about this with some of his colleagues. 'Short-term, short-sighted thinking,' he said about those who ruthlessly cleared their land just to fit a little more stock on it. Usually the same reply would follow: 'Farmers have a right to make the best use of their land.'

Peter said the risks were now well known and well documented. In fact, there was a fairly serious replanting programme to counteract the erosion, at least in Australia. But every second week, it seemed, Peter read in dismay of massive 'controlled burns' of rainforests in South America; of 'development' of new farming areas; of 'progress'. The spreading of civilisation, turning thousands of years of nature's rule into a short-sighted gain for man.

'Everywhere mankind is reaping the benefits of new technologies, new machines, new sciences, the benefits of progress,' people would say.

'Reaping? No, man is not reaping. Man is *raping!*' Peter would reply. Sometimes he wondered whether it was possible to take 'civilisation' too far. Will we ever learn from nature? Or even from our own mistakes? Occasionally nature reminds us of her power with an earthquake, or a volcanic eruption, or flood. Do we learn? Scientists proclaim that we do. But we still relentlessly clear forests, we still rebuild cities on fault lines or under volcanoes, and we still plan for short-term gain, ignoring long-term risks.

"We're coming in to land, better buckle up," Jack called, bringing Peter back from his reverie. Below now were Melbourne's western suburbs, some houses within metres of runways.

"Progress," he muttered disdainfully.

JULY 25

Peter woke still feeling the effects of the long flight from Ross Station. They had arrived at Essendon Airport, north-west of Melbourne, late yesterday afternoon, and the timing had meant he had to face a long taxi ride through peak traffic to get home. The driver skirted the northern suburbs and the trip took just over an hour. Other drivers on the road, aggressively weaving in and out of the heavy traffic, cursing and gesticulating just to get a few seconds ahead, seemed ridiculous to Peter. *They ought to spend some time where I've just been*, he thought.

The taxi left the M3 motorway at Ringwood, and soon suburbia gave way to the familiar smells of the native bush and larger semi-rural properties. Even with the windows up, the fresh, delicate fragrance of the great eucalypts on both sides of the road permeated the air vents. It was a comforting aroma. Much closer to home, navigating the quiet, leafy winding roads near Warrandyte, his oasis on the north-eastern fringe of Melbourne, Peter started to unwind.

He always felt more comfortable, more at peace, outside the city. Not that he hated the inner city; in fact, when he was lecturing more regularly he had often enjoyed long walks through the city or its surrounding gardens, and the many good cafés and restaurants. But he did like to leave it all behind sometimes. Living just outside Warrandyte was an excellent compromise. It was a picturesque and peaceful, almost *country* setting, within reasonable commuting distance of the sprawling and bustling city.

He looked at himself in the bathroom mirror and decided he had looked a lot better. He had four days of stubble and his eyes looked a little more grey than green. The dark circles under his eyes told him he needed another good night's sleep. His usually wavy dark hair was more or less sticking straight up, and he was due for a haircut. He mused that he would either have to shower and shave, or join a rock band. He smiled to himself, and the laughter lines creased his face around his deep-set eyes. *You're looking old*, he thought.

Half an hour later, he'd showered, had some breakfast and made himself a small pot of coffee, which he finished while staring out the kitchen window into the forest. The tranquil bush setting, particularly during winter and spring, always made him feel more relaxed. His reflection in the window looked slightly more presentable now, his squarish jawline clean-shaven and hair more under control. He pushed his mop back with his hands and stood to take his coffee cup to the sink.

His house was an old stone and timber cottage, originally built around the beginning of the last century, but several owners since, himself included, had made their own changes and additions. He turned around to survey his home, not really seeing the timber and plaster walls, nor the old Baltic Pine floorboards that needed a bit of putty here and there, nor the leadlight windows in the living room and kitchen. What he saw was his retreat, his sanctuary.

From where he stood, he could see most of the house. It was much better this way. When he had bought it, it had too many poky little rooms, like so many older houses. A couple of years ago, he'd got builders in to add some large and expensive supporting beams in the roof, and he'd spent one of the more enjoyable weekends of his adult life demolishing three internal walls with a chainsaw. He could picture the house full of exhaust fumes; he could almost smell it. It had lingered for days. The thought of it made him smile. No amount of education and conditioning can completely take the boy out of the man. He'd ripped out the small living room and kitchen window frames and replaced them with larger ones, too. The pieces of old framing timber that he couldn't recycle had given him months' worth of firewood.

The huge stone fireplace in the living room was beckoning him to light a fire, but although it was July, the coldest month of the year in Melbourne, he felt warm – probably after the Antarctic climate. The cottage had two large fireplaces, the other in the main bedroom. It used to have three, but when he'd had the kitchen rebuilt, the old wood-burning stove had been removed as well. He'd wanted to keep it, but it was totally impractical, and the kitchen *was* too small.

He unpacked his notes from Ross Station, found his reading glasses and took it all into his study to review. The big old oak desk was clean and tidy. It was part of the home's personality, too. He had found it in a local junk shop that advertised '*antiquities*'. Hardly an antique, but it *was* old, solid and full of character. He always tried to keep his desk tidy; he had found long ago that it was better to start something new without remnants of the last fifteen tasks lying about. His work was quite diversified anyway, so any new work was likely to be completely different and detached from the last.

Peter's tidiness was anathema to his colleagues. Most of them, Peter had often said, worked by the 'volcano principle' – their offices being utter chaos, desks piled from end to end with papers – the theory being that eventually everything flows in towards a crater in the centre, to be dealt with in its own time. 'That way,' he'd been told, 'everything is right there at hand.' He wasn't completely sure what he'd said, but it might have been 'Bullshit.'

Right now, the only things on his desk were the telephone, his laptop and an empty photo frame he'd meant to find a picture for. Perhaps this was a symbol of something missing in his life, although he didn't dwell on it. He liked working at home, even if he wasn't getting paid for it. He didn't need the money at the moment anyway. The regular income he received from occasional university lectures and book royalties was enough to sustain him.

He had written his book the year he and Sam had split up, living for four months in Meekatharra, on the edge of the Gibson Desert, to closely study the Aboriginal history and heritage of the area. That was another truly tough place. One of the driest, hottest environments in the world, he was sure, and it had taken him a long time to acclimatise. That wasn't all that had taken a long time; it took most of the four months he was there for the locals to accept him and really talk to him. When they had, he knew he'd made some good friends. One or two of them still wrote to him occasionally. That time also helped keep his mind from dwelling on the past.

He looked at the array in front of him and told himself he had enough material to justify spending some time investigating. He would offer his services to ANARE, and if he was lucky, they would fund his expenses. Of course, all he really had was a story about a frozen piece of grapevine, and some dirty ice that suggested maybe the Antarctic wasn't as cold and inhospitable thousands of years ago as was originally thought, and that didn't prove anything. In fact, there was a lot of scientific evidence, or at least well-founded theory, to prove him wrong. But it was interesting.

As he sat typing his notes on the laptop, a thought occurred to him. He rang Sydney University to find a former colleague who was lecturing in cultural anthropology and, to his surprise, located him almost right away.

"Hello, John, it's Peter here, Peter Hennessy." Professor John Morton was an excellent person to bounce ideas off. He always had another perspective, a different approach to consider.

"Ah, Peter, how nice to hear from you." They exchanged pleasantries and caught up briefly before Peter launched into his explanation.

"I've got something interesting here." Peter told him all about the ice cores, that their depth indicated their age to be about six to eight thousand years, and how they suggested a very different climate than expected. He explained about the *Vitis vinifera* which had been lost with the plane that went down.

"*Vitis vinifera*. Now *that's* interesting. Did you know that, as well as being one of the oldest fruits, the grape is one of the oldest known *cultivated* fruits."

His words excited Peter. Maybe he really *was* on to something.

"*Vitis vinifera* is more than just a grape, old man, it could be an indicator of a civilised community of winemakers! Wine has been around for millennia; perhaps even longer than we know," Morton said.

He's being rather optimistic, Peter thought.

"You'll need some good evidence, though, m'boy. I can't imagine our esteemed colleagues," – John often referred to the scientific establishment, for whom he often held much contempt, as *our esteemed colleagues* – "being too happy about this. It might shake some of their crusty foundations loose. I don't think there's been much work done anywhere on the possible existence of past civilisations on Antarctica. This may be a first, so I'd make sure you don't jump to any ill-founded conclusions, old chap."

John was in his late fifties, and he spoke like an old Oxford professor. He even had one of those jackets with leather elbow pads. If he'd smoked an old briar pipe, he'd have been in grave danger of becoming a caricature. They talked about ways Peter might continue his research, and John asked if there'd been any further news about the lost plane. He said it would be very valuable to have that piece of grapevine properly analysed.

"You can't even be sure it's not a hoax," he added, voicing Peter's own concerns.

John said goodbye after promising Peter he would see what he could dig up, although a hoax was certainly possible; it seemed the only piece of potential evidence for ancient human life on Antarctica had been destroyed. Still, it was a long stretch from finding a grapevine to proving there was a civilisation.

Peter then contacted ANARE down in Hobart. He spoke to an overly polite information officer who wasn't very informative, eventually getting through to Marc Richardson. Marc didn't sound as cheerful as he had the last time they had spoken. He apologised for the information officer's reticence, explaining that they had a 'situation' at their base at Macquarie Island, and the press were asking questions.

"Even the Australian and New Zealand governments are sticking their noses in, you know." Marc said he didn't have time to explain, as he was just about to be briefed on the developments. He told Peter he was flying to Melbourne the next morning for a special meeting, so if Peter wanted to link up with him at the airport, they would have about an hour to catch up. Peter thought of the long drive to and from Tullamarine, Melbourne's main passenger airport, and groaned inwardly.

After he'd taken down the flight details and hung up, he wondered what the hell the 'situation' was and what sort of meeting Marc had to rush to Melbourne for. He also wanted to know why New Zealand was getting involved. Macquarie Island used to be a New Zealand dependency, but he couldn't see why they'd want to be officially involved now. Unless it was the Ross Island connection; that *was* a New Zealand dependency.

Welcome back to the real world, he thought, the world where politics was everything and hardly any *real* work got done. He supposed that as a senior administrator for ANARE – an organisation dependent on government funding – Marc had a lot of politics to contend with. Even so, Peter looked forward to seeing him tomorrow. He *could* be a bit of a pain sometimes, but he was helpful, and might have some useful information. Even gossip could be useful sometimes.

He had almost finished sorting and typing his notes. Just the last two pages – his *unscientifics*, general thoughts and feelings – remained. It was time to take a walk to clear his head. He had long ago discovered that he did his most productive thinking while he was walking. He reread the unscientifics, so they were fresh in his mind, then put the two handwritten pages in his pocket. He found his old backpack, filled a water bottle, locked up and drove down to the local shops to pick up some sandwiches and fruit. He made a mental note to call at the supermarket on the way home to restock his kitchen. As he pulled out of the driveway, he thought he heard the phone ring. *Oh well, if it's important they'll call back, or call my mobile,* he thought. It was just after three o'clock when he finally parked the car near the national park and set out on foot.

5

"So why are you calling me?" As a microbiologist and medical professional, Dr Nicole Palmer currently worked at Wellington Hospital studying the effects of new chemotherapy drugs on patients with certain types of cancer.

This smooth-talking, emotionless voice had interrupted her at a patient's bedside. She was right in the middle of a consultation and interview with a leukaemia patient who was supposed to be in remission but was still clearly unwell. These interviews were hard enough without interruptions.

"Because we need someone with your experience to handle this delicate situation," came the glib reply.

Dr Palmer had recently worked on some interesting projects, it was true, including a complex investigation of the so-called *flesh-eating virus*, a nasty strain of the golden staphylococcus bacteria that could kill people by literally eating away skin and organ tissue – at the alarming rate of several centimetres an hour. Her current chemotherapy project was for the New Zealand health system, and the smooth-talker on the phone was one of the health minister's advisors, although Dr Palmer couldn't see the connection. And he'd said *Macquarie Island*. Where exactly is that?

But this 'delicate situation' seemed like it had political connotations, if a minister was involved. She was not interested in getting involved in any political machinations. Without more information, 'rubbish' was what she wanted to say, but her mother had brought up a girl who gave everyone at least one chance.

"But why *me*? There are other doctors here with far more experience than me … just a minute." She covered the phone and spoke to the gaunt-looking woman sitting on the hard plastic hospital chair. "I'm so sorry, Adele. I should have turned my phone off. I'll be back as quickly as I can." Her look of concern was tinged with annoyance at the caller's interruption. Just down the corridor she found an unoccupied room. "Okay, go ahead."

"Dr Palmer," the voice said, "it's because of your research into infectious diseases that we've called you. We have a situation on Macquarie Island that looks a little, ah, *delicate*. A man has died from a mystery disease, and no one seems to know what's caused it. And in the same week as another major incident – a plane crash on the island that killed three people."

She wondered what kind of man was she speaking with. Four dead bodies and a mysterious disease, and the situation is '*a little delicate*'. *And it seems you want someone who can just drop everything and jump when you say jump*, she thought.

"Where was the plane from?" Nicole Palmer asked, showing a mental agility that surprised her caller.

"An Australian research station in Antarctica. Although we don't know if they're linked," said the voice.

"Had there been any other contact with the rest of the world, say, two weeks prior to these deaths?" she asked.

"No," was the curt reply.

"Then I'd say it's very likely that the plane and the disease are directly related. Has anybody left Macquarie Island in the last two weeks? Or the Antarctic base, for that matter?"

"Yes, we've identified three passengers plus two crew now in Melbourne, and one is here in Wellington. He got in this morning."

"What's the situation at the base?" Just one of a hundred questions that flooded her mind, but the voice had no answers.

Dr Palmer took down the local man's details and agreed to visit him immediately to run some tests. The government man, Arnold Wood, said the Australians were checking the others out today. She rang her man, and arranged to meet him. Then she went back to Adele.

Adele Howard was patiently waiting when Nicole returned. She liked Nicole very much, mostly because she didn't treat her like a child, as others had since she got sick. Adele had been in and out of hospital for what seemed like years, and when she was 'in', most of her visitors, including her own daughter, had started to behave differently around her. Conversation was often stilted, and Adele hated it. She wished they would remember that she was still the same person, but no matter how many times she told them, they would always soon revert to the parent/child attitude.

But Nicole was different. On each of her three visits so far, she had talked to Adele just like people used to before she got sick; she was always so sincere and natural. There was a warmth and genuineness to the lovely smile that shone in her brown eyes. Adele knew Nicole cared about her, and they had become friends. The interviews and check-ups were supposed to take about fifteen minutes, but they always talked for about an hour. During their conversations, Nicole had told Adele a little about her life, and to Adele she seemed lonely.

Nicole had talked about missing her mother in Melbourne; that although they spoke on the phone every week, it wasn't the same as seeing her in person. She had also let slip that her marriage had broken up, although did not elaborate, and Adele did not wish to pry. Adele could tell from Nicole's eyes there was a depth to her soul that she did not often see in the other hospital staff members' faces.

Dr Palmer left the hospital just after eleven in the morning. The weather was unseasonably warm, and Riddiford Street was alive with people. The southbound traffic was backed up already. Luckily she was headed north, and within a few minutes she'd eased onto the motorway, reaching Lower Hutt less than fifteen minutes later. She quickly found the address she had been given, and by two o'clock had completed a thorough check on the man, a young mechanic. He said he felt fine, and he looked fine too. She asked him and his parents not to go out anywhere until the blood tests were completed, and warned them that she would need a detailed list of their movements for the last couple of days if any tests came back positive.

If this young man's blood returned any indication of infection, they would have to quickly identify, isolate and test everyone he'd come into contact with. Including herself. She quickly drove back to the hospital with the blood sample, grateful that traffic in Wellington was so much lighter than in Melbourne. It was possible that a serious epidemic could already be incubating in several cities right now. And what of the people at the Macquarie and Antarctic bases? And their families. And the passengers that shared the flight back from Antarctica.

She parked the car and hurried back to the laboratory. Thoughts swirled in her head as she completed the tests, but as each result came in, she started to relax. The man was apparently as healthy as he'd looked. Only a few results were still to come, and all so far had been negative. While she sat waiting, Arnold Wood called to check her progress, so she asked him again about the people in Melbourne. Wood said they had checked all but one of them, a doctor. Hennessy, he thought the name was. Nicole Palmer asked the man to call her as soon as he had all the results. With luck, they would confirm that the epidemic had not spread.

Dr Palmer, Nicki to her friends, was thirty-two years old. She'd been living in Wellington for a little over three years, having moved from Melbourne. She told all her friends in Melbourne, when she left, that she'd had an offer 'too good to pass up', and that was why she was moving to a new country. It was essentially the truth, and her friends had accepted it, knowing she'd never been afraid to eat life in big bites, but she had left out some important details.

Hennessy. A name from the past. Her mind wandered back to Melbourne, a few years earlier. At the time, she'd been doing some tutoring at Melbourne University and had made some good friends there. One of those was a lecturer in anthropology named Peter Hennessy. At first, she'd thought Peter was an abrupt, laconic sort of man. But over time she got to know him fairly well and found that, under the surface, Peter wasn't really like the aloof, reserved image he portrayed. Nicki could see through his defences. She remembered one particular day, only a few weeks after she first met him, when she was feeling a little stressed. She was sitting in a staffroom trying to concentrate on her notes, when Peter walked up to her and said hello. She hadn't heard him come in, and his deep voice almost made her jump out of her chair. He'd apologised and said 'you look like you need a break' and practically dragged her outside for a walk. They walked out into the warmth of a beautiful summer day, caught a tram down the bustling Swanston Street, engrossed in conversation. They'd walked couple of blocks before she wondered where he was leading her. They ended up in the Fitzroy Gardens, and she soon found that the shaded pathways surrounded by lush greenery and brightly coloured flowers somehow gave her some of their peace. And so did Peter.

They had walked and talked for almost two hours. They strolled past the conservatory, past Captain Cook's Cottage, which had been built in England more than two centuries earlier and transported out to Australia. She remembered the way the sunlight had trickled through the foliage above, the sound of the trees and the birds, and she could almost smell the freshly cut grass. As they meandered slowly along the paths, the conversation also wandered from the mundane to something much deeper. Peter talked of the day his father died, of his pain, of his sense of helplessness, of how unfair that fourteen-year-old boy felt the world was. It had touched her. Strange how two people who knew very little about each other could relate so easily, and so completely. He spoke as if they'd been friends for years, and she found herself doing the same thing. That was the day their friendship really started.

He'd been going through a rough time back then. He needed someone to talk to, and she was happy to oblige. They shared many a long conversation, about anything from the effects of scientific or medical discoveries on the human race, to more earthly matters, like friendships, and she found Peter thought in the same ways she did about many things. Peter Hennessy turned out to be the most unlikely friend. One day, over a cup of coffee and a shared piece of chocolate cake, she even told him about her past relationships that had failed and how they had hurt her.

Peter suggested the human mind should have an 'off button'; some thoughts were just too destructive. She remarked, only half seriously, that no man could be trusted, and he replied, also half seriously, that she just hadn't met the right one yet. He claimed, maybe with a hint of sadness, that some women want to suffocate their partners, and she had punched him on the arm, saying 'maybe you all deserve to be suffocated'. She smiled as she pictured him sitting in that café, his head tilted slightly to one side, as he'd tried to think of a response to that.

In many ways, Peter Hennessy was different to other men she had known. She remembered talking to him once about holidays, and places they wanted to see. She named places where she could go skiing, or islands, or beaches, and he said, 'But you can do all that stuff anywhere, even here. Where's your sense of adventure? Don't you want something different? I'd trek through the Himalayas or the Andes, or go to Wiltshire to see stone circles like Avebury or Stonehenge, just to watch the sun rise from inside and see what it *felt* like.'

Sometimes, in a group of people, or even across a room, she would catch his eye, and he'd smile at her, and she'd lose her train of thought. They had developed a real empathy. Before she realised what was happening, her feelings of friendship, her discovery of a kindred spirit, had evolved into something else. In fact, it was her mother who had said to her, 'Why don't you just admit it, girl, you're falling in love with him.' But deep in her heart she was sure Peter just thought of her as a friend. And she knew there was already someone in his life.

Nicole Palmer knew she was an enigma. She was a trained doctor and scientist, with a logical and analytical mind, but in matters of the heart she hardly ever felt logical. She believed dreams could come true if you wanted them *enough*, and she sometimes forgot that *real* people often don't behave rationally or logically. But she believed anyway, and had been that way since she was a little girl, always knowing there were some things we weren't meant to understand, they should just be accepted.

Nicki had never allowed her confused feelings for Peter to develop any further, and she had never told Peter how she felt, deciding that not only was his life already too complicated, but perhaps all they both needed was a friend to talk to.

The tutoring she'd been doing was only temporary anyway, so she started looking for another job. Time to move on. It didn't take her long to find an opportunity to move into research work, which she had been interested in for some time. One of her friends told her of an available tenure at a major public hospital, that she had a friend already working there, Tony Palmer, a doctor she had known for nearly four years.

New Zealand was a bit further away than she had in mind, but it was perfect timing, and it would be good for her career, so she jumped at it. She contacted Tony, and he told her who to talk to. Within a few weeks of her initial discussion and emailing her bio and references, she was on her way. It all happened pretty quickly, especially for a government institution. Maybe Tony had put in a good word for her.

Before she'd had time to think deeply about it, she had changed her whole life. She'd wrapped up her feelings and her dreams in a neat package and had taken them all to a new beginning. Only it wasn't a beginning, it was an ending.

"Are you all right, Dr Palmer?"

She looked up, but it wasn't Peter, it was Danny, the chief pathologist's assistant.

"Oh yes, I'm fine. I was miles away," she said in a small voice. "I was just thinking about some ancient history," she added dismissively.

Danny's a nice guy, she thought. He had worked with Nicki since she first started in Wellington, and they quickly developed a good rapport. At first Danny didn't seem too sure how to take Nicki; he could see she was very efficient and often seemed to be coolly professional, but they got on well and had now become firm friends. Danny helped Nicki settle into Wellington, and even helped with her wedding arrangements a year or so later. He probably deserved a better explanation.

"Actually, I was thinking about when I first arrived here, and how you, and Tony I guess, made me feel so welcome," she explained.

As she spoke, Danny remembered how touched she was when, on her first day in the job, someone had anonymously sent her a single, long-stemmed red rose. He knew Tony had been smitten by her, although he denied sending it. Danny told him it was a nice gesture anyway. It was a pity how things had worked out, he thought. He grinned at her, and tactfully changed the subject. "Well, the good news is that all the tests are all done. All negative," he said cheerfully.

"Oh, thank God," she muttered. She pulled her thoughts together, got up and rang Arnold Wood, confirming that their man had checked out. But Wood said he still had no word on Hennessy.

6

The message had been clear. Brief, but clear. His base was quarantined. No flights in or out. The doctor was to give everybody a check-up immediately; a report back, covering even so much as a common cold, was required later that day. The next flight back to Australia, scheduled in six days' time, was cancelled pending further investigation. Supplies would be airdropped when necessary only, which meant mail would be delayed, maybe for weeks. John Kelly was particularly annoyed by this, although he understood that there was really no choice.

It was damn hard to run a base like this, and telling the men they were temporarily quarantined was going to cause friction. Just not getting their mail might be problematic for some of them. But Kelly thought they would accept the news from him – as long as no one actually got sick. He was conscious that the months without sunlight could have strange effects on people. Tempers frayed more easily during the winter, and all it would take would be for someone to get a cold and trouble would start.

He had been running this base, on a rotation basis with another man from Sydney, for four years now. He knew the people and the environment very well, and he knew he was good at what he did. What he didn't know was what the immediate future held for the base. If there was a deadly epidemic on the loose, there was no doubt in his mind that his government would let them all die. Of course, there would probably be a public attempt to get help to them, but really, what else could they do? And Ross Station, Antarctica was far enough from 'civilisation' for them to let it happen.

A few minutes later, he called for the medical officer and sat down, scratching his long beard thoughtfully. *How will I tell the men? How can I reassure them?*

The doctor arrived. "You called, Ned?" a loud baritone voice asked.

Australians were well known for using nicknames, and any man named Kelly, especially one with a beard, would inevitably be called Ned, after the famous nineteenth-century bushranger. Martin Brinksma, the base doctor, wasn't born in Australia, but he had picked up a lot of innately Australian habits. Born in the Netherlands, his family migrated to Hawke's Bay in New Zealand when he was ten years old, so he spoke with a curious combination of Dutch and New Zealand accents. He looked a lot like Ned, at 178 centimetres, and with a luxuriant beard. At a distance, the only way the others could tell them apart was that Martin's hair was fairer.

"Is somting de metter?" Martin added.

"Marty, I need you to do a pretty thorough check-up on everyone. It seems a new kind of ... ah ... flu or something has hit Macquarie, and they say it may have come from here. In our plane." Kelly didn't have to remind Brinksma that the plane crashed there, and that three of their men had died in that crash. They had received the news within an hour of the discovery on Macquarie Island. He spoke slowly and thoughtfully. "Tell the men we're being checked for a new flu virus, and if they ask any more questions, tell 'em you don't know anything else, okay?

"Oh, and you could tell 'em that if it started here, we'll be famous. We'll call it the Ross Island flu." Ned looked pretty serious.

Martin didn't need to ask; he knew Ned wanted it done right now.

* * *

JULY 26 – MELBOURNE, AUSTRALIA

Peter arrived at the airport fifteen minutes before Marc Richardson's flight was due. He sat down in an uncomfortable lounge chair and was still there, reading a newspaper, forty-five minutes later when Marc finally walked in.

"Sorry I'm late, the flight was delayed in Hobart. Give me a lift to Collins Street, could you?" As they walked out to Peter's car, Marc started to explain what was going on.

"This Macquarie Island thing is causing quite a storm. It seems a plane from the Ross base crashed into the island a bit over a week ago. For some reason, it took the Macquarie people a while to find the wreck, and the guy who found it has died from some kind of flu."

Peter could see he was choosing his words carefully.

"The government's put a lid on the whole thing, and even the New Zealand Government have pushed themselves into the loop. It seems they had a guy at Ross recently, too."

Peter didn't see how Ross Station could be involved, because everyone down there had been healthy when he was there, and that was *after* the first plane had left. But Marc was obviously taking it all very seriously.

"Yeah, he flew back with me two days ago, but …"

"Well at least you all checked out okay," Marc interrupted.

"I haven't been 'checked out'?" Peter said.

Marc looked horrified. "You haven't been checked? They said they'd got hold of everyone!"

"Not me." Peter remembered the card he found stuck in his door when he got back home about nine last night. Just a name and a phone number and the word 'urgent'. There were about half a dozen cigarette butts near the front door. Someone had been waiting for a while. Now he wondered why the 'someone' hadn't waited for him, if it was as important as Marc made out. He'd taken the card inside and was about to call when John Morton had called from Sydney. He had put the card down next to the phone so he wouldn't forget to call later. But Morton's call had piqued his curiosity and made him forget nearly everything else.

"Shit, Peter, we'd better go to Fairfield right now," Marc interjected, jolting Peter back to the present. Fairfield Infectious Diseases Hospital was the only place Marc could think of that he and Peter could be quickly and safely tested. Marc looked paler.

"What about your meeting?" Peter asked.

"Fuck them, they can wait."

Marc seemed very agitated, so Peter drove to Fairfield, while Marc contacted someone on his mobile, stabbing the keys so aggressively Peter thought he'd push right through the phone. By the time they got to the hospital, the staff were prepared and Marc was pale and pretty jumpy. The hospital put them in an isolation area and a nurse came in. She couldn't get out quickly enough. Peter thought she was abrupt and rude. She found a vein almost immediately and filled two small tubes with Peter's blood.

"How long do you think the test will take?" Peter asked.

"You'll get the results as soon as we do," she answered tersely, and walked out.

Peter grimaced at Marc and got no reaction. Marc seemed totally preoccupied.

The next few hours felt like *days*. Marc paced nervously up and down the small cubicle, while Peter tried, largely unsuccessfully, to quiz him about the Macquarie Island situation. In the end, he gave up and threw him a magazine. "Read this. Maybe it'll take your mind off things." Marc was driving him crazy. "All we can do is wait."

Four interminably long hours later, they were released, and Marc raced off in a taxi to the government complex behind parliament house, at the top end of Collins Street, in the main business district. Peter was a little shaken by the whole incident, probably more by Marc's distress than anything else, it occurred to him afterwards. He was a far more pragmatic person than Marc; he understood there was nothing they could do except wait, so he had tried to wait as patiently as possible.

As Marc left, he said, "Peter, you mustn't talk to the media if they approach you."

Peter had agreed, thinking this was dramatic overkill on Marc's part.

By the time he got home, it was already dark and Peter felt drained but still a little jittery. He was running on nervous energy, he knew. It had been a full day, and what he needed now was to relax. He had almost stopped in at the Grand Hotel in Warrandyte for a meal.

The Grand was an old stone building, nestled amongst the craft shops of the little shopping village on the main road. It overlooked the Yarra River, and the sort of country he loved, the great ghostly, pale eucalypts with their bluish leaves, the lush green grasses, and of course the river's clear waters. It always amazed him that this was the same river that flowed, poisonous, brown and dead, through the city, only twenty kilometres downstream.

Peter often ate at the Grand. But not tonight. When he got home, he microwaved some frozen leftover lasagne. While it was cooking, he lit a fire and tried to wind down, without much success. Maybe the time he'd spent with Marc waiting for the test results had shaken him more than he had let on. It's not every day a man finds out he may have contracted a deadly disease.

The lasagne turned into a kind of edible rubber. He ate it at the dining table, wishing he'd had a meal at the hotel. After dinner, he poured himself a glass of wine, sat in his living room and relaxed, taking in the silence. An hour later he was still sitting there, when he thought he heard a noise in the study.

But there was nothing out of place. The windows were closed and still latched, and nothing had been disturbed. The stone was sitting on his desk, right in the middle, as if it was the focal point of the whole room, commanding everyone's attention.

"So! You're in charge now," he said to it.

When it didn't answer, he picked it up, and as he touched it, he thought he heard another noise. He was conscious of a vague feeling of danger; perhaps he was hearing things. He searched the whole house but could find no evidence of a break-in anywhere. The front door was securely locked – something he didn't always bother to do. He didn't think he had imagined the sound, so he went out and checked around outside too. No sign of any activity, not even a possum.

The whole experience left him wondering whether or not he had been living alone for too long, but he rationalised that it *had* been a tough day, and solitude had never affected him badly before. He decided he probably just needed a good night's sleep. He poured himself another glass of wine, a fine companion, he reflected, and turned on the television to get his mind off today's events. What a day! It was late, but he still needed to unwind. He found an old movie, stoked up the fire and settled into an armchair. Audrey Hepburn was about to leave for South America when the phone rang.

"Hi, Peter," said Marc Richardson, sounding a lot better. "Sorry I'm calling so late, but it was a long meeting. Look, the government guys are going to set up an investigation into the problems at Macquarie. There'll be a doctor from here, as well as a couple of other people, and I think the Kiwis are going to send someone, too. They asked me if I knew of anyone with a scientific background who had knowledge of the bases at Ross or Macquarie. I thought of you."

"I'm a bloody anthropologist, not a doctor. What good will I be?" Peter said, immediately wishing he hadn't, because this would give him the opportunity he wanted to further investigate the unusual discoveries at Ross. And besides, he was still an adventurer at heart.

"Well, no harm in talking to them, is there?" Marc said, and Peter allowed himself to be recruited. Marc gave him a number to call.

"Ask for Neil Colles, that's C-O-L-L-E-S." He pronounced it 'Collus'. "He wants you to ring him tonight."

Almost midnight, Peter thought, *but what the hell ...*

He turned *Breakfast at Tiffany's* off and rang the number.

"Colles." The deep voice almost barked, and then waited. Apparently Mr Colles had no time for social niceties.

"Peter Hennessy. Marc Richardson asked me to call." Peter could wait in silence too.

"Hennessy ... you're the anthropologist. Well, you might be able to help us. I understand you've just returned from Ross Station." He didn't wait for Peter to respond. "We have a meeting scheduled for tomorrow morning, it will be at ..." He gave Peter the details. "I trust you appreciate the importance of keeping everything confidential. See you here at 7 am."

And with that, Colles abruptly hung up. Peter felt like he'd just joined the army.

7

The telephone's loud, insistent ring woke Nicki up. She leaned across the bed and picked it up. "Yes?" *No need to be polite at one o'clock in the morning.*

Arnold Wood's taut, emotionless voice filled the receiver, and she groaned inwardly. "We've had confirmation that the last Australian on the flight checked out satisfactorily."

"Who?" she asked, in a sleepy daze.

"Hennessy. Peter Hennessy," Wood said dismissively.

"Oh, thanks for letting me know." Her attitude softened; she *had* asked him to call, after all. *Peter Hennessy?*

"Also, doctor, the Australian Government, with our assistance, are setting up an investigation team, and we'd like you to be involved," Wood went on. "Your background makes you a perfect candidate. As a practising doctor, and a microbiologist, I'm sure you'll be very valuable to them. I've made flight arrangements for you for tomorrow morning. I hope you don't mind." His attitude said *I don't care whether you mind or not.*

Ordinarily she would have told anyone off for making arrangements without consulting her first, but she could see the urgency, and ... "Okay. I'll do it."

Since Wood's first call, she had been reminiscing about her days at Melbourne University. In truth, she had been reminiscing about those times quite a bit lately. Funny how relationship troubles make people think about old times and old friends. 'What is it we look for?' she had asked herself. Reassurance that we're okay? Of course, time had dissipated her feelings, but it would be nice to see Peter again. When she left, she hadn't explained anything to him, not really knowing whether he'd care or not. She said it was a career opportunity not to be missed, and then more or less rearranged her schedule to avoid him for her last two weeks in Melbourne. He had congratulated her and wished her well. *I hope he hasn't completely forgotten me.*

She couldn't find a pen on the bedside table so had to get out of bed.

"You have a current passport?" Wood asked.

Nicki wondered what he would say if she said no. "Yes."

Wood took her personal email address and said he would email the details and ticket from the airport. All other costs would be met by the government.

"But you must have receipts, of course, and all expenses you claim must be justified." She smiled as he said it. You just can't get away from petty bureaucrats no matter what you do. How typical to be worried about expense receipts when the world might be about to have a deadly plague inflicted upon it.

She got back into bed but couldn't get to sleep again. Her thoughts were confused: she thought of old times and old friends; and of Tony. He was basically a good man, she had no doubt, but soon after they'd been married things had changed slightly; he had tried to make *her* change. It had been subtle, and she didn't think he even knew he was doing it. But he *was* doing it. It started when they moved in together, a month before the wedding. She'd put her doubts down to some sort of pre-wedding jitters – they were normal, weren't they?

Soon after they were married, Nicki had started making little compromises for him, until she became aware she was starting to give up her own dreams, her own goals, to make way for his. She'd changed her name to his just to avoid offending his family. Ultimately, the crunch had come when Tony was offered a lucrative position in Auckland. He badly wanted the job, and he wanted Nicki to give up hers and go with him. She flatly refused, telling him in the heat of the moment that she was not going to sacrifice her own needs for him anymore. 'You don't want a compromise,' she'd said to him, 'you want me to be your mother.' She also told him that he was too greedy, that he always thought of a problem's financial implications first. She would have taken it back if she hadn't been so mad at him. For Tony, that argument was the final straw. They had been married just on eighteen months, and it had occurred to her sometime afterwards that the human mind really is capable of misleading its owner.

She looked at the radio alarm. 3.17 am. Her plane was leaving in less than six hours. Lying next to the clock was her wedding ring. She wasn't sure why she still wore it. Maybe she didn't want other men asking her out. Maybe it seemed to help her get more respect from some of the male hospital staff. Of course, there were still men who hit on her anyway, not caring whether she was married or not, but they were easily dealt with.

Maybe the ring symbolised the little girl's dream she had grown up with – to be successful, to be happy, and to be married. It was silly, but perhaps she didn't want to let go of that dream. She just didn't know.

She *did* know that sleep was hopeless and got out of bed again to make herself a cup of hot chocolate, resolutely resisting the temptation to eat a spoonful of Milo straight out of the tin.

* * *

JULY 27, MACQUARIE ISLAND, SOUTHERN OCEAN

As he looked at his home, Gary Masters knew he had a big problem. Since he and Doc found Jimmy's body three days ago, his quiet and efficient research station had turned into almost total chaos. He sat in the moonlight on Wireless Hill going over the last few days' events, quietly wondering what the hell else could go wrong.

Once they'd found poor Jimmy, they quickly returned to the main base, where Gary detailed three men to go back to the hut with Doc. The men took a stretcher and a black polythene body bag up to Jimmy's hut. Both Doc and Masters knew an autopsy was required, but they both also knew the facilities at the station weren't adequate. Doc couldn't determine cause of death from his preliminary examination of the body, but he knew Jimmy looked like he'd aged ten years since they'd last seen him alive.

Of course, it was difficult to get a clear impression of exactly how Jimmy's face looked because he had fallen forward, evidently breaking his nose. That, coupled with the fact that his body had been lying face down, left most of his face and head a deep bluish-purple colour. Lividity like that was normal at the lowest point, or a pressure point, on a dead body, but Jimmy's eyes were also bloodshot and watery, and there was blood, as well as mucus, in his mouth and nose. He had clearly been coughing up blood before he drew his last breath.

They had advised ANARE that Jimmy Davis had died from what appeared to be acute pneumonia. A flight was arranged for the next day to collect the body, to return it to Hobart for the post-mortem. ANARE had instructed them to store Jimmy in the freezer until then. Masters acknowledged that there was no other real choice, so he got two of the men to store the body carefully, swearing them to secrecy. It wouldn't have mattered whether Jimmy had died from a disease or an accident, he knew most of the station would not want a body stored with their food. Quite understandable, Gary thought. He wasn't exactly thrilled about it himself.

Then yesterday morning, Doc and Macka had started to show signs of a cold, Doc with a fever as well. He'd gone straight to Masters and told him it was possible that whatever killed Jimmy was contagious. Gary recognised what that meant to his station – if it was some sort of highly infectious pneumonia, which had now spread to some of the others, they were obviously all in grave danger. This thing had killed Jimmy, who was young and fit, in just a few days. They wouldn't be able to risk contact with the rest of the world either, just in case.

Gary contacted ANARE again and was told the flight was already only two hundred kilometres north of the station. He explained the situation, and they turned the plane back. The Macquarie Research Station had just been quarantined.

Masters had reluctantly sent Josh and Mick back up to Jimmy's hut to check it out. He would have gone himself, but he wanted to maintain close contact with the mainland, and he also wanted to help Doc, who was by now administering high doses of antibiotics and vitamins B and C to the others. Doc hoped the vitamins would build up their immunity to the bug. Well, it would do no harm, anyway.

Josh and Mick searched in and around Jimmy's hut for anything to indicate how he had spent his last few days, any clue as to how he caught the bug. Masters particularly wanted them to check out the bird colonies Jimmy had been studying. He reasoned that if a new type of virus had hit the island, it had probably come from the birds. Some of them migrated freely from Macquarie to Antarctica, or New Zealand, Australia and even South America. So the two men checked the hut, finding nothing unusual except the remains of Jimmy's small radio antenna on the ground outside. There was nothing odd inside, and they didn't want to spend too much time in there.

They went up to the royal penguin rookery, carefully making their way up the slippery rocky slopes. All the birds looked to be in good health, but who – apart from Jimmy – could really tell? They went up a little higher to have a good look around and spotted the wrecked plane. Mick, the younger of the two men, ran back to notify Masters; the other went down to the crash site. Both knew they'd found the missing ANARE plane, even though it bore no specific names.

Mick called out as he hit the gravel road. "Gary! Gary! We found that Ross plane!"

Within minutes of his arrival, practically the whole base knew of the plane wreck, and most were speculating about it being the cause of the new 'plague'. That was all he needed!

Amongst the thirty-seven station people, Gary Masters knew he had a few born leaders, people who knew what to do in a crisis, and who many of the others looked up to. Nick Anakos and Cath Williams were two such people. Masters found them and filled them in with what he knew so far. He tasked Williams with talking to everyone and trying to maintain some sort of calm. A leader with an easy and friendly manner, she would have a good chance of getting the others to listen.

With that, Gary and Anakos, the base's senior meteorologist, went back to the wreck, Mick leading the way. Gary took Anakos because he had a pilot's licence and had often co-piloted flights to and from the mainland. Maybe he would be able to tell what had caused the crash.

The four of them spent several hours at the crash site, noting down the plane's registration details, the apparent damage, measurements and descriptions of the furrows it had dug in the ground as it slid, and the state of the bodies. By rights, Doc should have taken a look, but Masters wanted him focused on taking care of the living. Gary did note with some relief that, apart from obvious crash injuries, the plane's occupants did not seem to have any of the respiratory symptoms Jimmy had shown.

They could find no indication as to what had caused the crash. Their best guess was that it must have just been the bad weather, although Masters wasn't satisfied. He knew the weather at Ross Island was far worse than anything Macquarie could inflict. There were days when the pilots had to fly through blizzard conditions, but the fact that the pilot had come from Ross meant he knew how to land a plane on the ice – he was obviously not inexperienced.

"Notice anything strange?" Anakos said.

"No. Should I?" Gary answered.

"The seat belts. The passengers weren't wearing seat belts."

They left the bodies as they lay, justifying their decision by saying the government would probably want to thoroughly investigate the crash site. Masters knew that none of them wanted to touch the bodies, and frankly, neither did he.

They returned to the base just after three in the afternoon, and Gary had just begun to fully appreciate how fast this disaster was unfolding. He found Doc in the sickbay, not looking at all well. Macka wasn't quite as bad, but Doc looked pale and exhausted, and was sweating.

"Doc, what do you think we have here?" Gary asked.

"I don't know. It scares the hell out of me, though. Never seen any bug take hold so quick." Doc sounded pretty bad, Masters thought. "Even the bubonic plague takes at least thirty-six hours to incubate," he said. "I don't think the penicillin is making any difference. We need some help here. I've got no way to properly analyse this disease. I can't even be sure whether it's viral or bacterial, but I'm confident it's bacterial." Doc coughed violently. "You can hear the fluid building up in my lungs there, and I'm running a fever." His voice was laboured.

"Macka's only showing symptoms of a bad head cold, though, so maybe the penicillin is working for him, I really don't know yet," he continued. "What we've got to do is get blood and fluid samples back to the mainland for proper analysis."

From his stretcher bed behind a partition, David McKenna, 'Macka', spoke up. "At least it's cut me smokin' in half, Doc."

"And about time, too, Macka," Doc replied, trying in vain to sound cheerful.

"Okay, I'll see what I can do," Gary responded.

Masters now wondered about the body in the freezer. If the bug came from the Ross base, then it was possibly impervious to the cold. Maybe it was spreading to their food right now. He contacted ANARE by satellite phone again, explaining that they now had one dead man and two sick men. Without more hospital-grade medication, their doctor could not properly treat the sick, and the doctor himself was now also ill.

In fact, all they could do was to administer the antibiotics they had, along with high doses of vitamins, to everyone. Gary pressed the point about getting samples back to the Australian mainland for urgent analysis so they could find out what, exactly, they were dealing with, as soon as possible. The ANARE people didn't know how to deal with a situation like this, but they were very concerned and agreed to find out, and quickly make special arrangements.

Gary returned to the sickbay to update Doc. He tried to sound more optimistic than he felt. "They're going to alert medical authorities and get back to me. I'm hopeful we'll get some help soon."

"As long as they don't forget we're quarantined. We can't let this bug leave the island," Doc replied grimly.

"They know. We'll need to leave samples for them at the airstrip. They'll collect them and leave supplies, without coming into contact with anyone."

"This is unlike anything I've seen before, Gary," Doc rasped. "It seems like it incubates sufficiently to cause serious symptoms *within twenty-four hours.* That's almost unheard of."

"Spanish flu?" Gary asked.

"No. That was a very serious, but not entirely unusual influenza. And generally speaking, it was a *post*-flu infection, like pneumonia, that killed millions, not the virus itself. Plus that was before antibiotics, and in pretty awful conditions, just after World War One. Not the same." Doc's breathing had become more laboured.

"Spanish flu's incubation period was much longer, too. Could be almost a week before serious symptoms developed," Doc added, after a raucous bout of coughing.

Neither man wanted to say it, but both knew that Jimmy's plight indicated that this disease could *kill* within two to three days.

8

The waitress had brought out his meal of steamed rice and fish, and the man watched, not without envy, as she now brought his companion's meal. Naturally, she had brought him his meal first. Xeng Pang always expected, and always received, preferential treatment from almost everyone in the Chinese community.

He had ordered rice and fish because he had a peptic ulcer, and he knew that the more he enjoyed a meal, the more he would pay for it afterwards, so he always chose carefully. It was simply a matter of discipline, he knew, but it did nothing to improve his disposition. His companion, Lin Fan Cheng, was in his late twenties and felt privileged to be taken to dinner by his superior. Xeng was a formidable figure, and although he was now in charge of the Chinese Cultural Centre in Melbourne, his previous posting had been a senior one at the Chinese Embassy in Canberra.

It was understood that Xeng had been moved to Melbourne as a disciplinary measure following an indiscretion. And it was rumoured that that indiscretion was executing a former superior after a disagreement. The man had been found with his throat slashed so violently his head had almost been severed, but there had not been any hard evidence to convict

Xeng. In any case, with his diplomatic immunity, the police knew it would be almost impossible, so they probably didn't try all that hard.

Xeng had never made any attempt to deny the rumour. To Lin, he certainly looked as if he could kill someone. He was in his forties, fit and tough, his face carried scars from his youth, but he was not ugly. He could be a courteous and charming diplomat one moment, and ruthlessly devoid of conscience the next. He was said to be proficient in martial arts, and Lin knew from experience that Xeng had a gift for frightening people into submission, simply with a look. Even at his most charming, Xeng had cold, steely eyes that frightened Lin.

Lin waited for his superior to start eating, sitting in silence. If Xeng wanted him to speak, he would say something.

Then Xeng cleared his throat. "A billion Chinese, Lin Fan Cheng. There are a billion Chinese. More. We are the world's largest nation, and yet the people of this country see us as second-class citizens. They ridicule us, and they taunt us." Lin couldn't imagine anyone ever taunting Xeng.

"Each day, they throw away millions of dollars of food, while we can barely feed our great nation. Our *hosts*," he spat the word out, "do not appreciate the riches they have."

Lin wondered where Xeng was going, but did not dare ask.

"These peasants have it too easy, they don't understand the difficulties we, as one of the world's great nations, face." Lin was staring intently at Xeng as he paused to emphasise his next words. "*They are spoilt, they are lazy, they are selfish*," the older man continued, in a voice Lin found oddly menacing. "*They need to learn some respect.*"

He gave Lin his most predatory look, then his face softened a little. "Lin, you must not waste this excellent food. Eat, my friend." Lin was honoured; Xeng Pang had called him *friend*.

During the meal, the older man spoke only once. "The Australians criticise us constantly for the way we run our nation. They say we are a barbaric and oppressive regime, yet we know they are no different in many ways."

Xeng allowed his words to foment Lin's sentiments, not speaking at all for the remainder of the meal. When he'd finished, he knew he had Lin exactly where he wanted him. Lin held Xeng Pang in awe, he hung on his every word.

"Lin Fan Cheng, I have heard of an opportunity, a great opportunity for us to adjust this imbalance and make ourselves important men in the mother country. We will have work to do, an important and confidential mission, do you understand me?" Lin nodded obediently, as Xeng looked at him menacingly.

Then Xeng Pang smiled. "Good, good, my friend."

Lin was honoured and felt great pride that this powerful and important man had called him *friend* twice. He also fleetingly imagined an alligator having the same smile just before it dismembered and devoured its prey.

9

July 28, Macquarie Island, Southern Ocean

Just before dawn, ANARE contacted Masters and advised him arrangements had been made for 'emergency' collection of the samples. He wrote down the complicated instructions carefully and went to see Doc. He expected to find him in his quarters, but instead he was working in the sickbay.

"I was just about to come and get you," Doc said, looking a good deal worse than the day before. "Macka's pretty bad, and we've got another two sick men ..."

"Josh and Mick?" Gary interrupted, predicting it would be the last two of the stretcher-bearers.

"Yes," Doc confirmed his fears. "So it's definitely some sort of epidemic we've got on the island. They're both showing the same respiratory symptoms as Jimmy and me." Doc rasped out a tortured cough that made his red eyes water. "Samples ready for analysis, if you can get transport." Doc had nine sealed, labelled phials on the bench next to him, some containing a yellowish fluid, and some deep red with blood.

"Blood and mucus from myself and the other three, plus a blood sample I took from Jimmy's body yesterday. How about you, how do you feel?" Doc asked.

"I've felt better," Gary said. He had woken up with a bad headache and an odd feeling in his chest.

"I should get some of your blood, too, just to complete the set," Doc said, as he started to sway on his feet and almost collapsed.

Masters helped him to one of the beds, noticing that he was burning up and shivering at the same time.

As he lay there, Doc made Gary write down everything he done for the sick men, including himself, saying Masters had to get the information to whoever was going to analyse the samples. Just before he closed his eyes, he tried to push himself off the stretcher bed. "I've got to talk to Jenny and the kids," he muttered, falling back to where Gary had laid him.

"Gary, I want you to call Jenny if ..." Doc spoke as if he had accepted that he was going to die, and his words made Masters feel impotent and angry. Why did this have to happen *here*, to *his* people?

"Tell her I love her, and I miss her ... and the girls. We had a fight last time I called, you know. I want her to know I'm sorry." Doc closed his eyes.

Masters sat with Doc in the sickbay for a while before mustering his strength to get everyone together and tell them what he could. They had a right to know, and allowing rumours to spread wasn't going to help anyone. He could feel the anxiety building up. But his dilemma was that he was also aware that telling them what he knew would also make it harder to keep things under control.

Gary Masters pushed these thoughts down to a long-hidden place in his mind, and less than ten minutes later he walked into a noisy, crowded room. Those who had arrived first were seated at the tables, but many were standing at the back of the room. Normally he'd have to whistle loudly to get their attention. Today they had fallen silent as he walked in.

"You've probably heard a lot of different stories over the last twenty-four hours, and some of them may be true. I want to tell you exactly what's been happening, and what happens next."

He had their undivided attention, at least for now. He went on to tell them about finding Jimmy, and the wreck of the Ross Station plane, with its cargo of three bodies. He told them about Doc and the others getting sick, quickly reminding them that he'd been to Jimmy's hut, too, and yet he was okay. Silently he also told himself that he was okay *compared* to the others. He had felt better. As he spoke he could see some people getting nervous, making quiet comments to each other out of Gary's earshot.

"Where's Jimmy's body? I heard he's in the freezer," someone asked.

Gary confirmed that. They all knew there was no choice, but it did not help them to accept it.

By the time he had finished, he knew life was about to change dramatically on Macquarie Island. Most of them would stay fairly calm, he hoped, and many would pitch in and do whatever they could to help. But there were some who had not reacted well. They were afraid, and they felt trapped. They couldn't leave the island, and they knew there were no adequate medical facilities available. One or two were very angry with Masters for not telling them everything sooner, and they were the ones he was most worried about. Overall, his words had the effect of polarising the station into helpers and helpless, all with varying levels of confusion, frustration or anger.

The weather had also turned nasty, and rolling in ahead of the wind and rain was a dense fog. That meant the plane that was to collect the samples had to be delayed. Gary felt the descending fog in his bones. It was dissipating the foundation and social fabric of his base, and with it came a fear he hadn't felt in years. It had a profound effect on the others, too. As it slowly but tightly choked the island, blocking out the sky, the ocean, the hills and even the buildings, the Macquarie base seemed to be gripped by a kind of creeping fear. They were completely at the mercy of nature, and at the mercy of an unknown, invisible killer.

As if to crush any faint hope that the strongest amongst them might hold, at a quarter past two that afternoon came the worst omen of all. Dr Paul Holderay, friend, advisor and symbol of medical science, died without regaining consciousness.

Three hours later, Josh was dead and Mick was lying unconscious, gravely ill, next to him. And Gary Masters had quietly walked out of the sickbay, and out of the base.

By nightfall, the fog had dissipated enough for Masters to see the nearby Wireless Hill, the island's monument to past achievement. In the pale, veiled moonlight, he had slowly climbed the hill. His headache was worse too, and an unshakeable depression had beset him. The cold, damp air smelt of the sea that surrounded them, but there was something else. He decided it was the smell of *fear*.

Wireless Hill was important to Masters. It symbolised man's achievement against incredibly harsh conditions. In 1911, Sir Douglas Mawson, as part of his heroic Antarctic expedition, had built the wireless station, which first established communications with the rest of the world, atop Wireless Hill. The rusted remains of the steel cables that once held the radio mast in place were still there, standing testament to the engineers of the day. More than a century ago, Mawson, after the tragic death of his companions, had made that famous 160-kilometre trek across the Antarctic ice, alone. An Australian legend, and an impossible icon for Masters.

From where he sat, Masters looked back down through the remaining fog at his base, seeing the diffused lights shining through some of the windows. He tried to imagine he was looking at a small village, somewhere in the Australian outback, and could almost smell the smoke of imaginary log fires, in imaginary stone chimneys. For a brief moment, he was a pioneer in the gold-rush days, a great leader, a man others depended on. But the feeling soon passed, to be replaced by the inexorable and awful reality the whole station now faced.

Yesterday, he had called Susie Davis, Jimmy's sister. She hadn't taken the news at all well. First she had screamed at Gary that it wasn't true; she'd just spoken to Jimmy a couple of days ago, Gary was wrong. Then, from somewhere between distraught wailing and inconsolable sobbing, the smallest and most helpless voice Gary thought he'd ever heard asked how it happened. Masters had tears welling up in his eyes as he explained. He knew Susie must have loved Jimmy very much, and Masters wished he was with her, to be able to comfort her. After he had told her everything he could, she blamed him for letting Jimmy live so far away, and for not making sure he was all right, and for not caring about his people. And he had listened to her in a cold, stony silence, knowing that if he'd made Jimmy stay in the main camp, he might still be alive today. In fact, Doc might still be alive as well.

Now, sitting on the freezing rocks of Wireless Hill, the disintegration of his world seemed somehow distant, less real. He listened to the sound of his own breathing and watched his breath turn to vapour. There was a knot of fear in the pit of his stomach, and as it took hold, it dragged him back to the day his parents died. He was fifteen years old again, angry, afraid, uncomprehending. He could clearly remember – in fact, he could *feel* the grip of depression that had lasted for months – the almost overwhelming sense of loss. The terrible fear of being alone. And here he was, alone again, facing not only his own mortality, but having to watch his friends, his people, his *family* die.

The two worlds joined in Gary's mind, and he was a scared fifteen-year-old in charge of the Macquarie Island station. They needed a strong leader, and he was no longer that man. He would fail them, and failure had been his greatest fear since he'd dragged himself out of the dark place of his late teens and put himself through university. He placed his head in his hands and wept for the first time since he was that scared teenager.

He thought of his mother and father, he thought of Susie Davis, he thought of the families and loved ones of all the people under his care. He thought of Jenny Holderay. Tomorrow, he would have to find the courage to call her and tell her she was a widow. He would have to tell her that Paul loved her, that he was sorry, that their daughters would grow up without their father. The tears streamed down his face and onto his jacket. Gary sat still in the cold and let them flow.

Then, as if breaking the spell, he heard shouts coming from the base. It took a moment for the sounds to penetrate the emotion that had enveloped him. He shook himself off and stood, trying not to take notice of how much his legs ached, and trudged back down the hill. The damp smell of the sea had given way to something else. Smoke. It brought back the cold, hard reality of the situation, and Masters started to run. Was that fire he could see through the fog? It seemed like his home and his 'family' were going straight into hell.

10

Driving off the Eastern Freeway onto Hoddle Street, as he entered the slow-moving traffic, Peter thought about John Morton's interesting message. John said he'd checked around and heard of an old paper that suggested our accepted history of Antarctica might be wrong. Not '*not quite accurate*', not '*incomplete*', but '*wrong*'! It was based on some ancient maps, found many hundreds of years ago, although Morton said there weren't enough facts and far too much supposition, so the paper hadn't really been widely accepted.

Peter was keen to call him back, but it had seemed unsociable to phone him before dawn, so it would just have to wait. The more Peter thought about it, the more curious and excited he'd become. Was it possible that someone had discovered Antarctica before the date historians generally believed? What would that mean? Were they looking at the possibility of a hidden alternative history of Antarctica? This could be an incredible find, especially if this alternative theory was corroborated by evidence now surfacing in Antarctica. Peter had a hundred questions in his mind to discuss with John.

He parked in an underground car park off Flinders Lane, near Parliament House. He put the ticket in the back pocket of his jeans and briskly walked up three flights of stairs to street level. He crossed Spring Street, dodging the traffic, already busy before seven o'clock. He navigated the asphalt footpath around behind the old parliament building then through the Treasury Gardens to the more modern office complex behind. He walked straight in and, to his surprise, no one challenged him. The two Commonwealth Police officers at the front desk merely returned his nod. He had imagined they would have some heavy security. Perhaps if he'd been carrying a case or something ... Or perhaps he was expected. He took the lift to the sixth floor and went straight to the only desk he could see with someone sitting at it.

An attractive blonde girl was sorting what looked like expensive invitation cards, and checking off a long list. She started to cover them with a pile of folders and official-looking documents when he walked up to her, but she stopped her pretence when Peter smiled at her. She must have decided he was okay.

"Hi. I need to find Mr Colles. Can you help me?" he asked.

She returned a pretty smile. "Is he expecting you? He hates unexpected visitors. I can ring him for you if you want, he's got some others in there now ..." She reached for the phone with her left hand, flashing a large diamond ring. She looked about eighteen or nineteen, and Peter thought she was much too young to be getting married.

He held up a hand to stop her. "No, thanks, I'm expected."

"Okay, it's the fourth office on your right, just down there."

"Thank you very much," he said, smiling back at her. In the glass wall of the office directly in front he could see her watching him as he walked away. He smiled to himself. Maybe she liked his jeans, because that was where she was looking.

There was no name on the office door, but he could hear voices inside, so he knocked and waited.

"Yes," came the gruff reply.

He opened the door and stepped into the room. He saw four people he'd never seen before, seated in different coloured chairs, which he presumed had been dragged in especially for this meeting. He knew who

Colles was immediately, the voice matched a solidly built, fit-looking man, who seemed about fifty. His thinning hair was black flecked with grey, close-cropped military style, and he wore a neatly trimmed moustache. Opposite Colles, there was a balding man with untidy tufts of grey hair over his ears in an old-looking brown tweed jacket. With their backs half turned to Hennessy were two people in expensive-looking dark suits, one of whom was a woman. She looked about forty-five, although he couldn't be sure, and she had her hair pulled up in a tight bun which made her face look cold, harsh and somehow predatory. She had eyes like a snake. As Peter walked in, she closed her briefcase and stood up. Her suit was a navy pinstripe, cut like a man's, and it made Peter think of something funny someone had once said.

He'd been working at Melbourne University at the time, and was in a staffroom with a group of people, talking to a friend, a tutor. A member of the staff – an older man well known for his sexist attitude – had walked up to the young tutor, who was wearing matching jacket and slacks, and said, 'You almost look like a man.' The young woman, Nicki, had turned to him quickly and cheekily said, 'So do you.' Later she'd asked Peter if he thought she might have upset the man.

"It's up to you, Colles," the reptile woman said, and with that, the man in the suit stood and they both left, nodding curtly to Peter as they walked past.

"Peter Hennessy," he announced to Colles.

Colles didn't bother to introduce himself, Hennessy had obviously worked out who he was. "Professor Conrick," Colles gestured to the remaining man.

Conrick leaned over to shake Hennessy's hand. With his patches of unruly hair, he looked a little like a harmless old history professor.

Colles pointed to a vacant chair. "I've been instructed to keep this delicate matter out of the media. We don't want the public to panic, do we, Dr Hennessy?"

"I don't want anyone to panic," Hennessy said calmly, sitting down. "Exactly what is your 'delicate matter'?" He hoped to get more information than he'd already been given by Marc.

"Richardson has already told you that we appear to have some sort of highly contagious flu down on Macquarie Island ..." Colles paused to drink the last of his coffee, "... and I believe you know that a plane from Ross Station crashed on Macquarie recently." Peter was looking directly at Colles, waiting. "The professor here has advised me that the virus almost certainly couldn't have originated on Macquarie, so what I intend to find out is where the hell it did come from."

"Tell me how I can help," Hennessy said, following Colles's direct approach.

"Well, firstly," said Professor Conrick, in a quiet, controlled voice, with a trace of a Scots accent, "you can tell us exactly where you've bin during the past four weeks."

Peter told him Melbourne and Ross Island, Antarctica. The professor wrote something in his notebook, and as he wrote, Peter thought the differences in these two men were written all over them. If he announced that he had personally caused the epidemic, Professor Conrick would probably quietly ask him to explain why, out of scientific curiosity. Colles looked like he would probably kill Peter with his bare hands, possibly just for making his job more difficult.

"And tell us everything you can remember about your stay on Ross, starting from the trip down there."

So Peter carefully explained about the rough flight out of Melbourne, the other passengers, the discoveries in the ice cores – the fine sediment deposits, the frozen fragment of *Vitis vinifera*, the stones.

He covered everything he could think of, even how he'd felt during the flight home. The professor was extremely interested in the plant specimen. Colles interjected to say it wasn't recovered from the wreck yet.

Conrick suggested that the plant material opens up another possibility. The disease could be caused by some kind of fungus, or unknown botanical poison. Hennessy also detailed the state of health of everyone at Ross, including himself. He could see Colles was not happy with the results of the discussion. He wanted answers, and he wanted them now.

"It's possible the disease reached Macquarie Island in a food shipment," Professor Conrick suggested. "Or was introduced by migratory birds. The Ross Station flight is'na the only option."

It's the only logical option, though," Peter quickly countered. He wasn't exactly sure what his role was supposed to be, but he was used to speaking his mind and assumed Colles would expect a contribution.

"If it came in a food shipment, you would have sick people at the source. Here," Peter continued. "And if the birds had brought it, then likewise, it would not be contained to Macquarie Island."

Colles nodded, apparently appreciative of Peter's contribution.

"Well, if it were carried by one or two penguin species, it may not get any further north than Macquarie," Conrick said. "We're still checking people down at other Antarctic bases. We're also checking people at Heard Island, the Auckland Islands, the Kerguelen Islands, South Georgia and the Falklands, all with negative results, so far." Conrick seemed a bit annoyed.

"We're even checking with hospitals on the southern Argentinian mainland and Tierra del Fuego," Conrick added. "And if it were in the food, mebbe no one else has eaten any of the same food. It could be still lying in a freezer somewhere, untouched. Although I agree that's unlikely."

He explained to Peter that he didn't think the disease was viral, theorising that it would be a very careless virus indeed that killed its host so quickly. Bacteria and fungi, on the other hand, are independent life forms. They grow, multiply and die, just as any other living species. Peter wondered about the logic of this but kept his non-medical thoughts quiet. Conrick started to explain about the great plagues of the past, starting with *Pasteurella pestis* bacteria, carried by rats, which caused the Black Death that killed millions upon millions of people, when Colles interrupted again.

"We don't need a history lesson. The status is this: we have a highly contagious, lethal disease which we believe to be isolated to a remote island in the Southern Ocean. That island is home for numerous species of birds, many of which could carry a plague and are easily able to migrate to and from Australia and New Zealand, and other populated places. The disease hasn't responded to normal treatment so far, and it's probably only a matter of time before it reaches a highly populated area.

"The bacteria, or whatever the hell it is ..." he looked pointedly at Conrick "... may have come from our Ross Island base, or it may not. I've listened to the health officials, I've listened to medical people, now I want some fucking answers. I want to know where this plague came from! And I want to know how the fuck we stop it!" Colles was clearly a man used to getting results.

"Okay. What's been done so far?" Hennessy asked, following Colles's lead.

"I'm briefing you in, based on Richardson's vouching for you," Colles said bluntly. "You understand that this is covered by national security legislation?"

"Yes, I do."

"Ross and Macquarie are now quarantined. Medical samples are on their way back from Macquarie – they were delayed by a thick fog around the island until this morning. Professor Conrick will supervise the analysis of these, starting right after this meeting."

"And you, doctor, I want you to travel back to Ross base. We have a small team set up to run the investigation, and you will assist them." Colles said it like it was an order.

"Why me?" Peter asked.

Colles looked hard at him. He had the feeling Colles was assessing whether he was afraid or not.

"Three reasons, doctor. First, you're familiar with the environment and the people at Ross; second, you have scientific training and we know you have a practical approach to problems; and third – possibly most importantly – they may trust you enough to confide in you." Colles had done some homework, it seemed.

"What do you think has happened at Ross Station?" Hennessy asked. He wanted to know what Colles knew.

"We have no indication that anything has happened, and there's no sign of any infection. But I'm not ruling anything out," Colles replied bluntly and unhelpfully.

"I want blood samples from everyone at Ross," Conrick said. "And I think we should also get blood from all the bird colonies at Macquarie. We may have to exterminate them if they're carrying the disease," he added matter-of-factly.

And if *the people* are carrying the disease? Peter wondered.

When Hennessy got back home after the meeting with Colles and Conrick, his head was still swimming. Another trip to Antarctica, a mysterious plague on Macquarie Island, clandestine government involvement – it was turning into a hell of a week! He wondered how the strange findings at Ross fitted in to it all. No, actually he wondered *if* the strange findings at Ross fitted in to it all. Perhaps he, as a scientist, just wanted them to. Colles said there was no indication of infection at Ross, but obviously there was risk. Peter was excited and slightly nervous at the same time.

He made himself a coffee and called John Morton in Sydney, to see what else he'd found out. Maybe there was more startling news waiting for him. He got John's voicemail on the first attempt and assumed he was lecturing, but soon his friend called back.

"John! Your message has my curiosity piqued," Peter said enthusiastically.

"Yes, it's been very interesting. I did more research last night and again this morning. The two maps that really got me going are from the 1500s. Piri Reis and Oronteus Finaeus." John spelt the names out for Peter to do his own searching.

"Piri Reis was a Turkish pirate and admiral who compiled his map in 1513, and Oronteus Finaeus was a European cartographer who produced his in 1532. The most astonishing feature of these maps is that they both appear to depict Antarctica with reasonable accuracy, yet it was only discovered in 1820 and the maps were drawn three hundred years earlier!

It also seems to be widely believed that they were compiled from much older sources, as yet unidentified.

"The catch is that there are some inaccuracies, and they're quite difficult to interpret, which gives the sceptics fertile ground. They're not like any maps you've seen before, old boy."

"How did you come across these? You mentioned a paper?" Peter asked.

"Yes. They're easy to find if you know what to search for, but the paper I found was, in fact, a book written in the 1950s. Hapgood was the professor's name. He proposed a theory of 'Earth Crust Displacement', which has not been widely accepted. His theory offers a possible explanation for a *temperate* climate on Antarctica just a few millennia ago. *A climate where grapes might grow ...*" John paused to let that sink in.

"Wow, my head is spinning. Can we go back to those maps? Tell me more."

"Certainly, Peter. I've gleaned that the two maps have been reliably dated and that they were produced thousands of kilometres apart by two people unlikely to have had any contact. One in what is now modern-day Turkey, and the other in France. Both have well-defined sections of great accuracy – even longitude, which European cartographers and navigators could not reliably measure until the eighteenth century. Both also have some sections where the latitude and longitude errors are consistent.

"Both also have land masses that don't exist. Or at least don't exist *today*," John added. "If Hapgood was right, though, who knows what sort of havoc a displacement of the earth's crust would wreak on oceans and islands."

"I suppose if Piri Reis and Oronteus Finaeus both had similar ancient source maps, they could then have applied the crude map-making techniques of their own time to compile their maps. That might account for anomalies?" Peter suggested.

"Careful, m'boy. That's heresy!" John laughed. "There's also the unusual projection of these maps. Mercator didn't come along until a generation or two later. According to some sources, the makers of these old maps both seemed to have some method of map projection similar to modern spherical trigonometry. That's a mystery in its own right, because spherical trigonometry supposedly wasn't invented until hundreds of years later."

"John, this is just astonishing!"

"It does seem to be, but remember there are all manner of fringe theories all over the Internet. Evidence is what's needed," John cautioned.

"But surely the maps are solid evidence?" Peter countered.

"Not solid enough. There are sufficient errors in them that our esteemed colleagues are very reticent," John said resolutely. "Of one thing I'm certain, though: if Piri Reis and Oronteus Finaeus did have the map-making skills required to produce these maps themselves, they could not have got those skills from the world's best-known scholars, or even from Europe's finest universities. This, to me, has all the hallmarks of an excellent mystery."

"Agreed," Peter said emphatically. "I'm flying back to Antarctica tomorrow, so maybe I'll find out more."

"Good heavens, man. Two flights in a month. That's more than most people in a lifetime. Do take care."

Indeed. If only you knew why, Peter thought, not without some concern.

11

In the awkward mirror of the tiny lavatory, Dr Nicole Palmer thought her face looked a little pale, although that was probably just the plane's anaemic, low-voltage lighting. She took the tie out of her hair, shook it out, and then tied it back again, deciding it was okay. She didn't normally bother with much make-up, just the basics, but today, for some reason, she had taken more time. She touched up her lipstick and smiled into the mirror.

"Why are you doing this?" she asked her reflection.

As she returned to her seat, the seat belt sign lit up.

The New Zealand and Australian government people hadn't been completely clear about her role, other than that it was to investigate the potential new disease, so Nicki wasn't quite sure what to expect. Regardless, she looked forward to seeing her mum. The last time they had caught up in person was just after her marriage break-up. A couple of weeks off work to visit home, more for moral support than anything else, was just what she'd needed.

If there was time, it would be great to catch up with some of her old friends from university as well. But these were fleeting thoughts, in a sea of emotions stirred up by these recent events. The ordered structure of her

74

reality was being challenged by Arnold Wood's 'delicate' situation where people were dying, by names from the past, by unresolved feelings. It gave her a strange sense of some unseen force that somehow tied these things together. Logic and science, she knew, could not explain everything.

Perhaps it was simply her own experience that made her accept that logical analysis couldn't always provide answers. Hennessy. A name from the past. Peter Hennessy was one of the few people she'd told about the story of something that happened to her as a little girl. Something that had shaped at least part of her world view, and something she had trusted very few other people with ...

At eight years of age, she'd had what she would now term a 'paranormal' experience. In fact, it had happened twice. The first time, she'd dreamt her grandfather had died. It was vivid, and horribly frightening for a little girl who loved her grandfather very much. She had woken up screaming, and when her mother ran into her room, she had said, 'Mummy, Grandpa's dead.' Her mother had consoled her, of course, and told her it was only a dream. But two days later, her grandpa did die, unexpectedly. Nicki was distraught and blamed herself because she had dreamt it and therefore must have made it happen.

For months she had been despondent, she just couldn't get it out of her mind. She was afraid of going to sleep just in case it happened to somebody else, and her mother was extremely worried about her. Then, about three months later, lying half awake in bed, listening to the rain outside, she'd felt someone tapping on her shoulder. She looked around and no one was there. She remembered wondering why she wasn't scared, but somehow she had known there was no danger. She felt the tapping again, this time on her leg, and looked around to see her grandfather standing at the foot of her bed. He quietly told her it wasn't her fault he had died. It was just that it was time for him to go, and that she'd seen it earlier because she was special, and because he loved her. She had just seen the future a few days ahead, that was all it was, he said.

As she grew up, she soon learnt she couldn't tell that story to her friends. None of them believed her. Some girls had made fun of her, calling her names. But not Peter. He had listened intently, accepting her words as fact right away ...

She walked out of the secure customs area and looked for a sign with her name on it, or a familiar face. Seeing no one, she started towards the exit when a young blonde girl appeared almost in front of her. She was chewing gum and holding a small card which said 'Dr Palmer'.

"I'm Dr Palmer," Nicki said.

"Oh hi, I'm Donna. Mr Colles didn't tell me you were a woman. I mean, I just expected a man, an older man." Nicki wasn't too sure how to take the girl. "He said you're some sort of medical expert, and the other one is an old guy." The girl wasn't making much sense. "Come on, Dr Palmer, I'll help you with your stuff."

"Call me Nicki."

"Cool," the girl said, offering a pack of sugar-free chewing gum. "You want some?"

"No thanks."

Donna helped Nicki with her luggage, and they went out to the car. It was cold outside, and the sky was dark grey, but at least it wasn't raining. She had a new sedan, with red and white government registration plates. All the way into the city, Donna chatted about everything from her fiancé and their wedding plans to her boss and the people she met at work. She told Nicki that usually her boss only dealt with 'boring government types'.

"Although, today was different. We had the health minister," Nicki could tell Donna didn't think much of the health minister, "her assistant, an old guy who looked like a scientist, then this other guy came in wearing jeans. I liked him."

"Nice butt, too," she added.

Nicki just smiled politely and asked Donna about her accommodation arrangements. Donna didn't know what had been booked, so they left the luggage in the car for now and went directly to the government complex in Treasury Place.

Colles gave her the same information he had passed on to Hennessy hours earlier. He told her the first part of their work would be analysis of the fluid samples from Macquarie Island, that he'd just briefed Hennessy, the last man back from Ross Island to be cleared, and that Hennessy would be part of the team.

"I think I know him," was all she'd said.

The samples had apparently been taken to a special laboratory outside the city, outside Yea, more than an hour and a half's drive away. He told her to phone Professor Conrick, who was already out at the Yea facility, and he'd give her details of her accommodation. Donna would arrange for a car, and supplied her with contact phone numbers.

Nicki was very businesslike with Colles and he seemed to respect that. He was a direct man, so she knew where she stood. Also, he hadn't seemed the least bit surprised that she was a young woman, and she appreciated that. It all happened so quickly she barely had time to think. She called Conrick as Colles had instructed.

"Conrick." A quiet and controlled voice, with a mild Scottish accent.

"Professor, this is Dr Nicole Palmer. I'm about to leave for the laboratory. I believe you're expecting me."

"Ah, yes. I'll brief ye when ye get here, lass."

Lass?

"We'll be isolating what I'm expecting to be a new strain of bacteria from the Macquarie fluid samples. I'm hopeful we'll be able to keep it contained to the island."

"What about migratory birds? Insects?" She had a lot of questions for the man.

"Insects cannae travel that far," Conrick countered.

"Parasitic infestation?"

"Och, well it's possible, but it's a long way. Nonetheless, I've asked for samples from the bird life as well as the people."

"All right. I think I should be there in about an hour and a half, depending upon the traffic." Nicki ended the call.

The long drive out to Yea on her own was when Nicki really started to process everything she'd learnt. She accepted what the professor had said at face value but wasn't completely convinced. It was possible a virus could infect bacteria, as well as more advanced life forms like animals or birds. A harmless and common bacteria could simply be the carrier, while the real killer could be a virus.

Her loan car was a much older version of the government car she'd ridden in from the airport. She typed the motel's details into her phone as her destination. Donna had also given her the details of the government laboratory – which, in the navigation app, was misleadingly denoted as a 'Commonwealth Agricultural Research Facility' – and had helped her transfer her luggage from the other car.

It was unlikely she would get to Yea before dusk, but Conrick had wanted her to get to the lab tonight anyway. Any plans she'd had to catch up with people seemed to have fallen by the wayside. She drove out of the city, listening to the radio playing softly, her head filled with unanswered questions.

The sky was looking decidedly dark, the weather report telling her 'there were thunderstorms predicted 'on the nearby hills'. She assumed they were referring to the hills she was driving towards. In the distance, the mountains she could see were a kind of dark blue, and swirled in thick, blackening low cloud. Stratocumulus opacus, she knew, but the name didn't do them justice. It understated them. The mountains were shrouded in the storm's harbinger. Nicki had always liked storms. She liked to watch lightning, to hear the thunder, rain and hail. Even the smell of a storm was special, a sort of musty warning, and she could smell it in the air now.

The traffic thinned as she reached Melbourne's outer edge. She'd taken the M3 out to the east, and by the time she drove through Croydon, dense suburbia had been replaced by larger rural properties, and ultimately farmland. As she passed through the Yarra Valley the forest had started to thicken, and the traffic was much lighter. The quieter country roads helped clear her mind, and she'd started to think more about the difficulties they might be faced with.

Nicki had done a lot of research on unusual bacterial infections over the past few years. There had been an incident in Milwaukee, Wisconsin where 400,000 people had contracted a flu-like infection caused by cryptosporidium getting into the city's water supply. There was another lesser outbreak of cryptosporidium in Sydney's water supply a few years ago. Then there was the occasionally deadly legionella bacteria, legionnaires' disease, which preyed upon the old and infirm, and lived in water. It was much more common than most people thought, living invisibly in water tanks, air-conditioning cooling tanks, swimming pools and even soil. It was just that to most of the population legionella was relatively harmless.

There were hundreds of others, too, some without names. That was the thing with bacteria – its life cycle was so short, and it multiplied so rapidly, it could evolve into something completely different well within the normal lifespan of a human being, or the lifespan of a tiny insect, for that matter.

Many of the known bacteria were also becoming much more resistant to treatment, too. Since the discovery of penicillin in 1928, the wonder drug of the twentieth century, dozens of strains of new penicillin-resistant bacteria had emerged. Nothing had yet been discovered to kill these new tough microbes. And there were different ways in which they could change; sometimes with the aid of a bacteriophage – a virus that can attack a bacterium. More commonly, though, there was simple, spontaneous mutation; sometimes they just changed *because they could.*

And treatment could be complex. Part of the problem is, of course, that humans and animals are dependent on certain types of bacteria. The *Escherichia coli*, or *E. coli* bacterium, for example, billions of which live in the human digestive system, enabling the intestines to work effectively. The gut needs *E. coli* bacteria, so it's not just a simple matter of killing them all. Any treatment has to kill the *right* bacteria.

All these thoughts were still spinning through her mind when she pulled into the car park at the Riverside Motel. She walked in the light rain to the office, collected her key then moved her car to a spot outside room 17, her home for the next few days. Hers was the only car there, July apparently not being the peak period for this part of the country. If in fact there *was* a peak period for this part of the country ...

She dropped her luggage in the room and went into the bathroom to dry her hair. Then she opened her handbag and rummaged through it, eventually finding a small piece of paper with the phone numbers Donna had neatly written. She sat down on the bed, collecting her thoughts for a moment, and was about to make a call when there was a knock at the door.

"Hi," Nicki said to the boy standing outside. He was holding a small glass jug of milk and a menu. "You forgot your breakfast menu. Just fill it in, and drop it back at reception when you're ready, as long as it's before nine o'clock. Oh, and here's a jug of milk for your tea and coffee."

"Thank you." She took the jug and smiled at him. Then found the tea bags, which were next to a small pack of two biscuits of the kind that no one who really liked biscuits would buy, and made herself a cup of tea.

Okay, now don't put it off any longer, she thought. She took out her phone and dialled the number.

"Hello." A friendly and familiar voice.

"Peter ..." she said awkwardly. 'How have you been' just didn't seem the right thing to say. A second or two passed in silence.

"Hello?" he repeated.

"Hi, Peter. It's Nicki Palmer here. You knew me as Nicki Poulsen." She tried to sound more sure of herself.

"Nicki?"

Recognition. Surprise?

"Yes. Hi, Peter."

"How ... what are you doing ... ah ...?"

"What am I doing here?" she interrupted.

He laughed. "I'm sorry, you've taken me by surprise. I didn't think I'd ever see you again." His choice of words elicited a slightly sad smile but helped her to relax.

"I'm working for Conrick on this Macquarie Island thing. I've just arrived in Yea. I flew in from Wellington this morning." Another short pause. "How have you been?"

"Pretty good, I guess. But I've missed you terribly, of course." She couldn't tell whether he was being serious or not.

"We're on the same team, it seems. I thought I should call and say hello." Suddenly it seemed to Nicki that she should have been in touch with him a long time ago. They had been friends, after all, even though it had ended awkwardly.

"Well, you've surprised me! It's been what, over three years? I'm delighted to hear your voice again." He seemed genuinely pleased.

She hadn't known what to expect. It occurred to her only now that she'd possibly really hurt his feelings when she avoided him in those last two weeks they'd worked together.

"I'm sorry, I ..." This didn't seem the time to explain how she'd felt. *If* she could explain it to him. "I'm sorry I haven't been in touch sooner," she finished weakly.

"It's okay."

"Now that we're working together again, it would be great to catch up with you." She found herself wishing she could see his face. She wanted to know how he *felt*.

"Well, I'd love to catch up with you, but this morning I met a man who I think wants an expendable scientific observer, or maybe a guinea pig," he said "Anyway, he's sending me back to Ross Island tomorrow. He says I'll be able to help because the Ross people know me and trust me, but I'm not sure if that was the whole truth. Anyway, that means we'll have to postpone, I'm afraid."

"That sounds like the man I met today. Colles?" She tried to hide her disappointment.

"That's him."

"When will you get back?"

"I don't know. A few days, I guess. I'm not sure if it's exciting or reckless. Either way, I've already started to have some possibly crazy ideas." That sounded just like the Peter she remembered. "It's lovely to hear your voice again," he added. Nicki didn't know what to say.

After a few seconds of silence, Peter jumped in first. "I hope you don't mind me asking, but I think we have a bit to talk about. With this Macquarie thing. I have some things to fill you in on, and maybe you can help me fill in a few blanks – I'm not completely sure about what I'm getting into.

"Yea isn't that far from me, and it's not yet seven. I could be there in an hour or so." *What was he trying to say?* "Could I meet you there?"

"I'm staying at a motel. There's not even a restaurant. It's a bit depressing," Nicki said, wondering if they could meet at the facility.

"Okay, I understand. When I'm back we can talk more. I'm so glad you called."

"No. I don't mean ... I really do want to catch up with you. Maybe we can meet somewhere. They've given me a car." Oh no – did she sound too eager? Another pause.

"I hope you don't think me too forward, but do you want to come here? I mean, it might help to go over my notes and ideas. I'll even cook you some dinner. You're welcome to stay here. I have a spare room," he said. "And I'd like to see you," he added.

"Yes, I'd like that."

He gave her directions and warned her the weather was getting worse.

"It's the same here," she replied. "If I'm not there by dawn, you'd better send out a search party."

12

The office might have been an English nobleman's library, with its dark-timber bookshelves on all but one wall, dark-green carpet and the oversized antique mahogany desk, complete with tooled-leather inlay. It even had an antique brass banker's lamp. It smelt of opulence. The desk was kept meticulously tidy by its owner, with only current matters ever permitted to intrude. The large room's sole occupant sat in an expensive leather chair drinking a cup of steaming jasmine tea, which had just been brought to him by an attractive young assistant.

The man had never taken notice of the girl's looks, he was not interested in matters of the flesh. The girl always noticed the man's looks, though; he could have been an attractive man, she thought, but there was something cold and disturbing in his eyes. She was afraid of him. She hated going into his office, it felt like she was entering a spider's lair.

The phone rang, and the man looked at it disdainfully. He allowed it to ring four times before carefully putting down his tea and picking up the receiver. "Yes."

"I think I have your man," the caller said. "He has access. And he's greedy." There was a lot of background noise. It sounded as though the caller was in a crowd.

"Excellent," the man in the leather chair said. "When will he be contacted?"

"Tomorrow morning."

"See that it goes well."

Xeng Pang put the receiver down. He decided everything was going extremely well. From the time he had obtained information about the plague, he had orchestrated events perfectly. Soon he would be in a position to execute his brilliant plan, and prove once and for all that Xeng Pang was not a man to be buried in this pathetically ineffectual diplomatic role.

He was in complete control, and he was a brilliant tactician, capable of bold, decisive action. His plan was foolproof, no one could suspect the truth. Not even Lin Fan Cheng. Xeng knew he could trust Lin completely at this moment; Lin was utterly under his spell. And it did not matter what Lin would think of the next stage. Once the plan had progressed that far, Lin was of no further use anyway. Xeng sat in his office with a smile on his face that would have sent a terrible chill down the spine of the young female assistant. He knew he was approaching the greatest moment of his life.

After his call to Xeng, Lin felt exhilarated. He had pleased Xeng with his achievements; he had delivered all that had been asked, and within the time Xeng had allowed. He walked down the bustling Little Bourke Street to The Dragon's Kingdom. Little Bourke Street was Melbourne's Chinatown, and today, like any other weekday, it was alive with people. Australians, Malaysians, even camera-laden Japanese tourists, but mostly Chinese. Lin walked through the crowds purposefully carrying his black leather portfolio and mobile phone. He attracted no undue attention, he was just another young Chinese businessman going about his business.

He stepped confidently into the restaurant, past the other people standing and waiting, and gave his name to the arrogant-looking young host. The Dragon's Kingdom was one of the most popular and exclusive

Chinese restaurants in Melbourne, but the staff knew Lin and had seen him dine with Xeng Pang recently. He was seated immediately, at a table screened off from the main area. He had told the head waiter he had an important business meeting, and he wanted some privacy. He rehearsed the words he would use in this historic meeting.

Lin was outraged when Xeng had told him the Australian authorities were concealing a dangerous plague and allowing their own people to die. Lin understood that Xeng wanted to embarrass the Australian Government, but he also agreed with Xeng that the world should be informed of what was happening. Then the government would have to ensure appropriate measures were taken. Of course, this would require irrefutable proof, and that was where Lin came in.

A few minutes later, the head waiter showed Lin's 'business associate', *a rude American*, he thought, through the flimsy bright red and gold screens to the table.

Lin Fan Cheng ordered a cup of Chinese tea while his companion had a glass of bourbon on the rocks. Lin's guest had towered over most of the other people in the restaurant, his long blond hair making him all the more obvious amongst the shorter, dark-haired Chinese. He had a scar on his left cheek, visible through his untidy beard. Lin thought he could tell why Xeng had chosen him; at first glance he had the look of the 'greenies' and environmental activists Lin had seen in the Australian newspapers so often. But on closer inspection, there was a hard coldness in his eyes that Lin had not expected.

After the waiter had brought the drinks, Lin opened his portfolio and took out a sheet of paper and a photograph. "This is the man," he said, handing the photograph and paper to Kevacic. "You should be able to contact him at one of those phone numbers tomorrow morning." There was a name, two phone numbers and two addresses.

"You will represent the IHRF, the International Human Rights Force. They are a US-based, privately funded organisation who expose government acts that disregard human rights. They have had fairly public involvement in Cambodia with the Khmer Rouge, in East Timor with the

Indonesians and, more recently, in Haiti." Lin paused to take some tea.

"They have also exposed an Australian Government incident before. Atomic device tests that affected innocent native Australians at Maralinga, South Australia in the 1950s. The target will know the IHRF."

"You can tell him that you've heard of an outbreak of a highly contagious disease on an Australian island, which the government are concealing. Your organisation believes the government are risking the lives of civilians with their secrecy. You will say it is your target's duty to give you the information."

As Kevacic was listening to him, with a level of disdain or disinterest that seemed downright rude, Lin started to wonder about Xeng's choice. To Lin, the man now looked more like a dangerous drug dealer than an environmental activist. Still, it was not his place to question his leader.

"Your target will not be interested in any of this and will probably deny it all. You will not reveal your sources. You are then to offer him some money for information."

"How much money?" Kevacic would probably base his own fee on the amount of money involved, Lin knew.

Lin withdrew a manila envelope from his inside pocket and handed it to Kevacic. "Start with five thousand dollars. Tell him you will pay him that for information about the disease and its location. We do not believe it will be enough, but the man will be interested. Draw him out; perhaps you will find out how much he knows.

"Eventually, you may offer him twenty thousand dollars for complete details of the island, the number of deaths, government involvement, and you must also tell him you will pay another *fifty thousand dollars* if he can provide you with a sample of the disease. That is most important."

Xeng had been adamant about that. 'I must have proof,' he had said. Lin had readily agreed with Xeng – the Australians had been criticising China's human rights record for years, ever since Tian'anmen Square, and Lin agreed they should obtain irrefutable proof that Australia was concealing a deadly plague; that perhaps the Australians' word should not be blindly accepted after all.

"My fee will be five thousand dollars," Kevacic said. Lin must not have looked annoyed enough, for he added, "For each meeting. And a further twenty thousand for your sample."

"Very well," Lin eventually answered, knowing Xeng would be satisfied.

13

Gary ran down Wireless Hill as quickly as he could in the darkness. As he got closer to the sickbay, he saw two sides of the building engulfed in flames. Nick Anakos was already there with two men, all with fire extinguishers, spraying the walls, to little effect. The fire seemed to have spread quickly and really taken hold. He stood there dumbfounded for a moment, then asked the obvious question. "What happened?"

"Smell it?" said Anakos, and Gary noticed the unmistakable fumes in the air.

Someone had deliberately started the fire. But why? Several more people came to throw buckets of water at the flames, but it wasn't much use. The sickbay building was made of steel panels, but it was lined with a thick plastic insulation, which was feeding the blaze very effectively. Clouds of pungent black smoke were billowing up into the fog above.

"It's no use!" someone shouted.

"Keep at it!" Anakos snapped back. He and Masters both knew that most of their medical supplies were stored in that building.

"Go to the supply shed and get me the spare extinguishers," Anakos roared at two of the men. Gary ran with them, not knowing what else to do.

He shoved the shed door open and burst inside. He found the light switch and flooded the supply shelves with a bright fluorescent glow.

They all looked around, then one of the men asked, "Which ones?" pointing at three red and three yellow fire extinguishers.

Their indecision suddenly snapped Gary back into action. "Doesn't matter, fire's not electrical. Get one each and throw me one."

They ran back to the sickbay, but by the time they got there the whole building was alight. They turned their extinguishers onto the flames, struggling valiantly with the fire, but they knew they were going to lose. Within fifteen hot, sweaty, heartbreaking minutes, their sickbay, doctor's quarters and most of their medical supplies had been destroyed.

From outside the twisted wreckage, the warped steel panels and the pools of foam, Gary could see the charred bodies of two men. He looked at Anakos, and the two of them carefully walked through the debris.

Gary touched some of the steel roofing. "Shit!" he snatched his hand away, leaving burnt skin sizzling on the hot metal. They saw the bodies of Mick and Josh, and knew that further in they would find Macka and Doc.

"Jesus Christ," said Anakos, echoing Masters' thoughts.

The last time Gary had seen Mick he was still breathing. He might have been burnt alive. The smell of the charred flesh and the whole scene before his eyes suddenly took control of him. He ran out of the wreckage and vomited. It was all too much. What kind of people would burn a man to death, even if he was dying already?

They had no real choice but to leave the bodies in the sickbay. They couldn't bury them – there would have to be autopsies – and it was certain no one was going to touch them. The sick were now using one of the dormitories. It had become a sort of leper colony, no one healthy going anywhere near it. If any of them ventured out, others would scream at them from a distance to get back inside. Fear was overriding everything else at the base. All work had stopped. If anyone so much as sneezed, he was immediately ostracised. Everyone watched everyone else.

After the fire had been put out, Masters and Anakos stood near the smoking wreckage, drawing warmth from it.

"Where the fuck were you?" Anakos said, without animosity.

"Wireless Hill. I needed time to think," Gary said inadequately, his voice strangely emotionless.

"It was the bodies, I suppose. Someone must have decided to burn the bodies, after Mick died. A medieval cleansing."

"Well, they've burnt most of our medical supplies as well," Masters muttered sullenly. "Now we're in even deeper shit." He shook his head slowly. "Fuck!"

Masters went to his room in the communications hut. He didn't know what to do. Anakos had done his job for him at the fire earlier, and they both knew it. The others knew it, too. It was true that Masters by now felt pretty sick, but he had not developed much of a fever yet, and he knew in his heart that illness wasn't the reason for his failure.

All his life, Masters had fought to prove himself. He had tackled many difficult tasks, the odds often against him, and he had always prevailed. He had a deep need to succeed against harsh conditions, a need to prove himself as a good leader, a defiant refusal to fail. All these things were now laughing in his face. He felt like his whole life was disintegrating before him, all the successes of the past becoming irrelevant. He was losing everything he had worked for since he was fifteen.

He now had more than dozen sick people on the base, including himself, and about twenty still healthy. And they had now polarised completely into opposing sides in a war. The sick were herded into one building and not allowed to venture out. They had been given enough food to last a few days, but the healthy ones had more or less written them off as dead. Thousands of years of civilisation had been undone by the most basic of emotions – fear. Cold, unreasoning fear. Friendships, rational thought, common sense were now all things of the past. A primal, tribal world had taken over. Masters had no doubt that if one of the sick ventured into a 'healthy area', he would be killed rather than be allowed to get too close.

Nick Anakos was worried about Gary. He knew Masters was showing some signs of the bug, but he had never seen him be anything but strong with his people before, and tonight Masters had been weak and ineffectual. He had stood there like an idiot and watched the fire, until Nick screamed out some orders. Anakos knew Macquarie base needed a leader now more than it ever had, and he didn't think Gary was up to the job. He had to try to galvanise Masters' strength, help him in any way he could. He doggedly went into the communications building, looking for the man they all needed right now.

"Gary." Anakos knocked on the door as he called. There was no answer so he went inside.

Masters was sitting on his bed. He looked up at Nick. "I know why you're here. You think I fucked up badly tonight."

"You've had to deal with a hell of a lot over the past couple of days. I know it can't have been easy, and I know you haven't had much sleep." Anakos grinned at Masters. "You do look like shit, you know." Masters didn't smile back.

"Do you want me to contact Jenny Holderay for you?" Nick thought that might relieve some of the strain.

"Don't you think I can handle it?" Masters asked accusingly, his tone taking Anakos by surprise; he had never seen Masters so defensive.

"Look, Gary, you're still the boss, I'm only here to offer my help. What do you think we should do?" Nick noticed a flare gun next to Masters' bed and had a fleeting thought that Masters was losing it.

"I think *we*," Masters sneered the word, "should get some sort of order back into this place. Tell me how you would do *that*." Masters had a wild look in his eyes.

"I don't know, Gary," Nick said in a calm voice.

"Get the fuck out of here. This is my base." Masters glanced at the flare gun as he stood up. Anakos was fairly solidly built and could hold his own in a fight, but Masters was much bigger.

"Come on, Gary, I'm here to help. I work for you, remember?" Nick walked a little closer to Masters, again seeing a glazed expression in his eyes. "We should work together." Anakos was inching toward Masters.

They had never been the greatest of friends, but they had certainly never been enemies. Nick respected Masters and he believed Gary respected him. The scene unfolding in the hut was almost surreal to Nick, and he had to push his rational thoughts aside to focus on what needed to be done. Masters was falling apart, and Nick believed he might be a danger to himself and maybe others.

Moving toward Masters seemed to aggravate him more, but Nick wanted to get between him and the flare gun. Maybe then he could back off a little and defuse the situation.

"Fuck off, you lying bastard!"

Gary looked away for a second as he moved to pick up the gun, and Anakos grabbed the opportunity. He jumped forward and hit him under the jaw as hard as he could. For a couple of seconds he thought Masters was going to shoot him, but then the big man's legs buckled and he fell to the floor.

Anakos was sweating and shaking. The whole incident had frightened the hell out of him, and he wasn't too sure what to do next. They had no lock-up to put Masters in. Maybe he'd regain consciousness and be more coherent, maybe not. As he thought out his next move, he rationalised that he had behaved the best way he could in the situation; he couldn't think of any other way.

He took the loaded flare pistol from the bed and put it in his jacket pocket. Then he tried to get Masters onto the bed, without success, so he took a blanket and covered him, placing a pillow under his head. He prised Masters' mouth open to make sure he hadn't bitten through his tongue in the fall, or when he'd hit him. Anakos was thankful Masters was far from at his best, otherwise the result could have been very different.

He left the room, taking the only key he could find, and locked the door. He was both glad and sorry that Gary kept the liquor in his quarters; it meant he had the only lockable sleeping quarters on the base, but it also meant Gary could get himself drunk. He'd never seen Gary violently drunk, but it wasn't a happy thought.

Nick set off for the main communications room to contact ANARE and give them a clear picture of the events so far. He decided to omit the fight. His news was going to shock them enough without that, he knew. Instead, he would tell them Gary was delirious with fever. He hoped they could help him work out what the hell to do next. At the very least, he could make sure they would get new medical supplies, including antibiotics, airdropped to them. Ideally they would have a medical team flown in, but it seemed unlikely, since it meant risking more lives.

Nick was not a religious man, but he found himself quietly praying that Masters would be rational and calm when he regained consciousness. He needed all the help he could get.

14

"Get Ned down here quick!" Bob Jacks shouted to his partner. Something had happened to the equipment. He wasn't sure what, but either they had struck something really hard, or something odd had gone wrong with the drill.

They were at 789 metres, and that was about the level where they had found the stones and the piece of grapevine. Bob remembered when they'd found the first stone, the drill had bucked noticeably, and they thought something had snapped. In fact, he'd been very surprised when all it turned out to be was a baseball-sized rock. It was their first drill malfunction, and they'd taken ice cores at a lot of different sites on Ross Island. To the men operating the equipment, these problems were causing a lot of speculation.

Drilling core samples was a relatively straightforward process, much easier than, say, drilling through many different types of earth and rock for oil. Sure, the ice was damn hard, but at least it was consistent. He went over to look at the drill housing assembly, which stood about four metres tall. To a layman, he knew, it looked a lot like steel spaghetti, with cables and cogs everywhere. But Bob knew his job.

Bob Jacks had been working with this sort of machinery for the best part of twenty years, and he was getting pretty concerned about these unexplained difficulties. The drill's engine appeared to have seized, but he had always maintained it with meticulous loving care; he was certain it was not the result of carelessness or normal wear. Ten minutes ago the machine had been fine, plenty of oil, all cabling properly lubricated, and there was no unusual strain on any part of it.

"Did you break your drill again, Bob?" Kelly called out good-naturedly, as he walked into the portable drilling hut, snow falling from his beard.

"Dunno what's wrong, Neddy." Bob was practically shouting to be heard over the combined noise of the generator and the wind blasting the hut outside. "She should be workin' fine. I've checked the core drill out and it's not stuck, and a few minutes ago the motor was purrin' like a kitten. It's as if she's just decided to stop by herself."

"What could've caused it?" Kelly asked, going over to have a closer look.

"No idea, mate. It's bloody weird. I first thought we musta' hit somethin' really hard, but that's not it. See, I can move the core drill manually." Bob showed Ned that the shaft still seemed to move a little as he levered it. "Anyway," he went on, "the clutch that releases the shaft if it gets stuck is still workin'."

Kelly knew that meant that, even if the drill had hit something as hard as steel, the clutch would have disengaged the engine. Striking hard rock hadn't been the cause. "Can you fix it?"

"Maybe. But I reckon the Hand o' God musta stopped 'er."

Kelly asked Bob to keep him informed of his progress and to find out what had happened, then went back to the main base. As Kelly was hanging his coat up, young Jamie came running up to say he had a call waiting from Australia.

"Okay, thanks Jamie, I'll be right there." Kelly hurried after the young red-haired communications officer into a small room with benches along two walls and two tired old chairs. Though they still called it the 'radio room', the days of the old-fashioned short-wave radio sets were long gone. The benches were littered with telephone and satellite communications equipment, two PCs, an old fax machine that seemed to still work and a rat's nest of cables.

He picked up the phone. "Kelly."

"John, Marc Richardson here. We've got a flight leaving for Ross from Melbourne tomorrow morning." Kelly didn't like Richardson much. He was too much of a politician. "Dr Hennessy is coming back, and he'll be bringing another doctor with him. Routine investigation of this infection at Macquarie."

Routine investigation of a plague! That was an interesting turn of phrase. "Okay, I'll expect them by tomorrow night. How are things at Macquarie?" Kelly asked.

"I believe as well as can be expected," Richardson replied cautiously.

What kind of answer was that? Kelly wondered. "Uh-huh. Well, let me know if we can help. And you'll see that our supplies and mail are on the flight, won't you?"

Kelly had been relieved to find out that their regular supply and mail deliveries were now reinstated. The only quarantine condition remaining was that no one could leave without clearance from Melbourne. He wondered how they justified flying guests in and out of his base, even if they were doctors. Maybe doctors and government people were somehow immune ...

* * *

JULY 28, MELBOURNE, AUSTRALIA

Colles sat in his office on the sixth floor and looked out the window. He could see the storm developing over the ranges thirty kilometres away. It was almost nightfall, and the sky over the east of Melbourne looked threatening and oppressive. It was exactly the right sort of sky for a night like this, Colles thought grimly.

He had just completed his report on Macquarie to the health minister. She wasn't going to like it, but he didn't much care. He would present the truth, warts and all, and he had no intention of dressing it up to make anyone happy, least of all the Praying Mantis.

He had once heard one of his staff refer to the minister as a *praying mantis,* and he had thought the description entirely appropriate. The female praying mantis devours the male after mating. Of course, he had told his staff member off, knowing what would happen if the man had been overheard by someone else, but he had chuckled about it in his office afterwards.

Colles picked up the report and read it through once more, ensuring there could be no misinterpretation.

Macquarie Island
Situation Report
28 July, 19:00

1. MEDICAL

    1.1 Presenting symptoms (unchanged)
- Acute common cold symptoms and headache
- Respiratory tract inflammation
- High fever
- Severe pulmonary oedema
- Death

    1.2 Incubation
- Infection by close proximity, physical/body fluid contact may not be necessary (unconfirmed)
- Incubation within twenty-four hours
- All symptoms (including death) can manifest within thirty-six to ninety-six hours
- Not known whether carried by non-human subjects

    1.3 Biological Hazard
- Level 3–4 (preliminary assessment)
- *Pathogen appears impervious to penicillin. Other tests pending.*

2. SUBJECT STATUS

    2.1 Macquarie Island[1]
- Eight dead. Five confirmed from infection, three from plane crash 21/7 Crash victims' bodies show no evidence of disease (unconfirmed)
- Approximately twelve live subjects in varying stages of infection (unconfirmed)
- Approximately twenty subjects in good health (unconfirmed)

- Base leader Masters infected. Symptoms include delirium
- Local situation volatile. Incidents of violence reported, medical facilities and supplies destroyed, four bodies have been burnt
- *Medical supplies required urgently*

2.2 Ross Island[2]

- Crashed flight originated from Ross Island base, Antarctica 21/7. Plane situated at Ross for eleven days prior to departure
- All personnel reported to be in good health
- Ross Island considered stable, currently quarantined
- *No other instances have been reported*

3. POSSIBLE SOURCES (Conrick verbal report 28/7 07:00)

3.1 Bacterial. Possible sources:

- Ross Island (considered unlikely)
- Macquarie wildlife. Includes royal penguin, king penguin, rockhopper penguin, Antarctic petrel, sooty albatross, fur seal, elephant seal
- Food supplies. Last shipment arrived 5/7. Source Hobart. Same shipment also went on to Ross Island base, via ship and helicopter (considered unlikely)
- Insects. Advised as possibility by Conrick at 18:00 (particularly parasitic infestations of migratory birds)

3.2 Viral. Possible sources as for 3.1

- Now considered less likely

3.3 Fungal. Possible sources as for 3.1, additionally:

- Partial botanic specimen[3] found at Ross Island in ice core (800 m) 11/7

3.4 Artificial Toxin (airborne or otherwise)

- Not considered by Conrick as realistic possibility but cannot be ruled out

3.5 Hypothesis

1) New strain of bacteria, unfamiliar to human immune system
2) New fungal infection, unfamiliar to human immune system

4. ACTIONS TO DATE

26/7 Macquarie Island and Ross Island quarantined, and personal communications to both islands disallowed

27/7 Blood and fluid samples prepared by Macquarie doctor (now deceased) Tests completed on all six persons departed from Ross Island (five in Melbourne, one in Wellington). All cleared

28/7 Macquarie samples flown to Melbourne for analysis (delayed by adverse weather conditions)
Conrick requests body fluid samples from all Ross Island personnel and from birdlife at Macquarie

5. RECOMMENDATION

- Maintain suspension of non-official communications from Macquarie and Ross
- If situation not resolved within 72 hours of this report:
- Exterminate all animal and bird life on island, unless excluded by confirmed tests
- Exterminate all bird life on all other islands within migratory path, unless excluded by confirmed tests
- Actions for personnel to be determined

Alternate option of allowing disease to run its course without action deemed unsuitable

---

[1] Verbal report by Nick Anakos, senior meteorologist, Macquarie, 28/7, 18:15

[2] Verbal report by John Kelly, Ross base leader, Antarctica, 28/7, 16:30

[3] Exact nature of specimen unconfirmed. Preliminary analysis at Ross Island indicates *Vitis vinifera* (common grape). **Specimen lost in plane crash at Macquarie.**

Colles didn't bother to reread the last section of the report. He had already been over that three times. In any case, the health minister could work out the risks for herself.

He knew exactly what his report meant to the people living on the island. Biological hazard level three to four. That put it somewhere between anthrax and Ebola – both deadly – and it might prove to be worse. Technically, it was level four, as there was no known treatment at this point. If Conrick's team was unsuccessful in isolating the disease and developing a cure within the next three days, Colles had just recommended the death of every animal and bird on the island. This did not exclude the extermination of human life on the island, either.

He did not feel callous about it; he knew there was no other choice. If this plague got to the mainland somehow, it could wipe out much of the population within a matter of days. Colles also knew that producing and issuing enough of a new antibiotic, or immunisation, for nearly thirty million people in Australia and New Zealand within that time was far from the realms of possibility. He intended to personally explain that to the minister. It would not go in the report. At least not yet.

He looked out the window again and saw heavy rain pouring down on the eastern suburbs. As he watched, sheet lightning flashed over the mountains, momentarily bathing them in brilliant light. A flash too quick to see anything in detail, then back into darkness. A few seconds later he heard the loud crack of thunder explode into the night.

He got up to hand-deliver the report to the Praying Mantis, whom he knew would be in her office waiting impatiently for it. She would read it cursorily, then quiz him on his recommendations, as she assessed how they could affect her chances of re-election. As he stepped out of the elevator onto the plush, leather-furnished, thickly carpeted ninth floor, he found himself hoping like hell that Conrick was good at what he did.

*   *   *

The temperature had dropped a few more degrees as the wind turned more southerly, and the light rain had turned into a heavy downpour. Peter Hennessy had hardly noticed, though. Speaking to Nicki had brought back memories of a painful time in his life. Memories and feelings he thought he had left behind a long time ago, most of them centred around the end of his marriage to Sam. It was odd how a voice from the past could spark such things, he reflected.

As he made up the bed in the spare room, he also found himself wondering how Nicki had been. Would they still have the same rapport? Three years! Anything could have happened in that time. When they had been friends, he'd been emotionally drained. He was sure he was a different person now. 'Palmer' she had said; she must have got married since they'd last seen each other. Peter wanted to be happy for her.

It was going to be a cold night, and the firewood supply in the living room was low. He went out the front door, not bothering with a jacket, since the short path leading to the woodshed at the side of the house was sheltered. As he walked, an explosive cracking sound, rising above the howling wind, came from above. He stopped and listened, but it was too dark to see where it had come from. The clouds had completely obscured the moon and stars – the night was black as pitch. He couldn't make any sense of the sounds around him, the wind and rain screaming through the trees filling his ears. Perhaps he had imagined it.

But then it came a second time, the same violent wrenching sound, punctuating the wind and rain, but this time it was followed by a series of explosions, Thor wielding his mighty hammer again. Then, with a deep, earth-shaking thud, a huge tree limb landed across the driveway.

Peter's heart raced, and he was sure he'd cried out involuntarily. The branch had landed no more than ten metres from where he had been standing. He hadn't even seen it until it had practically hit the ground. He stood there for a few seconds just staring at it.

He was shaken, but his rational mind reminded him that it wasn't the first time one of the big gum trees had dropped a limb. The trees were colloquially known as 'widow-makers', and they were very common in the area. He'd been told a few times to get rid of them, but he liked the shade they provided, and he liked living in a 'real' bush setting.

He took a closer look to find that the branch had blocked the driveway completely. As his eyes got more accustomed to the darkness, he was able to see the trees above. They looked fairly safe – there were no more limbs overhanging the drive, but he could picture Nicki coming in and crashing into the debris. They had spoken well over half an hour ago so she would arrive soon. He ran back through the rain to the woodshed to get an axe, and returned to clear some of the smaller branches away.

As he worked, he wondered what his neighbours would think if they came down the road now, a madman with an axe running around in the middle of a violent storm.

15

Heavy rain kept visibility down to not much more than eight to ten metres. As cars approached, Nicki could see the faint and diffuse glow from oncoming headlights, and then suddenly, as if emerging from a dark ocean, a car would appear only a few metres ahead. The appalling driving conditions didn't seem to slow other drivers down too much, though; quite a few of them had passed her, even on corners. No doubt mostly locals who knew the road well, or were just plain reckless, she assumed.

She had given up on the radio – reception was practically non-existent, either from the weather or the mountains all around her, so she was driving to the sound of the rain beating down on the roof of the car. Occasionally a flash of lightning would light up a few more metres of road, as well as momentarily and eerily illuminating the huge trees that surrounded her.

Sometimes she thought she could see glistening eyes staring at her car when a flash lit up the trees ahead. Possums, she told herself. With the poor visibility, she was relying heavily on the road signs, as well as the reflectors on the roadside posts, red on the right and white on the left. And although she was tired, there was little chance of falling asleep at the wheel tonight, she told herself; staying on the road required all the concentration she could muster.

As she drove, she wondered what Peter's house would be like. She wondered how she would feel, and how he felt about her. She was apprehensive about seeing him after all this time. Three years ago she'd still been in her twenties. They were only seven years apart, but that seemed a lot. Peter was so much more settled, and *married*. She'd told herself it was just a crush, but she knew it was deeper than that. They'd got to know each other and developed a real bond.

As the weather threw its worst at her, she also wondered about the wisdom of driving these roads at night. Every time she saw a faint glow ahead – probably just headlights – she slowed a little and had to concentrate hard on the road. There were no street lights on these country roads, so she was reliant on the roadside reflectors. She drove past what appeared to be a road sign, or at least the white painted steel post of a road sign which had been knocked over. Immediately she slowed down, and as she did she saw the road ahead disappear.

Too late! Instinctively, she swerved right, barely registering that the white roadside reflectors veered sharply around a bend, and at that moment the oncoming car appeared, headlights almost blinding her. The lights were way up high. She still couldn't see the road, just blinding lights. A horn blared, and then it was dark again.

A truck roared past. She was half on the road and half off, and had jammed on the brakes. The car had started to slide sideways. She screamed as she skidded towards a dark, imposing stand of trees. Turning the wheel furiously, she pounded the brake pedal again, but nothing helped. As she braced herself for the inevitable impact, the car gently came to a complete stop, and the engine cut out. Silence.

She was shaking, but wasn't about to fall apart. She steeled herself as best she could. "I'm okay," she told herself, more than once. She hadn't hit anything. Or anyone. In the pale headlights she could see the road not far away and was quickly getting her bearings. She turned the key and heard the starter whining but the car didn't start.

"Oh, you've got to be kidding," she said to the trees, taking a deep breath. She switched off the headlights, tried the key again. This time the car started. She slowly drove forward to the road, hoping not to get bogged, and within a couple of minutes was safely back on the tarmac. It was still cold, but she was sweating. *Why am I doing this tonight?* she wondered.

Now soaking wet, Peter had almost finished work on the fallen tree. He'd been at it for at least twenty minutes when he saw headlights approaching through the driving rain. The car had slowed to look for house numbers.

Nicki saw Peter as she pulled into the driveway, and stopped half a metre short of the mess. He watched as she stepped out of the car. He couldn't help but smile as he looked at her. It was wonderful to see her again. She was wearing jeans and a woollen jersey, and she didn't bother with an umbrella.

"Hi." Her smile was still the same. It would melt the iciest of hearts.

"Hi," he said, wrapping her in a wet bear hug for a moment. "Oh, sorry. I'm a bit damp."

"Great night for a bit of gardening," she said, bending down to help him move some of the smaller branches in the bright glow of the headlights. A few minutes later, she was able to drive the car into his yard. He helped her with her gear. She'd brought a small overnight bag, he noticed.

They stood in Peter's living room, both dripping wet, looking at each other and laughing. *He looks happier than I remember*, she thought. *There's a peace in his eyes. More than I remember from three years ago anyway. His hair's longer.*

He was looking at her face, his eyes holding hers. She wanted to say she had missed him, the moments they'd shared all that time ago suddenly back in her mind. Were these rational thoughts? They had never been more than friends. Still, it was very good to see him again.

"Did you bring a change of clothes?" he asked, breaking the spell.

"Only for work tomorrow. I didn't expect to be helping a demented late-night gardener," she said, still smiling at him.

"Come on, I'll find you something." He went out through the open living room toward the bedrooms, and Nicki followed, still feeling slightly anxious.

"How was the drive?" he called over his shoulder.

"Hair-raising," came her reply. She was taking a little time to look at his home as she followed him. The more she saw, the more she liked it. She hadn't quite known what to expect. She didn't even know if he had a partner or not, although she'd noticed that he'd said *I* have a spare room, not *we*. His home seemed like a lovely lived-in cottage.

Halfway down the hall he pointed into a small room with a single bed and very little else. "That's yours. Sorry it's so bare, I've never bothered to buy any furniture for it. Never really known what to buy."

She felt slightly nervous and wasn't quite sure why. As he stepped into his bedroom, she waited in the hallway outside.

"Come on in. You'll need to choose something." He led her through the bedroom to the walk-in wardrobe. She loved the room, the simple queen-sized bed with a dark-timber and black iron head, a subtle, smallish print of Monet's *Rocks at Belle-Île* hanging on one wall. It was a peaceful room, she thought.

"Okay, pick a shirt. I'll see if I can find some trackpants – that's probably all I have that'll come close to fitting you."

She picked a warm-looking checked flannel shirt and held it in front of herself, showing him. "What do you think?"

"Beautiful. No question," he grinned.

"You must have been a lumberjack in a former life."

He laughed. "I'm going to have a quick shower," he said, "then I'd better get a fire going."

She took the clothes and left him alone.

"Hey!" he called, as she walked out the door, throwing her a pair of grey pants.

Ten minutes later, he came back into the living room to find Nicki standing in front of a good fire, her clothes drying on a kitchen chair she'd carried over.

"I hope you don't mind. I couldn't wait."

He didn't mind. And he liked her in his shirt. "I'll go and get some more firewood."

"Okay. Try not to be killed by a tree. I hear they're falling out of the sky tonight."

Half an hour later, she sat in front of the fire finishing off a ham, tomato and basil omelette he'd made for them both.

"Shall I open a bottle of wine?" he called from the kitchen.

"Um, actually, I'd love a cup of hot chocolate, if that's okay with you," she said.

Good idea, he thought. He noticed she was wearing a wedding ring, which she was idly twisting with the fingers of her right hand.

"Still a 'chocoholic' then?"

"Of course!" she grinned.

So he made the hot chocolate while Nicki sat by the fire. She felt there was something hanging in the air above them, like there was something that needed saying.

"Did you say your name is Palmer now?" Peter called out from the kitchen. "Does that mean congratulations are in order?" he added, trying hard to mean it.

"Um, well I don't know about that, but yes, I got married two years ago," she said a little shyly.

He turned around so she couldn't see his face and decided that perhaps she didn't want to discuss it any further. He brought the hot chocolate out and sat down with her, changing the subject.

"Now, what about the 'hair-raising drive'? The locals can be a bit impatient sometimes."

Nicki told Peter about her near miss on the road, making light of the whole thing. He listened and could tell it had obviously shaken her up.

"And I made you do the gardening and build a fire when you got here! Apparently chivalry really *is* dead!"

Nicki laughed and her eyes drew Peter in as well, he couldn't help but join in.

"You still do it," she said.

"Do what?"

"When you're thinking about something, you tilt your head to one side and look up, as if for divine inspiration," she replied.

He laughed again. "I've always done that, ever since I was a kid."

They went on to discuss her move to New Zealand, how she'd settled in, what it was like moving to another country. She told him she'd felt welcome from the first day. She had made a lot of friends at the hospital and enjoyed most of her work.

They chatted for almost an hour, neither one taking any notice that the connection, the friendship they had had three years ago was not only still alive, but maybe even stronger. In the occasional moments of relaxed silence, they listened to the rain on the metal roof, the wind in the trees and the comforting crackling of the fire. Peter watched the firelight glow on her face and dance in her eyes.

"Everyone in Wellington made me feel so welcome. It's a wonderful place. Do you know that on my first day at the hospital I got a lovely welcoming gift. A nice, simple gesture." She didn't say it was from Tony. "A beautiful, single ..."

"...long-stemmed red rose," Peter completed. "Unfortunately, the sender was too stupid to include a card. He didn't know what to say."

She looked almost stunned. "That was you?" she asked in a small voice.

"I missed you, you know, even before you left, I think. I never really got a chance to say goodbye. I almost called you a few times," he said lightly. *More like a few dozen times*, he thought.

"I missed you too," she said softly. "Um, would you mind if I had another one of those delicious cups of hot chocolate?" she said, quickly changing the subject.

"At your service, ma'am," Peter said with a wink.

He returned in a few minutes with fresh mugs of chocolate and carefully set them down on the side table. He looked at Nicki, and could see tears in her eyes. He didn't say anything at first, just held her eyes with his.

"You can't cry. If you cry, I'm completely in your power. I am your slave and I cannot resist your will."

"Still an idiot," she laughed through the tears. Peter felt a lump in his throat. "Anyway, it was a lovely gift," she added.

A moment of silence passed them both by, unnoticed.

"It didn't work out," Nicki said awkwardly. "My marriage," she added, responding to Peter's unasked question. "I think I was still finding myself."

"You don't have to explain anything to me," Peter said. But Nicki felt comfortable telling him; in fact; she *wanted* to explain it to him. She told him how the relationship had got derailed, with Tony trying to mould her into his life, wanting her to adapt, compromise, give up her ambitions. "You know, I even remember picturing myself, somewhere, sometime in the future, and Tony wasn't in the picture. We can be blind sometimes, can't we?"

How true that was, he thought. "It's impossible to be objective when you're the subject."

"I think it took me a long time to find myself after I left Melbourne. Partly I was running away."

Peter looked at her curiously, head tilted to one side. "Running from *what*?"

"You." She coloured slightly and hoped he didn't notice. "Well, maybe I was running away from something I didn't understand," she added quickly. "I didn't know where our friendship was going, you were still married and ..."

"Separated," he corrected.

"Well, yes, but it was bad timing, and ... oh, I don't know any more."

A big flash of lightning outside caused the lights to flicker, then came the huge crash of thunder, barely a second later. Nicki jumped.

"I'd better stoke that fire," he said, throwing a couple of small logs on.

"Well, we'd better do some work, too," Nicki said. "That *is* why I'm here, after all. Do you want to take me through your notes and thoughts from Ross Island?"

"Okay. I'll show you my notes," he said, taking her lead. "And my souvenir," he added, giving her his best naughty-little-boy look.

"Come on." He held out his hand.

In the study, he proudly showed her a pile of uncharacteristically messy papers. "My notes!" he said with a flourish.

She laughed, as he explained that he now had it all on the laptop and just hadn't tidied his desk up yet. He told her briefly about the *Vitis vinifera* specimen that had been lost in the plane crash on Macquarie. She surprised him with how quickly she slipped back into her 'professional' role. In fact, he was a little disappointed as the conversation became more business-like. She was particularly interested in what had been done with the plant specimen at Ross Station. Had the Ross people examined it? Had they handled it much? Had it thawed while still there? Peter answered 'yes' to each of her questions.

"Well, I think we can rule that out as a source of the infection. Conrick's not so sure, but I'm not sure about *him* yet."

Peter also explained to her about the unexpected sediment brought up in the ice cores. Sediment that suggested water erosion, not glacial. She was fascinated, and he was excited to have someone to share his theories with. He told her about the old maps supposedly compiled three hundred years before Antarctica was discovered. Sixteenth-century maps possibly reconstructed from some much older maps, perhaps dating back millennia!

Nicki's curiosity was a delight. She wanted to see the maps, so they looked on the web, but the laptop screen was not ideal. John Morton had sent high-resolution copies by courier, but they hadn't arrived yet. Peter told her what he knew about 'continental drift', the movement of the earth's tectonic plates and the shifting of the magnetic poles. He outlined his rough theory of the possibility of a habitable Antarctica existing around eight thousand years ago, acknowledging that it did sound implausible.

He acknowledged also that climate science dictates that a change of the required magnitude would take much, much longer than a few thousand years. Still, Nicki was enthralled; she agreed it was a fascinating theory.

He finished by showing her his souvenir. He picked up the stone and pointed out to her how symmetrical it was, how he thought it looked artificial and even polished. "If this had been found anywhere else, I think most people would assume it was man-made." He handed it to Nicki, and she took it with both hands.

As she grasped it, she drew in her breath sharply, and the look on her face changed instantly to one of horror.

Suddenly Peter's study disappeared. The whole world disappeared. Nicki was engulfed in darkness and an immense, crushing heaviness. She stood completely still, frozen with fear, trying to take it all in. Where am I? What happened? She couldn't speak. She couldn't breathe. A deathly, dark world, not quite lit by a large pale moon, had completely enveloped her. That strangely oversized moon was the only thing she could see. And the only thing she could feel was fear – no, *dread*. It was like the life was being leached out of her.

Somehow the air smelt different. Darkly oppressive, suffocating. Everything was different. Nothing made any sense. She couldn't comprehend, and she couldn't fight it. As each second passed, she felt her strength, her very life, being sapped away. Something horrific was about to happen. She felt her body moving and she screamed. She was going to die here. But she could vaguely hear someone calling her from miles away. If only she could see.

She felt herself being pulled toward the voice ...

16

Peter watched in horror as Nicki cried out and gripped the stone with both hands, so tight her fingers turned white. He reacted quickly, prising the stone out of her grasp as she lost consciousness. He carried her back to the living room, and as he picked her up, she let out a faint cry. He laid her down gently on the couch and sat on the edge next to her, searching her face for a sign that she would be all right. What the hell had just happened?

"Nicki. Nicki. It's okay. It's all right."

Her face was ghostly pale, even in the warm, orange glow of the fire. Slowly she opened her eyes and looked vaguely at him as he came into focus. She was shivering as he stroked her face and hair. "What happened? It was ... I don't know ... *terrifying.*" Her voice was unsteady. She looked stricken, lost. Her breath came in short gasps.

"You're okay," Peter said. "Breathe." He stroked her face gently.

She took slow, deep breaths as she tried to regain her composure, pausing to look at herself, and at Peter, as if to make sure she was really here in his house, safe, with him.

Peter didn't have any words; he was too shocked to say anything, so he just stroked her head, holding her hand, searching her eyes for the answer.

"I felt truly afraid, like I could feel death. I couldn't breathe."

Peter wanted to just hold her close and calm her, but he stopped himself. What the hell was that stone? As crazy as it seemed, it just had to be that stone. Did it have some sort of ... who knows what ... that Nicki was sensitive to? Something that affected brainwaves somehow? That seemed crazy. Was it 'possessed'? Why wasn't Peter affected?

That last thought struck Peter. Perhaps he *was* mildly affected. There was definitely something special about that stone. He thought back to his strange dreams on the flight back from Ross Island.

Nicki was now starting to recover. "It was so, so ... unbelievable. I don't know where all those feelings came from, but they were so *real*. I don't know how to describe it," she said, and her face gave Peter all the description he needed. Her breath was still coming in gasps, but at least she sounded like she'd be okay.

"There was one of those stones on the plane that crashed, too," Peter said, and he went on to explain the nightmare he had on his return flight.

"It felt like death." She shook her head slowly. "I can't believe it did that to me. Maybe it wasn't the stone. Maybe I'm just exhausted," she rationalised but didn't sound at all convinced. "I should touch it again and see what happens," she added.

"No," Peter said firmly. "I don't think that's a good idea," he added in a gentler tone.

"Where did you say it came from?"

"They found it under thousands of years of ice at Ross Island," he answered automatically, apparently deep in thought. Then, slowly, he went on. "I wonder what its history really is."

A long pause.

"Have you ever heard of psychometry?" He knew there were people who could supposedly 'read' inanimate objects to learn their past, their secrets. And it seemed that the stone might have some awful secrets.

Nicki was obviously still shaken by the strong feelings it had given her, but she was calmer now.

She had heard of psychometry and had even read about it, but she was certain she'd never experienced it before. In fact, the only genuinely unexplainable event in her life had been with her grandfather ... She'd had strong intuitions before, but never anything like this. Peter was still sitting next to her, holding both her hands, with nothing but concern on his face.

"My head hurts," Nicki said, still looking pale, and now even more exhausted.

"Let me get you something." Peter went into the bathroom and found a packet of paracetamol tablets and returned with a glass of water.

Nicki took the tablets and yawned. "Sorry. It's been a very long day," she said. "I think I need to get some sleep."

JULY 29

Peter woke up feeling cold, the duvet now lying mostly on the floor. He had obviously been tossing and turning, although he couldn't remember any specific dream. And now he just felt restless, as he thought of Nicki sleeping next door. His mouth was dry, so he got up quietly and went to the kitchen. The storm had abated a little since he had helped her get settled in her room. He'd been shaken up by the whole thing as well, but he hadn't wanted to admit it.

The fire had almost died out and the house was cold. The kitchen floor felt like ice under his feet. The kitchen clock read 3.17. He drank a glass of water and walked back down the hall. *Crack!* Another branch falling? *Crack!* It sounded close. There was a loud ripping sound, followed by a deep thud as something hit the ground outside.

Peter went back to his bedroom and grabbed his bathrobe and torch and walked quickly but quietly to the front door. He hoped Nicki was still sleeping. Outside he pulled his boots on and had a quick look around the yard and driveway. Nothing. There were a lot of big trees around, and it could have come from anywhere. Maybe he would have time to look around in the morning. He went back inside and saw Nicki standing in the hall. She was still wearing his shirt, he noticed, and the look of relief on her face didn't match the concern in her eyes.

"Is everything all right?" she asked anxiously. "I heard a crash ..." She was clearly unsettled.

"It's fine, just another branch coming down, I think," Peter said, in his most calming voice. "Don't worry, none of them overhang the house. Are you okay?"

"I woke up a while ago and couldn't get back to sleep. I can't get that stone out of my mind. I've been thinking about what happened. I remember getting a shock when I first touched it. I felt terrified, like I couldn't breathe, but I think that was just the shock. It was as if I was thrown from being wide awake into a black nightmare, instantly. I want to touch that stone again," she said, her resolve returning.

"No!" Peter said, too quickly. "I mean ... are you sure? You said you could feel death," he added gently.

"Did I?" She stared past him as she tried to remember. "Fear. Fear and anguish; I think that was what I felt."

Without actually saying it, they knew the stone had something to tell them. She was courageous, of that he had no doubt, but he was deeply concerned for her. She took herself off determinedly into the study, and Peter quickly followed. It seemed even colder in there. Nicki did not waste any time. Without visible apprehension, she went straight to the stone and picked it up with both hands. Peter hurried over, ready to hold her again if she fainted.

There was the same sudden intake of breath as last time. The colour again quickly drained from her face. He wished there was some other way, that *he* could do it this time instead. He stood there with her, not knowing whether to let her continue or not. She looked around the room unseeing, with a frightened expression on her face, and then Peter saw that she'd stopped breathing again. He managed to wrench the stone free with both hands. As he took it, he felt the hairs on the back of his neck stand up, but it was nothing like Nicki obviously felt. He dropped it on the floor and the sensation passed as he held Nicki, trying to soothe her.

He helped her back to the living room, not bothering to turn on a lamp.

The fire's embers bathed the room in a pale red glow. He set her down gently on the couch again. She recovered more quickly this time, and as she found words, he threw some small kindling into the embers and watched them catch alight.

"Peter, it was so unreal. Nothing was clear, but I know I felt fear and some kind of powerless anger and sense of doom." She paused again to collect her thoughts. "I felt like I couldn't breathe again, too."

"You weren't breathing," Peter said, as he added some larger pieces of wood.

"My head hurts again, though not as much as last time," she said, absently rubbing her eyes, as he sat down. Peter saw that this time there were tears in her eyes. He could not stop himself reaching out and holding her.

"I don't know what I was seeing, it was all vague, or muddy," she said quietly. "The feelings were so real, though. It was so sudden, and so powerful, I couldn't control it."

Peter released her. "Don't stop." He turned to face her, his head just inches from hers.

Nicki leaned forward and kissed him gently. "Hold me."

She shivered against him, as they held on to each other. Peter worried that she was still clearly shaken, although she had recovered more quickly this time. Nonetheless, he was concerned for her.

"Fear, anguish, helplessness, all at once. It was like being thrown into a hostile world of darkness." She spoke slowly, choosing her words carefully, still holding Peter close. "Does that make any sense?" she added.

"I'm not sure." He wanted to just hold her, to give her comfort. His emotions were in control.

"Maybe if I tried it again ..."

Peter could see she didn't relish the thought, but he could see she meant what she said. Clearly a very determined woman. "I'd feel much happier if we waited until morning," he said.

Nicki had started to relax and was now just looking at him, with an expression that truly warmed his heart. She opened her mouth slightly and leaned into him again. Her kiss was soft and warm and, as he responded, became more insistent. Peter held back. He was still worried about her, and, if he was honest with himself, worried that this was an emotional reaction to the awful experience she'd just had. As he thought it, it seemed foolish.

Nicki seemed to sense what was in his mind. "Peter, I'm okay, *really*. I'm not *fragile*." Her smile, and the expression in her eyes as they locked on his, put his fear to rest and ignited something in him that he could not tame. She took his hand and touched it to her bare skin under the flannel shirt, and he felt her intake of breath. As he kissed her again, she pushed him back on the sofa, her hands inside his bathrobe. Her touch on his skin electrified him, and he pulled the flannel shirt over her head.

Nicki woke to hear the radio in the distance somewhere. She was still on the couch, covered in a duvet that hadn't been there earlier. She could hear a shower running. She smiled to herself as she remembered last night. The feelings of uncertainty and anticipation that she felt yesterday and hadn't understood now made perfect sense. She hadn't expected the night to end the way it had, but now it seemed like it had been inevitable.

She was very tempted to join Peter in the shower, but he'd obviously got up very quietly and hadn't woken her. Did he have regrets? She pushed that thought from her mind as she climbed off the sofa and wrapped herself in Peter's bathrobe. He'd apparently left it for her. She put another log on the fire.

In the light of day, Peter's home was very warm and inviting. She felt more at peace here than she'd felt in some time. A remarkable thing, she reflected, given the reason she was here was a deadly plague that threatened the human race!

It was almost eight o'clock. Peter came in, freshly showered, his face ruddy from the hot water, and his hair completely and rather amusingly out of control. He kissed her warmly, dispelling her fears.

"New look?" she enquired, smiling.

He looked mystified for a few seconds. "Oh, yes." He roughly ran his fingers through his hair and made it look presentable. "I'm sorry about breakfast. I'm supposed to be at the airport by nine-thirty," he said. "You looked so peacefully asleep I didn't have the heart to wake you." Actually he'd had to resist a strong desire to wake her.

"I've just booked a ride," he said. "It will be here in about ten minutes. Got to finish packing!" He dashed off down the hallway. She wasn't sure whether she should stay or not, but Peter seemed to expect it.

"Help yourself to some breakfast, and you're very welcome to go through my notes if you like," he called.

He returned a few minutes later with his bag and handed her a key he'd retrieved from a kitchen drawer. "Please, help yourself to everything and stay as long as you want."

"Be careful. I ..." She paused for a second, not sure what to say next. "Will you call me when you get back?"

"Of course! As soon as. I wish I didn't have to go now." He pulled her close and kissed her again as a car horn beeped outside. He released her and raced back into the study, bringing back a thick book she hadn't seen before. He stuffed it into his bag. "I'm so glad ..." his voice trailed off as he wasn't sure quite what to say.

"Me too," she replied with a delightful smile.

"Bye. I wish I didn't have to rush off like this."

And with that he was gone.

Nicki watched the car leave, seeing Peter in the back rummaging through this bag for something. She hoped he hadn't forgotten anything important.

She went into the kitchen, found a cup in the first cupboard she looked in, and tackled Peter's espresso machine.

Then she phoned Conrick to tell him she had met with Peter this morning. That was true, after all, and the fact that she'd arrived last night wasn't any of Conrick's business. "I'll be back at the lab by about nine-thirty," she told him, ending the call before he had time to admonish her.

She treated herself to a quick tour of the house, deciding Peter wouldn't mind. The first things she noticed were his paintings. He had a few interesting prints, but in the living room were a couple of original watercolours – landscapes, but their most striking feature was the moody, stormy sky they both depicted. She loved them.

As she walked into the study, she saw the stone lying on the floor where Peter had dropped it last night. She wondered whether she should pick it up again and see if the images got any clearer. She bent down to take another look. *It's very symmetrical*, she thought, *and almost polished enough to be some kind of ornament. Strangely beautiful.* She wondered what it was, and where it had come from. What had given it its energy, its *memory*. She was tempted to reach out and touch it, just quickly, and ...

But what if she couldn't let go? She remembered how bad it had made her feel. And Peter did say she'd stopped breathing. She moved her hand closer to it. Nothing. *Better leave it alone*, she thought. She held both hands, palms open, around the stone, not quite touching it. Still nothing. She had felt afraid before touching it the second time last night, but with Peter there with her, it had seemed safe enough. She heard light rain on the roof. Maybe in daylight it wouldn't be so bad.

17

Harper, the director, was not listening, Marc knew. The man was just being polite, or perhaps just humouring Marc.

"I ... I feel as though all my authority has been withdrawn," Marc Richardson went on. "Can't you do something about it?"

"Neil Colles is a very capable man, Richardson, and he has my complete agreement on this matter." Harper had the voice of a statesman, a president, and he loved the sound of it, Marc thought unkindly.

"His department has experience in this sort of thing, whereas we do not. Additionally, Colles has the minister's full authority to act as he sees fit. She telephoned me personally to make that clear."

Richardson did not want to step on the director's toes, he was the boss after all, but Marc did not like being pushed around by these heavy-handed, self-important government people. Surely they could see a senior administrator was quite capable of making his own decisions?

"I understand, but perhaps I can assist Colles in managing the situation," Marc said.

"It's a relatively straightforward matter, Marc." Harper was starting to get annoyed with Richardson's petty attitude. He hardly ever used first names. "Colles has simply taken control of communications with the

Macquarie station, he hasn't taken over your job, man." Harper had been none too happy when the minister had forced his hand, but Marc hadn't taken the hint.

"Maybe not, but he's banned all communication, and all flights to and from both Macquarie and Ross have to be cleared through him. Even supplies, for God's sake." Marc felt as though they didn't trust him, and he didn't like it at all. "And he instructed me to contact Macquarie and tell them they were to remain 'cut off'."

Harper had heard enough. "Firstly, all personal communication is banned, and that's for public safety. Secondly, all flights are banned because there may be a plague down there – a *deadly* plague I might add. And thirdly, I suggested to Colles that *you* should maintain contact with Macquarie and Ross, rather than him. They know you. Now, I will hear no more on the matter of Colles's activities. Suffice to say that he has my, and the minister's, absolute authority. That's all."

Richardson left Harper's office sulkily, as the director shook his head.

Earlier, he had gone into Harper's office to advise of a disturbing call from Nick Anakos on Macquarie Island. Anakos wanted to know when the medical supplies he'd asked for would be arriving; he had more than sixteen sick people now, and he'd started to develop symptoms himself. The base leader, Masters, also presenting symptoms, had apparently had some kind of breakdown and disappeared altogether. There were eight others who could not be accounted for. The place had turned into utter chaos.

Harper felt sorry for the people trapped down there. He had contacted Colles in Melbourne immediately and given him an update. Colles had said he would contact Macquarie himself, but Harper suggested it might be better if all communications came from ANARE in Hobart, and Colles had reluctantly agreed. Colles wanted to ensure that no communication was made from the base, except for reports to ANARE by the leader. He also wanted to know when the birds' blood samples would be available for collection; he'd been particularly concerned about that. To Harper, that collection seemed like an unnecessary risk, even though he knew the airstrip was isolated from the base. In the end, he accepted that Colles knew what he was doing. Those samples must be important.

Harper had gone back into Richardson's office, instructed him to contact Anakos again and waited while Anakos told Richardson that he hadn't heard of any request for blood samples, and that he wasn't sure he could get them anyway. He didn't think many of their medical supplies had survived the fire. Anakos suggested they fly in medical supplies as soon as possible, and he'd arrange for samples from all bird colonies, and seals as well, as best he could, by the next morning.

He'd reminded Richardson that they had no doctor or vet but would do their best. The island's airstrip was more than a kilometre from the base, so it seemed safe enough. Richardson said he would clear that with the 'health people'.

Harper had left at that point to confirm the arrangements with Colles. An aircraft would be despatched to Macquarie Island that afternoon to drop the required supplies, and the plane returning from Ross Station would collect the samples the next day. It would take longer than Colles wanted, but at least it was fairly safe. Harper relayed that to Richardson, who was just wrapping up the call and making some rough notes. Anakos confirmed there would be no one within one kilometre of the airstrip.

Harper had then instructed Richardson to complete a brief but concise report and bring it to him within the hour. And now it seemed Richardson had spent a good part of that time brooding over Colles's involvement.

Fifteen minutes later, Richardson returned with a laser-printed report.

Harper read it quickly, learning little more than he already knew, except that sometime since yesterday afternoon, eight men had stolen survival equipment, clothing and enough food to last for weeks, and disappeared. Anakos had advised that they might have gone to a place called Green Gorge, which would probably offer them the best shelter. Harper wondered whether there was some risk of these men getting close to the plane, so he checked the map. He penned a note on Richardson's report for Colles, noting that, according to his map, Green Gorge was about two kilometres over rough terrain from the airstrip, and there was no way these men could know there was a plane coming. All in all, Richardson's report was clear and concise, and Harper told him so. It wouldn't do to have the man fretting unnecessarily. Then he sent the report to Colles.

Harper sat at his desk trying to imagine what it would be like to be living in a tent, in freezing conditions, knowing your friends were dying of a terrible disease and you might be next. Or what it would be like to realise that you'd contracted this plague and know that you could be dead in less than two days. To make it even worse for the people on the island, they were not allowed to contact their loved ones. He couldn't imagine how any of these things must feel. All he could do was be grateful he wasn't there himself.

18

Dr Palmer arrived at the Yea lab at around a quarter to ten, parked her car on the gravel out front and called Professor Conrick to let her in. The facility was an ugly concrete bunker with a low roof and very few windows. She hadn't seen any identifying signs outside, but the directions were clear and she was sure she was in the right place. Momentarily, Conrick opened the secure door, his disapproval showing on his face. He'd been short with her last night when she'd phoned to say she would not be coming in until the morning.

The professor handed her an electronically encoded pass card and gave her the PIN number. He swiped his card and entered his PIN and told her to do the same.

"Everyone who enters needs to swipe. No tailgating," he said gruffly.

Nicki did as instructed, and they both entered the building. It was well lit inside, in spite of the impression the tinted one-way glass of the security door had given her.

"Did you find anything useful in Hennessy's notes?" Conrick asked. No time for pleasantries it seemed.

"I think we can rule out the *Vitis vinifera* specimen as a cause, or even as a carrier. The Ross people handled it extensively," she answered.

123

"Nothing else?" Conrick asked bluntly.

"Nothing that specifically relates to our work, professor," she said, a little testily. She was not going to be talked down to by this man, or anyone else.

"Well, we've got no further here. All we've done so far is make the test cultures. It's definitely bacterial, though, you can see the little buggers." Conrick pointed to the eyepiece of the microscope-like device attached to one of the windows in the lab's airtight 'cell'.

Nicki went to look for herself and could indeed see the 'little buggers'. They were the same size as most other bacteria she had studied, but it was there that any similarity ended. They were a brownish yellow with a small black or very dark-blue spot near the centre. She had expected them to be vaguely similar to pneumococcus, or at least something she'd seen before.

A young man came over and pressed a few keys on the console. The large monitor lit up, and she was able to stand back and watch the bacteria multiply in high-resolution colour. She stared at them, transfixed. Amazing how such a tiny organism could cause so much harm. The young man was saying something, but she wasn't listening.

"This is frightening, I've never seen any bacteria multiply quite as quickly as these!" Nicki was shocked. A sea of dirty yellow death growing in front of her eyes, faster than even the most rampant bugs she'd seen before.

"They're obviously very resilient; they've survived being frozen for who knows how many thousands of years," the young man observed quietly, almost to himself.

The 'cell' was located at the back of the lab's main room. It was about three metres square and had three thick Perspex windows in one side, each with its own fully movable microscope controlled by a computer console. Each of the microscopes had miniature cameras whose images could be displayed on any of the three video monitors above the console. The whole set-up was controlled and monitored by a central computer system. Conrick had explained briefly, in his usual condescending manner, that the system kept a check on the cell's door, seals and atmospheric pressure, and all instructions input to the consoles were recorded.

"It also has built-in safety checks, so it's idiot-proof." Conrick somehow managed to convey an impression that he was surrounded by idiots, as he explained about the airlock and scrub/suit room through which the cell could be entered. There were also a few manual controls, although access to these was still controlled by the system.

Nicki could see rows of Petri dishes behind the windows, each with a number, starting with Ma001 to her left. There were more than a hundred of them. She wondered what would happen if the computers malfunctioned. She'd half expected the lab to be deep underground so if anything went wrong, it could be completely sealed.

'We can deal with any kind of biologically hazardous material at the Yea facility,' Colles had told her. Anything except infected *people*, she now reflected. She wondered what they would do if anyone inside the lab was infected.

The young man walked up to the window she was standing directly in front of. "Hello, I'm Philip."

"Hi, Philip. Nicole Palmer," she said, extending her hand.

"I'm the lab technician," Philip said. "Conrick's slave, in other words." He looked to be roughly her age and was just a little taller than her, which made him about 170 centimetres. He had pale blue eyes, which Nicki thought had a hungry look in them.

"Then I guess you'll be helping me out, too. It's nice to meet you, Philip." She left him at the cell, returning to Conrick.

"I've asked for more blood samples from Macquarie," Conrick told her. "Birds this time. They should be here tomorrow.

"Now, some new hospital-grade antibiotics arrived this morning. The cultures are growing very quickly, so you can start testing today." He handed her a printed sheet with a number of columns, the left showing culture numbers, then called Philip over.

"Philip, start unpacking those boxes, lad. Start with the tetracyclines, since they've already tried penicillin on the island."

Nicki knew all the drug names. While Philip unpacked and prepared the medications, Nicki went over the safety procedures with Conrick.

He showed her five lockable control switches placed around the lab, located rather unobtrusively on the centre of each wall at about eye level. Or at least she assumed they were, because one of the walls had a row of large cabinets obscuring the place where the switch should be. She raised her eyebrows. That seemed a little careless, but Conrick said nothing. There was also one on the cell's main control panel. Each one had a key in it, and to activate them one simply had to turn the key and flip a switch. They would immediately shut off the air-conditioning system, seal the air-intake and outlet vents and the cell's airlock. They also sealed and locked the labs' external doors.

Conrick explained that the two labs, theirs and the vacant one next door, had their own independent negative-pressure air-conditioning systems to ensure that the atmospheric pressure inside the labs was always at least five kilopascals below the outside pressure, to allow a few extra seconds to seal the building.

"Be careful with them. You cannae turn it off from inside; we'd have to call in security and Colles to get us out," Conrick said. He went on to explain that the cell was kept at a lower pressure still, somewhere around eighty kilopascals, or about four-fifths of an atmosphere. Any sudden inrush of air would activate the security system. Nicki understood why the place was referred to as an 'Agricultural Research Facility'. If the local citizens knew its real purpose, there would be a public outcry.

And so it went, adding antibiotics to dishes filled with slimy bacterial jellies, watching the bacteria's reaction and marking the test sheets accordingly. So far, the bacteria had been impervious to the medicines. It was frighteningly resilient. Each test required fairly careful monitoring, so they could only safely do a few at a time. It was going to be a long day.

They settled into a routine, pausing each hour to check all results and document everything. Philip was entering the information from the sheets into the system for detailed analysis and reporting; Conrick had advised him that Colles would want precise progress reports regularly. *Hurry up and wait.* While Nicki worked, she reflected that what they were trying to do was like trying to find an old key that might unlock a new kind of lock. Only there were thousands upon thousands of keys and none of them were made by the maker of this lock. And maybe it was not made to be unlocked at all.

They were dealing with bacteria that was probably eight thousand years old, almost certainly frozen all that time. Modern humanity had never seen it. Nicki knew bacteria could form spores, making them impervious to freezing, even to boiling. In that dormant state, they could live without food indefinitely. She also knew that viable bacteria had been retrieved from sealed Egyptian tombs.

The big question in Nicki's mind was *where had these bacteria come from?* She'd made the assumption that it probably *only* existed in Antarctica, her reasoning being that had it existed anywhere else, humanity would have developed antibodies to attack it or we probably would not be here today. Additionally, she knew that bacteria, like any other living organism in our complex ecosystem, tended to evolve into something that could coexist with other life forms. Less than five per cent of known bacteria were harmful to human life. But it seemed that *Macquarius,* as they'd come to call it, could not coexist happily with humanity.

She thought of Peter's theory on possible life in the Antarctic eight thousand years ago. Maybe there had been a great plague, *this* plague, and maybe it killed the people of Antarctica. Was that the oppressive and ominous sense of doom she had felt? Was the stone connected somehow to the bacteria? Perhaps it was a good thing she'd decided to leave it alone this morning.

Of course, she kept these theories to herself. The 'evidence' that she and Peter had discussed could hardly be called conclusive, and it wasn't very scientific. Nonetheless, following that line of thought, it was possible that the bacteria had done its deed in Antarctica, then become dormant as it froze, to be unearthed and thawed by man, thousands of years later. But none of that could explain *how* it had come to be 'snap-frozen', and where it had come from.

Conrick still thought Macquarie Island was the source, but Nicki couldn't see how that was possible. It *surely* had to have come from the Ross Island ice.

They took a break for lunch at one o'clock, and Conrick told Philip to arrange for sandwiches to be delivered. One of the security guards brought them in about twenty minutes later, along with a large bottle of orange juice and some fruit. At least they were being fed reasonably well. Philip had started to annoy Nicki a little. He talked incessantly about his girlfriend, about their house in *Malvern*, making the point that they weren't renting it. Nicki thought he lived well for a laboratory technician, Malvern being one of Melbourne's more fashionable inner suburbs.

She ventured out into the lab's grounds for some fresh air after lunch, and strolled around for about half an hour. When she walked back, Philip was talking to a girl she hadn't seen before, and as she went past, she heard him mention the house in *Malvern* again.

It seemed to her that Philip was probably insecure, but he also seemed quite shallow. If he wanted to impress Nicki, then having an expensive house wasn't going to do it. Being a good lab technician was the best way she could think of for him to do that.

She continued to stroll back to the lab, idly thinking about Peter. It made her smile. Even this morning, rushing around, but still such a lovely man, just as he was three years ago. She had his house key in her pocket and it connected him to her. It was silly, she knew, but it somehow comforted her. She couldn't help but wonder how he was feeling on the trek back to Ross Island. She remembered the book he'd packed at the last minute. Not a novel to read on the long flight, but an *atlas*. That was Peter. It made her smile again.

She hoped he would be back soon. They had so much more to talk about. And she wanted him to hold her close again. She hoped he would come back safe. And *healthy*.

19

The driver had left Peter and his luggage in the rain outside the old terminal building at Essendon Airport. Inside, he'd gone straight over to the snack bar to buy a toasted sandwich for breakfast. He'd been surprised to see Colles standing close by with a younger, very fit-looking man. Both were drinking coffee from paper cups.

"Hennessy, Melville," Colles said economically. "He'll be taking blood samples with the base doctor while you talk to the people down there."

They shook hands. Melville looked more like an athlete than a doctor, and Hennessy wondered why another doctor had to tag along. *Surely the base doctor can handle this?*

"I want you to question everyone, informally. Get their confidence, and find out everything you can about life at Ross for the past month. I want to know about anything unusual that's happened. *Anything* at all." Colles spoke to Hennessy as though he was a subordinate, but Peter didn't take offence. He was sure Colles spoke to everyone that way.

"You don't have long, your flight back is scheduled for tomorrow morning, oh-eight-hundred. Oh, and you'll be stopping at Macquarie for a few minutes to collect some medical samples." Colles looked directly at Peter as he said the last words. "Appropriate safety protocols are in place.

You won't leave the aircraft, and the airstrip is some distance from the quarantined base."

Peter wasn't overly concerned; he didn't think these people would risk several lives unnecessarily, and if there was some risk, they would not be allowing the plane to return to Melbourne.

"If anything turns up, you can give me a call from Ross Station. If not, you can give me a report as soon as you return." Colles was issuing orders again.

"Okay, I'll come and see you when I get back," Peter said.

"Your flight will be landing at an airstrip near Yea, so a call from the lab will be fine. Melville or Conrick will get you into the place. Good luck." Colles nodded to both men and walked away.

While Melville finished his coffee, Peter found a quiet spot and made a quick call.

As the two men walked towards the plane, Melville extended his hand. "David Melville," he said.

"Peter Hennessy."

They boarded the flight, escorted by ground staff across the tarmac. It looked like the same Hercules as last time, Peter thought. Seated on board, Melville took a paperback out of his briefcase. There was a semi-naked woman on the cover; evidently Melville wasn't a fan of literary masterpieces. Well, everything had its place, Peter supposed. Then he remembered his own book, realising he had left it in his bag. Now he'd have to wait until after take-off to retrieve it.

He tried to relax as he waited for the plane to taxi out onto the runway, but he couldn't. He was not looking forward to flying back into the cold darkness that waited for him at the bottom of the world. Nevertheless, he felt buoyant. That was about Nicki. As soon as he heard her voice on the phone yesterday, all the feelings he'd had three years ago came flooding back. He'd never really known what had happened. Just a sense that she'd avoided him, which hurt a little at the time, although he hadn't wanted to admit it.

She'd become more than a friend in his mind. It had happened rather unexpectedly and took him by surprise, but he hadn't known she felt the same way. And then last night, it was as if they hadn't been away from each other at all. The closeness, the conversation, the laughter, the episodes with the stone, and then, well, *boom*. All the suppressed, withheld feelings seemed to explode at once, and there was no holding back.

"Happy memories?" Melville asked.

Peter realised he had big smile on his face. "You might say that." He did not elaborate, and Melville did not ask any questions.

Peter remembered what Nicki had said after touching the stone. She couldn't see anything clearly, it was 'vague or muddy'. Did that mean she was seeing the dark Antarctic winter? Or was it something else? Maybe it had just given her the *feelings* but no images. He wished he understood more about psychometry. If that's what it was.

No, he wished he'd felt it himself instead.

But no matter what she'd felt, there was an obvious problem. It was inconceivable that any civilisation, even an advanced one, could have survived the Antarctic weather we know today. What would they have eaten? How could plants, or livestock, have existed in those conditions? The discovery of *Vitis vinifera* was strong evidence that the Antarctic, or at least the Ross Island region, once had a more temperate climate.

And there was the unexplained sediment in the ice cores. Not the expected glacial scrapings, but fine-grained sediment that implied a more gentle *liquid* water erosion. It was further evidence of that more temperate climate. *But how was that possible?* Current continental drift theory and plate tectonics could not explain the climatic change over a geological 'moment' of just six to eight millennia. According to geologists, Antarctica broke away from the giant land mass Gondwanaland about sixty or seventy *million* years ago, and had been very slowly drifting south ever since. But that didn't explain anything at all.

Could there have been some other unknown event that caused a sudden shift much more recently? But *what* could do that? And that wouldn't explain the plague, if its source really was Ross Island, of which they had no proof. In fact, the scientists – except for Nicki – were all looking at Macquarie Island, but Hennessy felt Ross Island, and maybe those strange stones, were part of it.

As the pilot raced the engines for take-off, so too raced Peter's thoughts. There were quite a few pieces missing, although the plague's source was still foremost in his mind. Could it have been *manufactured*? Some kind of ancient biological warfare gone horribly wrong? That didn't seem likely – any race equipped with technology to engineer bacteria surely couldn't have disappeared without a trace. Unless maybe it destroyed itself in some ancient holocaust? It seemed far-fetched.

Whether or not they had such destructive technology, if he was right about the maps, they at least had some fairly advanced mathematics. And the darkness, or 'muddiness', that Nicki had talked about, did she *feel* it or did she *see* it? The old plane shuddered as it took to the air, rattling every one of its thousands of steel rivets. After ten minutes or so, Peter felt the pilot turn the aircraft south and level off.

He got up and retrieved his book. As he made his way back to his seat, Melville glanced up, looked at the book, then at Hennessy, raised his eyebrows then went back to his paperback.

Peter sat, took his reading glasses out of his pocket and opened the book. It was a geographical history and atlas of the world. He had no books specifically on Antarctica, so he hoped to find what he was looking for in this volume.

He quickly found references to Antarctica's huge mountain ranges and spectacular valleys: the Eternity Range and the Transantarctic Mountains, the latter extending very close to Ross Island. There were numerous volcanoes, many of which were still active, including Mount Erebus and Mount Terror. In general, it was, unsurprisingly, very rough and inhospitable terrain.

Antarctica was one of the most mountainous continents of the world, the book told him, and one of the planet's most rugged places, but nothing he read jumped out at him. True, he wasn't sure exactly what he was looking for; there was just something nagging, hidden away in a corner of his mind. Maybe the answer was hidden away from modern science as well.

After all, he didn't even have all the pieces to the *question*, let alone the answer. And if there was something he was missing, it was probably buried under 'almost thirty million cubic kilometres of ice'!

He put the book down, put his glasses back in his pocket and closed his eyes. Maybe the old maps John had sent down from Sydney would help him find whatever it was he was after. Hopefully he would have them by tomorrow.

* * *

"This is Kevacic."

"Yes," Lin replied.

"I've made contact. Your man was interested. He has a copy of a top-secret report that sounds like what you want, and he says he'll be able to get a 'culture' out," the American said. "This will cost you one hundred and fifty thousand dollars," he added. Kevacic evidently had an idea of the value of what he was getting. A confidential government report, with irrefutable proof of a major government conspiracy. He knew the Chinese would pay a lot for it. Lin was furious, he could imagine Xeng's reaction.

"That was not agreed! We will not pay that much!" Lin shouted, knowing he had no authority to negotiate with this man.

"Okay. Goodbye."

"Wait! I will talk to ... my superiors. Call me again in one hour." Lin slammed the phone down, now very worried. He knew Xeng would blame him for this. Had he let Kevacic know too much? He must have said something wrong. He went over their first conversation in his mind, trying to anticipate Xeng's questions. He could feel a knot forming in his stomach as he slowly dialled Xeng's number. He was so nervous he had to punch the numbers in twice, and he had started to sweat.

"Yes," Xeng answered.

Lin Fan Cheng nervously explained exactly what Kevacic had said, and Xeng listened without making a sound. For all Lin could tell, Xeng may have been about to explode with anger. Then he surprised Lin.

"It does not matter. Tell him we will pay. Let me know when and where it will be available." Xeng hung up, and Lin felt a great wave of relief. He thought he was going to vomit, but it soon passed. He was astounded at Xeng's response; he had expected to be censured scathingly. It occurred to him that Xeng must have anticipated Kevacic's action. Either that, or he had a backup plan.

Xeng sat in his office waiting for his jasmine tea to be brought in. He looked at the small potted plant on his immaculate desk. It had been moved slightly. A sour look of displeasure flashed across his face. He expected, *demanded*, perfection. His ulcer had been acting up again, and this sort of carelessness irritated him. It was a mark of disrespect and not to be tolerated.

As he waited, with even less patience than usual, he congratulated himself on anticipating everything brilliantly. He had known Kevacic would want more money, and he had expected their target to ask for more. He thought one hundred and fifty thousand dollars was a small price to pay. Not that he was going to pay. He had chosen Kevacic for two reasons. Firstly, the man had been a known 'associate' of Lin's previous superior, and one could draw the conclusion that he was known to Lin, rather than Xeng. Secondly, he was efficient and ruthless, but not too smart. Lin would have to give Kevacic the required amount to make the initial exchange, but the final exchange would not work out as Kevacic planned.

Xeng pictured the exchange in his mind, wondering whether Lin would realise how foolish he had been. Lin blindly trusted his superior, a mistake that Xeng had never made. Maybe Lin would have time to realise, maybe not. Xeng didn't care either way; Lin was of no importance now. To the police it would be clear cut; another sordid drug deal gone wrong. Lin would be disgraced, of course, and Kevacic was already known to the police, but the mother country and Xeng himself would come out of it clean. And no one would know what had really occurred.

A girl knocked on his door nervously and waited.

"Enter." He watched her in silence as she placed his tea directly in front of him, just as always, her eyes averted the whole time.

"The plant." He nodded toward the pot on the desk. "Straighten it."

The girl did not know what to do. She turned the pot so it was aligned to one side of the desk, hoping that was correct.

"No!" he barked, suddenly standing. The girl stood perfectly still as Xeng leaned toward her and slapped her face hard. "Insolence."

She stood in fear as Xeng lined up the plant slowly and meticulously. Precisely aligned to the corner and equidistant from each edge.

"Now get out."

The girl quickly walked out and softly closed the door.

Xeng sipped his tea and put the girl out of his mind. Momentarily he wondered how his fool would feel when he found out who he'd sold the bacteria to. Perhaps he'd simply wish he'd demanded more money. Xeng smiled. They were all so stupid. And within a few hours, Xeng would have what he was after.

This is going to be the easiest money I've ever made, the blond man thought. All he had to do was meet his mark tonight, hand over seventy-five thousand dollars of the Chinese money, and then meet Lin, who would pay him another fifty thousand for his 'brokerage' fee. Seventy-five thousand dollars for a day's work. *Not bad*, Kevacic thought. *Not bad at all.*

He had called the mark this morning, and everything had gone exactly as expected. The man wasn't interested in 'doing the right thing', but was very interested in the money. He had said he could provide information, in the form of a confidential government report, for the fifty thousand dollars Kevacic had eventually offered. But, for seventy-five thousand, he would give Kevacic the report *and* a sample.

Kevacic had decided the Chinese would go for it, and had agreed, adding a small bonus, twenty-five thousand extra for himself. He hadn't even bothered to try to beat the man down; after all, it wasn't his money, was it? All he had to do was meet the man at the Commerce Hotel in Yea at six o'clock tonight. He would call Lin back in a few minutes and arrange to meet him at eight, preferably at some location a little closer to the airport.

Kevacic had booked himself a flight to Brisbane, more than twelve hundred kilometres north, for that night. He wasn't exactly sure what the Chinese were up to, but he didn't want to stick around and find out. And it would be nice to get some sun for a change, too. He called Lin's mobile number.

"This is Lin speaking."

"Your decision?"

"We will pay. On delivery," Lin said.

"I need one hundred thousand in advance to pay for what you want. You have to get it to me by four o'clock this afternoon."

They arranged to meet outside an address in Chinatown. Lin would hand Kevacic a briefcase with the money. He wouldn't need to check it; no cash no deal, and Lin knew it. Kevacic was about to start a long, relaxing holiday, funded by the Chinese.

20

The Hercules landed on the slick, icy Ross Island airstrip in the late afternoon, greeted by darkness, freezing wind and snow. It was a cloudy night, so dark this time that Peter had to look hard to see the bright-orange nylon markers, even in the artificial lights. Flying into Antarctica was like flying into a forbidden, bleak world, like entering a land where time stopped in an endless night. The flight, at least, had not been too bad. The Hercules seats weren't great, but they weren't as bad as others made out. And there was always plenty of room to walk around and stretch one's legs.

Just over halfway through the flight, around where the Southern Ocean meets the Pacific, there had been some fierce turbulence, and it was noisy as hell, but, with something to read, a light meal of sandwiches and lukewarm tea, the hours had seemed to pass more quickly this time.

John Kelly was waiting for them at the main doors of the base. He did look like a bushranger, Peter thought. The pilot went straight inside, stopping briefly to nod at Kelly.

"Good to see you again, Ned," Hennessy said. "This is David Melville." Peter wasn't sure whether the man was a doctor or not, and Melville didn't offer any explanation.

Kelly quickly ushered them inside, where a wave of heat hit them. In reality, it wasn't that hot inside, it was just so cold outside.

"We're not here for long, Ned," Peter started to explain, "and Colles wants me to talk to everyone."

"Yeah, I know. They told me, and I've told all the men to give you as much time as you need. Make yourself at home." Kelly apparently didn't mind the intrusion. "Just make sure you leave enough time to fill me in before you leave."

"Sure."

Kelly showed Hennessy and Melville to their quarters, where they left their bags, and set off with Melville to find the doctor.

Melville and Martin Brinksma started their rounds, taking blood samples from some willing, and some slightly less-willing patients. Each container was carefully labelled, sealed and placed in a sturdy aluminium case Melville had brought with him.

Hennessy decided to start his interviews with the most likely possible source – the drilling team. For each person he started a fresh page, writing their full name, and the date and time of the interview, in true empirical tradition. He intended to be as thorough as possible, knowing that time was short for the remaining people on Macquarie Island. There was no time for mistakes or oversights.

The third man he got to was Bob Jacks. Jacks was manning the drilling rig when they'd brought up the first of the stones and the piece of grapevine. Bob was a tough character; he'd worked hard all his life and had never backed away from a challenge. But Peter knew that beneath the rough exterior was a good man who would always go the extra mile for a friend. The salt of the earth.

"The bloody drill shook itself right out of me 'ands," Bob began. "Never usually 'appens," he added for clarity. "I'da swore we'd 'it some seriously 'ard rock, but it was just a bloody pebble. Funny business, this ice drillin', y'know. Ice is like steel down there – all that pressure – but some rock is softer than the ice and some is 'arder. That little bugger was a 'ard one. The cold can play hell with the m'lec'lar structure of steel too, ya know.

"When I was workin' in Canada, way up in the north, we hit all kindsa frozen stuff diggin' out foundations an' that, but not like this fella. Can't tell ya 'ow surprised I was when all we brought up was a shiny, egg-shaped stone. Bloody lucky the little bugger fitted in the core tube, I'd say, otherwise we coulda had a serious fuck-up with the drill. Dunno why the drill didn't rip up the stone, either. Doesn't make sense." Bob scratched his head thoughtfully. "The drill was playin' up that day, though, an' we never did figure out why."

Peter listened as Bob went on to point out that later on they had brought up some black mushy-looking stuff which he'd been told was a piece of some plant. Bob didn't believe it, though. "Plants? Here? Yeah right, mate."

That was certainly an unusual day, Peter reflected, but there was nothing out of the ordinary in Bob's story. Jacks went on to tell Peter that the other man on the drill, who had also been his friend, was killed in the Macquarie plane crash. The drill had played up twice since. He wasn't sure when the first time was, but he knew he hadn't been on duty when it happened. The second time was yesterday, when everything just stopped.

"I told Ned it was the 'and o' God that stopped 'er," Bob lamented. "I checked every inch of 'er and couldn't find nothin' the matter with anythin'."

Peter had to start a new page in his notebook.

"I care for 'er as good as any woman I've known, ya know. Maybe better." Bob was obviously a dedicated mechanic, Peter thought, or maybe a very lonely man ... He smiled at that thought but Jacks didn't notice.

"I just can't unnerstan' it." He went on to explain that all ice core extraction activities had been suspended temporarily, until they could work out what had happened. The equipment was too expensive to risk damage. Hennessy found himself feeling a little relieved that, at least for the moment, nothing more was being taken out of the ice.

That evening they sat down to a huge meal of roast beef and vegetables, with the teams split into two separate dinner shifts, as always. Last time he had been there, he'd been surprised at the size of their meals, and Ned had mentioned that the average man needs about five thousand calories a day to cope with the freezing Antarctic conditions. At Peter's dinner shift, the nature of his and Melville's business was the main topic of conversation, and the men had a hundred questions. So many that Kelly had to ask them all to leave Peter in peace while he ate his meal.

When he'd finished, he quietly asked Kelly if he could tell the men what he knew. Kelly had no objections, so Peter briefly conveyed all he thought he could about the plague at Macquarie. Most of them had already heard something anyway. He explained that the health people wanted to run a final check on everyone at Ross base, because that was one of the possible sources. He finished by saying that, to all intents and purposes, Ross base had been 'cleared', but these blood tests would be final confirmation. The tests should be completed by the end of tomorrow.

He wasn't actually sure of the last point, but he knew Nicki and Conrick's team would run the tests as soon as possible. He was going to ask Colles to advise Kelly of the results as soon as he could. Kelly was grateful to Hennessy for easing some of the unrest.

After dinner, Peter got through another few interviews, and this time one of the men told him about a couple of strange dreams he'd had. The man couldn't think of the last time he'd remembered a dream after waking up – maybe it was when he was a kid – so he thought this was unusual enough to mention. These were very unsettling dreams, too. A dark, unfamiliar place, where people had fear in their eyes, and it was hard to breathe.

By midnight, Peter had interviewed most of the remaining men, leaving only a few, including Kelly himself, for the morning. During his rounds, some of the men told him Melville was asking questions, too, and he wondered again exactly what Melville was there for. Colles didn't seem like a man to do things unnecessarily.

Peter set his phone alarm for six o'clock. By the time he got to his quarters to turn in, he was utterly exhausted. He fell asleep within minutes of hitting the pillow.

21

Six-fifteen, according to Nicki's watch. *Time to go home,* she thought. It had been a long day, and her eyes were hurting. The work was urgent, but they all knew that pushing themselves to the limit would lead to mistakes. They had checked one hundred and twenty different test substances, and had had one hundred and twenty negative results. All of it had been slow and painstaking, with system controls, safety checks and double-checks. The precautions were all necessary, of course, but they turned even the simplest task into a complex series of procedures and commands.

Philip had just finished preparing the next one hundred and twenty Petri dishes for tomorrow's tests and those needed several hours to incubate beforehand. He'd just emerged from the cell to de-suit. Nicki wasn't feeling confident about the results. The bacteria had shown extraordinary resistance to everything they'd thrown at it. If there had been a plague on Antarctica thousands of years ago, it seemed likely no one had survived. No immunity at all. An entire race wiped out *in a matter of days.* It was a frightening thought.

Conrick was more positive, saying that if a cure existed, they'd find it.

"If we do, I doubt it will be in time for the people on Macquarie,' she reminded him, thinking he was just looking for the solution to a puzzle, rather than an antibiotic to save the life of dozens, or maybe thousands, *or millions*, of people. She packed up her notes, taking care to leave the last sheet separate from the rest. Philip had not had time to enter it into the system yet. He would update the data tomorrow, he said.

"Goodnight, Dr Palmer," Philip said, not quite meeting her eye.

Conrick had left at around five-thirty but said he would be back after dinner to start the next tests. Nicki was a little worried about him. She conceded he was probably at his best on the theoretical side, but his methods lacked a little on the practical side. He wasn't as meticulous as she, and that bothered her a lot; human lives were at stake. She'd also noticed that he didn't like it when she pointed out things he hadn't thought of, especially if anyone else was around. She overheard him on the phone earlier referring to her as '*that New Zealand doctor*'. All she wanted to do was find the cure, quickly, and hopefully save some lives. If Conrick wanted to be petty, or wanted to take the credit, then so be it.

For Nicki, there would be no need to return to the lab tonight. With Conrick setting up later, they would have results by morning. Her first task tomorrow would be examining the samples and logging the results. Later in the afternoon, they expected test samples from Ross and Macquarie to arrive. With Peter.

In fact, she thought that spending some time away from the lab, mulling over everything in her mind, might even be more productive than some of their tests. Fleming's discovery of penicillin had come about because of a lab *accident*, after all. They'd be running all kinds of tests on those samples until well into the next night, she knew. She felt the new Macquarie or Ross samples were more likely to hold the key they were looking for.

She put on her coat, checked the cell, noting that each one of the console screens were locked – waiting for a password before anything could be done – and left, making sure the electronic security locks on the doors clicked shut. She drove out, wishing the guard a goodnight as she went.

In the main part of town, she didn't find a nice-looking restaurant, but she did find a nice-looking hotel. There was even a perfectly reasonable Sauvignon Blanc from New Zealand on the wine list, so she treated herself to a small glass with her meal. The best-sounding item on the menu was Chicken Chasseur. She sat down at a table set for two and sipped her wine, thinking of Peter. He'd told her the people at Ross Station had already been checked for the plague, and it was safe, but she still didn't like him being there. The girl behind the bar brought her meal over and asked her if someone would be joining her.

"No. I'm on my own tonight." *Most nights, as it happens ...*

There were a couple of others eating at tables near her, and the bar next door was quite rowdy. She would much preferred to have found a nice little restaurant. As she ate, she tried to sort out her thoughts from the last two days' events, realising it had become a conversation in her head. A conversation she would have had with Peter, were he there. She gently shook her head. She'd seen him once, the first time in three years, and was already missing him! "Don't be silly, girl," she told herself.

She didn't linger at the hotel after dinner. Peter had called her this morning from the airport and asked if she'd mind collecting his mail. He hadn't wanted to impose, but he wanted to get those maps as soon as possible, so they could go over them at the lab when he returned. He'd been very enthusiastic about what they might find, and she readily agreed.

She drove back to Warrandyte, noticing the weather for the first time since the morning. The air was clear, and she could see the stars in the sky. The weather had been fine since late morning. Maybe that was a good omen. This time she enjoyed the quiet drive through the mountains; it was hard to believe it was the same piece of road she drove last night. She looked but couldn't find the spot where the car had spun off the road. Safely at Peter's house less than an hour after dinner, Nicki parked the car near the fallen tree. Sitting on a chair on the front porch, she found a bulky package from a Prof. J Morton. She unlocked the door with the help of the pale moonlight and stepped inside to the faint, welcoming aroma of the fireplace. It made her smile.

After helping herself to a glass of water, she took the mail into the living room. The place seemed cold tonight. Perhaps it was the cold, long-dead ashes in the fireplace. She thought of Peter, down in the endless frozen winter in the planet's wasteland. *He'll be fine,* she told herself for the twentieth time today.

Nicki put the junk mail and a letter from the telephone company aside, and carefully opened Prof. J Morton's letter, so as not to damage the contents. Spreading the maps out on Peter's dining table, she was more than a little disappointed. They did not look like any maps she was familiar with. They had a kind of amateurish look about them, a lot of copperplate handwriting in a foreign language she did not recognise and some very elaborate and ornate drawings. At least Morton had included a few pages of notes and explanations, along with some photocopied text about portolans – thirteenth- and fourteenth-century 'port to port' maps used by medieval sailors.

The text explained that these maps did not appear to use modern grids of latitude and longitude, but Morton's handwritten notes said he had done his own calculations and believed the maps were fairly accurate. Much more so than the maps used by, say, Marco Polo in the thirteenth century. He said in his notes that the Piri Reis map fairly accurately detailed the Antarctic coastline along Queen Maud Land and around the Weddell Sea, to 'within a few degrees'. Apparently it was common for the maps of that time to be out by several hundred miles, longitudinally. Morton had also included a copy of something called the Dulcert Portolano, which Nicki found even more difficult to read.

The Oronteus Finaeus map was much more interesting, though. It showed almost the entire globe, with Antarctica clearly visible. She studied it for a few minutes, but she found it too busy to properly understand. She went back to Morton's notes. His theory was that the precursor maps could have been produced in pre-Hellenic times, before the early Greek map-makers, even before Ptolemy's maps – which were actually far less accurate, Morton's notes said – although much more famous.

Professor Morton's hypothesis was that the earlier precursor maps could have been produced by ancient Phoenician or Carthaginian navigators and these, in turn, from even more ancient source maps. The repeated transcriptions could account for the areas of remarkable accuracy being interspersed with fairly obvious errors. But Morton's theory could not explain how the map-making technology could have been lost. Nicki could feel another headache coming on.

She went into the study to have another look at the stone. She fumbled for the light switch and, a split second before it clicked on, she was sure she saw a faint glow coming from Peter's laptop screen. She shivered again. Had the laptop been turned on? She went over to the device, being careful not to touch the stone, which was on the floor almost directly under it. The laptop was cold to touch and apparently switched off. What could make a screen 'glow in the dark'? Some kind of energy field? Or simply a trick of the pale moonlight outside?

She felt cold all over. Looking around, she could see no earthly reason why the screen might glow. It was eerie. She was glad she had resisted the temptation to touch the stone this morning. She wondered whether Peter had talked to John about it. She knew Peter wanted to have it analysed, and ...

On an impulse, she took out her phone and searched the Sydney telephone directory for Professor John Morton. Thankfully there was only one J Morton with 'Prof.' in front of his name. Moments later she was dialling his number.

"Hello."

"Professor Morton?"

"Yes. Can I help you?"

"Professor, my name is Nicole Palmer, I'm a friend of Peter Hennessy. I believe he's spoken to you about his trip to Antarctica."

"Ah ... yes, that's right." Morton's voice sounded a little guarded.

"Um, I'm a doctor, I used to work with Peter at Melbourne University a few years ago. I'm calling from Peter's place now; he's back at Ross Station again." She hoped that would break the ice a bit.

"Oh. I see ..." Nicki could tell that he didn't see anything at all. "How can I help you?"

"Did Peter tell you about the stone he brought back?" she asked.

"He mentioned it, but I don't know anything about it."

"Well, it's a very unusual piece of rock. I hope you don't think I'm crazy, but ..." Nicki plunged right in to explain last night's mysterious experience to him, hoping he didn't think she was a fool. At least Peter trusted him, she knew that. And maybe it would help him to trust her.

He listened in silence, asking, when she'd finished, if she'd ever had any other similar experiences. She said she hadn't.

"This may sound crazy, too, but in the study here a few minutes ago I thought I saw a faint glow coming from Peter's laptop screen. The stone is very close to it." Morton hadn't said much, and she was now wondering whether he thought her a fool.

"Look, I've been thinking about coming down to Melbourne ever since Peter first called me. He's got me intrigued, you know. Anyway, I've been meaning to catch up with old friends for a while now, and this is just the excuse I need."

Nicki was encouraged by the boyish enthusiasm in his voice. It made him sound like an older version of Peter.

"I want to have a look at that stone, and talk to you both. When's Peter due back?"

"Tomorrow. I'd like to talk to you, too, about those maps."

Morton said he would try to fly in to Melbourne tomorrow, and Nicki gave him her number. She hung up, and a vague feeling of uneasiness returned. She put the maps back into the envelope and stepped out into the darkness. She allowed her eyes to adjust and took a long look at the house after she had locked up. It was a lovely country cottage, she thought. So peaceful, so relaxing. She loved it.

She walked past the remaining debris of last night's storm back to her car, and headed back toward Yea. As she drove, she was busily sorting through the information in the maps and Morton's notes.

22

When Nicki arrived back at the Riverside Motel, she noticed another car parked there this time. A new-looking Japanese sports car of some kind.

She took off her shoes, put the kettle on, made a cup of tea and relaxed on the bed.

Ten o'clock. The other car drove off noisily. Her mind was still overactive, so she turned the television on, settling on an old movie. She watched it for a little while, and then the phone rang.

"Have you seen Philip anywhere? He's staying at your motel." Conrick. He sounded flustered.

"No, I haven't." *What was he getting at?* "Why?"

"I've just checked the Petris for tonight's tests, and there may be one missing," Conrick said.

"What? Are you sure? Maybe Philip miscounted. There are a lot of them."

"Och, I hope you're right. I'll keep trying his room just in case." Conrick hung up.

She turned off the television and went to bed, trying not to worry too much about Conrick's call. She'd left the lab locked, and the place was

147

guarded. *This must be a mistake.* What kind of thief would want to steal dangerous bacteria?

"Conrick here. We may have a problem. I've just checked the Petri dishes and there might be one missing."

"What the hell do you mean? One of the bacteria cultures *might* be missing?" Colles barked.

"Well, I've counted them twice and we're one short, but there could have been a mishap or mistake with one. I won't know for sure till I can get hold of Philip, the lab technician."

"Where is he?"

"I don't know. I spoke to Dr Palmer, she was the last one here. She said Philip must have made a mistake." Conrick's subtle way of pointing the finger at Dr Palmer didn't escape Colles. "It could be a mistake, but I thought ye ought to know."

"You're damned right. And check the place thoroughly for anything else that might have gone missing." Colles sounded like he needed sleep. "Call me on this number if anything else is found to be missing. The call will follow me if I'm not here, so just let it ring. And call me when you find Philip."

"You know what it means, if a culture's been stolen, don't you ..."

"Yes, I know exactly what it means, professor. It means you'd better find a cure, and you'd better do it very fucking quickly." Colles hung up.

The man really was annoying sometimes. Still, at least he had the sense to report it right away, just in case. Colles hoped Philip had a good explanation, but in case he didn't, his mind was already considering the possibilities. Assuming the thief knew what he, or she, had, that bacteria could be used to extort large sums of money from almost any of the world's governments. Or worse, it would be a powerful terrorist weapon, which could be unleashed virtually anywhere, with dire consequences. Terrorists with a virulent biological weapon, the worst-case scenario.

If it had been stolen by someone who didn't know what they had, the prospects could be just as bad, but that seemed unlikely with all the security controls at the lab – the thief would have to either have the required passes, PINs and passwords, or would have to be some kind of computer and security system genius. He contemplated whether to wake the Praying Mantis but decided against it, at least until he heard from Conrick again.

Colles resolved to have all Melbourne hospitals contacted early the next morning, asking them to advise – and immediately isolate – any serious influenza or pneumonia cases. He had to be careful how this was done, of course; he couldn't panic the public. He was sure the minister would allow him to conscript some more immunologists, or whatever Conrick thought he needed, from Fairfield or any other medical facility.

He would also arrange a more detailed investigation of all of Conrick's original team, including the professor himself. Maybe they missed something the first time.

* * *

Fifteen minutes earlier, Senior Detective Mike Barker had been sitting at his desk expecting a quiet night. In fact, he'd even ordered a pizza a few minutes before. He planned to eat his pizza while clearing a backlog of paperwork before the busy nights coming up. Friday and Saturday were always busy nights. But the phone had rung. A restaurant owner in Chinatown had found two bodies. Naturally he'd seen nothing, heard nothing and knew nothing, which didn't surprise Barker at all.

At five past ten he got to the poorly named Celestial Avenue, which was merely a narrow cobblestone alley in Chinatown. He'd walked down from the Russell Street Police Headquarters, a few blocks away, with two other detectives.

"The shittiest part of town," Barker growled, to no one in particular. Neither of his colleagues made any comment. They knew there was no point.

As their eyes adjusted to the relative darkness of the alley, they saw two men lying on the cobbles, one Caucasian, and one Asian.

"Whitey's been shot, and the chink sliced," Barker observed. The Asian victim had had his throat brutally slashed and was lying in a large, elongated pool of blood. "Took this joker a while to die, I reckon," Barker added callously, pointing at the blood.

"Hello." Barker again. The other two knew his routine and said nothing. "What's this?" Barker feigned surprise. "As if we fuckin' don't know," he added, almost to himself, pointing to a briefcase containing four small plastic bags of white powder.

"Another fuckin' chink drug dealer out of the way," Barker muttered. The Chinese were not Barker's favourite people; they kept to themselves, they never saw or heard anything. In fact, he just didn't like them at all. Sen. Det. Mike Barker was one of the 'ugly Australians'. To Barker, the whole thing looked straightforward – a drug deal had gone wrong.

"Looks like this chink wanted the money *and* the merchandise." Naturally, in Barker's mind, the Asian was the drug dealer and the Australian was the victim.

"Could have been the other way around," the younger of Barker's colleagues ventured.

"Yeah right, of course it was," Barker sneered.

He told the other two detectives to search the alley and surrounding area, hoping to find the weapons, although he had assumed they would be long gone, taken by some other lowlife opportunist, no doubt soon to be used in other crimes.

Barker overheard the other two talking as they walked away.

"Doesn't look like they killed each other to me," said the younger detective.

"That Asian guy just doesn't look right for this ... not a drug dealer, I'd say," replied the other, almost out of Barker's earshot.

He scowled in their general direction. But he had to admit that maybe they were right. There could have been an accomplice who'd taken the money, and the gun and knife, and run.

The Chinese had a credit card and an international driver's licence in his wallet that said his name was Lin Fan Cheng, which Barker would check later, and would no doubt find they had been stolen. The blond man had no ID. Maybe his prints were on file. He didn't expect to solve this one. And he expected the police to take a beating for it in the press too. He read the headlines in his mind: 'ANOTHER DRUG MURDER IN CHINATOWN', 'POLICE ILL-EQUIPPED TO DEAL WITH GANG VIOLENCE', 'COPS CAN'T CLEAN UP CITY'.

Then he pictured 'ROGUE DETECTIVE KILLS REPORTERS' and smiled.

High above Barker and the detectives, Xeng sat in his immaculate office, quietly considering his brightening future. Everything had gone exactly as he had predicted. He had what he wanted. Soon, he told himself. Soon.

23

Something was really, terribly wrong. It was impossible to see clearly, and there was a strange kind of confusion everywhere. It wasn't blind panic, it was more like a chaotic bewilderment. Nicki's heart was beating quickly, and she could only take shallow breaths, each one hurting a little more than the last. It was dark, but she could make out vague features around her. The big moon provided a dull light, more like very faint candlelight than normal moonlight. She knew she was lost. Lost in a totally alien place.

From the distance, someone was approaching her. She didn't want him to, but he kept coming anyway. *He's going to do something horrible,* she somehow knew. She wished him away as hard as she could, but he kept coming. She could feel her heart racing, beating its way out of her chest, and something inside her head was screaming. She tried to run, but she couldn't. Her legs were rooted to the ground and refused to move. She felt so weak, and a terrible foreboding had started to overwhelm her.

"Get away! Leave me alone!" Shouting was no good either, he just kept on coming toward her. She tried to see his face but it was too dark. She tried to scream but no sound came out. She gasped for breath as the man kept walking.

It was ... it was ...

Nicki woke up sweating, her head pounding like a battering ram. It took her a few minutes to realise where she was. Lying still, she allowed her mind to slowly come back to reality, to let the grip of fear release her and dissipate. Then after a few moments, she rolled over and checked her phone. 2.15. Her mouth was dry, so she climbed out of bed for a glass of water. Hopefully it would help with the headache.

It had been almost the same vision again. Just a dream this time, just her mind trying to decipher that vision, she told herself. The stone must have had a big impact on her. She was still feeling shaken and more than a little jumpy. She slowly drank the water and absently ate one of the motel biscuits. She tried to go over what had happened again, trying to compare it to the images she'd seen in Peter's study last night. It was all so unclear, but she started to remember, realising that this time she'd been able to remember more than she could the first time. Or at least she had been able to *feel* more.

At first, it was something like being dazed, or utterly confused, like being completely lost in a strange and unfamiliar place. Maybe as the fear she'd initially felt subsided, or maybe as she got more used to it, some of the other things became clearer. There had been a man coming towards her this time, and she remembered that she didn't want him to. She'd felt afraid ... No, that wasn't it; it was more like *anguish* than fear. What was that all about? He might have had something with him. Something terrible. And the darkness, the fear and the feeling of being suffocated, they weren't new. She tried to go over it again, but she couldn't concentrate. She would tell Peter about it tomorrow. *Today.*

She wrote it all down on a piece of paper, reread it to make sure it was all there, and then went back to bed. It was like trying to piece together a jigsaw in the dark. She lay still again for a few minutes as the headache started to ease, and with each minute she relaxed a little bit more. She lay there a while, letting the warmth of the bed seep back into her body. A vision of the terrible dark place returned, but she was determined she wasn't going to let the nightmare take hold again.

Instead, she imagined herself sitting by a warm fire on a deserted beach at night. She started to build up a lovely tranquil picture, piece by piece, just as her mother had taught her to do as a child. A moonlit bay with half a dozen small boats, dinghies, moored just offshore. She imagined the gentle sound of the calm sea. Stars shared the clear night sky with the moon. Familiar city lights glittered in the distance, comforting her somehow. Small, gentle waves, just ripples, rolled quietly in to shore. Peter pulled her closer. *Peter, why are you here? This is my dream*, she thought sleepily. She drifted off to sleep with a soft smile on her lips.

* * *

Po liked this job so far. Xeng had given him accurate information. He had waited in the alley, concealing himself in a doorway until the moment came. Wearing all black clothing, and without his sneakers, he emerged from his hiding place and was able to get to within a metre of the round-eye before either man knew he was there. The round-eye had turned and reached for a gun, but Po was too good for him. The bullet had entered the man's left eye and exited through the side of his skull, taking pieces of bone and flesh with it. The young Chinese had just stood there, face splattered with blood, looking like a confused and frightened little boy. Po laughed as he slashed his throat. He watched the man's face turn ashen and his eyes bulge with horror as he realised what had just happened.

They always look the same, he thought, like they hardly felt the blade, and then the expression of bewilderment on their faces was quickly replaced with abject fear as they realised they were about to die. Po always enjoyed that part of his work. It was why he was better than all the others, and it was why men like Xeng hired him. He had retrieved and photographed the container, and he had already attached the small device to it.

Po worked carefully to carry out Xeng's instructions, almost to the letter, knowing Xeng would not pay if he didn't. Xeng had never accepted excuses. The dashboard clock showed 3.10 am as he drove south-east out of Melbourne, along Wellington Road, using a van he had 'borrowed' from a city restaurant owner. The restaurant would not miss it, and even if they did, he knew they would not report it.

Earlier that afternoon he had stolen an old pair of pants and a hoodie from a cleaner's cupboard in one of the city's office buildings, and in the back of the van he had found a small fishing net and a bucket. Perfect! After a brief stopover, he carefully concealed the plastic container. If he was stopped on the way, or at the reservoir, he would say he worked for the restaurant and he was out catching yabbies, a type of small, local freshwater crayfish, considered a delicacy in some restaurants.

Xeng had told him the container must not be damaged in any way. Should anything happen to it, he was to be contacted immediately. Po left suburbia about thirty kilometres from the city, following the main road out another twenty kilometres through the moonlight. He was glad there was a moon tonight. Last night's weather had been entirely inappropriate – no one would have believed his yabbie story, if he'd needed it. He arrived just before four o'clock, and with half an hour's work in the pale moonlight, he had secured the device to his satisfaction. He was sure he hadn't been seen. Time to return to the city, get his money from Xeng and hand over the film.

On the way back, Po did not see the police car waiting just around a bend near Rowville, one of Melbourne's outer suburbs. The speed limit had changed from one hundred kilometres an hour down to sixty, and Po didn't take any notice. The two young cops in the police car were drinking coffee from a thermos flask, and eating burgers they'd just bought from a nearby takeaway. They watched Po hurtle past doing at least thirty kilometres over the speed limit and looked at each other.

"Whaddya think?"

"I guess we'd better." They turned on the siren, gave chase and soon overtook the van.

The young Chinese driver was very apologetic. "Did I do something wrong, officers?" Po said, subserviently. "I am very sorry." He had a knife taped to his left forearm. If these policemen tried to arrest him, he would kill them. He hoped they would let him go. He didn't really have time to kill them, and it would be inconvenient.

"Where's the fire?" asked one of the officers, wishing he had a dollar for every time he'd asked that.

"I did not see a sign. What is speed along here, please?" Po asked, and the officer told him sixty. Po looked concerned, and he apologised again, offering to give them both a free meal at his restaurant whenever they were next in the city. He pointed to the restaurant name on the side of the van. The police officers eventually let him off with a warning, both thinking a free Chinese meal wasn't a bad idea.

"What are you doing out here at this time of night?"

"Catching some yabbie. Good food."

A few minutes later the officers let him go, and he drove carefully back to the city.

24

The interviews were all but complete, with only Ned remaining. All, except for Bob Jacks, had been relatively uninformative, although Jamie, the young radio man, had told Peter about a strange dream he'd had the night they found the first stone. He admitted to being a little shaken by it, although all he remembered was a terrible blackness and confusion. Peter thought everyone had been very helpful. Most of them had questioned him, too. *Did he think their crashed plane was involved somehow? What was the plague like? What happens next?* and so on.

Ned took him into the radio room, and closed the door. "Okay, tell me straight, are we at risk or not?"

"I don't think so. Officially, Macquarie Island is the source of the plague, and it's the only place where people are sick," Hennessy said.

"Unofficially? You must have an opinion, Pete."

"Yes, I do, but I think I'm almost the only one who agrees with it."

"Try me," Kelly said.

"I think your base is probably the source of the plague. I think it may have come out of the ice. Either something to do with those stones, or maybe the grapevine segment you brought up." Kelly listened in silence. "Bacteria can remain dormant for thousands of years, and beneath hundreds of metres of ice would be the perfect place for that." He didn't want to tell Kelly about Nicki's experience with the stone.

"What about the stone you took back last time, have you had that analysed yet?" Kelly asked.

"No, not yet." Peter wanted to try to unlock more of its 'secrets' before subjecting it to too many laboratory tests, some of which he knew would be destructive. Kelly looked concerned, and Peter guessed he had a right to know a little more. He thought for a moment, then went on. "To tell you the truth, I'm not sure what sort of tests I should get done. Something tells me that an analysis of its composition is not going to help, and we already know how old it must be.

"Bob Jacks told me there have been some unexplained troubles with the drilling equipment. Some sort of interference maybe. Have you given that much thought?"

"Well, I've wondered what the hell's going on, if that's what you mean."

"I guess it is." Hennessy chose his next words carefully. "I wouldn't be surprised if that stone has some sort of energy field, some sort of 'charge'. I think the first one might have interfered with the aircraft's instruments, and I think maybe that energy is what's affecting your drill now." He hoped it hadn't sounded too far-fetched.

Kelly looked at Peter then slowly nodded his head. "Yeah, I wondered about those stones, too," he said. "The day we brought up the first one, everyone started acting a little weird. I didn't think too much of it at first, but it happened again when the second stone came up."

"What sort of weird?" Peter asked.

"Well, we had a couple of fights start, which almost never happens, and the next day, a lot of the men said they'd slept badly. I heard talk of strange dreams as well. Most of the men played it down, but I could see some looked a bit shaken. It was the same both times.

"Marty and I thought maybe the shock of the plane crash could have been a contributing factor, but I'm not convinced. Maybe it's a good thing the drill's stopped working," Kelly said.

"I think maybe it is," Hennessy replied.

They left the radio room and went to find the two doctors. Hennessy hadn't seen much of Melville since the flight. They found them both in the sickbay packing the neatly labelled blood samples into Melville's special case. It seemed that Brinksma and Melville had got on quite well.

"Tenks for your help, David," Brinksma was saying. "You'll let Ned and me know de results soon as you ken?"

"Of course. And don't worry, if I thought the plague was here, we wouldn't be leaving." Melville said the words very seriously, making Peter think perhaps that was why he was there; to ensure no one left if they found the plague. Peter wondered what his and Colles's real jobs were. It seemed unlikely to Peter that they just worked in government health.

Out in the freezing darkness, they crossed the ice to the plane. A small bulldozer was clearing snow from the landing strip, and the pilot was helping another man do something to the engines. Peter was reminded again of the constant effort required to carry out even the simplest task down here. It was a never-ending contest of man versus the elements, and if man let up for a moment, the environment would quickly swamp him.

After he and Melville had taken their seats, Peter leaned across and called to the other man. "You weren't here just to help Marty, were you?"

"What makes you say that?" Melville answered, offering no explanation.

Try another approach, Peter thought. "How long have you worked for Colles?"

"Well, I've known him for a few years, but I'm basically just a doctor, just trying to help get this thing contained." Not 'resolved', not 'cured', but 'contained'. That was something Colles would say. Hennessy decided he would get no more information from Melville.

"You'll be helping them at Yea?"

"Yes," said Melville, taking out his worn paperback.

25

It was five-twenty, and Nicki had just got out of the shower. Her breakfast wouldn't be arriving until six, but she had woken up early and couldn't get back to sleep. Conrick's call last night had been worrying her. She didn't think anyone would actually have stolen a culture, but if they had, she had no illusions about what it might mean. She dressed and was drying her hair when she heard a car driving up. Through the window, in the pale electric light of the car park, she saw Philip get out of the red sports car and step onto the glistening asphalt. She opened the door. "Philip!"

He looked over and didn't seem too sure what to do at first, although he soon recovered. "Hi. What a night I've had!" He looked dishevelled.

"Did Conrick catch up with you?" she asked, ignoring the remark.

"No." He pushed the hair back from his face. "Why, what's wrong?"

"He rang me last night. He thinks there's a Petri dish missing. He could only account for one hundred and nineteen of the new set you prepared yesterday," she explained.

"Well, he's wrong. I made up a hundred and twenty, and I numbered them all. Mb001 to Mb120." He looked certain about it. "Your hair looks great like that," he added, leering at her.

"I'll call Conrick," she said tersely, and Philip followed her into her room. She rang the lab but there was no answer. She hadn't really expected him to work all night after an early start yesterday. "We'll have to go into the lab now. Can you get ready in a couple of minutes?"

"For you, anything," he answered.

"Good. I'll try Conrick again." She stood there and waited for him to leave. After quickly brushing her hair and tying it back, she rang the motel office, apologised and cancelled her breakfast order.

Waiting for them in the lab's car park was another government car with a man sitting in it. As Nicki got out of her car, he climbed out of his. She recognised the solidly built military-looking man. He stood and watched Philip get out of his car, and the look on his face showed he was mentally noting every detail.

"Dr Palmer," Colles said.

"Good morning, Mr Colles. This is Philip Barnes, our lab technician." They shook hands, and Colles noted Philip's Longines watch and his gold signet ring.

"Ah, the wayward assistant. Conrick has been trying to contact you since last night. Where were you?" He looked directly into Philip's eyes, seeing that the man needed some sleep, and if he wasn't mistaken, there was the hint of a grin on his face.

"Well, to be honest, I met someone last night. At the hotel. I spent the night at her place." Philip winked at Nicki and she scowled back at him.

"Her name?" Colles asked, none too politely. Philip gave him her first name and her address. He didn't know her last name. They went into the lab building, Colles watching as Nicki and Philip scanned their passes to enter. Philip went straight over to the cell, and Colles followed ominously, carrying a black portfolio. He checked the Petri dishes, reading all numbers and verifying them against the list.

"Well, the professor's been doing some tests, on at least the first fifty dishes." Philip paused nervously to recount them. "But it looks like Mb117 is missing. I'd say Professor Conrick is right."

"Show me how you could get it out of this." Colles pointed at the cell. Philip showed him how the console worked, and the filtered airlock system they used to get things in and out. Colles didn't seem to be listening, but he watched intently while Philip went over everything, including the airlock and scrub room.

Then he stepped back and took a mobile phone out of his satchel, and dialled a number. No answer. He dialled another number. "Colles. Where is he?" A brief pause. "I see." He put the phone away. "Conrick should be here in a few minutes," he said. *Did Colles have someone watching Conrick?* Nicki wondered. *Or perhaps all of them?*

Colles started towards the small, unused lab next door. "You come with me," he instructed Philip. He seemed to know the layout of the facility well.

A few minutes later Conrick arrived.

"Looks like we do have a missing culture," Nicki said.

"Yes," Conrick said solemnly.

Nicki showed him what Philip had checked and told him Mb117 was the missing culture.

Conrick seemed to be fairly cool about the whole thing. "I wonder why anyone would steal a bacteria culture."

"God knows. I just hope it's someone who understands what they've got. If it's been exposed to air, then we may already have a plague incubating in at least one subject right now."

Conrick had no comment.

A little later Philip returned to the main lab looking pale. "That Nazi wants you next, doctor," he said to Nicki.

She went straight in, not quite knowing what to expect, but found Colles to be reasonable.

"I think you scared Philip," she said.

"You're not worried?" he asked directly.

"Yes, of course I'm worried; we could have a plague starting in Melbourne right now."

Colles asked her a lot of questions about her work, the hospital in

Wellington, her financial situation, where she'd been the night before, who she'd seen at the hotel, how long the drive to and from Peter's was. His questions were clinically logical, and Nicki understood that he had to ask them, but she felt a little embarrassed. Colles seemed to be able to look into her mind.

"So you're involved with Hennessy, then?" he asked pointedly, and her face gave away the answer before she spoke.

"Well ..." she started nervously. Lying to this man would be a mistake. "Dr Hennessy and I are old friends, and ..." she wasn't sure how to put it, so she just said it plainly, "... I stayed at his house on Wednesday night." She felt her face flush, but Colles took no notice. He just nodded and made a note in his notebook.

"Did you see Philip last night?"

"Is he involved in this?"

"Did you see him?" Colles repeated. He clearly did not wish to be questioned.

"No."

"He's staying at your motel. What about his car, that red Nissan, it's hard not to see."

"Well, I think I heard his car leave the motel last night just after ten. There weren't any others in the car park when I got there, and when I saw him pull up in it this morning, I assumed it must have been him leaving last night. You don't think he's involved in this, do you?" She didn't think Philip was that stupid.

Colles looked directly at her. "I'm not ruling anyone out." *Not even you or Peter Hennessy,* his expression said. He looked back at his notes. "Send Conrick in please." Apparently she was dismissed.

Conrick emerged about half an hour later, looking very annoyed and more than a little flustered. He sat down in front of the main computer console.

Colles came back into the room, his presence commanding everyone's attention. "I don't have to remind any of you how serious this situation is. We need a cure to be found, and quickly." He spoke like a military commander, Nicki thought. "Professor, how are those printouts out coming along?"

Conrick silently walked over to the printer and retrieved half a dozen sheets of paper. He handed them to Colles.

"Now, is there anything that can be done to help you here?" He looked at Nicki.

"Yes," she said, "I'd like to know the current medical status of everyone on Macquarie Island, I'd like their medical histories, and if possible, fresh blood samples as well." She wasn't sure whether their medical histories would help, but it would be wise to check everything. "We could use some more people, too. Doctors to go over the medical records, a ... another microbiologist." She looked at Conrick. "To get through it faster," she added.

Colles stood there in silence while he completed his notes. "What about equipment?" he asked.

"I think we have all we need. Professor?" Nicki had already made sure they had all the equipment she might want.

"It's all here," Conrick said abruptly.

Colles looked up at Conrick, staring for a moment. "I've got another doctor coming in from Macquarie with the samples already, and I've asked the health minister to give me some of the people you've just asked for. I'll arrange the rest before the end of the day." He walked out, extracting his phone from his satchel.

Conrick looked very annoyed now and didn't make any secret of it. He glared at Nicki. "Well, let's get on with it!" he snapped.

Colles contacted the health minister, quickly explaining to her that he was on a mobile phone, hoping she would take the hint. Mobile phones were just not secure enough for *this* conversation. The minister confirmed his request to draft additional medical people, and he told her subtly that 'a sample was missing'.

She was silent for a moment. "So there is a major risk then," she asked, confirming that she'd heard correctly.

"Yes."

He had skimmed through the system reports Conrick had given him, merely confirming what he had already assumed. He drove back into the city, where he could start making the necessary arrangements as quickly and discreetly as possible. He had started making calls from the car by nine and was back in the city before nine-thirty. He hoped Melville and Hennessy had some good news. They were due back by mid-afternoon.

26

They resumed work after Colles left, almost back into the routine established yesterday. Nicki reviewed the notes, looking for anything they might have missed. Conrick and Philip were already into last night's samples. Philip was very subdued and looking immersed in his work, not making eye contact with anyone. Apparently Colles had really unnerved him.

Nicki's phone vibrated itself to life.

"Dr Palmer?" *A familiar male voice.*

"Yes. Hello, professor."

"I hope I'm not disturbing you."

"No, it's okay. Go ahead."

"Well, I'm in Melbourne. I managed to get the early flight. I'm in the city. Will I be able to see you and Peter today?"

"Peter's due back this afternoon, yes, so tonight should be fine. Can I call you later?" Nicki said.

"Oh ... ah, good, good." He sounded disappointed. "Ah, actually I was rather hoping I could start right away."

"Well ..." Nicki did a quick calculation in her head. "I can't do much here, other than review yesterday's results, until Peter gets back with the

166

new samples. I could meet you at his place in an hour." *Provided I'm allowed to,* she thought.

"Wonderful. I'll see you there," Morton said.

"Do you want the address?" Nicki said, thinking the man was a little absent-minded.

"He hasn't moved in the last year, has he?" he asked.

She gave him the address anyway.

"Yes, that's the same place," Morton added unnecessarily.

"Good. See you there at …" she checked her watch, "… ten thirty."

At ten twenty-five, she parked in the street outside Peter's home, seeing Morton's rental car parked almost on top of the fallen branch. Conrick had grudgingly agreed that she could leave, *briefly*, but was going to inform Colles, he had said. She walked up to the house. On the front porch, a man wearing a brown tweed jacket and badly creased black slacks stood waiting. His hair was long and untidy, Nicki thought, and he had a distinct paunch.

"Professor Morton," she said, and held out her hand.

He shook it a little more vigorously than his relaxed manner suggested. "Very nice to meet you, doctor." He was looking at her intently but said nothing. She wondered if he was thinking she was too young to be a scientist. It wouldn't be the first time an older man had made that annoying assumption. Or maybe he was just wondering why she had Peter's house key.

She opened the front door. "The stone's in the study," she said, and Morton set off in the right direction, with Nicki following.

"I stayed here a few days last time I was in Melbourne," he said by way of explanation. "In the Room Without Furniture." He was pointing down the hall. Nicki was glad she'd put Peter's duvet back in his bedroom this morning.

"You say this screen appeared to be illuminated last night?"

Nicki didn't feel so sure of herself now. It somehow seemed less likely in the cold light of day. "Well, I can't be sure, but, yes, I thought it was."

"I'm not sure what could do that, but I'll try to find out," he said.

"Maybe I should try touching the stone again," she ventured, and Morton looked horrified.

"No. Please don't, my dear. I'm not sure I'll be as good a nurse as Peter."

Nicki didn't think so either, but didn't say so.

Morton bent down and touched the stone tentatively, then picked it up. "Well I guess I'm safe with it," he said. It was evident that Professor Morton had taken at face value what she'd told him on the phone. She was relieved. "Now, where are those maps I sent down?"

"Oh, I collected them last night. They're in Yea. I didn't think to bring them back. I'm sorry." She didn't have time to discuss them now, in any case. "I have to get back to the lab soon."

"Yes, yes of course. Do you know if Peter had any specific tests in mind for this stone? I've persuaded a colleague to lend a hand for a day or two."

"No, I'm not sure. Do you have any ideas?" She hoped it wouldn't be damaged. She wanted to know more of its secrets.

"Not really. I'm a cultural anthropologist, you know, geology is not my forte, but I did a bit of research last night." He looked thoughtfully at the stone. "I was looking for references on unusual pieces of rock, and I found some interesting information about the stone circles in England that might give us a starting point.

"Have you heard of the Rollright Stones in Oxfordshire?" Nicki shook her head. "It's a circle like Stonehenge. The stones apparently emit measurable ultrasonic radiation." He looked more excited now. "Apparently, this megalithic conversation occurs at dawn, for a few hours, and it peaks twice a year at each equinox. It's just one of the many stone circles on which ultrasonic detectors, Geiger counters, as well as highly sensitive magnetometers, have been used, often with surprising results." He looked at Nicki, almost conspiratorially. "I'll steer clear of tests that use radiation. We don't want to irradiate the thing, do we now.

It might have more to tell you!"

Nicki was relieved to hear that. "Yes, I think it might. When Peter's back, I'll try it again."

"Anyway, carbon-14 dating only works on organic matter, so it's probably of little use. Oh, I also reread what I have on psychometry. It's quite fascinating. Did you know it's been used reasonably reliably by archaeologists since the turn of the century, even by the awfully conservative British Museum!

"In 1941, a chap named Stefan Ossowiecki examined some ancient stone tools in Warsaw and made some quite remarkable statements contradicting anthropological and archaeological opinion of the day. But they were confirmed later by archaeological finds made in the Dordogne and Czechoslovakia! I wrote down one quote I thought summed it all up rather well." He rummaged around in his jacket and pulled out a small piece of paper. "Ah yes, here it is. One hundred and fifty years ago, Joseph Rodes Buchanan, who was a dean of medicine in Kentucky, described readable traces in objects as 'mental fossils' and said 'the past is entombed in the present'. He's the chap who named it psychometry."

Nicki was fascinated, but she had to get back to the lab. Right now, the plague was the most important thing in her life. She looked at her watch. Ten fifty-five. "Professor, I'm going to have to get back to Yea. Can I call you this afternoon?"

"Yes, of course. Please do." Morton looked disappointed that their meeting was ending so soon, but with stone still in hand, he walked purposefully to his car.

* * *

Back at his office, Colles worked feverishly. By ten o'clock he had arranged for three more people to be sent to the Yea lab, and he had briefed them all. A detailed investigation of all six people, including Barnes, Palmer and Conrick, was under way, covering everything from previous offences and current or past political affiliations, to financial and domestic situations. He was looking for anything that might even remotely indicate impropriety or potentially allow someone to be blackmailed.

The security system printouts Conrick supplied had confirmed that Dr Palmer's security code had been used to gain access to the system at 10.25 last night, but there was no record of any activity after logging in. The system had recorded that Dr Palmer had logged in but didn't do anything – didn't log off and didn't leave – so clearly someone must have altered the log.

This would have required some considerable skill with security systems. In Colles's mind, the fact that Dr Palmer's code had been used suggested she was probably in the clear; if the thief knew how to alter the system log, then surely he or she would not have left such an obvious calling card. He also knew, painfully well, that no matter how much you drummed security procedures into people, they still sometimes allowed others to use their passwords, and they still often chose passwords easily remembered and therefore often easily guessed.

Colles shook his head as he recalled an investigation he had run some years ago, where he had to determine who had accessed a secure systems environment. By reviewing all users' personnel files, he had been able to correctly guess thirty-two of the forty-seven passwords in use, many of them on the first attempt.

All that the Yea security system reports *really* confirmed was that someone on the 'inside' was involved.

Donna had provided the three new medical scientists with a car and a driver. Two of them had been recruited from the Fairfield Infectious Diseases Hospital, and one from the Royal Melbourne. All had signed standard declarations under the Official Secrets Act, and all understood the seriousness of the situation and were now on their way to Yea. Colles's briefing had been deliberately robust.

He had elected to keep the theft to himself at this stage. That had been a tough decision, since he had no doubt there was a serious biohazard on the loose. He was also technically obliged to contact the World Health Organisation. But in this case, he knew it had to be an 'insider' and that involving WHO would also involve the police. That would only further increase the risk of information leaking out. Besides, he was already doing everything he thought WHO could possibly do.

His investigation clearly pointed to one of Conrick's people. But Barnes' and Palmer's cars and rooms at the Riverside Motel had already been thoroughly searched, without success. He was now just waiting on the report on Conrick's quarters at the lab. He had personally briefed the minister and had been told again that it was up to him.

Now it was almost twelve, and he had just returned to his desk when the phone rang. *Conrick to say he'd found a cure?* "Colles."

"Nicole Palmer. We've just received a ... a *demand*." She sounded shaky. "They are going to release the bacteria unless we do what they say."

"Who?" Colles barked.

"There's no ident- ..."

"What do they want?" Colles cut in.

"It doesn't say, just that they'll contact us again." She read the note to him. "There's a photo, too. It's one of our hermetic containers." She paused momentarily. "I think whoever took it knew how to use the equipment here."

"How did it arrive?"

"Looks like hand-delivery, but I didn't see anyone." Colles heard her call out to someone. "... Philip saw no one either."

"Take a photo and send it to me, and touch it as little as possible," he instructed. "Where's Conrick?"

"He had a bad headache. Went for a walk about ten minutes ago."

Less than two minutes later, Colles had the photo on his phone and was printing the image. *Not much to it*, he thought, *but clear enough.*

BACTERIA WILL BE RELEASED INTO A MAJOR
CITY WATER SUPPLY IF OUR DEMANDS ARE NOT
FULLY COMPLIED WITH

TWENTY MILLION US DOLLARS IN USED ONE
HUNDRED DOLLAR BILLS WILL BE REQUIRED
WITHIN 24 HOURS
DETAILS FOR DELIVERY WILL FOLLOW

TREACHERY WILL RESULT IN AUTOMATIC
RELEASE

27

John Morton had taken the stone straight back to Melbourne University to meet up with his old friend, Pat Hammond. Walking through the corridors of the university brought back fond memories for him, and he was tempted to drop in on a few old colleagues, but he resisted that temptation. He could do that later. Right now, he wanted to get started on analysing this extraordinary stone.

He found Pat in his lab with a couple of students. Pat was a geologist whose main field of expertise was igneous petrology, which Morton thought was perfect because the stone appeared to be basalt, a volcanic rock. At 186 centimetres, Pat was a little taller than Morton, and he was ten years younger and twenty years fitter. Morton thought Pat would be better placed working in the field, rather than lecturing at a university, but Pat liked to stay close to his wife and family so the academic job suited him well.

"John. Good to see you!" Pat said enthusiastically. They shook hands, and Pat clapped John on the back. "How's the rat race going?" Sydney was always 'the rat race'.

"The rats are winning." It was the expected response.

"John, I'd like you meet Kevin Hodge and Beth Willard, two of my star students," Pat said.

"If you believe Dr Hammond, we're all 'star students'," Kevin said in a confident voice, smiling and extending his hand.

Beth Willard stepped forward and shook Morton's hand, with a surprisingly firm grip.

"Pleased to meet you, Professor Morton," she said quietly.

"Beth's specialty is geophysics, and mine is mineralogy," Kevin said. "When Dr Hammond told us what you had, we both asked if we could help. It's not every day an 8,000-year-old stone surfaces in Antarctica."

"Well, I don't know whether Pat told you, but I have some fairly unorthodox testing in mind. Also, we can't damage the specimen in any way, so I understand we're a little limited. I hope that doesn't dampen your enthusiasm. And please call me John."

"Exactly what haven't you told us, John?" Pat asked.

* * *

Barker had got nowhere with his investigation. He had talked to every business owner in the vicinity of Celestial Avenue, and none of them had seen or heard anything. He found the knife in a nearby rubbish skip, but it hadn't told him anything – no prints on it, just the Chinese victim's blood. There had been no sign of the gun. He didn't know why he even bothered. Barker believed Australia would be a better place if all the Chinese went back to China. It was of no consequence to him that many of the Chinese he referred to were actually born in Australia. Nor did he care that they were part of a very important sector of the Australian economy.

He tried the Chinese name in their criminal records database, without success. Then he contacted the bank named on the back of the credit card. They said the card had not been reported stolen and had dutifully placed a stop on the account, pending Barker's investigation and identification of the body. They had also given Barker the man's address.

The credit card had been obtained with the assistance of the Chinese Embassy in Melbourne, although the bank had no current record of where the man worked. Barker had called the embassy and they had been most unhelpful. It never occurred to him that his attitude didn't exactly inspire friendliness. The police had found nothing at the man's apartment; he looked clean. The driver's licence had been of no help either.

His chief was telling him to get results quickly, and he was getting increasingly annoyed with the news media ringing him. He couldn't tell them much, and he knew some of them would make up their own versions of what happened and print them as fact. He decided he would give them what he could and use them to help him. He told his chief what he intended, and the chief grudgingly agreed, muttering that he wished it was someone other than Barker. He'd also given Barker a hard time about the state of his clothes. His shirt wasn't ironed, his suit badly needed dry-cleaning, and it was at least two sizes too small.

Barker gave the newspapers photographs of the dead men and a couple of morsels of information to chew on. Maybe someone knew these men, or saw them yesterday, and would come forward, though he didn't really expect it.

When the afternoon editions of the papers came out, he sent one of the detectives out to get copies. The stories he read covered all the facts he wanted covered. They named Celestial Avenue, the Moonflower Restaurant, and Barker himself as the senior detective in charge of the investigation. They also speculated that it was another drug-related murder in Chinatown and said the police were 'baffled', but all in all, it wasn't too bad.

He hoped the television news coverage didn't make the department look any worse. He had done his best in the interview, he thought, but the television networks edited them considerably and only kept the most newsworthy bits, which of course meant the most *sensational* bits. Not that Barker minded that sort of thing personally, but it would be another reason for his chief to come down on him even harder.

He sent one of the others out to get him a burger for an early dinner, reflecting that it was a shame his wife had left him; he hated ironing and cooking. Then the phone rang. "Barker."

"Jackson. We've just received a driver's licence photo that looks like your dead guy. His name's Franklin Michael Kevacic, and he's a US citizen. Been here for a few years." Detective Constable Jackson went on to explain that a routine check on an illegally parked vehicle had turned up the name. The car had been towed and its owner notified.

Barker inspected the photo Jackson had sent through and confirmed the identification. Then he went back to get his burger. He wasn't going to miss dinner again tonight. He headed down to the pound, meal in hand. The car was old and had seen better days. Barker guessed its value at no more than a thousand dollars. Either Kevacic was very low in the pecking order, or his money was elsewhere. Barker chose the former because, in his experience, people high up in the drug trade were after a quick dollar and usually liked to show off their money.

He had the uniformed officer from the yard break into the vehicle, and he roughly searched it. It didn't take him long to confirm his suspicions. Under the front passenger seat, he found a small travel bag containing twenty-five thousand dollars in cash, and a ticket to Brisbane, Flight 456, scheduled to leave at ten-thirty last night from Tullamarine Airport.

Barker wasn't sure what it meant exactly, but he figured this Kevacic had got out of his league in a big way. He arranged for an immediate and thorough examination of the vehicle. He wanted it taken apart, fingerprinted, registration history, everything. Then he arranged to check the money against their records of unsolved robberies. Then finally, calls to all motels near Brisbane Airport searching for bookings in Kevacic's name, or for confirmation that a blond American had checked in, just in case. Once again, his night was shot to hell.

Back at Russell Street headquarters, he had almost finished clearing the mountain of paper this case had so far required, when someone yelled for him.

"Hey, Barker, I got a call for you. She wants to speak to you personally." The other detective leered at him.

"Put it through, arsehole."

"That's *detective* arsehole, sir." Just the right sort of sneer in the 'sir'.

"Barker!" he snapped into the phone, scowling at the other man.

"Um, Senior Detective Barker?" a small voice said.

"You got me," he said, wondering who the hell it was.

"Um, my name is Carol Connell. I work at the Commerce Hotel in Yea," she said, and Barker had to restrain himself from telling her to get to the point.

"I saw the man on TV," she went on, "the blond-haired man. He was here last night in the hotel."

"Are you sure?" Barker was suddenly interested.

"I remember his blond hair. And the scar on his face." She had gained a little momentum now. "And I remember he was wearing blue jeans." *Like about five million other people in this country, including nearly all of the hotel's customers*, Barker thought.

"And he had an American accent." That clinched it for Barker; the newspapers didn't know anything about him being American.

28

"*Treachery?*" Who the hell uses that word today? Colles wondered.

The demand appeared to be neatly laser-printed on plain white paper, with no visible distinguishing features. No surprise there. The photo of the container wasn't all that clear – no surprise there either. It was a photo of a photo. He took Dr Palmer's word that it showed an authentic lab container. He wondered who might be responsible. *Terrorists?* Not *impossible,* but unlikely; they would release the bacteria and *then* send a note, he thought grimly. *Extortionists?* More likely. He needed to find out who was the inside man. Or woman.

He advised the minister, then made another call to have two additional men despatched to watch the lab and Conrick's group. Maybe they'd get lucky and catch the messenger next time, but he didn't think so. This looked to be the work of professionals. They could easily have acquired the information, there must be twenty people outside Macquarie Island who knew about the plague, but for them to find an insider and execute the whole thing so quickly showed Colles that he wasn't up against fools. Twenty million US dollars! He wondered whether they had any idea how difficult it would be to get that much cash in a foreign currency. Maybe even impossible in twenty-four hours.

A middle-aged woman knocked on Colles's door and entered without waiting. She was a senior NSO officer assigned by Colles and had the same level of security clearance as her boss. They had worked together many times before.

"Something interesting, boss." She knew Colles trusted her instincts. She handed him a two-page report, one page of which was a bank statement.

"Our friends in Auckland turned this up about an hour ago." It was a report on Tony Palmer.

"Shit." Nicole Palmer had not been on his mental list of primary suspects, but now ...

"Her ex, Tony Palmer, has been living well beyond his means for more than a year now. The Auckland people's assessment is that when he moved to Auckland he bought into a very expensive area with an eye-watering mortgage, and has been living it up – well, that might be a bit strong, but he's had a number of expensive overseas holidays, and just look at that debt."

Colles flipped the page and whistled. "Jesus. What does he do again?"

"Doctor."

"What kind?" Colles barked.

"Consultant. In private practice. The report doesn't say which field, but the bank statement shows a fortnightly salary which doesn't sustain his lifestyle. The thinking is that he's a bit showy, and 'in' with a wealthy crowd, so has just kept overextending to stay 'in'. That makes sense to me," the NSO officer said.

"Is there any indication that he's in touch in any way with his ex?"

"No."

"Either way, this makes her a primary suspect. Dammit." Colles was not happy. He trusted Nicki more than he trusted Conrick, and this was going to get in the way. At the very least, he would have to interview her again, and this time it would be much more pointed. "And the checks on the others?" he asked.

"Almost done. One has some offshore affairs, which is taking a little longer, but that doesn't mean anything in particular," the NSO officer replied.

Colles dismissed her. He then contacted Taylor, his security man in charge at the lab, and filled him in, telling him to arrange for two more men, and to find Conrick and to keep a closer eye on Dr Palmer. Then he diverted his office telephone to the mobile, grabbed his coat and satchel and walked out briskly. He drove out of the government car park moments later, heading north-east toward the Commonwealth Agricultural Research Facility.

During his long career, he had been a soldier, from where he'd transferred to Australia's limited military intelligence service. In MI, he'd spent much of his time supervising and analysing surveillance, and he'd really missed the action. From there, he'd gone on to the NSO, the National Security Organisation, where he had worked for the past five years, generally on loan to one government department or another, seeking out the more hands-on assignments.

Within the higher echelons, it hadn't taken long for Colles to gain a reputation as a man who could get quick and decisive results *discreetly*. He'd been assigned to the health ministry immediately when the possible plague situation had first been advised by ANARE. The minister had made it very clear she wanted results, and she didn't necessarily want to know how he got them. It was the way he liked to work. Neil Colles wasn't very good at being subordinate.

Conrick seemed preoccupied, Nicki thought. He was still doing his share of the work, but he had stopped giving orders to Philip and was just working quietly, keeping to himself. Philip was not quite himself either; he seemed much more subdued and was now taking his work more seriously. They had almost finished the second set of Petri dishes, still without any success, and Philip had started preparing the next batch. He was walking around inside the cell in his airtight suit, like an astronaut, occasionally looking at Nicki through the window.

Nicki knew they were getting nowhere. This new bacteria was impervious to all the usual antibacterial test substances, all the known antibiotics. There wasn't much she could do until the samples arrived from Macquarie, and she hated just waiting around. "Have those medical history files arrived yet?" she asked of no one in particular.

No one answered. She stepped towards Conrick and repeated her question. "Medical history files?"

"Och," Conrick almost spat the word out, "over there." He glared at her, irritably pointing to the printer. There were fifty or so pages in its tray. She wondered how long they'd been sitting there and was about to tackle him about it when she realised she could have just as easily checked it for herself. Maybe the stress was starting to get to all of them.

The documents in the tray were copies of medical reports for everyone on Macquarie. Each and every one had to have a complete physical exam prior to signing on. The first page was a note from Donna, who said if Nicki needed actual histories for anyone, she'd 'do her absolute best'. Nicki knew there would be little chance of getting good information. Ever since the 24-hour bulk-billing clinics had sprung up, the days of the family doctor who knew all about a patient's history were long gone.

It took her about twenty minutes to read through all the reports. There was nothing useful in any of them. Everyone was apparently in good health, none had reported unusual conditions, past or present, that she thought warranted further investigation. She bundled up the reports, hand-writing a single-page summary to attach to them. Another long shot ruled out. *Now what to do?* The extra people should be arriving soon, but until they did, all she could do was wait. She wished she could contact Colles and ask when the plane would be arriving.

The door opened and she looked over, but it wasn't Colles. Two security men walked in carrying some cages. Lab rats. Use of rodents was one of the distasteful realities of Nicki's profession. She didn't like it, but she knew very well it *did* save human lives. In this case, rats were known carriers of many types of dangerous bacteria, including the infamous

Pasteurella pestis, but they had their own natural resistance to it. Nicki thought there was a reasonable chance that these little creatures could help save lives and could survive the process themselves. She hoped so.

If *Macquarius* was introduced to laboratory rats, then possibly they would have, or would quickly develop, antibodies to fight it. It was another long shot, but they had to try everything. And if the rats weren't immune, it still gave them an opportunity to properly monitor how the disease attacks a living animal.

Lunch arrived with the new people. Nicki introduced herself and the others to the newcomers. Loh was the senior of them, he looked to be in his sixties, his hair was almost white, and he had a droopy moustache. He spoke with a slight accent. Hart was probably twenty years his junior, looked badly out of shape, and at least twenty kilograms overweight. They had trouble finding a lab coat to fit him. The last was Chris Telford. Chris was in her early thirties, and was the only one who asked questions as Nicki summarised their work to date.

They ate their sandwiches, Hart having twice everyone else's share, and sweating while he sat and ate. Nicki finished hers, poured some coffee and went to look at the rats. They reminded her of a time working with Tony a few years ago. She was standing there with a half-smile on her face when Chris Telford walked up to her.

"I don't like experimenting on them either, but I didn't know rats were funny," Dr Telford said.

"I'm sorry, they just reminded me of someone I knew, and I realised that was an awful thing to think." But it was true – when she'd first met Tony they'd been working together using white lab rats. Animal rights activists would call the scientists involved 'murderers', but where rats could be sacrificed to save human lives, Nicki, like most others in her type of work, believed it was necessary. That was something she and Tony both completely agreed on. It was just that the rats themselves were kind of cute. They were nothing like the slimy gutter rats seen in the movies; they were much more like big white mice, or guinea pigs, and she found it hard to be coldly scientific about them. But people's lives were at stake.

* * *

JULY 30, MACQUARIE ISLAND, SOUTHERN OCEAN

The flight back from Ross Station had been more peaceful than the first, the prevailing weather being more moderate this time. In fact, at Macquarie Island, it was mild and sunny. As they approached, Peter noticed how lush and green the place looked. On the coast he saw hundreds of penguins with yellow markings on their heads, all them scurrying out of the path of the aircraft.

The island rose up sharply out of the water in some places, many rocky outcrops pushing out above the long grasses. He could see no signs of life. No buildings, no people, nothing. It was bigger than he thought it would be; he had pictured the place as a tiny speck of land in the middle of a dark-grey, raging, freezing ocean. Today it was sunny and picturesque; the sea was blue and looked fairly calm.

Once they'd landed, Melville donned his jacket and snapped into action. The pilot kept the engines running while Melville jumped off with a medium-sized crate marked with a red cross. Medical supplies for the base. Hennessy remembered that he had to pick up some blood samples taken from birds and animals, too. He had offered to assist Melville, but the man declined, saying it was bad enough that one of them had to get off the plane.

As Peter waited in his seat, he wondered how far away the people were. What would they be thinking, seeing a plane land, then take off again without offering to help them, without offering to take them to a hospital somewhere? And what of the remaining healthy people, who must know they're probably next?

Peter thought he heard voices outside, but it was hard to tell above the noise of the engines. About five full minutes had passed since Melville got off, and he started to wonder if something was wrong. Maybe the man needed help. He stood up to see if there was anything he could do, and as he walked to the door, a solidly built, bearded man burst in. He looked as though he hadn't slept or washed in days, and he was holding two oddly shaped, large-barrelled pistols, one of which he pointed at Hennessy's chest.

The man had a wild look in his eyes, and Peter didn't doubt he would use the guns if provoked. Another man jumped in behind him carrying a knife and looking just as menacing.

29

Colles walked into the lab, the usual thick file satchel in hand, and a stony expression on his face. "Dr Palmer, a word please." There was no hint of 'please' in his manner. He led her into the small lab next door and pushed the door closed. "When did you last see your husband?"

"Ex. Nearly eighteen months ago," Nicki was surprised by the question. "We went our separate ways. Why?"

"We're checking your phone records. Do you stand by that answer?"

"Yes, of course. What's this about?" Nicki was now getting concerned. "Is Tony all right?"

"Has he ever asked you for money?"

"What? No, of course not." *What the hell?* "What has he done?"

"Have you ever provided him with *any* kind of financial support?" Colles went on, ignoring her questions.

"No. He earns way more than I do. That seemed important to him." *Did that sound a little bitter?* "What is this? What's going on?" Nicki was more insistent this time.

"We are also checking your bank records. Now's the time to tell me if something might have slipped your mind." Colles was starting to frighten her.

"Help yourself. I have no secrets. And if you want me to answer any more questions, you can damn well tell me what you're accusing me of. I don't do witch-hunts," she said firmly, forcing herself to hold Colles's relentless and commanding gaze.

Colles looked at her for almost half a minute. It seemed like an eternity to Nicki. He made a decision he hoped he would not regret later. "Dr Tony Palmer is in significant financial difficulty. That gives you motive."

"*Motive to steal some lethal bacteria? Are you insane?*" She was shocked. Could Colles *really* think that? *Could Tony be that stupid?* Shock and anger were vying for control of her emotional state. "I can't believe you think that."

Colles took a slightly more gentle approach. "Tell me about your separation."

Nicki explained about the changes in Tony, the slowly increasing pressure to adapt her life to his, the well-paid offer that lured him to Auckland. Colles could see her shock and anger starting to give way to concern for Tony. She seemed completely genuine, and he believed her that she had no idea of Tony Palmer's situation. Nicki told him the split was sad for them both, but was amicable, and *final.*

"I believe you," Colles replied, with an unexpected change in demeanour. "Those phone and bank records are being checked, of course, but I believe you."

"Is Tony all right?"

"I can't say. I've already told you more than I am supposed to, but many years of this work have taught me to trust my instincts. He's dug himself a big hole." Nicki was holding back tears now. Maybe it was due to the emotional roller coaster Colles had just put her through, but part of it was sadness for Tony. He wasn't a bad person really, just the product of his upbringing.

As Colles closed his bag, his mobile phone vibrated aggressively. "Colles." He listened for a moment. "Yes, I know who you are, man," he snapped. "Go ahead." Then signalled for Nicki to leave the room and close the door behind her.

She heard Colles explode as she pulled the door shut.

"FUCK!"

* * *

One hundred and forty kilometres from the Commonwealth Agricultural Research Facility at Yea, Lieutenant Brad Hughes, a military communications officer attached to the NSO, sat in a control room next to a radar operator. Five minutes earlier, a cryptic message had come through from the pilot of the Ross/Macquarie flight. They were just out of range, but Hughes had picked up a few words: '... been hijack ... repeat ... -jacked'. He had no doubt as to what that meant. He contacted the number he had been given immediately.

"Colles."

"Lieutenant Brad Hughes, sir. Communications officer at ..."

"I know who you are, man. Go ahead," Colles snapped.

"Sir, I've just received a message that the Ross/Macquarie flight has been ... well, *hijacked*, sir," Hughes said nervously.

"FUCK!" Colles exploded. "Where is it now? *Exactly.*"

"About eight hundred kilometres south of Hobart, sir, flying north. ETA Hobart is approximately two hours."

"Can you contact them?" Colles snapped.

"No, sir. I've tried a few times," Hughes said quickly.

"Try again. Now," Colles ordered and waited, contemplating his next order. If they couldn't get hold of Melville, he would have no alternative.

"Nothing, sir, but I thought I heard a few seconds of cockpit noise. As if someone hit transmit but didn't say anything." Almost a full minute passed in silence as Colles considered what he was about to do.

"Sir?"

"Send the encrypted signal, Lieutenant Hughes." In a clear, measured voice, Colles gave Hughes an authorisation code and confirmed his full name and rank.

"Yes, sir." Hughes put the phone down and Colles heard voices in the background, ending when someone said '*Do it!*' After ten seconds, Colles heard loud voices at the other end, and Hughes came breathlessly back on the line.

"Sir, the flight has just disappeared off the radar screen!" Hughes thought he heard Colles say 'I know', before the phone went dead.

* * *

Kevin Hodge, honours student in mineralogy, generally confident and decisive, was flummoxed. He didn't know where to start. The types of tests he would normally have conducted were destructive, and Morton had been clear that he didn't want the stone damaged. It was undoubtedly basalt, which was consistent with its point of origin. Antarctica is volcanically active, and has been for millions of years, so it has the mineral-rich lava flows required for the creation of basaltic rock.

There was nothing unusual about that – eighty to ninety per cent of the planet's volcanic rock is basalt. Kevin was keen to understand more about its composition, in particular the silica content, which would tell him more about its origin. But without drilling into it, or at least grinding off some dust, all he could do was guess. He stood at the bench looking at it, willing it to give up its secrets, rubbing his tanned chin.

"Let's go back to what John told us," Beth suggested.

Morton had instantly stimulated their curiosity, simply with his opening statement: 'Well, I'm not sure where to begin, or how much I'm *allowed* to say.' That got their undivided attention immediately.

Beth, a geophysics student, was more interested in the processes that might have created such a beautifully symmetrical volcanic stone, as well as its external physical properties. For Beth, its chemical composition was less important. She also wanted to know more about how and where it was found. All Morton said was that it had been brought up from beneath eight hundred metres of ice, thousands of years old, on Ross Island, not far from Mount Erebus. She knew the mountain was one of more than eighty Antarctic volcanoes, and that it had been continuously erupting for more than forty years.

Morton had also explained that this stone was one of two brought up, both identical, at least as far as base personnel could determine. He told them the two stones were at the centre of some strange and unexplained goings-on. Of course, there was no scientific basis for that, but it was certainly *interesting*, he'd said. Pat was enthralled, too, but had since left Kevin and Beth to their investigation as he departed to give a lecture.

Beth asked Morton what he meant by 'strange and unexplained goings-on'.

The professor had been slightly circumspect. "Let's say they may have had an effect on people's health, and on some types of electronic equipment, although I'm not aware of any hard evidence of that."

"What do you mean by 'health effects'?" Beth wanted as much contextual information as Morton could provide.

Morton had not been willing to describe Nicki's experience to two science students, so he talked about it being associated with effects on mood and possibly behaviour, as well as potentially inducing strange dreams – something Peter had suggested.

He had closed by trying to bring the somewhat ethereal back to hard science. "Of course, we have no evidence that any of this is anything other than pure coincidence, but I wonder whether they might radiate some sort of electromagnetic or other form of energy. And there's also the question of their symmetry. I wonder what the odds are against natural formation of two perfectly elliptical stones like these being found, more or less together, under thousands of years of ice, where this is supposed to only be glacial moraine?"

With that final question posed, Professor John Morton left them alone.

"Well, staring at it isn't going to give us any answers, so how about we start where John left off. Let's see if it has any measurable field," Beth suggested, pushing her glasses back up towards the bridge of her nose.

"Sure, that's as good a place as any," Kevin agreed. "Let's go see the physics department."

They started with the most pervasive, although possibly most benign, force they could think of. The stone's magnetic potential was just slightly above 'normal' at around 0.8 gauss. Beth knew the earth's geomagnetic force ranges from 0.3 to 0.7 gauss at the equator and the poles, respectively. At any point, it might fluctuate by no more than 0.1 per cent. This stone was more than ten per cent higher than the geomagnetic force, but that could be explained by any number of factors, including its trip back from Antarctica. It didn't seem anomalous. Well, not anomalous *enough*, anyway.

The ultrasonic tests proved more interesting. They spent an hour, after agreeing to calibrate the ultrasonic detector to its most sensitive, slowly checking frequencies from just above the range of the human ear, at 20,000 Hz, in steps of 50 Hz. This was slow, painstaking work, and after some initial excitement, they realised that the rustling of their clothing and the sound of their breathing was being picked up by the detector. In the end, they took the equipment into a soundproof recording studio and operated the detector from the control room, watching through the plate-glass window between the two rooms.

At 26,350 Hz, something started to register. They progressed further up the spectrum, and the 'noise' peaked at 27,100 Hz and disappeared altogether at 28,000. They had no idea what it meant, and of course there was no way to 'listen' to it.

"Dogs can hear those frequencies," Beth told Kevin.

"Great. I'll have my dog write us a report," Kevin joked.

Beth gave him a look that said 'idiot'.

Mystified by the high-frequency result, they retrieved a few samples of rock, metamorphic, sedimentary and igneous – including basalt samples – from the geology lab, as well as two similarly sized 'honeycomb' rocks – the type found in every second suburban garden –

figuring they would probably have been handled less than the geology lab's samples, just in case that made a difference.

It didn't. None of the other rocks emitted so much as a peep. They weren't sure what the high frequency meant. 27,000 Hz was about a thousand times higher than most human brainwaves. All it really told them was that the stone radiated a very faint ultra-high frequency 'white noise'. But so what?

Kevin set off for physics again to borrow a Geiger counter.

"You guys are opening a shop, are you?" the physics professor had asked.

"Yeah, we got fifty dollars for your ultrasonic detector. I owe you a beer."

"Very funny."

"Now I need your Geiger counter," Kevin said.

"Geiger-*Müller* counter, actually," the physicist corrected him.

"I need your Geiger-*Müller* counter then."

"What the hell have you guys got over there?"

"Just a piece of rock. Pat's got us all thinking of how many different tests we can run on a plain, ordinary piece of rock. I think I'm winning," Kevin said. The professor gave him a wry smile and pointed to a locked cupboard at the back of his lab. He threw Kevin the keys. "Make sure you bring it back," he called. "Don't know what it is about them," he added abstractedly, "but we've had two Geiger counters stolen this year."

"Geiger-*Müller* counters," Kevin corrected.

But the Geiger counter was of no use. They had carefully calibrated the device and tested every aspect, and there was no measurable ionisation.

Feeling more than a little stumped, Beth went in search of research papers analysing Antarctica's geophysical characteristics to see if that might prompt any useful ideas. Kevin was still itching to drill into the stone to be able to test its mineral composition in detail but resisted the urge. He set about devising alternative tests that might help them build a clearer picture of what they had. A half-hour later, he discovered something he didn't expect.

"Hey, this is a little odd," he said.

Beth put down the papers she had been studying and went over to take a look.

"I'm trying to roughly determine its constitution without chipping a bit off," he explained. "I think its weight is all wrong."

"Very scientific, Kevin," Beth said sarcastically, looking at the stone sitting in a large jug of water.

"Well," Kevin went on unperturbed, "its displacement is 345 millilitres, or 345 cubic centimetres. According to my workings, that volume of aphanitic basalt should weigh 510 grams, plus or minus about three per cent."

Beth raised her eyebrows and waited for Kevin to continue.

"Even allowing for it to be composed of different types of basalt, which I consider improbable, its weight shouldn't vary by more than around six per cent. Our stone weighs in at 363 grams. It's thirty per cent underweight."

"So what are you telling me?" Beth asked.

"I think it's either partly hollow or there's something in it a lot less dense than basalt," Kevin said as Beth stared. "And that's not the weirdest thing. I've measured it every way I can, and it's a perfect ellipsoid. Well, oblate spheroid. Not approximately, but *perfectly symmetrical*."

30

Conrick, Palmer, the gimlet-eyed Hart and the others were all staring at Colles, looking for an explanation. They had heard his expletive as Nicki emerged from the small lab, and then heard his raised voice from behind the closed door. They couldn't make out exactly what he said, but it was obvious *something* had happened.

Colles paused for a moment as he surveyed the room and quickly assessed what he needed to tell them. He knew there was no point in trying to dress it up. "The flight back from Ross Station and Macquarie Island has crashed," he announced matter-of-factly.

"*No!*" Nicki cried out involuntarily.

"I'm very sorry," Colles said. And he was. He'd just detonated the explosive device on the plane, and almost certainly killed a number of people. He didn't even know how many, but he assumed at least four. Melville, Hennessy, the pilot and at least one hijacker. He wondered what the hell had gone wrong. They must have been ambushed at the Macquarie airstrip somehow, and Melville must have been killed, or at least overpowered. That probably implied at least two hijackers, maybe three. Melville was a very capable agent, as well as being a trained doctor.

The situation was far from ideal, but Colles knew he'd had no choice.

One of Melville's primary roles had been to make sure there was no way the plane could get back to the mainland if it had been exposed to the plague. Colles had also taken an 'insurance' measure – planting an explosive device on the plane that could be detonated by an encoded signal that only Colles could authorise.

Nicki couldn't believe it. *Wouldn't* believe it. Chris walked her over to a chair and sat her down. Her face was ashen, and she was too stunned even to cry. Colles's words hit her like a body blow. She couldn't stand up, and she could hear her own breathing coming in short gasps. She felt physically sick. How could this have happened? *It's just routine*, he'd said. *I'll be safe.* Someone was telling her to breathe slowly. She couldn't think properly. Peter had been due back in just a few hours.

"No," she murmured again.

Someone was stroking her hair. Peter had told *her* to 'take care'. She vaguely heard someone asking 'what's going on?' This was nothing like when her grandfather had died. She felt cold all over. That was awful, but this felt like ... she didn't know what it felt like ... It felt like part of her had died with him. She felt like throwing up.

As she tried to process the awful news, anger started to well up inside her. She hated Colles. He'd sent Peter down there. Peter had even said he thought Colles wanted someone 'expendable'.

Colles was walking toward her. "I'm very sorry," he said again.

"Get away from me!" she cried.

Colles walked right up to her chair anyway, put his hands on her shoulders and spoke softly but very firmly. "I'm very sorry this has happened, but we need you to keep going. There's a deadly plague somewhere in this city, and a cure must be found. We need you."

His steely eyes were holding hers. "Peter Hennessy and David Melville died trying to help save millions of lives. Don't let them die for nothing." It was trite, he knew, but it was true, nonetheless. "Come with me."

He was suddenly more of a father figure than a military man. And deep inside, she knew he was right, but she just couldn't deal with it right now.

He took both her hands and pulled her out of the chair, forcefully leading her outside. She didn't fight him. He walked her through the car park and onto the lawn beyond, not speaking, leaving her alone with her thoughts for a moment. Somewhere in the middle of the flood of emotion, she was shocked at the intensity of her reaction.

Colles interrupted her despondency, speaking in the same quiet but firm voice. "They told me the plane disappeared off the radar in an instant. It would have been over in seconds." That was the truth. "I know it hurts, and I know it seems unfair, but you must go on with the work we've all been doing. You know he would want you to. *I* need you to."

He led her towards an old oak tree. Her mind raced, trying to process what he'd said. As they walked, she started to realise what had happened to her since Wednesday night. Peter had burst back into her life, and it felt like he had always been there, like she'd been somehow incomplete for years, and when he came back, she'd realised what had been missing all that time.

"Oh, Peter. *Why?*" she murmured, as the tears started to come.

Her tears rolled silently down her cheeks, and Colles saw the almost uncomprehending sense of loss in her face. She would need time, but that was a commodity they did not have. Colles looked at her again, and something in her eyes, something behind her grief, told him she was also a strong young woman.

"I'm truly sorry." Colles was sorry, too, but there had been no other choice. He also knew there was a chance Hennessy or Melville were still alive, but he couldn't tell Nicki that right now. The chance seemed tiny, at least for Hennessy, and if he were wrong, it would be even harder on her.

Colles stood there with her for almost ten minutes while she silently mustered her strength. She knew he was right; Peter would want her to continue. But how? Right now, she needed someone to hold her, but that someone was probably at the bottom of a deep, cold, dark ocean. She shuddered as the sobs racked her body.

Colles had his hands on her shoulders again. "Dr Palmer, we *need* you."

In the distance, Nicki heard someone calling.

"Colles! Colles! There's another note!" Conrick called.

Colles squeezed Nicki's shoulders and nodded to her, trying to convey his confidence in her. He released her and marched over to Conrick to take the note from his outstretched hand. Professor Conrick was very pale and obviously disturbed.

Colles read the note. The demands had just got harder to meet.

The note demanded that the money *and* a mid-sized aircraft be readied for a long flight, by midday tomorrow. Colles knew the aircraft added millions more dollars to this extortion and might be rather difficult. 'No crew needed' meant that at least one of the perpetrators was a pilot. That could help him narrow suspects down, but at this stage they had no suspects anyway.

There was a minimum specification of the required plane, which would need a range of twelve thousand kilometres. Not a light plane, clearly. That distance would take the perpetrators well into Asia, or even South America.

Less than an hour later, Colles had arranged for acquisition and preparation of the specified aircraft. He'd had to use the landline in the small lab to dial in to an emergency cabinet meeting in order to brief ministers. It was an occasion where he was glad the health minister was blunt and forceful.

His organisation had already commenced arrangements for the acquisition of twenty million US dollars in cash. In fact, the money would be flown in early tomorrow morning, direct from the States. That had involved pulling some very large strings, and he had been told to 'just stop this maniac!'. He was grateful the US hadn't insisted on sending their own investigator. He'd then have to brief someone who would try to run the whole show; the Americans always liked to run the show. Fortunately, they knew Colles well.

He had given the note to Taylor who would arrange for a thorough but discreet forensic check on it, but he expected to learn nothing. He'd also had the grounds and immediate area searched. The man who delivered the mail to Conrick had been questioned, but all he could say was that it was with the mail delivered by the postman. Taylor's officers had found the postman, some five kilometres away and still completing his rounds, but he didn't know anything either. They were trying to trace its entry point into the mail system, but that was probably another needle in a haystack.

Colles stepped out of the detail for a moment to assess what they had. This whole thing had only been unfolding for nine days, and it wasn't until five days ago that they knew about the plague. That information had been well contained, at least until Colles had set up the lab team and briefed them. That was only *two* days ago.

So whoever it was had obtained access to top-secret government reports three to five days ago and had then been able to infiltrate the lab team – at least so Colles believed – to get a physical report and a sample of the deadly plague. They were remarkably resourceful. Among them was a pilot, and they evidently had a long-distance escape plan in mind. But were they extortionists or *terrorists*? If the latter, then it seemed to Colles it was possible they could take the money and release the bacteria anyway. He hoped it was just plain old greed.

Twenty million dollars would go a hell of a long way in many parts of the world. The logistics of that amount in hundred-dollar bills were interesting also. Colles knew it would not fit into a standard-sized briefcase, as most people might imagine. He wondered whether the extortionists had done their homework. It would weigh somewhere around 25 kilograms and completely fill *two large suitcases*. If the perpetrators wanted to check it all at handover, that was going to be totally impractical and time-consuming.

The release of the bacteria into the water supply was, of course, another problematic needle in a haystack. Melbourne has many reservoirs and waterways, and he would need a thousand men to check every possible site. He believed that a remotely controlled or timed lock release, or even a tiny explosive charge, could be used. That would be the way he would do it.

If it were a radio-controlled device, he hoped it required an encoded signal and couldn't be set off by a wayward two-way radio, phone or other transmission. If it were a timed device, that would mean someone probably had to retrieve and disable it. Of course, there may be no device at all, but Colles knew the bacteria was out there somewhere so he couldn't take that chance. What he had to do was locate the 'insider' and find out everything he knew. Quickly.

He called his office to get an update on the checks on Conrick's people and learnt that Barnes, the sleazy young lab technician, had a wealthy girlfriend. He seemed to be sponging off her, so he was evidently strongly motivated by cash, but Colles thought Barnes wasn't smart enough to fool him, if he was guilty. Palmer had checked out clean, and his instinct told him to trust her, so Conrick appeared the most likely candidate. The difficulty with the background check on Conrick had arisen because he had some overseas investments or funds. That was not necessarily an indication of guilt; the man was, after all, not originally from Australia.

Unfortunately, the search of Conrick's and the others' rooms had proved fruitless. Colles's people had only received the judicial order necessary to get access to financial records and would advise as soon as they got a result. The New Zealand authorities and the banks had been more helpful. They needed more information. Colles needed to do *something*. He was not able to just wait.

He decided to visit the town and see what he could find. If he was lucky, someone had seen something useful. He drove into the township and parked near one of the local pubs. It was the afternoon shift for most hotel staff, but for many, the afternoon shift carried on until closing time, so he was hopeful he'd be able to talk to the right people. They should remember strangers; at this time of year almost all their trade was locals.

At the second hotel he checked, the Commerce, he came across someone who remembered Nicki. It wasn't often an attractive stranger walked in, the young man had said. He also remembered a couple of 'outsiders' coming in, but they seemed like 'regular people', just drinking and having a good time. There were only two staff working and it was a busy time. Colles cornered the other staff member as she returned to the kitchen balancing several plates.

Carol Connell told Colles she remembered an American man coming in. "He was tall and blond, with a beard," she said, "and he was wearing jeans. That's all I can remember."

Colles asked whether the American had met anyone there, but the girl couldn't remember. She did say he hadn't stayed long. Colles gave the girl the same card he'd given the others, with a contact number to call anytime if she remembered anything else. Carol rushed off as someone from the kitchen yelled to her.

As Colles walked back to his car, his mobile phone rang. "Colles."

"Your man owes about eight hundred thousand dollars." *Straight to business.* "Payments are regular, though," the voice said. "All the others look okay." Eight hundred thousand dollars ... That was a lot of debt for someone in the government's employ ... That fact gave him a new prime suspect, at least for the insider.

Colles drove back to the lab; everyone was working at a feverish pace. Nicki told him they still needed to have blood samples from everyone at Macquarie. Was there any way to get them? Colles was trying to work that one out when Conrick called him over.

"Urgent call fer you. Said they've been trying your mobile, but reception out here might be patchy."

Colles took the call.

"Hughes again, sir. We've received another message. Routed from ANARE in Hobart. I'm not sure what to make of this one either, sir." He spoke slowly and clearly. "All I got was 'Melville ... Macquarie ... plane hijacked and must be stopped ... repeat must ... there are ... need equipment ... chance ... please get ...'. That was it, sir. I can't re-establish contact."

"Are you sure about the wording?"

"No, sir. But ANARE said they're pretty sure, sir."

"Keep trying to raise them, and good work, son."

Melville might be still alive! He wrote the message down verbatim.

Then he rang Hughes back. The man answered quickly, and Colles cut him off. "Hughes, you said the message was routed from ANARE in Hobart. So it was definitely from Macquarie Island?" Obviously not from the plane, now likely at the bottom of the ocean. Colles realised he must be getting tired.

"That's right, sir. The island's usual satellite communications, though the signal was unusually poor."

"All right, thank you, Hughes."

"Yes, sir."

So, Melville, and possibly Hennessy, might be alive on the island.

Need equipment ... He would need medical advice on what they might require. Dammit. Conrick was still under investigation, and now more of a suspect, and he wasn't sure yet how he wanted to use that information.

Somewhat reluctantly, Colles handed the note to Nicki. "That message was just received from Macquarie. Their communication equipment is evidently playing up. I can't be sure what it all means, but someone has said they 'need equipment'. What do you make of it?" he asked.

"Could it mean they're still alive?" Nicki had her heart in her mouth.

"It could indicate Melville's still alive. Can't say about any others. Don't get your hopes up, we don't know what's happened, and no one's heard from Hennessy." But she didn't hear him, all she could think about was that Peter might still be alive. She closed her eyes for a moment as her mind, and her heart, raced.

"Doctor, the note," Colles prompted quietly but firmly.

Nicki did not hear him. This news might mean Peter didn't die in the plane crash. He might be on the island. Which would mean he was in the midst of a deadly plague!

Nicki also realised that if the plane from Macquarie Island hadn't crashed, it was very likely the plague would now be in Hobart or

Melbourne, where it would quickly, and unstoppably, spread. Unless they could find a cure for it and somehow distribute it in time. And without the Macquarie blood samples, that now seemed far less likely. Even if Macquarie was kept isolated, there were the migratory birds. They had no blood samples from them, either. It was a dire situation.

"Doctor Palmer, the note. What equipment would you want if you were there?"

"I don't know what Melville would want," she said automatically.

"He's a doctor, too. He'll want to continue the work you're doing here, as much as possible. If you were there, what would *you* want?" Colles pressed.

"Equipment to analyse blood samples down there on the island. That's what I'd want," Nicki said emotionlessly.

"Make me a list," Colles said firmly, picking up his phone again.

31

"Get out!" the man yelled. Hennessy grabbed his jacket and did as he was told. There was no doubt in his mind that these men were desperate enough to kill. Outside, Melville lay on the hard, gravelly landing strip, nursing a bleeding right arm, surrounded by six dishevelled, unshaven and tired-looking men.

The apparent leader, the first man Hennessy had seen, leaned out through the open door of the Hercules. There was wild look in his eyes. "Get in," the man shouted impatiently.

Hennessy knew he wasn't included. He went over to Melville, as the six men climbed aboard, then turned back to the plane. "You can't go back! You'll kill millions of people; you're probably carrying the plague!" Hennessy yelled at the man.

"Shut the fuck up!" The man pointed one of the strange pistols at Hennessy's chest.

"I'm not sick, and I'm not going to die!"

The man was beyond reason, but Hennessy knew he had to try anyway. "You can't risk it! Let the pilot take the samples back and keep us here. He's a doctor." He pointed at Melville, who was still on the ground holding a badly bleeding arm.

"*I said shut the fuck up!*" The man fired the pistol.

Hennessy jumped back and felt the hefty 'thunk' as a flare embedded itself in the ground at his feet. Thick, acrid smoke with a red tinge billowed from it as he stepped away from its heat. Through the smoke he saw the plane's door slam shut, as the engines roared in readiness for take-off.

"We've got to stop them," Melville said quietly.

"How? We're unarmed, you're injured."

They couldn't stop the plane from leaving, but Melville had a different idea. "We'll have to get to the main base and get a message to Colles. That plane's got to be stopped."

Melville had been knifed in the upper arm, through his thick jacket, now wet with blood. Hennessy quickly helped him remove the jacket, and ripped the crimson sleeve from his shirt. He tied a makeshift tourniquet around the bleeding arm. He worked as quickly as he could, while they both watched the plane ascend towards the north. Towards millions of vulnerable people.

Melville seemed to be all right, and he was certainly tough and determined enough, although he had lost some blood.

Peter hoped they would get help at the base, and of course, communications with the mainland. The crate of medical supplies was still on the ground where Melville had dropped it. He started to open it to find a bandage and some antiseptic, but Melville stopped him.

"There's no time for that. We've got to get to the radio now!" he said vehemently.

"This tourniquet is enough for the moment," Melville added, looking at the bloody sleeve tied around his arm. "Flight time to Hobart isn't all that long, so I need to get a message out *fast*."

"Okay, any idea which way?" Hennessy asked.

"North-east. The station should be about twenty minutes that way," he said, pointing down a grassy hill. Another surprise. *Has Melville been here before?*

Hennessy picked up the heavy crate and they set off. He wondered what Colles could do about the plane. *Have it shot down?* He knew Melville was right; that plane could be carrying the plague.

The track was well defined, and on any other day, they might have been walking through a national park, perhaps a wildlife sanctuary. As they left the grass and packed gravel of the landing field, the track took them into some low vegetation. Peter had been to many such places during his childhood, and even in his adult life, sometimes through his work and sometimes just for relaxation.

A long time ago, Peter's father had taken him to South Gippsland, in Victoria, where they had walked through bush tracks near the beach. Of course, it had been warmer there, and there were no snow-covered hills in South Gippsland, but the vegetation was similar, at least according to his memory. There were no trees, just the low scrub and hardy grasses, and very few signs of human life.

"Let me help," Melville said, as Peter stumbled with the weight of the supplies. They swapped sides, and Melville took half the weight with his good arm.

On the way back to the station Peter had a chance to think about their new predicament. They had to warn the mainland, but who knew what they would find at the base. If the men he'd seen get on that plane were any indication, they could be heading into a miniature civil war. At best, there had to be some kind of horror awaiting them. He knew many had already died from the plague. If he and Melville weren't already infected, they were almost certainly about to be.

Peter's mind conjured up an image of medieval Europe in the grip of the fourteenth-century plague. A plague that had wiped out millions and changed life forever. Sick, frightened people wandering around waiting for death. People who had lost their loved ones – in many cases, their entire families. The sick being ostracised, or killed off ... Bodies being burnt. Perhaps oddly, it had also strengthened humanity, in the sense that those who survived had a greater immunity.

"You okay?" Melville asked, as they marched doggedly along the track, both men now slightly out of breath.

"Sure," Peter replied half-heartedly. "I was just wondering what to expect at the station."

A little further along, Hennessy spotted a deserted-looking shack a few hundred metres from the track. The sun reflected off the small window, looking for a second like something moving inside. He was about to run to it, hoping they could make contact with the mainland without actually having to get to the base, but Melville stopped him.

"We need the main base. That's just an old hut, there's no communications equipment there." Melville explained it was the birdwatcher's hut. "He was the first victim. The plane wreck that probably started all of this is somewhere near here."

Peter shivered at the thought, or perhaps just at the cold, mustering his strength as best he could. There were millions of lives at stake, and there was clearly no alternative.

Ten minutes later, they strode down the gravel track into the main Macquarie Island base, shouting to anyone who'd listen. They passed a makeshift sign some comedian had erected. *Scientific Reserve – Please Do Not Feed The Scientists.*

Hennessy looked around at the base, seeing the burnt-out remains of two buildings. The rest of the place appeared to be more or less intact. He roughly counted about fifteen buildings of different sizes. Most of them looked like sheds of some sort. He was surprised to see two small four-wheel drive vehicles and a motorbike parked nearby.

Melville took a closer look at them as they passed. There was no one around, the whole place looked deserted, like a partially bombed-out village from a war somewhere. Hennessy smelt something strangely unpleasant in the air, and looked at Melville. He'd noticed it, too, and the look in his eyes hardened.

"I've smelt it before, a few years ago, in the Gulf. It's the smell of death," Melville reflected. "Come on."

He led Peter to a larger building with a communications mast attached to one side, extending towards the deceptively blue sky. As they walked, Melville quietly said that he thought the vehicles and bike had been disabled. "Stay alert, this looks like a war zone," he whispered as they entered.

They saw eight bodies lying on mattresses on the floor. Hennessy felt sick. *These poor bastards,* he thought. He put the crate down.

Then one of the poor bastards moved. "Get away," came the croaky, laboured voice. "Get away from here while you can."

"We can't. We're probably already infected," Melville said, as if he was saying 'well we're here now, might as well stay for tea'.

"Who are you?" Melville asked.

"Nick Anakos." The man could hardly speak, although he was able to half sit up.

"The radio?" Melville asked.

"Satellite phone's dead," Anakos told him. "Some of the sick tried to contact the mainland. They were going to say people were recovering. Thought they'd get help that way. I couldn't let them."

Melville nodded.

"Well, it looks like eight of them are heading back to Australia now in our plane, and we can't warn anyone," Melville said, without censure.

By now another three people were moving, and they all looked like they'd been to hell and back.

Peter opened the medical supplies. "Is there anything we can give these people?" he asked Melville, who had checked all of them and was pulling four of the blankets up to cover their heads. He administered large doses of penicillin to the four who were still alive, not really knowing what else might help. One of them had bad burns to his hands, and Melville gave him a shot of morphine as well. The poor man was in a bad way, clearly in pain and unable to move. Peter didn't think he would survive much longer.

"Is there communications equipment anywhere else?" Melville asked.

"Spare parts in a storage shed, but I don't know whether they're any good. Since we've had the satellite phone, we haven't used radio gear. There also a VHF set in Jimmy's hut, but that won't get you far. Only good for a few hundred kilometres." Anakos was sweating.

Melville ran into the comms room, and a few seconds later came back out. "You did a pretty good job on the equipment," he told Anakos. "But maybe I can fix it. Where's that shed?"

While Melville looked for tools and spare parts, Peter brought some water to the sick, and asked if they wanted food as well. All shook their heads. He helped them take a drink and started asking questions about the plague, while Melville went off to find the spare communications equipment. Peter had momentarily forgotten his fear of infection and instinctively started to help.

"I'll see if I can find anyone else," Peter said. *Anyone else alive*, he thought.

He walked outside and went into the nearest building. A sign over the door read 'Macquarie Hilton'. It was a dormitory with three separate rooms. The first room he entered had only various personal effects in it; no people. He saw photographs pinned to the walls. Happy, smiling faces of children and other loved ones looked back at him. One of the shelves above the beds had a collection of books, mostly poetry. He recognised an old volume of W B Yeats's works that he had a copy of at home. There was also a Robert Burns, and a book of famous quotations.

Another shelf revealed a pile of handwritten letters to 'My Micky', from someone named Cathy. He didn't read them, but he saw that they were all signed with lots of kisses and hugs. There was a picture of a young man with his arm around a dark-haired, bright-eyed young girl of about twenty, and a big ugly bull mastiff sitting next to her.

As he looked around, he felt almost suffocated. He could imagine the lives of these people, the little bits of home and mementos they'd brought with them. Families and loved ones who probably didn't even know yet that they would never see their partners, sons, daughters or parents again. The room was the saddest place he thought he'd ever seen.

He went into the next room and saw three occupied single beds. The first had a man and a woman lying close together holding each other's hands, reddened eyes open but not seeing. Their faces looked terrible. Unearthly pale skin, bluish-grey cracked lips and dark, dried blood on their skin and clothing. Each of the other beds had a man on it, both with the same pained faces. All were dead. They had died painful, lonely deaths, with no one around to help them. The room seemed to have a presence of its own. Almost as if their souls were still waiting there, waiting to understand why. Why had this happened to them? What had they done to deserve it?

With the phone out of action, they hadn't even been able to tell their families they loved them, or say goodbye. Or find out whether the mainland had been hit by the plague. They must have just lain down and waited to die, wondering what the hell was happening. Peter revised his assessment of the first room. There was a gut-wrenching, overwhelming pall of anguish pervading this space.

The next one also had two bodies in it. He went back outside with his stomach turning somersaults, steeled himself and checked the four remaining dormitories that hadn't been burnt out. They had names like 'South Pacific Sheraton', or 'Club Med Macquarie'. And they all had bodies in them, but in the last he discovered a man still alive, although unconscious. He counted fourteen dead bodies and one survivor.

He spotted Melville breaking into a locked shed near the main building. He asked him to help carry the unconscious man back to the other four survivors.

"There are supposed to be thirty-seven people here. How many did you find?" Melville asked.

"Fifteen. Fourteen dead. Plus the eight on the plane and eight here," Hennessy said. "That makes thirty-one. Six unaccounted for."

"Gary disappeared two days ago. Don't know about the others," Anakos said, sounding a little better. Or perhaps that was just Peter's hopeful imagination. "Sorry about the phone. Do you think they'll get back to the mainland?"

"Not if I can help it." Melville was now feverishly working on the transmitter. He had to know that Colles had received his message. That plane must be stopped.

"Peter Hennessy," Hennessy said to the two men. "David Melville," he added, nodding in Melville's direction.

The man next to Anakos spoke in a gravelly voice. "Mick Wilson. No offence, but …" Mick paused as he coughed painfully, "… what the fuck are you two doing here?"

Hennessy thought he recognised the man from one of the photographs he'd seen, but he wasn't sure.

"Micky got sick the night before last, then I got it yesterday morning. Those two …" Anakos pointed to the other two who seemed to be sleeping, "… about two days ago."

Hennessy didn't know what to say. They all knew they were probably going to die. He and Melville likely only had days to live themselves.

32

"But it's the best chance we've got!" Nicki argued.

"No! We need you here," Colles countered. "Melville is quite capable." Colles was unaccustomed to defending his position, just as he was unaccustomed to listening to the arguments of others. But he felt the woman deserved some respect.

"No, you don't need me here, you need me on the island," Nicki implored him. "Look, we're getting nowhere here. Not even a glimmer of success. You know the bacteria is out there somewhere, and for all you know, it might already have been released."

"You could be risking your life for nothing. I can't see how that can help," Colles said, now beginning to get annoyed with her persistence. "Melville can handle it."

"My life is at risk *here*. And so are millions of others. It's only a matter of time before birds or *something* bring the bacteria to a populated area." Nicki paused briefly to let that point sink in. "Dr Melville doesn't have the equipment he needs, and he's not a microbiologist or pathologist!" That had been a guess, but Nicki could tell by Colles's face that she was right. "And he might not be familiar with the equipment. Look, if we don't discover a cure ..." Her words trailed off, as she could see Colles was starting to see her point of view.

"You really believe there's a better chance of success on the island?"

"Absolutely," she said without hesitation. "Provided there are survivors," she added slowly, hoping her face did not betray her confident veneer.

"Why can't you do it here?"

"No, it can't be done here," she insisted. "Someone has to go there to collect the samples anyway, risking infection. And it's *more* dangerous to bring the samples back to the mainland. Any delay now may have disastrous consequences. I think we have to go there. Now."

"What are the chances of finding a cure within a few days?" he asked.

"Moderate," she said, with more hope than conviction. But it was their best shot, she told herself. Even if the extortionists didn't release the bacteria, she knew in her heart that a global pandemic would still be almost inevitable.

"All right, Dr Palmer." Colles held her with a steely gaze. "But you understand that if there's no cure, you will not be leaving the island." He watched her face closely as he said those words.

"I know."

Colles admired her resolve. She had convinced him she was right, and she was about to risk her life, for what Colles saw as a slim chance of success. But if courage and determination were the only prerequisites, then she'd succeed for sure.

By late that afternoon, Colles had amassed all the equipment Nicki had listed – most of it already at the lab facility. All he'd had to do was get a more-portable gas chromatograph and centrifuge. Melville would have to help carry the equipment to the station. Colles had arranged for a flight, and this time there would be no communication with the island, so nobody could know it was coming. The pilot was military and understood his orders. He would not leave the plane, his job was to simply deliver Nicki and the equipment then get out as fast as possible. He was also armed.

The equipment was ready, along with some basic supplies that Colles knew may or may not be needed, depending upon the number of people still breathing. The NSO security people, led by the burly Taylor, were loading the equipment into an SUV just outside the main lab. The flight would leave at three o'clock the next morning so that it would arrive at dawn on Macquarie Island.

Colles could only hope he was doing the right thing, allowing Dr Palmer to go. He did not relish the thought of another death on his hands.

In spite of her earlier resolve, Nicki was now beginning to wonder whether she was doing the right thing. She had mentally debated the whole thing back and forth in her head many times over. On the one hand, there was no better place to investigate than 'ground zero', where it all seemed to start, and which had had very little scientific analysis so far. But on the other hand, she was still marvelling at the unexpected intensity of her reaction to the news about Peter's plane crash. Had that played a part in her decision?

There was no guarantee she could do any better on Macquarie Island than anyone at the lab had already done. There might be no survivors, except for the deadly bacteria, of course, maybe now spreading via the large bird population. A number of cases of birds spreading human diseases, particularly flu-like diseases, were well documented.

She was about to leave for the motel to pack and get some rest, or at least try to rest, when her mobile rang. She picked it up absently. "Hello."

"Hello, Nicole, It's John Morton here. I have some interesting news about that stone. When can I meet with you and Peter?"

Nicki didn't know what to say. She tried to explain about the plane crash, but the words wouldn't come out. "He's not ..."

"Are you all right?" Morton asked.

"The plane crashed." She held back the tears. "They don't know if he's alive or not."

"Oh my God!" Morton was stunned, lost for words.

After a few seconds of silence, Nicki spoke quietly. "Someone sent a message back from the island, and there's a chance ... a chance that Peter's there. I'm flying down there tomorrow morning. I hope ... I hope that ..."

"I hope he's all right too, my dear," he said gently. "But you're flying down to *Antarctica?*"

"No, Macquarie Island. That's where the message ... oh, it's a long story ..." She faltered a little, then the words started to flow. She felt she needed someone to talk to. "We've known each other for years."

"I know," Morton said. So Peter must have told him about her.

"I hadn't seen him in three years, and last night ... two nights ago, well, it was like we'd always been ... I've just got to find out if he's okay. *I have to know*," she cried.

"Nicole, you know Peter, he's a pretty tough sort of fellow. If there was any chance, you know he'll be okay." Morton could hear her softly sobbing, and he wanted to give her any little comfort he could. "Last year, when I stayed at Peter's, we talked for a while one night over a bottle of port. He told me about an intelligent, strong-willed young woman that he had known some time before. He thought about you more than you might know." John hoped he wasn't betraying a confidence. "Peter said that if ever there was someone who could change the world by sheer strength of will, it was she. Don't let your faith dissolve now."

Morton felt his words sounded contrived, but Nicki seemed to take some comfort from them. "Thanks. I guess I'm feeling the stress of it all."

"No doubt." Morton hoped he'd said the right things, but he felt he wasn't very good at this.

Nicki wanted to tell him about the plague. In fact, she just wanted someone to talk to about *everything* she was feeling, but she knew she couldn't.

"Tell me about that stone, so I can tell Peter tomorrow," she said as optimistically as she could manage.

"Well, my friends think it's probably hollow, possibly a vessel of some kind. They worked that out from its volume-to-weight ratio. And it emits some kind of low-intensity ultrasonic radiation." Silence. "We don't know what it means yet, but we've at least proven it's not just an ordinary stone."

"Yes, we'd assumed that, too, so it's good to have at least a little bit of proof."

"And they've carefully measured it. It is *precisely* symmetrical. A perfect ellipse. They don't think it could possibly have been naturally formed."

There was silence on the line as Nicki thought about that. "I *knew* it was special. I wonder what its purpose is."

"Hmm. That's the big question," Morton replied.

Nicki thanked him, and they said their goodbyes, he wishing her safe travels and both of them the very best of luck.

Nicki went back to her motel and packed a carry bag with her warmest clothing and some other things Colles might have considered a waste of time ... Colles had said he would arrange for wet-weather gear to be packed for her and would give her some specific instructions before the flight. She put the bag near the door. Still hours to go before the flight, and she felt she needed some company.

Nicki decided to call her mother. She just needed to talk, even if not face to face.

She dialled the number and her mother answered on the second ring, as if she'd been waiting for Nicki to phone. "Hi, Mum."

"Nicki! Lovely to hear from you. Where are you?"

"Actually, I'm in Melbourne, working on a special project."

"Oh, lovely. You'll have to come for dinner."

They chatted about this and that for a few minutes, but her mother could hear the worry in Nicki's voice. "There's something the matter, isn't there."

Mothers always know, Nicki thought. *Where to begin?*

"Do you remember me talking about Peter? Peter Hennessy, when I was working at Melbourne University?"

"Yes, dear, of course."

Nicki went on to explain how Peter had come back into her life unexpectedly. She struggled to find the right words, but her mother, as ever, had intuitively helped her out.

"You haven't seen him for three years, but it sounds to me as though, in your heart, Peter never left," her mother said, knowingly. "You wouldn't admit it three years ago," she added gently.

"It was complicated ..." Nicki said weakly.

"It always is."

Nicki was holding back her emotions, and her mother could hear it.

"What's wrong, dear?"

"Oh, I'm just feeling ... lonely." *No, that would not do.* "I'm not supposed to tell you this, but Peter had to fly back from, well, it doesn't matter where from, and I'm not allowed to say ..." She knew she had to keep Macquarie Island and the bacteria out of it. "... and the plane has disappeared."

Her mother gasped. "Oh, dear, I'm so sorry."

Soon they were both in tears.

Her mother asked if Nicki could come to stay with her. Nicki tried to explain that it was a very important project and she couldn't get away, but all she succeeded in doing was to give the impression that she worked for a cruel, heartless boss. Of course she'd had to leave out her own impending flight into danger, but she told her mother as much as she could.

Nicki promised she would let her know as soon as there was news about Peter, and that she would come and stay as soon as it was possible. She finished the call and lay on her lonely motel bed letting the tears flow down her cheeks. She was sure she was doing the right thing, even though the chances of finding a cure in time were probably slim. That could take weeks, months, or even years.

If there were no survivors from the Macquarie base, the chances grew even smaller. But she knew that if they failed, it was very possible that her mother, her friends and everyone else could be dead within days. She thought of Peter, maybe stuck on the island, infected. She was trying not to get her hopes up for him, and even if he was alive, the odds were certainly stacked against him. She'd argued with Colles rationally, and she knew he believed she was right or he'd never have given in and risked another flight. But she also knew that her emotions were so tangled up that maybe she wasn't thinking completely clearly.

She lay down on the bed and tried to sleep, without success.

33

Colles had driven back into Melbourne in the evening gloom. He'd arranged an eight o'clock meeting with the minister, and his director at NSO. He hadn't prepared any notes for the meeting, knowing that no one present would want the subject recorded on paper. It was going to be difficult, and he went over his report in his mind. Since the last one, he had a lot to advise, and a lot to consider. The minister would want him to tell her how he would solve the problem, and the director would want to know about leads and suspects. Colles didn't have answers for either of them.

He had no idea where the bacteria *was*, or in whose hands it was, and he had only vague suspicions about who might be involved. Hell, he couldn't even prove there was *inside* involvement. It was just *very* likely. And he would have to advise that they were no closer to a cure, although he could at least outline some positive action in that area, even if results weren't by any means certain.

The minister would be concerned that he had already risked the life of one civilian, and was about to risk another's. More likely, he thought uncharitably, she would be concerned that the media might find out about it – how things *look* always being more important than how they

217

are. Colles didn't have much time for most politicians, and even less patience.

He got back to Treasury Place at ten minutes after eight and reached the minister's luxury office by eight-twenty. The minister and the director were both waiting for him, sharing an expensive bottle of brandy. *Taxpayers' brandy*, Colles thought.

"I'm sorry I'm late," he said without meaning it.

"Any further demands?" the director asked coldly.

"No."

"Leads?"

"No. All staff have checked out clean so far."

"Suspicions then?" the director pushed.

"Just a hunch, and we're checking it out thoroughly now." Colles did not want to elaborate.

"And the cure?" The minister spoke for the first time, and Colles was relieved not to be questioned further about his hunch.

"Nothing yet. All tests have proved negative." He elucidated briefly, explaining that over three hundred tests had so far been done, including many involving laboratory rats. "We're also conducting some tests at Macquarie Island," he finished, wondering which one of them would pick this point up.

"Who exactly is running tests on the island?" the director asked, quickly zeroing in.

"Dr Melville. One of mine." At least he hoped Melville was still alive and running tests. "And one of the research team is flying down there tomorrow morning." Colles knew he had to tell them.

"Who? Another of *your* people?" the minister asked pointedly.

"Dr Palmer. On loan from New Zealand's health people." *Dammit.*

"A *civilian*? From *New Zealand*?" The health minister was agitated.

"Yes, a civilian. Australian citizen. Checked and cleared. She volunteered for the job without even being asked. I see no choice. She's our best chance." Colles rattled off some of the points Nicki had made earlier. "The other staff, government and civilians, heard her volunteer, and heard me warn her of the risks." Colles almost gritted his teeth as he spoke; he hadn't cared who had heard, as long as Dr Palmer was aware of the risks herself, but he knew the minister would have headlines churning over in her mind. 'Brave doctor risks life to save others', or 'Government and medicos work together to save world'. As long as it wasn't 'Government sends young doctor to her death'.

The minister considered his words for a few moments then spoke slowly. "I am advised that there is little chance of finding a cure for this plague quickly enough, but I agree it's an acceptable risk. One life for many." The director nodded solemnly as the minister said it. "I understand Dr Palmer has made her decision fully aware of the risks."

"Yes, she's a brave young woman," Colles said sincerely.

Both the NSO director and the minister wanted Colles's view on what would happen if the bacteria were released in Melbourne.

Colles pulled no punches. "It divides and spreads very quickly. Best case is hundreds of casualties within three to five days; potentially hundreds of thousands infected within one to two weeks. Without information from Macquarie Island we can only surmise over the mortality rate. At this stage, the assessment is close to one hundred per cent." Colles paused to let those words sink in.

"If we can develop a cure, it might take weeks, or even months, to mass-produce and distribute, by which time Australia's population would likely be decimated. The worst case is more than a million people dead within one to two weeks. The plague will spread to all other cities, and will spread to other nations. If there's no cure to be found, if no one's immune – and it looks that way so far – then the human race may have just met its destiny." It was theatrical, Colles knew, but it had its effect on the minister, if not the director.

"Then we do not evacuate the city," the director said.

"No," the minister agreed. Both knew there was no possible way of getting more than four million people out of the city in time, and the ensuing panic could kill thousands anyway.

"Well then, we'll maintain the media blackout, and leave it to you,

Colles. Find the missing culture, and find a cure," the minister stated. "Is there anything else you need from me?"

"No." Colles could not tell whether she was genuine, or whether she was seeking to absolve herself of further responsibility.

"And track down your man before that money is handed over," the director added, making Colles wonder whether it was the millions of lives, or the millions of dollars that were most important to the man.

He went back down to his office, took off his jacket and lay down on the leather settee.

Track down *your* man, the director had said. He had a none-too-subtle way of letting Colles know that this problem was *his, personally.*

Colles went back to the small sleeping quarters in his office and set an alarm for one o'clock the next morning. That would give him four hours' sleep, making a total of eight in the past forty-eight hours.

*   *   *

JULY 30, YEA, AUSTRALIA

Carol Connell's Friday shift was more or less the same as usual. It was always the busiest day of the week. Earlier in the day there had been a bit of drama with Frog, one of the local lads. He'd been drinking heavily again and got into a fight with a tourist. Apparently, the tourist had started talking to a local girl whom Frog had taken a fancy to. Carol had to call the police when he threatened the tourist with a broken glass. *Poor Frog,* she thought, *he'll be locked up again.* He was so easily aggravated. And a bit sensitive sometimes for the tough image he liked to portray.

Of course, the poor bugger didn't get his name from being the most handsome man in town, Carol thought. His large beer gut didn't help, either. It was something Carol saw a lot of since she starting working in country pubs. Fortunately, the other guy could look after himself, and Frog *was* drunk.

Now, as she finished cleaning up, she remembered the man who called in looking for information. It was surprising that he was the second person who'd expressed interest in the American guy, and she was fairly sure that in the rush she hadn't mentioned the detective to the second man. *Surely they knew each other, both asking about the same guy?* But perhaps not.

The second man was much nicer than the detective she'd phoned, and now that she had more time to think, she reflected that the second man seemed to have no idea of the television news story. He'd said to call him anytime if she remembered anything, no matter how small or trivial. Perhaps she should, just in case.

Carol retrieved the number from her handbag and dialled. It rang six or seven times, and she almost gave up when it finally answered.

"Colles."

"Um, this is Carol Connell from the Commerce Hotel, Mr Colles. We spoke today."

"Yes, I remember."

"Did that detective call you?"

"What detective?" he asked.

Carol went on to explain everything, even down to phoning Barker. He was annoyed that she hadn't called him earlier, but he held back. He knew a lot of people wouldn't have bothered at all.

It was nearly ten-thirty, and it looked to Colles like he would get no more sleep tonight. But he now had a connection to a related crime. A new lead that he *really* needed. A simple connection made by a worker in a country pub, not by his own people, or the police. That fact aggravated him, but he decided to leave it until tomorrow.

He tried to get hold of Barker and was told the man was 'out of the office but expected back very soon', and 'No, Barker had this case to himself'. Colles left a number and made it clear that he wanted to be called *immediately* when Barker returned, no matter what time it was.

Jackson wrote a note for Barker, thinking that if it had been another cop, he would have explained that Barker had just gone out for a cup of coffee and a smoke.

He left the note on top of a pile of others, marking it 'urgent' and went home to his wife and four-month-old daughter.

34

Peter Hennessy and David Melville had settled into a busy routine on the island, and that kept Hennessy's mind off their plight. They had made the sick people as comfortable as possible, and Peter had searched all the remaining buildings. He'd found no more people, dead or alive. He had fixed a meal for everyone who could eat – simple tinned meat, biscuits and the last of their fruit supply. Anakos and Micky had eaten a little, but he could see it was difficult for them both. The other two weren't able to eat anything, so Peter had just made sure they had enough water.

Melville was working in the comms room again, without success. He'd done the best he could and had sufficiently repaired the equipment that he hoped he'd got a message out. Unfortunately, he had no way of knowing, because he still couldn't receive.

For the rest of the afternoon, Melville had been analysing blood samples, although that was hardly the right term; with only a microscope, all he could do was watch the bacteria multiply and flourish in every sample, a little faster in some than others. He had taken Peter up to some of the bird rookeries, and after much careful coaxing, followed by some rather unpleasant force, had taken blood samples from five birds of different species.

It was a long walk and the weather had turned. It was now wet and gloomy outside. With the light rain, visibility had also reduced. When they had returned to the main building, they were both soaking wet and cold.

"Do you want to see if you can lay your hands on some dry clothing?" Melville asked Peter, as he set to work on the samples.

Peter was not comfortable with taking clothing belonging to dead men, even if it was clean, fresh from the cupboards in the dormitories. But he did it anyway, knowing they had to stay warm and keep themselves healthy as long as possible.

The analysis of these samples took longer, but it showed the birds were immune, or at least it proved bacteria had not yet attacked them. Given that Jimmy was the first victim and had been in close contact with the bird colonies, they took that as a positive sign.

"I hope we haven't just infected the birds ourselves," Melville said to Hennessy.

Peter was Melville's lab assistant for the afternoon and had helped him document all the results, albeit in a somewhat rudimentary manner.

Later, they had visited nearby seal colonies, where they collected more samples. That was an undertaking that proved difficult and dangerous. The seals were not afraid of humans, but they were not pleased when Melville jabbed them with a needle. Both men had avoided being bitten, more by luck than skill.

As they returned to the station, the weather worsened again. Large, heavy drops of rain were now giving way to hail and sleet as the wind started to scream. Peter had to go out in it again to get the generator restarted when it cut out, but at least he was dressed properly this time. He was glad he had borrowed the extra clothing. The generator was necessary for Melville to finish the blood tests.

The lighting was poor, but at least they were warm, Peter thought. It must have been absolute hell for the men who'd hijacked the plane. If Anakos was right, they'd been out in that weather for two days. It amazed Peter just how quickly it turned today. Even more remarkable than Melbourne's 'four seasons in one day'.

Melville's examination of the seals' blood showed they had not been infected by the plague, either – or, as with the birds, all they could deduce was that the ones he tested had not been infected, *yet*. They were getting nowhere, and it was hard not to begin to feel depressed.

On the positive side, Anakos didn't seem to be any worse, and both David and Peter felt fine, but Micky was asleep. They could hear his laboured breathing as well as the other two who had been more or less comatose for several hours.

By eleven o'clock, both Peter and David were totally exhausted and decided they'd better get some rest. They went out in the rain to fetch some more bedding, finding some clean blankets in one of the dormitories. They made sure the sick were as comfortable as possible and lay down on the floor close to the gas heater.

It was then that the reality of their predicament hit home. They were stuck on a quarantined island, in the middle of the Southern Ocean, surrounded by dead bodies and lethal bacteria. There work so far had been essentially futile, other than confirming that the local wildlife appeared not to be carrying the disease. They had no way of knowing whether the plague had been spread to Australia, or New Zealand, or wherever those desperate men had taken the plane.

"God help the rest of the world if that plane got back," Peter said quietly to Melville.

Both men gained a lot of respect for each other that day. Both had accepted the situation as being unchangeable and got on with the job at hand. It was only now they really had time to reflect.

"Where do you think this bug came from?" Melville asked, almost conversationally.

"The crashed plane from Ross base, most likely." Peter was thinking of the stones again.

They went over the possibilities again, getting no further. Melville wasn't the sort of man, Peter thought, who would be interested in wild speculation about strange old maps or stones with mysterious powers.

"You're a pretty tough sort of bastard, Hennessy," said Melville, using the word 'bastard' as a term of endearment, as many Australians did.

Peter didn't feel very tough at the moment, though. "I'm a fatalist. We're here. Moping about it won't help. Besides, I haven't given up on a cure yet," Peter said, but Melville saw his weak smile and knew that Hennessy, like himself, realised it was almost hopeless.

"I'm glad we didn't bring any of the Ross crew back with us," Peter went on, "or ..."

"You married?" Melville asked, after a long silence.

"Was once. It didn't work out."

"Kids?"

"No," Peter answered. "You?"

"No. Never met the right woman."

Peter thought about Nicki, and they sat there for a few moments in silence.

"Well, let's not give up hope. They *could* find the cure back at Yea and arrive tomorrow morning, for all we know," Melville said.

"Yeah, you're right," Peter replied, giving Melville a half-hearted smile, half snapping out of his reverie.

He felt utterly drained. He laid his head on his jacket and thought about Nicki again. In his heart, he hadn't yet given up hope of a cure. Their situation didn't look too good, but it wasn't totally hopeless.

A few hours later, Hennessy awoke feeling cold. The heater had stopped working, and his blanket had ended up to one side. Outside, he heard the wind shrieking and the rain beating hard on the metal roof. He roused himself, got up, found the torch and, with a little effort, changed the gas bottle and restarted the heater. All the others seemed to be asleep. He then went back to his makeshift bed and rolled himself up in the blanket. But he couldn't get back to sleep. His mind was too busy.

He thought about Nicki's vision, the things she described after holding that stone. She'd felt powerless, and breathing was difficult. That could be the plague. And 'a sense of doom'. Well, it wasn't hard to relate that to the plague and what he'd seen here. But *the darkness*? Admittedly, he didn't know whether that was really part of the picture, whether she'd really 'seen' it, or not.

There were also a number of other unresolved problems with their emerging theory, such as the 'snap-freezing' of the Antarctic, or at least Ross Island. *What the hell happened to the civilisation there?* Could a civilisation *really* have even existed? Could there be any other logical explanation for the stones and the plant specimen? Or had he and Nicki added two and two to get five?

Peter had been disappointed to read in his atlas that Australia and the Antarctic were drifting apart at the breakneck speed of just under three centimetres per year. So, in eight thousand years, that would be two hundred and forty metres. Hardly enough to account for climate change.

But what if something had helped things along? Some sort of mega-disaster, like whatever destroyed the fabled Atlantis? He'd heard a lot of speculation about Atlantis. Wild and unsubstantiated theories. He'd seen a lot of these fringe theories pop up in his Internet searches over the past few days. But even the believers couldn't agree on how such a civilisation could have disappeared without a trace.

One theory that kept recurring in the searches and the literature he read was the speculation that Atlantis may have been destroyed when Santorini erupted violently, around three and a half thousand years ago. That would have caused unimaginable tsunamis and quakes all around the Mediterranean Sea.

But what could have caused a cataclysm like this on Antarctica? And how could it have been significant enough to turn a liveable climate into a frozen wasteland? A sudden shifting of the poles? He'd read that the North Pole had moved before, but how? And what effect would that have on Antarctica, if any? What about the kind of event that wiped out the dinosaurs? As he lay there, a wild thought slowly came into focus.

The prevailing theory about the dinosaurs' extinction was that an asteroid had struck the Yucatan Peninsula in Mexico. The asteroid was only about nine kilometres wide, but it struck with such unbelievable force that the crater was an incredible one hundred and eighty kilometres in diameter. Its outline is clearly visible from space. Scientists speculated that the impact would have thrown enough debris into the atmosphere to block out light to the whole planet for decades. Enough destructive power to obliterate Hiroshima many millions of times. Palaeontologists had generally agreed that this event could have wiped out the dinosaurs sixty-five million years ago.

The Shoemaker–Levy comet was another example. It crashed spectacularly into Jupiter in the nineties – fragments of less than a thousand metres in diameter had generated an unimaginable amount of energy when they struck the planet. More than a million megatons. He had seen some evidence of this phenomena himself, at the Wolfe Creek Crater in Western Australia. Could this type of catastrophic event have occurred somewhere in Antarctica? If an asteroid one-tenth the size of Yucatan had hit Antarctica, it would have created a vast fireball and shock wave.

Peter's knowledge of astrophysics wasn't particularly strong, but he had read a lot of material on this type of phenomena since visiting Wolfe Creek. Chemistry also taught him that if a large object burned through the atmosphere, heat would combine oxygen and nitrogen to form nitric acid. This would turn into acid rain, killing off crops in the vicinity. The force of the impact, like a massive volcanic explosion, would throw a huge amount of earth into the atmosphere. The dust and debris would shroud much of the planet for some time, effectively blocking out all light. Could that explain the darkness and death Nicki saw?

Peter's mind was racing now. He'd seen recent research proving that ancient oak trees preserved in peat bogs in Ireland had no growth rings for two or three years after the Santorini eruption. Solid evidence of a lack of sunlight, and probably very severe frosts throughout the summer. In an already-cooling Antarctica, it might have been only one or two winters before the whole place started to freeze and all crops and animals perished. Anyone wanting evidence of how cosmic collisions cause catastrophic damage merely needed to look at the moon. Even through a cheap telescope, a vast number of craters are clearly visible.

Hennessy didn't know whether such a force could cause sudden movement of tectonic plates, but he guessed it probably could. He reckoned that, at the very least, the ice shelves would rapidly grow in the cold darkness, and as they grew, they would cool the air even more. With each feeding the other, by the time the sun eventually returned, the ice would reflect most of the solar radiation. The cooler winds would then aid freezing, and the whole process would sustain and perpetuate itself.

The temperature only had to drop by a couple of degrees on average. Ross Island was, after all, just a few degrees colder than northern parts of Scandinavia, which were inhabited. Hell, the Vikings settled on Greenland centuries ago, and it consists largely of glaciers and ice shelves. A comet or an asteroid. It seemed plausible.

There was also another reason why a cosmic impact could make sense. When Halley's Comet passed in 1986, a space probe analysed its composition and found that its nucleus was an icy body covered in a cocktail of *organic* chemicals.

It was widely believed that, over many millennia, comets played an important part in the evolution of life on earth. Maybe that was where the bacteria had come from, or maybe it was the catalyst that started the whole chain of events. Some sort of radiation could have affected common bacteria which mutated into this plague. It all seemed as though it could fit together.

As these disjointed thoughts swirled around in Peter's mind, he was starting to doze again when he thought he could see something. He opened his eyes wide and pushed himself up on one elbow to look out the window. "What the ...?"

He could see a faint red glow through the rain, subtly lighting up the dark night sky.

There was someone else alive on the island with them.

35

Nicki dozed for perhaps a few minutes during the hours she lay on her lonely motel bed. She went over and over her motives for doing this. She couldn't see a better chance of finding a cure for the plague, but at the same time she knew it could cost her her life. *But someone has to do it,* she rationalised, and she was certainly well-equipped for the job. Colles and the others had seen her logic. She told herself that if she didn't do it, there was a reasonably strong chance the plague would spread. *Quickly.* It just *had* to be done.

And she thought of Peter. He might be on the island, injured or sick, or he might have died in the plane crash. She knew he was quite capable of looking after himself, but she wanted to be with him anyway. Were these thoughts rational after seeing him only yesterday for the first time in three years? Maybe tiredness and her emotional state had taken control, but she thought she saw things with a remarkable clarity.

Three years ago, she had followed her head. She had chosen a new chapter for her life, turning her back on the old. Tony had fitted in very neatly. At heart, he was a good man. He had made her laugh, and he made her feel *comfortable.* They had such busy lives, it never occurred to her to wonder whether she *really* loved him. Had she stopped to take a breath, she might have found the air to be stale a little sooner.

She knew now that she should have followed her heart. Instead, she had run away, maybe because Peter was still trying to sort his own life out, and she hadn't known where that would leave her.

Yesterday, for the first time in her life, she'd been able to look forward into the future and see something that made her feel somehow unchained. Anything seemed possible. In the past, she had always focused on where she was heading, and even with Tony, she pictured him as having a kind of separate existence from her. She was only on the fringe of his world, and he on the fringe of hers. But whatever she saw ahead now, she could see Peter there with her. She *hoped* he could be there with her.

*   *   *

July 31, Melbourne, Australia

Colles had finally got hold of Barker, after calling again twice. Barker had grudgingly explained all about Kevacic, his car, the air ticket and the money. Colles sprinted around to police headquarters to read Barker's notes and see the files. Barker hadn't been all that helpful at first, but Colles soon got the help he needed – he simply suggested that he might have the NSO director contact Barker's chief and demand immediate and full co-operation.

Also, it had taken Barker a full day to find out that the body carrying Lin Fan Cheng's identification really *was* Lin Fan Cheng, a mid-level official from the Chinese Cultural Centre. The man simply hadn't checked the name properly, and Colles had berated him for it. Didn't the fool know the Chinese put the surname first?

To Colles's knowledge, the Chinese Cultural Centre people were not known to be involved in any covert activities, and certainly not with drugs. In fact, he thought they were generally good people with a genuine interest in their community. The NSO gave Colles a list of all officials and staff at the CCC and confirmed that all appeared to be clean. They were currently checking whether any of the Chinese had just arrived in the country or had just left in the last twenty-four hours. He also had them checking the list of names with the airlines for any bookings.

He instructed Barker to keep the new developments completely to himself, but that it was still to be considered a routine drug-related case, as far as the media were concerned. Colles had left Barker in no doubt as to what he would *personally* do to him if he failed to follow his instructions. Barker sullenly promised to contact Colles with any developments, no matter how small they seemed.

Colles was now quite sure that Kevacic had collected the bacteria from his inside man in Yea and had then returned to deliver it to Lin Fan Cheng. The way he figured it, either Kevacic had an accomplice who was smarter than he was, or the Chinese had a partner who wanted both men silenced. He favoured the latter, but either way, he didn't like what he had. It wasn't enough. He didn't know for sure who had sold the bacteria and, most importantly, he didn't know where it was now. Maybe they'd get lucky again, and Barker's *brilliant* investigative ploy of asking the *entire* city, via the media, might pay off further. Colles thought they'd been lucky the first time.

He carefully went over all the information in his head, knowing that he was tired and might have missed something. But nothing else came to mind. At least he now knew his instincts about Dr Palmer must have been right. The entry in the lab's log for 10.25 pm *had* to be a fake. Firstly, the exchange must have been made about four hours *before* the log entry, and secondly, he was sure Palmer was either with Hennessy, or on her way to his house about a hundred and thirty kilometres away when the culture was stolen.

It was now almost two in the morning, and he had arranged to meet Dr Palmer before her flight, to personally ensure all arrangements had been made properly. Ordinarily, after the latest developments, he would have had someone else do it, but he had really started to respect her. He'd never had time in his life for a family, but if he had, he'd have been very proud to have a daughter like Nicole Palmer. She was about to risk her life on a chance that she might be able to save thousands of others. Colles couldn't think of many other civilians he knew who would do that.

He sped out to Yea, pleased that there was almost no traffic at this time of night. On the way, he called Nicki to say he would pick her up from the motel himself. He had made sure everything she had asked for – and a few things she hadn't – were packed on the plane and could be readily unloaded. He had spoken to the pilot and instructed him to try to make regular contact with the Macquarie base on the way there and to circle the base a few times until someone came out. If there was no sign of life, he was not to land under any circumstances. Dr Palmer was to be brought back, regardless of any protests, restrained if necessary. He would not let her risk her life for nothing.

He had made sure the plane was equipped with the same 'insurance' device as Melville's and, as with the last flight, the pilot would be given coded messages to send if there was any risk of contamination. Colles would give the pilot these instructions in person. He would not tell the man what could happen if he sent the coded message. He couldn't take that risk. He would also give the pilot strict instructions to assist Dr Palmer unload the equipment then leave her at the landing strip immediately. He hoped he wasn't sending two more people to their deaths.

Colles arrived at the Riverside Motel at three o'clock, to find Nicki ready to go. She looked like she needed sleep, and she looked nervous. The cold was starting to seep through his clothing as he stood outside the motel room door. At least it wasn't raining, he thought.

"Ready as I'll ever be," she said with a weak grin.

Colles smiled back and said nothing. He just picked up her bag and carried it out to his car.

They sat in silence almost all the way to the airfield, some fifteen minutes away. For her sake, he hoped Hennessy hadn't been on that last plane.

Nicki didn't have any doubts that she was doing the right thing, but she was now feeling very nervous about it. There was a knot in the pit of her stomach, and she steeled herself as best she could. But ... "What if there are no survivors on the island?" she asked Colles, and the thought of Peter's probable death struck her again.

"Don't worry. The pilot will only land if there are people there." But how will he know? she wondered.

They drove into the poorly lit airfield, and Nicki saw an old, tired-looking plane waiting for them. They loaded her bag on board, and she half expected Colles to say 'last chance to change your mind'. But he didn't. He had accepted that she was right, and as far as he was concerned, the decision was made. Colles escorted her onto the plane, pointing out the equipment she had requested, and explained that the pilot would help her unload it but was not permitted to leave the landing strip.

Nicki would be on her own. He gave her a map of the island, a photocopied A4 page, sealed in a plastic sleeve and carefully folded in half. A track was marked in bright yellow to show her where she'd have to go. The pilot would circle the base until someone signalled back, if he hadn't already successfully made radio contact during the flight. The pilot had also been told to ensure that there was at least one able-bodied person on the island to assist with the equipment.

"Good luck, doctor," he said. "I'm glad you're part of my team." It was almost a display of emotion, and it touched Nicki.

"Thanks," she said. "I'll see you in a few days."

"I hope you do."

"Oh, how will I get a message to you?" she asked.

"Don't worry, there's portable transmission equipment in one of the boxes, and Melville knows how to use it. If he's ... ah ... not around, it's set so we can contact you. All you have to do is switch it on."

She watched in silence as Colles got off the plane and slammed the hatch behind him. The pilot checked the hatch and secured it, and within a few minutes the plane was in the air. There was no turning back now. Nicki was not religious at all, but she prayed to anyone who was listening that she was doing the right thing.

Watching the plane disappear into the cold night sky, Colles reflected again that Dr Palmer was a brave young woman. In the past few days, she had been working closely with bacteria that could kill her if she made a mistake, she had probably lost the man she loved and she was about to risk her own life to save others. He admired her courage.

* * *

"Yes."

"I have some information."

"Go on," Xeng snapped.

"Colles has made a connection between the lab and…" the man referred to a crumpled scrap of paper in his hand "… your man, Lin something. Apparently he was carrying identification when he died." The soft-voiced man heard the other curse in a guttural, explosive tongue that he didn't understand.

"Also, he knows someone at the lab is, er, involved," the soft voice added.

"And the plague? There is no cure yet?" Xeng spat the words out.

"No cure."

"You have no more information?"

"No."

Xeng was furious. If Po was in his office, Xeng would have crushed his throat with his bare hands. *The fool! Leaving behind some identification!* Xeng didn't care if Lin was identified later, but he didn't want it to happen so *soon*. Po had always been very efficient, and totally ruthless, but a psychopath who enjoyed his work was not a man to be relied on too heavily. It was now only a matter of time before Colles found the connection to the bacteria's source, and there was no way to know whether Kevacic had said too much. Xeng couldn't even be sure of what Lin may have told Kevacic. *Curse the fool Po.*

There was really only one safe course of action. The source had to be silenced. This was an unfortunate development but, Xeng reflected, it was not a disaster. It merely added a degree of difficulty that would make his victory even sweeter. He went through the next steps in his mind meticulously, allowing for every nuance he could imagine, and when he'd decided what he must do, he started to relax slowly. Yin and yang; it was the way of the world, and he was still very much in control.

He picked up the phone and demanded a glass of milk to take with his ulcer medication and reminded himself again of the successes so far. As he waited, he also reflected on how helpful it was that mobile phone use had become so ubiquitous. Nearly everyone now used mobile phones indiscriminately. So much easier to listen in undetected.

Anyway, this new problem did not matter much. Today was *The Day*. This day would appear in the history books of the future. Some would say he was taking a major gamble, but it was a small price to pay, and it was the only way to *win*. Xeng did not care if a few million Australians died before a cure was found. But he had no doubt in his mind that a cure *would* be found. After all, it could only be some new strain of the influenza virus. What else could it possibly be?

Just a few more pieces to be put in place, and within hours Xeng would be on his way, far from this contemptible and stupid country. Far from these bigoted, good-for-nothing slobs who thought they were better than everybody else. Far from the pathetic and lazy, whom he'd had to endure for years, while his own weak government had allowed them to defile and slander his great country. And far from the plague he was about to unleash.

Power was surely the greatest sensation any man could feel, he thought. And right now, Xeng thought he had more power than any man in the world. Still, he had to tie up all the loose ends. He telephoned Po and cursed him for leaving Lin's wallet. Po made no apology. The arrogant dog. He obviously knew Xeng still needed him.

"You have compromised the contact in Yea," Xeng said bluntly. "Take care of it. *Now*." The sky was just beginning to show the first glimmer of the new day.

36

Nicki sat in the worn seat of the noisy old plane, looking out into the darkness occasionally, feeling lonelier than she had ever felt before. More than once, tears formed in her eyes, but she steeled herself each time with the knowledge that this simply *had* to be done. *Someone* had to do it, and she was best placed for the job.

She was nervous but determined not to let it show. She had to be strong, she had to think clearly and quickly. She had to be the cool professional her colleagues had often said she was.

She knew she had the necessary equipment and believed Colles would provide all the support he could, but there were still so many unanswered questions. What if they found no sign of life on the island? The pilot would just fly her straight back, and she would have lost another day. What if there were survivors, but Peter *wasn't* one of them? What if there was no cure to be found? What if ...? What if ...?

Her mind was spinning like one of those amusement park rides. But this one had become detached from its moorings and was whirling out of control. She *had* to somehow make herself relax. Maybe she should have brought a book. Any distraction would do. Then she remembered the notes she had for Peter. Morton's notes. Perhaps that would be enough to stop the morose, morbid thoughts that were circling in her head like vultures.

She retrieved the papers from her bag and started to thumb through them. She had to use the light from her mobile phone, the cabin lighting was just too dim. The high-resolution printout of one of the maps stood out. The Oronteus Finaeus map. She stared at it for a few minutes as she became used to the strange way it was marked and captioned. It was certainly an odd-looking and captivating piece of work.

Holding the light a little closer, she could see there was something about its markings that didn't quite make sense. She grappled with it for a minute or two but found she just couldn't concentrate. She put the chart down and closed her eyes.

Maybe John Morton would be able to explain what she thought she was seeing. Or maybe, when this was all over, they would find out there was no big mystery about these maps at all. Perhaps they were simply the product of poorly skilled or overly imaginative, medieval map-makers, just like the sceptics said.

Perhaps she was simply too tired to think properly, though sleep was impossible. She still had vague pictures in her mind of a vast city, a mysterious place filled with bizarre buildings, and golden temples and statues. Her mind must be filling in the blanks from stories she'd heard as a child about lost Mayan, Incan or Aztec cities of gold.

But it fitted the nightmare she had a few nights ago. She could picture the city, although it had been shrouded in darkness. And there was the man carrying something to her, something awful. She wished she knew what it all meant. What was it that was so *wrong* with the place?

Out of the small window she saw the faint beginnings of the dawn's eerie pale light, the coming of a new day. A day that would change her life forever, one way or another. Her stomach was tied up in knots.

"Hi. Can I pour you a coffee?" She almost jumped out of her seat. "Sorry. Didn't mean to startle you," the pilot said, proffering a thermos and a plastic cup, and smiling at her.

"Thank you," she said. "I guess I'm a little jumpy. And I'm not used to this," she said, looking around at their spartan surroundings, then back at the man.

"This is new to me, too. We don't often get attractive young passengers on these flights. Most are crusty old scientific types," he said, still smiling. "My lucky day."

Great, she thought, *people are dying and my life's falling apart, and this guy's going to ask for my phone number ...*

"We'll be landing soon, provided there's someone there to welcome us."

Sobering words.

"Do you know someone on the island?" he asked.

"Yes ... er ... I hope so," she replied slowly.

"Well, we'll know soon." He put his hand on her shoulder and gently squeezed. "I hope everything's all right." He left his hand on her shoulder a little too long. "If you need anything ..." His words trailed away.

"It's okay," she told him, as he poured her a cup of milky coffee.

He turned and headed back to the cockpit.

"Thanks for the coffee," Nicki called after him. Whatever his motives were, she appreciated the coffee and the brief conversation. As she drank, she stared out the window and thought of what she had just left behind. Her mother, her friends. She thought about what she might find on the island. But mostly she thought about Peter.

Peter. She'd never met anyone else like him. *Oh, here I go again,* she thought. *I'm overthinking this ...* But she couldn't shake the thoughts. Peter seemed to understand her at a deeper level. At school, she'd always known she was a little different to the other girls. She had an almost insatiable curiosity that drove her, even today. And Peter was the same.

It had taken her months to let her feelings go after she left Melbourne. She had wanted to call him, to see how he was, to hear his voice, but she hadn't. Then Tony filled that void in her life. Or at least he had filled some part of it. She remembered a friend telling her, 'You never really just get over it, time just slowly erodes it away. You just have to get on with your life, even when – no, *especially* when – it doesn't go the way you planned.'

In the distance, she saw land. Small, grey-green and partly obscured by mist or fog, and it put her heart in her mouth.

Another plane. The big man looked up angrily at the pale dawn sky. He'd been alone, isolated, for two days now, without food. He was tired and weakened by hunger and the cold that had seeped into his bones, but in his mind his situation had become clear. His base was lost, his people were probably already dead, and he was no doubt dying too. "I'm not afraid!" he yelled to the plane.

Gary Masters had not felt like this since he was fifteen. Everything he had achieved, every success, every obstacle overcome, it was now all gone. Meaningless. It had all unravelled. *He* had unravelled. He was a lost teenage orphan all over again.

I know they're laughing at me, he thought. *They know how badly I've failed.*

Masters could feel inexorable forces closing in around him. Strength, courage, defiance were no longer enough. He remembered exactly how he felt when they'd come to put him into a foster-care home. He fought, but he lost.

"Now they're coming to get me again," he muttered to himself disconsolately. "Well they won't be able to say I'm a coward."

He knew what he had to do.

"You're not taking me off my island. I'll die here with my people," he wailed at the droning engines.

Standing on the cold, hard landing strip, Nicki watched the plane take off in the dawn light. The pilot said he'd spotted two people at the station as he'd flown by, one of whom had waved at the plane. *Good enough*, he'd said.

Nicki had asked, but he hadn't been able to describe them. They were too far away. She could only hope ... Having overflown the base and given its occupants an additional five minutes' warning of their arrival, the pilot told Nicki it would be a very quick stop. He had his pistol holstered as he helped her unload. But no one had come.

On the airstrip next to her were her bag and the small crates of equipment. Still not a soul in sight, and it was freezing cold, the traces of mist in the air chilling her face. She drew the cold air into her lungs. *Bracing, to say the least*, she thought. The lush hills around her glistened with the night's rain. She had put on the thick green jacket and gloves Colles had found for her, and she had her map in hand.

The track led off into a hazy, weak, cold sun struggling to rise above the hills. It felt like an omen of some kind. This sun was not the one she was used to; it looked almost the same, but it wasn't as bright and there was no warmth in it. *This place doesn't quite seem real*, she thought. Was this *The Land That Time Forgot*? Maybe a dinosaur would raise its scaly head above the mist.

Her map indicated that the station was about a half-hour's walk to the north-east. She slung her bag onto her shoulders, her arms looped through its grips, picked up the small gas chromatograph and set off down the lonely track. The box was heavier than it looked. The rest of the equipment would have to wait. She hoped the men the pilot had seen would meet her on the way, to help carry it. And she hoped that one of those men had dark hair that ought to be cut, and deep green eyes ...

Peter woke up just after dawn. The weather had almost completely cleared. Anakos and the others were still asleep. Or so he hoped. Peter checked them more closely and could hear laboured breathing. A small mercy. Melville was already awake. Last night, when they'd seen the flare, Melville had leapt up and looked out the window, but it was too late and he hadn't been able to make out which direction the light had come from. He and Peter had watched for another half hour, but there was nothing more. Eventually they'd drifted back to sleep.

Peter put on his jacket and went to make breakfast for everyone. As he walked outside, he thought he caught the sound of aircraft engines in the distance and wondered whether he was hearing things. By the time he started to make some porridge, the plane's sound was so close he went outside for another look. He saw it turning almost above the station, and waved madly at it, yelling at them not to land.

Melville followed him outside. "You know they can't hear you."

"I know. But ..." Peter's voice trailed away. But *what*?

"I'll get up to the airstrip and tell them to go back." Peter knew what Melville was thinking, but neither would say it. *Unless they're here because they've found a cure.*

"No, I'll go. You keep going with breakfast; we've got to keep our strength up," Melville said, and started on his way.

Peter went back inside and finished making the simple breakfast, carrying the large pot back to the main building. Anakos and Micky were awake but didn't look too good. He set the pot down and went back to get some bowls and a tin of powdered milk, calling to Anakos as he walked out. "Nick, see if you can wake up the other two. They've got to have some water at least."

"They're dead," Anakos said matter-of-factly.

Peter looked back at Anakos without speaking, then turned and left. There was nothing to be said.

Anakos heard him coughing outside.

37

Nicki's feet were now freezing, the mud and the grass of the track ensuring she was soaked to her knees. A small hut sat just off the track, but it didn't look like the settlement on the map. Surely it must be part of the station? Maybe her map was wrong, or maybe she'd gone in the wrong direction. She took out the map again, and she was pretty sure she had to keep following the track.

She put the box down and stretched her arms, wringing her hands as she did. They were starting to ache from gripping the box. Her feet were aching, too, from the penetrating cold. *Okay, time to press on.* Then she heard it. The unmistakable sound of a glass smashing, and it sounded like it came from that hut.

"Don't come any closer!" a man yelled.

Nicki whirled away from the hut and saw a man standing further down the track. He must have come from the station. "We're quarantined!" he shouted at her.

"I know," she called back. "That's why I'm here. Colles sent me," she added.

The man looked surprised.

"I'm a doctor," she called. Melville walked up the track to her.

"Actually, I'm a microbiologist." She extended her hand. "Nicki Palmer."

"David Melville," he answered, as he recoiled and took a few steps back. "I'm almost certainly infected," he said. "Why no suit, no protection? Are you *crazy?*"

"I need to work with your equipment, your people. It's not possible any other way. And from what I understand, not everyone suffers the same effects. Maybe ..."

"Yes, but eventually they all ..."

They heard a crashing sound coming from the hut.

"Stay here," Melville said firmly. He ran up to the hut, and a big bear of a man emerged through the door, holding a large-barrelled flare pistol.

"Who the fuck are you?" the big man bellowed. He had blood streaming from jagged cuts on both wrists.

"I'm a doctor. We're both doctors," he said, looking back at Nicki. "We're here to help."

The big man looked at him strangely, a wild look in his eyes. "You can't help. My station, my people, all dead. Can't help. Don't want your help." Waving the pistol menacingly, he looked at Melville. "Just fuck off!" He turned and went back inside the hut, slamming the door in Melville's face. "Get away from here. Let me die in peace."

Nicki looked at Melville, a question on her face.

"Gary Masters, station leader, I think," Melville said quietly, retracing his steps back towards Nicki. "We'd better get him down to the station."

"Any idea how?" Nicki asked, walking up to the hut.

"Gary?" she called.

"*Fuck off!*" came back through the door.

Melville had come up behind her.

Nicki called through the door. "Gary! We're not going to leave you here to die. There are people down there who need our help. Dr Melville's help, my help, and your help."

"Just leave me alone! I can't help anyone."

"No!" Nicki said defiantly. "I don't give up so easily."

Silence.

Nicki waited, while Melville was staring at her, admiring her forthright approach.

"There's nothing you can do except watch people die. It's all gone to hell. We're *in* hell!" Masters added vehemently. "Why can't you just fuck off." His voice started to shake. "... spent my whole life ... now ... time to pay ..." He was muttering almost to himself.

"That's bullshit!" Nicki shouted through the door. "Stop feeling sorry for yourself! People here need you! We need you!" She wasn't thinking about her words, they just flowed out.

"I can't help anyone!"

Nicki decided to change tack. "If you believe in hell, then you must believe in God." Was he a religious man? "Maybe God kept you alive to help the others," she cried, her anger and frustration showing in her voice. She hoped he wasn't some kind of religious zealot; this was totally unfamiliar territory for her. Her words were met with a stony silence from the hut.

"Gary! You're their leader, and they need you more than ever now," she said firmly. Melville let her keep going. She was obviously a quick thinker, too.

"Who needs me? My people are already dead. I've watched them die. I let my people die already," Masters said, a little less aggressively.

"Gary, some of your people are still alive. And we're still alive," Melville said firmly.

"Who are you?" Masters asked again, the taut edge beginning to leave his voice.

"A doctor. We're both doctors," Melville replied through the door, mentally preparing himself to kick the door open and drag the big man out.

Then they heard shuffling feet and Masters opened the door. He looked awful and his eyes were swollen and red, but he had no other signs of the plague. He had evidently put the flare gun down inside.

Nicki's heart went out to him; he had the look of a lost little boy. A little boy who had had to watch his friends, *his people*, suffer and slowly die. He didn't say anything. Nicki looked at the bleeding wounds on his arms and ran past him into the hut. She pulled the sheet off the bed, tore strips from it, and quickly went back outside to Masters, not without noticing the bloodstained broken glass on the floor. Masters was just standing there in silence, watching her. He had done a reasonably good job on his arms, slashing diagonally across the inside of his wrists.

Despite the mess, he hadn't lost too much blood yet; there simply hadn't been enough time. Nicki took a roll of surgical tape from her bag and taped the wounds tightly. They were ragged but fortunately not too deep. Luckily he hadn't had a good knife or scalpel handy. She then firmly bandaged his arms with strips from the sheet. Masters didn't speak. He stood silently and let her do her work.

Melville spoke to him quietly. "I've seen some of what happened down at the station. It must have been sheer bloody hell. I'm sorry we didn't get here sooner. But people are still alive and they need our help."

Masters looked at Nicki, almost like a sick child looks at his mother. Nicki thought he was starting to come back to reality. Maybe it was simply knowing that not everyone was dead, and just having human contact again.

Nicki touched Melville's arm. "There are still two heavy boxes at the airstrip. We'll need them at the station as soon as possible." She wanted to get her work started.

Masters had remained calm while Nicki treated him. He looked as though his irrational state of mind was passing. It had only been fifteen minutes or so, but Nicki was optimistic.

"Gary can take me to the station, while you get the boxes," she said to Melville, looking Masters in the eye. She wanted to stitch his wounds properly before they opened again, although she wasn't sure whether going off alone with this man was her best idea this week. She decided to trust her instincts. And today *was* a day for risk-taking.

"I'll help," Masters said quietly.

"You can't carry anything until we treat those wrists properly," Nicki said sternly, and Masters retreated into the hut. She wondered whether she should have been more gentle with him. He was probably still close to the edge. Masters returned directly with a large backpack and started walking silently to the airstrip.

Melville winked at Nicki and told her to follow the main track down to the station. He jogged away to catch up with Masters. They could certainly use the big man's help, Nicki thought.

She picked up the bag and case, thinking how unreal the whole encounter had been. What kind of hell must it have been for the people stuck here? she wondered. They'd have to tend Masters' wounds as soon as he got down to the station. It was damned lucky they found him when they did, and not a few hours later.

She hadn't had a chance to ask about Peter yet, everything had happened so fast. She turned and called out. "Hey!" but they had already disappeared over the hill. Melville had said, '*We've* been looking after a couple of sick people.' Who else could he have been talking about?

38

Somewhere in the distance there was a loud, explosive banging sound. In his mind, he was a soldier once again. In the action. The explosions kept coming. He knew he had to open his eyes, he had to react to it, but he couldn't. Not explosions, just very loud banging. Must be getting old. Too old for *this* anyway, he thought, as he shrugged off the brief sleep. Colles had been sleeping on a sofa in the small side lab, trying to get a few more hours before the busy day ahead. Knocking. Then someone burst into the room.

"Sir!" Taylor, breathing hard.

"Sir, Conrick's dead. We got the guy who did it."

Colles leapt up, still in yesterday's clothes, and wearily slipped his shoes on. "Where is he?" he demanded, shaking off his fatigue.

"He's dead. I'm sorry." Taylor was well aware that Colles would have wanted the man alive. "He stabbed one of my men and went for me with his knife. I tried to stop him with a shot to the shoulder, but he moved so fast. Bullet pierced the carotid artery."

Colles knew Taylor was a capable man. A good shot, and he'd never seen him panic. He was sure it wasn't his fault.

"Sorry, sir," Taylor added again.

"What happened?"

"Looks like the man broke through security somehow – we're on that right now. Got to Conrick's quarters and slit his throat while he slept."

Taylor quickly explained how his man had found the killer as he tried to make his escape, drawn his gun a little too slowly and taken a knife in the gut for his trouble. If it hadn't been for Taylor walking down the corridor at the right time, the man would have been dead, and the killer would probably have got away clean.

In Conrick's quarters, Colles saw his body lying on the bed, right hand on his slashed throat, and a look of shock and horror on his face, captured forever in his bulging eyes.

The other man was out in the corridor, around near the lab, sprawled out in the middle of the floor. There was a river of blood seeping towards one wall.

"Find out who he is!" Colles barked at Taylor. As he walked away, Colles overheard one of Taylor's men telling him the man had no ID. On his way out, he saw Hart, one of the extra lab people. The obese man looked up at him rather nervously.

"What happened?" Hart wheezed.

"Your work just got more important," Colles barked, and told him that the man who had just killed Conrick had been shot.

He remembered the stunned look on Hart's face as he walked out into the freezing morning air.

A light rain had started to fall.

* * *

"You can tell him," said the young police officer to his partner.

He had just read about the Moonflower Restaurant in yesterday's paper, and they knew Barker had to be told about the young Chinese man they had stopped on the road. Barker would be really pissed off; it had happened on their previous shift, the night before last. They had just returned to the station after an uneventful night, and it was only by chance that Smith had picked up the paper.

"All right, all right, I'll go tell him now," Constable Smith said.

Barker was at his desk, scowling at a large pile of paper in front of him. "Excuse me, sir."

"What?"

"Er, yesterday morning, just before five o'clock, my partner and I pulled a van over for speeding, out near Rowville." Smith was nervous; he could see Barker was impatient and in a worse mood than usual.

"Get to the point!" he snapped.

"Sir, he was a young Chinese driving a Moonflower Restaurant van. We read in the paper ..."

"*Fuck!* That was two nights ago! Where the hell have you been?" Barker's face turned red. "Get me a copy of the ticket and get back in here!"

"Sir ..." Smith's voice faltered slightly, "... I didn't book him, I just warned him."

Barker looked like he was about to explode.

"*Sit!*" he roared, pointing at the chair. He rummaged through the papers in front of him and found a phone number, dialled and waited until Colles's gruff voice answered. "Barker. Might have something you want in the Chinese killing." He put the call on speaker. "Repeat what you just told me, constable," he barked at the hapless Smith.

"Ah, well sir ..." Constable Smith told his story to Colles as concisely as he could.

"What was his explanation for being out there?" Colles asked.

"Said he was catching yabbies, sir. He had some fishing gear in the back of the van. Out in the reservoir, I assume, sir."

"His name?" Colles asked.

"I'm sorry, sir ..." Smith started when Barker interrupted.

"They decided to let the guy go!" he said scornfully.

"Go to the restaurant. Find me the van, and find me the driver!" Colles voice cut through the air, as did the loud click when he slammed the phone down.

"You heard the arsehole, get your partner and we're going down there. You better hope there's someone there this early."

Smith was about to say they were off duty, but he thought better of it.

* * *

The young officers were not really to blame, Colles knew, they were just doing their job. But he was still furious. More than a day had been lost. He didn't think they had a hope of tracking down the van's driver, and it was probably too late now to match tyre imprints, and find out exactly where the van had been. However, it wasn't all bad news. Given that the van was spotted in the outer eastern suburbs, and assuming that this van is involved, they could narrow down the target location to just one likely choice – Cardinia Reservoir – part of Melbourne's water supply.

Colles wondered who it was he was up against. He still didn't have a clear idea whether they were facing extortion or terrorism, or just some well-organised lunatic with a grudge. He took the list of Chinese Cultural Centre staff names from his satchel – it was the only list he had. On a hunch, he called the NSO and asked them to check how current that list was and, to his dismay, discovered it was almost a year old. He told the woman on the phone to have a current list to his office within the hour.

It might not be important, but he had so little to go on, he wanted everything checked and rechecked. He now felt sure there was a Chinese connection somewhere. The van driver, the dead Chinese diplomat and the American 'enforcer'; all now seemed to be connected to a restaurant in Chinatown. And now they had a dead Chinese assassin in Yea.

His mobile interrupted his thoughts. "Colles."

"Do you have the money, my friend?" a cultured English accent asked.

"Who is this?" Colles snapped.

"That does not matter. I will collect my money and my plane at midday today. If you fail, you will kill millions of people."

"I need more time," Colles said quickly. "The banks are closed today." Would the man buy that? he wondered. It *was* Saturday, after all.

"The banks will open for you, my friend," the calmly controlled voice said.

"I have to open a lot of banks to get what you want. You'll get your money, but I need until tonight."

The voice at the other end laughed, an ugly, guttural laugh. "You are most predictable, Colles. My money will already be on its way from the United States of America. We both know that no bank here carries that much in United States currency. But I'm a reasonable man, I have planned for this. You have until four o'clock. You may need it." Xeng coolly and quickly gave Colles a short list of additional requirements for the plane and ended the call.

Colles retrieved the recording of the conversation and played it over. He decided that the man spoke very carefully, and very properly. 'United States of America', he had said. It was almost as if the man was showing off his perfect mastery of the English language. He also obviously enjoyed having power and wielding it. He certainly *could* be a foreign diplomat.

Colles made another call, ensuring all inward calls to his line were being traced. Unsurprisingly, the caller had not been on the line for long enough. He also thought it likely he would have taken precautions in any case, but they had to try everything. A new list of names had arrived in his inbox on the phone, thankfully with a brief note that listed the three differences from the old list. He immediately recognised one of the names.

Xeng Pang had been a senior figure at the Chinese Embassy in Canberra until a few years ago. He was a well-educated, charming sociopath, known to Colles, although they had never spoken. Xeng had first come to Colles's attention for being a major suspect in a diplomatic murder investigation several years ago.

Colles recalled that Xeng's superior had apparently issued an order to kill a courier – a man suspected of working for the Australian Government – and then, after the fact, when some of the ugly details had surfaced, the man had berated Xeng and publicly humiliated him, demoting him at the embassy. A clear signal to the Australians as to where blame lay. Two days later, the senior man was discovered in his bed, with his head almost cut off, three gaping slashes exposing jagged pink flesh.

The forensic report said the knife, a small instrument with a curved blade, had not been very sharp, and great strength would have been required to tear the man's neck open. Xeng was the most logical suspect, but there was no proof, and the Chinese officials would not assist. Colles also remembered that Xeng Pang had been educated at Cambridge.

Barker, along with Detective Constables Smith and Dawes, found the Moonflower Restaurant deserted. In the gloomy, wet alley, a few metres from where they'd found the two bodies, they came across the van. Smith confirmed it was the same vehicle, spotting the fishing gear and the same yellow bucket in the back.

Barker rapped loudly on the Moonflower's back door, until he heard someone muttering curses on the other side.

"What you want?" a small Chinese man asked.

"It's illegal to live here, old man," Barker snapped. "Do you want me to get the health department?"

The old man now looked frightened. "I help you. What you want?" the old man repeated, much more obediently.

That's better, Barker thought.

"Two nights ago, someone was out catching yabbies in that van. Who?"

"No. No. No one fishing. Van here all night."

Smith watched as Barker's expression changed to something malevolent, and the old Chinese shrank away. "Listen, you piece of slant-eyed shit, that van was out. Who took it?" Barker screamed.

"Nobody bring yabbie to restaurant. Nobody use van since Wenzay. I get keys."

The old man was extremely nervous and wasn't going to volunteer anything he didn't need to, Smith thought.

Barker really could be a prick when he wanted something, but Smith wasn't going to tell him.

"Smith! Did your man have any yabbies?"

"Er ... I don't know, sir, we didn't check."

"You didn't check! Excellent police work, Smith," Barker sneered.

The old man returned with the keys, and Smith was glad of the interruption.

"Open it," Barker growled.

The stench in the van almost made them sick. They found a dozen dead yabbies in the bucket.

"Someone went yabbying, old man," Barker snapped.

"Sir," Dawes said, "that's only about fifteen minutes' work. In a couple of hours you could catch about a hundred of these things." Barker looked at Dawes but said nothing. "Could be just a cover, sir," Dawes added superfluously, and Barker glared at him.

"Can I ask some questions, sir?" Dawes asked, and Barker grunted his assent.

Dawes decided he would play the good cop, to Barker's bad cop; it always worked on TV. He carefully described the man he had seen, and the old man said he didn't know anyone like that, but Dawes saw the fear in the old man's eyes. Barker went into the restaurant, saying 'no one touches the van', leading the old man inside roughly.

"Where do you keep the keys?" The old man showed him a hook near the kitchen door, about two metres from the alley door. "It's unlocked at night, isn't it?"

"We go in and out. We get delivvy ..." the old man had trouble with the last word.

"What?" Barker snapped.

"Delivvy. People bring thing. We take trash out. It stay open."

Barker gave the old man a look of contempt as he cursed under his breath. He called Colles, who told him not to touch anything in the van, that he would get his own forensic people out there.

"And tell the old man not to go anywhere," Colles added.

"This is my murder investigation, Colles." Barker was annoyed. He was being used like one of Colles's junior staff, and he didn't like it.

"I know what this is, Barker," Colles interjected coldly, "and you'll do as you're fucking told. Get all the employees' names, and get them down to the restaurant!" The phone went dead.

"Fuck you!" Barker shoved the phone back into his pocket.

39

"Hello!" A woman's voice called. Peter thought he must have imagined it. He had given Anakos some food, but the man couldn't swallow much. Micky could only take a small drink of water. He was waiting for Melville to get back to help move the two bodies to another building. Maybe the horror of their situation was making him hallucinate.

"Hello?"

There it was again, this time a little louder. It sounded like ... "Hello!" He ran outside to see a figure in a thick green jacket, laden with a bag and case, almost stumbling towards the main building. The figure saw him and stopped.

"Peter!" she called, quickly putting down the case and running to him. He could see her eyes glistening as he backed away.

"*What are you doing here?*" He was surprised by the intensity of his own voice.

Nicki stopped in her tracks.

"How could they send you here?" It wasn't a question. She was barely two metres away. Still safe, if she went back to her plane and ... But the plane was already gone, he'd heard it leave. He didn't know what to do.

256

Then Nicki practically threw herself at him. Before he could stop her, she had her arms around his neck. "I thought you were ... Oh, thank God you're all right."

But Peter pushed her away. "Why?" he implored.

"I had to. I have to find a cure for this plague before it spreads to the mainland somewhere."

Peter just stared at her.

"Melville's message," she continued, "he needed supplies, we thought there must be some survivors here."

Peter just stood there, trying hard not to think of her dying slowly like those people inside. He saw a determined look forming on her face.

"I came here to find a cure. I didn't come here to die."

"Nicki, I ..." He couldn't find the right words. All he could think of was that she was now infected with the disease.

She walked back determinedly to pick up the crate. Peter ran after her.

"I'm sorry. Let me carry it," he said. She put it down again and started walking.

"I've watched people die here," he said as he followed her. "All I could think of when I saw you was you getting sick."

Nicki turned to face him, and her expression softened a little as she saw his eyes.

"Sorry. I was just shocked," Peter said. "I'm sure it was a very difficult decision to come down here, and it's probably the most courageous thing I've seen." His eyes moistened. Before she had a chance to reply, they heard approaching footsteps, and Peter looked up to see Melville and a man he hadn't seen before coming towards them.

* * *

July 31 – Ross Island, Antarctica

"Better go get Ned," Bob Jacks said. They had just retrieved the drill head from the ice, a painstaking piece of work that had taken several hours. There was something wedged in it. Bob started to dismantle the head, chipping away the ice, as the other man headed back through the darkness to the main building. It was early morning, the young man's watch said, but they were just about to finish a shift, and that always made it seem like night.

The young mechanic located Ned chatting to Marty Brinksma in the mess. "Bob's found something. The drill brought something up."

"I told you there was to be no more drilling!" Kelly said angrily.

"We were just retrieving the head," the man answered defensively.

Kelly followed him out, grabbing a thick coat on the way. He wondered what kind of trouble he was about to find.

In the drill hut, Jacks was prizing a piece of rock out of the drill head.

"Don't touch it!" Kelly said loudly, startling Jacks, who spun around, dropping the head on the rock-hard ice. Kelly watched horrified as the whole thing hit the floor, exposing another symmetrical shiny black stone. Bob instinctively bent down to pick the mess up.

"Don't touch! Kelly roared, and he reeled back.

The three of them peered down at the stone.

"Look at that there," Bob said, pointing just to the left of the stone's centre, and they saw a perfectly straight hairline crack, right through the stone.

"Everybody out," he said firmly. He ushered the other two men through the door, picked up his torch, killed the generator and stepped outside.

"No one goes into this hut, no matter what!" Kelly said firmly, locking up. Bob walked up to the door.

"I'll just get me stuff, Ned, okay?"

"No, not okay. What've you left?"

"Jus' me smokes, an' me magazine."

"Well, you'll have to do without them. You got more smokes?"

"Yeah, but I was readin' about the Royals. Now I'm not gunna know 'ow it turns out!"

"Sorry, Bob. No one goes back in."

"S'only a stone," Bob said, a little defiantly. He liked his gossip.

"Bob, look me in the eye and tell me you won't go in there," Kelly said.

"Okay, I won't, I promise," Bob said. The younger man noticed that Bob had crossed his fingers behind his back when he made the promise, just like a child, but he didn't say anything. Bob was his friend, and his boss, and it *was* only a stone.

Kelly phoned Marc Richardson and told him about the latest find. Richardson didn't seem to think it was at all important but said he would advise 'the right people'.

"Does that include Peter Hennessy?" Kelly asked.

"Ah ... John, I'm sorry to have to tell you that Hennessy's plane crashed. He's dead," Richardson said.

"Oh God." Kelly paused for a moment. "How?"

"We don't know. The plane stopped at Macquarie on the way back, and I don't know what happened after that. The security people have got it all locked up tight. They won't tell me anything."

Kelly suddenly felt very much alone, stuck in a quarantine base thousands of kilometres from civilisation. He liked Hennessy, and he thought that if anyone could work out what was going on, on both Ross and Macquarie, it would have be Hennessy.

Bob Jacks lay down on his bed and lit up a smoke. It was one of the few places he was allowed to smoke, and even there it was strongly discouraged. He felt tired but he couldn't sleep. He picked up an old magazine from beside the bed and thumbed his way through. It was no good, he'd already read it a few times. Surely he could just get his bag from the drill hut? He stubbed out his cigarette, got up and wandered down to the mess, passing no one on the way. He thought Ned was being far too cautious, not letting anyone back into the drilling hut; *what harm could it do?* All they'd done was pull up another stone, just like the first two. And they were all frozen solid.

He passed the drying area and the outside doors. "It won't matter," he said to himself. "I'll just duck in, grab me mag and duck out." Looking around and seeing no one else, he quietly opened the door and went out.

The drilling hut now had a padlock on it. Bob smiled, knowing no lock was going to beat him. Twenty years working in tough surroundings had taught him a thing or two, and he took his keys out of his pocket. On the keyring he had a small jeweller's tool that often came in handy. Even with his hands shivering, he had the lock open in less than a minute.

"Who's there?" he whispered cautiously. As soon as he'd shut the door behind him, he had a feeling he was not alone. No answer. He flicked his cigarette lighter and looked around. No one, but the hairs on the back of his neck were still standing up. His eyes fixed on the stone.

"Jesus, what the ..." He could swear he saw something dripping from the crack in it. Something thick and dark, like blood. He went for a closer look, but there was nothing. Up close it looked the same as it had before, and it looked dry. Just to prove a point, more to himself than Kelly or anyone else, he reached out and touched the surface of the stone.

There! Not so scary, was it! He stood up and almost fell back down again, suddenly light-headed. *Must've stood up too quick*, he thought, as his head cleared. He grabbed his magazine, quickly left and clicked the padlock back into place. And he was glad to get the hell out of there. He stuffed the magazine inside his shirt and hurried back through the ice to the main building.

40

After seeing Dr Nicole Palmer off to Macquarie Island, Colles had had one of his men drive him back into Melbourne. That gave him the luxury of an hour's sleep on the way. There were still many leads and loose ends, but when he arrived back, he decided he could switch his phone to silent and take another two hours' sleep before the critical day ahead. It was a trade-off, like everything in this job, he reflected, but excessively fatigued officers made fatal mistakes. Fleetingly, he wondered when he would next sleep at home.

After a brief but sound nap, his alarm woke him at six-thirty. He switched his phone back on to see a missed call from Marc Richardson. He grimaced and decided to get coffee before calling the man back.

"Hello, Richardson here."

"Colles."

"Ah, good. I was just calling to ... ah, *check in.* The situation is fine down at Ross. I spoke to Kelly this morning. Everyone's in good health. And they found another one of those stones, too. How're things going at Macquarie?"

"What stones?" Colles said, not bothering to hide his weariness and choosing to ignore Richardson's question.

"Those stones they brought up from the ice, you know, the eight-thousand-year-old stones, there was one in the ..."

"Thank you, Richardson. Let me know if anything important happens." He hung up before the man could go on, and dialled another number. Next chance he got, he would have to talk to Harper about Richardson.

"Colles here. I need that plane prepared by four this afternoon at the latest. No problems?"

"No problems, sir. Everything as you asked."

"Good." Colles hung up. Then he called in another of his staff to make sure all arrangements for the money were in order.

With a clearer head, now he had time to think. There was something confusing here. Colles tried to put himself in Xeng's position. If he had an inside man, he didn't think he'd want that man dead until *after* he'd got his money. He would want to know whether a cure had been found, or if the stolen bacteria had been located. Yes, if either of those happened, he'd *definitely* want to know. So why silence Conrick? Was Conrick trying to extort more money? Was he threatening to expose his contacts?

Surely Conrick had never heard of Xeng Pang, he probably only knew his contact, the American. And Kevacic had already been found dead – the man's picture had been in the newspapers. No, extortion didn't seem likely; Conrick simply didn't know enough. A sudden attack of conscience? But then why would Conrick let Xeng's people know he was about to talk? Colles was certain Conrick was involved; his murder proved it.

Maybe the answer was that Conrick wasn't the only one; perhaps Xeng had another person on the inside. The man was certainly very resourceful and very well connected. The security checks on the new lab people had shown nothing unusual. But that was the only thing Colles could think of that could have made Conrick expendable. So who was it?

He called Taylor and briefed him, then he called Barker to tell him about the dead Chinese in Yea, thinking it might help the investigation if they could get Barker and the young constable a picture as well. Also, he decided he had enough information to get Barker to start searching the reservoir for something unusual. Possibly a long shot, but worth a try.

"Homicide," the unknown voice said.

"Colles. Get me Barker, quickly please." He heard the phone hit the desk, and the man mutter something, before yelling to Barker. A few moments later, Barker came on the line. Colles economically filled him in.

"And I want you to send a team out to Cardinia Reservoir and start looking for anything unusual. I expect it to be in the water."

"Shit, you want divers? What's going on, Colles?"

"I think you'll find a package. Drugs maybe," Colles lied. "And if you do find anything, make sure no one touches it, seal off the entire area and call me immediately. I'm sending you a photo of a container we know they've used."

"And it's possible it's wired to an explosive device," Colles added.

"How do you know all this, Colles?" Barker asked.

"Not your concern. And I'm deadly serious about the explosive, Barker, so make sure all your men get proper instructions." Colles sent the photo with an instruction that it was for the reservoir team's eyes only.

With as much as possible now on track, Colles thought about Nicki. He hoped she would be all right on the island. She *had* to succeed; thousands of lives might soon depend upon her. The pilot had confirmed successful 'delivery'. Colles reflected that he didn't often meet people like Palmer and Hennessy in his line of work; most people either didn't want to get involved, or they wanted to get paid a lot of money. It was often the good people who made his job worthwhile, and there were so few of them.

* * *

Barker had no difficulty getting four police divers immediately assigned. Colles had obviously pulled the necessary strings. They were now out at the reservoir, along with a team scouring the roads and car parks for anything remotely helpful. It was plain to Barker that that aggressive prick Colles had a great deal of clout. He was intruding all over police business. Still, on the plus side it meant that for Barker there was far less paperwork.

It was a dark and dismal morning, with a persistent drizzle making sure Barker and the ground team were as wet as his divers. The men on the ground had collected a large number of samples, though nothing promising. Nothing that told them where the van had been. He closed the park and had his men get the few diehard picnickers out. He also told the divers to be careful, but he hadn't taken Colles's idea of a bomb seriously – who in their right mind would booby-trap their own cache of drugs? And why risk damaging the dam and potentially flooding their escape route? It was crazy. When the bomb squad people turned up, he'd tell them it was crazy.

He wondered what this mess was really about. Why should a man like Colles be involved if it was just another drug bust. The police dealt with that every other day, and Barker was often involved because where there were large drug deals, there were often dead people.

"I've found something!" one of the divers yelled.

Barker ran over to the wall where two of the divers were waiting for him.

"Looks like a small case of some sort, down on the bottom," one of them said.

Barker looked down into the water but couldn't see anything. "How deep?" he grunted.

"'Bout six metres," the man replied. "It looks like it's been there a while, just sitting there."

"Bring it up." The man nodded to his partner. "Carefully," he added.

The two men disappeared from sight in the murky water. Barker watched as the other divers climbed onto the wall for a rest about a hundred metres away. He was shivering with cold and soaked through to his skin. "Fuck you, Colles," he muttered to himself. He could picture the man sitting in a warm office sipping a cup of steaming coffee. "Fuck you very much."

His divers surfaced at his feet, one of them holding a small, dirty vinyl case. They put it on the stone wall and Barker bent down to touch it. The brown surface was slimy to touch, and the silt rubbed off on his finger. It was a small make-up case, and under all the dirt, it was a pale pink. This couldn't be it, he thought. He picked it up and started to open it.

"Sir! Shouldn't you be more careful?" one of the divers said, looking very concerned.

"This isn't our drugs, man; are you blind? It's been in the water far too long!" he barked, as he prised the case open. He tipped the contents onto the ground. There was a lump of paper that looked like it used to be some letters and cards, tied with a piece of brownish ribbon, a couple of photos he couldn't make out, and a silver ring. He picked up the ring, rubbed off the slime and fresh gravel, and read the inscription. "Robert and Sally, 21-2-97." He threw it back on the ground, cursing. *No luck, just some sad person's life in here,* he thought.

"Well, what are you looking at? Get back to work," he snapped at the diver, leaving the man staring at the case as Barker strode back to his car.

"Get me something to eat, and some coffee," he said to the uniformed man waiting by the cars. "And a packet of these," he added, throwing the man an empty packet of cigarettes, as he put the last one to his lips. Almost lunchtime, and nothing yet.

"And this fucking rain is getting heavier," he cursed, as he realised his last cigarette was too wet to light. "Shit!"

* * *

For a man who'd had less than eight hours' sleep in more than three days,

Colles was remarkably focused, his staff thought. He was also getting more and more short-tempered with them, and many were now steering well clear of him, but they knew it wasn't personal. It was just his way with this sort of operation. He controlled the information flows, and he called the shots. He never left impossible decisions to others, and they knew he had their backs if things went wrong. This time, he was carrying a great deal of weight, though, and his closest few could see it in his face.

So far, this morning he had made all the necessary arrangements for the plane. He had confirmed that the money would be arriving by about 2.00 pm, now not far away, and he had demanded telephone records for all phones at the Yea facility. The last was, of course, a long shot, but it was worth a try. He had also reported in to the health minister, at her insistence. She had looked more than ever like a cross between a reptile and an angry insect.

She had caustically asked him whether he knew that Cardinia Reservoir was not the city's main water supply and could relatively easily be isolated. 'Of course I know,' he'd said tersely, and pointed out that it didn't matter – the bacteria would be in the air within days anyway. But she had been preoccupied with how the 'situation' would affect the public's view of her, not really listening to anything that didn't sound like 'we found a cure'. *Politicians. Too many of them are like spoilt children,* Colles thought, as the phone rang.

"Yes!" he snapped into it, having snatched it from his pocket before the first ring ended.

"Taylor, sir. Five forty-two this morning a call was placed from the lab phone to an unlisted number that we traced to the Chinese Cultural Centre. The lab security system shows that the only people here were Conrick and Hart. I thought it must have been Conrick, but while I was searching the log, Hart was asking too many questions, so I challenged him. We're holding him, sir; he admitted to the call."

"Does he know anything?" Colles asked.

"I don't think so, sir. He's just sitting there sweating and talking about deals," Taylor replied.

"Deals!" Colles exploded. "Tell him if this plague gets to any settled area, even another island, we'll charge him as an accessory to mass murder – if he's still alive! And put an armed guard on him. If the man so much as sneezes, tell the guard to point the gun at him. That'll make him sweat a bit more."

"Yes, sir."

"I want to know exactly what he told his contact, and I want a signed statement, including everything he knows about the contact, including the sound of his voice and the way he talks. Specifics."

"Shouldn't take too long. He already thinks I want to kill him," Taylor added wryly.

"Good." Colles put the phone down. Taylor was a good asset. He picked up the phone again and told Donna to send up some sandwiches and more coffee, and 'get someone to check in with that *idiot* Barker'.

41

Anakos seemed to be fading out. His face had an awful grey pallor, his breathing was laboured, his eyes red and rheumy. Micky was even worse; he was in and out of consciousness, struggling for breath. Melville came over to check on them, while Nicki kept working in her makeshift lab. It looked to Peter like some kind of old-fashioned portable computer gone wrong, and some sci-fi kitchen appliances.

Nicki had already tended Masters' arms, stitching them and dressing them properly. She had pronounced him 'tacked and ready for the tailor', a little too light-heartedly. There had been no anaesthetic available, and while he'd been tough and stoic about it, he'd gone very pale and had to lie down afterwards.

Peter now knew for sure that he was infected, his head ached terribly, and the pain relief he'd taken made no difference. He was coughing and wheezing a little. Melville was no better, but neither man complained. Nicki was concerned about them both and had marvelled at how quickly the infection had developed into these symptoms.

Melville was pleased to see that the apparent tension between Peter and Nicki had eased, and she was obviously very concerned for him. Nonetheless, Melville noticed that when she took Peter's blood earlier she hadn't been particularly gentle. She was now busily analysing their samples, first separating the serum in the 'blender', then using the chromatograph.

The conditions she was working under were spartan at best. Melville said 'welcome to the nineteenth century' when it was all set up, but Nicki didn't complain. Peter and Melville bagged the two dead men and carried the first clumsily outside, towards the Macquarie Hilton.

It was still overcast, and the air, although fairly still, had a bite to it. At least it wasn't raining. Near the door, Peter slipped on an icy patch, and his left foot slid sideways, making a cracking sound. He fell forward, putting his arm out to break the fall, and ended up half on top of the dead man, but with his arm pinned underneath.

He slowly struggled free, noticing the coldness of the body bag. It brought home the reality of their situation. *We'll likely all be that cold in a day or two, Anakos, Melville, me and Nicki ...*

"I think I'll be okay," he said to Melville. His ankle wasn't broken, he didn't think, but it didn't feel quite right either. He got up, carefully applying weight to it, and it held, although painfully. He and Melville carefully picked up their grim cargo and struggled on.

After they'd completed their second trip, neither man knew what to say. It was like a burial, but not quite. They laid the two men to rest as best they could and went quietly out into the rain.

Back in the main building they found Masters in slightly better spirits. Oddly enough, being stitched back together without anaesthesia had done him some good, as if he felt like a man again. He was talking to Anakos, to whom Nicki had just given water and more antibiotics.

"You're a tough bastard, Gary," Anakos rasped. "I thought you were going to kill me. You were pretty sick, you know. I thought it had made you crazy enough to do it."

"Guess I was lucky. Lucky again today, too." He glanced across at Nicki, who was now staring at them both.

"You were sick?" she asked sharply, interrupting Masters.

"Yeah. Guess it wasn't the plague, though. I'm still alive." Nicki put aside the blood sample she was about to start work on and found the one crudely labelled 'GM'. She knew she shouldn't get her hopes up, but maybe, just maybe ...

Small beads of sweat were forming on Nicki's neck, despite the cold. They were working furiously, separating the antibodies in Masters' blood to make antiserum. It was a painstaking process, and they were racing against bacteria that were trying to kill them all. And possibly worse, they had no way of letting Colles know. What if she didn't make it in time? The cure might die with them – Colles would probably burn the whole island, and what if the maniac released the plague on the mainland? How many more would die before they found another person with antibodies? How long would it take to make enough antiserum for *a whole population?*

Anakos was lapsing in and out of consciousness; Peter was obviously getting worse. She had to put those things out of her mind and try to concentrate. They were so close. As if to drive the point home, thunder crashed outside, shaking the walls of the building.

There was nothing for Peter to do but wait. He felt helpless and weak and wished he could do something, despite Melville telling him to rest, at least for the moment. *Rest? How?* He paced back and forth until Melville again told him to sit.

"Morton's maps are in there," Nicki said, pointing to her bag. "Sit down and read them if you need something to do. You're distracting me."

Obediently, he retrieved the ancient map papers from Nicki's bag and forced himself to start reading. *Funny,* he thought humourlessly, *here we are trying to prevent a plague that may have wiped out an entire civilisation, and I'm trying to make sense of a strange, four-century-old map.* He couldn't concentrate properly. Perhaps it was just his mental state, but he was sure some markings just didn't make any sense. *Were they just the idle doodlings of Oronteus Finaeus?* Peter stared at the map, willing it to reveal its secrets. He closed his eyes and maybe it was just a trick of a tired mind, but something was coming into focus. *Yes! Perhaps those odd markings really do make sense! But how ...*

"How is this possible?" he muttered to himself, now becoming more enthralled by what he thought he was seeing. He'd got up to retrieve his atlas, getting a sharp pain in his ankle for his trouble. The strange arrow-shaped markings on the old map looked like they might signify mountains. Perhaps it was only his imagination, his tiredness, or the headache that wouldn't let go. In less than a minute, he'd found the map he wanted, and incredibly, the mountain ranges matched almost perfectly with the ancient map.

Unbelievable, he thought. Nearly five hundred years ago, Oronteus Finaeus had not only known that Antarctica existed, but had *mapped* the numerous mountain ranges near the coast of Wilkes Land and other ranges which the new atlas told him had only recently been discovered! It was remarkable – the Ellsworth Mountains, the Mühlig-Hofmann Mountains, all there! This looked like proof that Antarctica had been 'discovered' well before the nineteenth century. *But how can this be possible?* Peter could not see any means by which Oronteus Finaeus could have got anywhere near Antarctica five centuries ago, so how could he possibly have charted its mountains? Maybe that was why the establishment hadn't accepted these maps; they raised many more questions than answers.

Peter remembered that the evidence suggested these sixteenth-century maps were copied from a number of much older originals. But no one knew where the originals might have come from, and how old they might have been. They had never been found. Morton's notes said they could have been produced before the Greek scholars, by map-makers of some ancient civilisation. He'd added a handwritten comment, in red ink, for Peter:

Check Andean civilisations. Early South American civilisations, such as the Norte Chico, started from around 3,000–4,000 BC. Many advanced cultures living high in Andes, spanning west coast of South America. Modern farming techniques (irrigation etc.), large cities, well-ordered societies, roads.

Some say human occupation of area might have started 20,000 years ago, but it was around 8,000 years ago that a much more advanced or specialised agriculture was developed, or introduced. [He had circled the word 'introduced'.]

Also, the Andean people all chose to live at the higher altitudes – from 2,500 to 4,000 metres, where cold nights and winters made their crops more susceptible to freezing conditions and frosts. Maybe they were used to a cold climate ... Or maybe they feared the sea ...

If one were to set off for the nearest major land mass from the Antarctic, there could only really be one clear choice: South America. Chile, and the southern end of the Andes in particular! Interesting?

"Yes, professor, *very* interesting," Peter said aloud. "What else can Oronteus Finaeus tell me?"

42

Xeng left his diplomatic car in the car park at Essendon Airport. He was used to being chauffeured, and escorted through a special security channel at Tullamarine, but on this occasion he'd driven himself and he now walked resolutely through the older Essendon terminal building. He carried only his briefcase. He remembered when he first visited Melbourne, many years earlier, that Essendon had been Melbourne's international airport. He had come to this country to make a difference, for his mother country, to show these lazy people what fearless and powerful leadership could do. Now, more than a generation later, he was about to make that difference.

A solid, military man in civilian clothing strode up to him. "Xeng." The military man made no attempt to hide his hostility.

"Ah, Mr Colles," Xeng smiled politely. "We finally meet. Please show me my aircraft." Colles silently led him out of the building and across the tarmac to a small jet, a Beechcraft Premier. Xeng estimated its age at ten to twelve years. *Older than I wanted, but satisfactory,* Xeng thought.

"Show me how you disarm your device," Colles said sternly.

"You don't trust me?" Xeng gave Colles a coldly menacing smile that did not reach his eyes. "I am disappointed."

Colles waited while Xeng calmly placed his case on the plane's ladder. In his hand was another device with a keypad.

"First of all, this is my insurance," Xeng announced, showing Colles the handheld device. "This excellent device communicates with the transmitter at close range. Each hour it reminds me to type in my code. If I don't do that, it will release the bacteria."

Xeng opened the briefcase to reveal a small radio transmitter attached to a nickel metal hydride battery of almost the same size. Colles was familiar with this type of transmitter and knew it could do the job, provided Xeng didn't leave it until he was too far away. Or perhaps, more precisely, provided Xeng truly intended to disarm the bomb.

"How do I know you won't use that to detonate?" Colles asked.

"It seems you will have to trust me after all."

"Why don't I just kill you now?" Colles calmly asked Xeng, half expecting the answer.

"Neither one of us is that stupid, Mr Colles. This is one of two steps required. The other will be executed by my colleague after I contact him." *Plausible, but uncheckable.* "I hope you have ensured that my plane can travel twelve thousand kilometres. If I do not reach my destination safely, you will be killing a lot of innocent people." Xeng seemed very relaxed.

If he *did* release the bacteria, Colles reasoned to himself, he could be killing more than a million Chinese living in Australia. *Would Xeng kill his own people?* Presumably, he could find a safe haven somewhere in China, but that would be difficult if he murdered millions of his countrymen. Could he take the risk that Xeng was either bluffing or intent on releasing the bacteria whether or not he got his money?

Of course, it was possible that the device had no radio receiver, that it would go off an hour or two after Xeng was clear, but Colles could not take the chance. There was no alternative; Colles would let this man leave with the money. He took little comfort from the fact that he still had a few tricks up his sleeve.

Xeng's flight started just as Colles had anticipated; he was heading roughly north-north-west. Colles reasoned that he could easily have arranged a refuel at a remote airfield, then continued across the Timor Sea to South East Asia, where almost any man with Asian features, in fact, almost anyone, could quickly disappear into total anonymity. But this wasn't right, he wasn't heading where Colles expected. Xeng had demanded a range of up to twelve thousand kilometres. That could take him all the way across the Pacific.

Or had the navigation equipment failed too soon? Had Colles made a mistake? Perhaps Xeng was not an experienced pilot in bad weather. His plane was now heading east and slowly turning further south. Colles was glad he'd installed the tracking signal emitter. The fact was, had Colles been relying solely on radar, the plane would be damned hard to find at all, Xeng was flying so low.

The way Colles had planned it, Xeng would fly across Australia, and after four hours in the air, the navigation equipment would fail. This would leave Xeng stranded somewhere far from his fuel source, far out of range of the bacteria release device, and waiting helplessly for Colles to track him down. It had been a calculated risk.

But twenty minutes in the air, Xeng dropped down to a low altitude and turned about 120 degrees east. The transmitter signal was weak due to the altitude, but it now appeared Xeng must be heading for the South Pacific islands. If he continued to turn eastward, he'd cross New Zealand's North Island.

Xeng was pleased with his work so far. He had his money, he was far from the land of the round-eyed fools. He was on his way to the first rendezvous. He laughed out loud. There was no bomb. The device he'd had Po set up was nothing more than a simple timer that would release the bacteria into the water. For all Xeng knew, it was already done. If Po set the device before heading out to the water supply, the forty-eight hours could already have expired.

The secure transmitter Xeng carried was real enough but was actually for a different purpose – he needed to communicate with the boat without anyone listening in. In two days, he would be across Chile and in Argentina, where a wealthy man could live like a king, *be protected* like a king, and not have to hide like a common criminal. Colles would no doubt have placed some sort of tracking device on the plane, so he would probably be looking for a plane wreck somewhere in the Pacific. The man smiled. A cold, evil smile. *Fools.*

The rain was now driving into the plane with some force, and it was getting colder. Xeng had never doubted his abilities in the past, although he now had to concede that he hadn't had much experience flying in storms. He was not worried, though; he knew he was smart and resourceful, and the plane had good navigation systems. He decided to change course to the south to avoid the worst of the storm up ahead. And just as he'd set his new course, without warning, the navigation systems stopped working. Xeng reached forward to tap the instrumentation, but as he did he smelt a faintly acrid odour of burnt plastic.

"*Colles!*" he cursed.

An hour later, Xeng had passed the edge of the storm and could now see the moonlight reflecting from the ocean, two hundred metres below. Two hundred metres was possibly elevated enough for radar detection, but in the bad weather, Xeng couldn't safely keep the plane any lower. Anyway, he reasoned, Colles had probably lost him hours ago. Xeng still had most of his instruments, he knew his altitude, his airspeed, and he had the stars to navigate by.

Xeng had recovered his confidence quickly after Colles's trick. "You cannot win, Colles," he said. He knew that when the New Zealand coastline came into view, which should be very soon, he'd be able to safely reset his course.

Xeng checked his fuel supply. It was a little lower than it should be, so he rechecked his watch and calculated he should have crossed the New Zealand coast an hour ago. *There couldn't have been that much of a headwind.* Now he started to feel disoriented. An *unacceptable* feeling. He looked again at the moon, and now he thought it seemed to be in the wrong place. *Was he off course?*

He shook his head vigorously and growled like a caged animal. He had to focus his mind. Discipline was required, and Xeng was extremely disciplined. "When the mind *must* focus, give the mind *a focus.*" He remembered these words from his childhood. He took a small knife from the briefcase by his side and determinedly pressed the point into his right thigh. There was nothing like pain to focus the mind. As the blood raced to the small puncture in his skin, his mind started to race too. *Options. There are always options.*

His calculations indicated that he must have run just south of New Zealand. No doubt due to the stormy weather. He had also calculated that he had enough fuel to get back to land. If he almost doubled back, three hundred and fifteen degrees to port, he would reach New Zealand. There would be ample places to land the small aircraft on the Otago plains, and he knew the population was so sparse, he might be able to land undetected. Then it was just a matter of finding a suitable farmhouse and disposing of its occupants. After that, he would have time to plan the next leg of his journey.

"You are a wily dog, Mr Colles," Xeng thought aloud. "One day I will take much pleasure in slicing your throat and watching you die."

This is very inconvenient, Xeng thought, but he knew he would prevail. He was a winner. He knew making a seven-eighths turn would be difficult without navigation instruments, but he could see the moon clearly enough through the clouds to do it. He was ready to make the course change now, and he scanned the night sky as much as possible – more from habit than need – there would be no one else in the air anywhere near him.

In the distance, he thought he spotted land ahead, slightly to starboard. Yes, a small, dull pimple on the moonlit horizon a few kilometres in front. An island. He must have passed just to the south of New Zealand's South Island. He was flying over the Foveaux Strait. This would be Stewart Island. It would do.

43

Six hours after drifting off to sleep, Bob Jacks woke up feeling thirsty. He dragged himself out of bed and went to the kitchen for a glass of water. He drank deeply, refilled the glass, drank again and coughed. *Whoever was on kitchen duty this week hasn't done much of a job,* he reflected. Glasses, plates, cutlery looked like they'd been washed, but were all soaking in a sink half full of water. He added his empty glass to the pile and shuffled back to his bunk, seeing no one on the way. Nearly end of shift. It was always quiet near the end of the 'night' shift, but despite the quiet, he couldn't get back to sleep. He picked up the magazine he'd retrieved from the hut and started to thumb through its already-worn pages.

"Wish this headache'd bugger off," he mumbled to himself.

* * *

AUGUST 1 – MACQUARIE ISLAND

Nicki was physically and mentally drained. The room they were confined to had become a claustrophobic prison, and for the past few hours all

279

they had been able to do was wait. Peter seemed deep in thought. Melville clearly didn't like the inaction but was obviously a man who knew how to follow procedure and wait, even if he didn't like it much. *It's time*, Nicki thought. *Well, it's near enough, anyway, I have to do something!* Dawn was still some hours away.

She stood up and went over to the bench then placed the latest bacterial culture under the microscope and studied it for a few seconds.

"Come and look at this," Nicki beckoned urgently to Melville.

He walked quickly over to the microscope, squinted and peered through the lens. Nicki was staring at him, waiting.

"Dead cells?"

"Dead bacteria cells," she said excitedly. "This proves it! Gary's blood has produced antibodies!" She gave Melville a hug as tears of relief started to roll down her cheeks.

They'd drawn a good deal more blood from Gary, as much as was safe, given his condition. Nicki knew they wouldn't need that much antiserum on the island, but she wanted to make sure there was enough to start production en masse. She thought it would take weeks to prepare enough for an entire population, let alone administer it to millions of people.

With Melville's help, Nicki had separated the blood plasma and made up a rather crude antiserum, the best they could do, bearing in mind the equipment available. They had then given liberal doses to everyone still alive on the island, starting with Anakos. She'd roused him from his semi-comatose state and tried to wake Micky, only to find, to her horror, that the man was dead. She held back her tears as she told Anakos to hang on as long as he could; that the antiserum should start to take effect within just a few hours.

As soon as they had completed preparation of the remaining antiserum, she and Melville could rest. They had worked non-stop for what seemed like days and badly needed sleep. Masters was snoring on one of the makeshift beds, and Peter, after napping a couple of times, was awake and again reading the maps and other stuff from Professor Morton. He had started to explain something excitedly about an hour ago, but she and Melville were so busy neither heard what he said.

Nicki looked across at Peter. He looked totally absorbed in whatever he was reading. Occasionally he looked upwards, but remained oblivious to his surroundings, then back to the papers. She wanted to ask him what was going through his mind but decided to let him be, reasoning that it was good that he had a distraction. Then he coughed involuntarily, making a rasping sound, jolting Nicki back to their situation.

Peter had indeed become engrossed in what he was reading. What had really shocked him was the most remarkable of all the map's features. Oronteus Finaeus had mapped the mountain ranges of Antarctica, and even *rivers*! The Oronteus Finaeus map showed the continent of Antarctica without ice! Most of the mountains depicted in his map were today completely buried under hundreds of metres, or even *kilometres*, of ice. As were the rivers. Not glaciers, but *rivers*! Sure, the map wasn't perfect, but it had some eerily accurate details that just could not have been known five hundred years ago.

Morton had pointed out that the entire continent was shown by the old map to be much larger than its real size, but he had theorised that Oronteus Finaeus had copied it from other much older maps, and that he had mistakenly depicted the 80th parallel of latitude as the Circulus Antarcticus.

For Peter, these ancient maps were solid evidence that it *was* possible. Possible that an ancient civilisation could have existed on Antarctica *before* it was frozen, and could, therefore, have produced these maps, or their precursors. It wasn't a big leap to accept that the stones could be linked to that civilisation!

Morton's final note pointed out very clearly that none of these theories had ever been widely accepted by 'the establishment' and could not be proved. Nor could they be disproved. Apparently, Gerardus Mercator, the most famous of history's map-makers, published a number of works on the creation of the world and its history. He also published scores of maps that had originally been presented to Ptolemy during the second century AD.

Mercator's atlas was published in 1569, and it too depicted the as-yet-undiscovered Antarctica. His map, almost incredibly, included the same errors of scale as the Oronteus Finaeus map. Peter's mind was reeling; he was perhaps piecing together one of the greatest anthropological discoveries of all time!

Of course, there was still one glaring problem – Peter did not know of any geophysical phenomena that could account in any way for the snap-freezing of the Antarctic region. Nor a sudden significant increase in sea level. It was no wonder the scientific establishment had more or less ignored these strange maps.

44

Kevin woke in a cold sweat. He looked around to see the familiar walls of his room, his messy desk, with reference books piled to one side. It was only a dream. Darkness closing in all around him. He felt panic setting in; an ominous feeling that everything he knew, everything he loved, was gone. Kevin Hodge hardly ever dreamt, or at least if he did, he hardly ever remembered it. But this nightmare had been so vivid he was still a little shaken. Perhaps it was just a combination of a couple of drinks, a late-night pizza and the mystery of that stone. He looked at the clock. 3.10 am. He'd only been asleep a few hours.

In the morning he would find out what the stone was made of. On Friday, he'd figured out it wasn't what it seemed; it couldn't be a solid piece of basalt. He wanted to cut into it. Morton had initially been against it, but Kevin believed it was the only way forward. They were all curious about it and had been lobbying Morton relentlessly.

Yesterday afternoon, Kevin played a football match, although he hadn't played very well. One of his teammates had criticised him for being preoccupied. He supposed the guy was right; usually he was very competitive. After the game, he'd arranged to go out with a few friends. He went home for a quick meal and, to his surprise, John Morton had called and left a message. Kevin phoned him back immediately. After a long discussion, he managed to convince the reluctant professor that the *only* way to find out exactly what that stone was made of was to drill into it. Morton was strongly against it at first, saying he was looking after it for his friend, but Kevin had been extremely persuasive. And Morton knew he was right; there was no other way either of them could see. He was meeting Morton at the lab at eleven. He rolled over and tried to go back to sleep.

* * *

AUGUST 1, MACQUARIE ISLAND, SOUTHERN OCEAN

Nicki and Melville had finally finished their work. All they could do now was wait. And hope. Peter had put away the papers he'd been so engrossed in and limped off to find additional blankets. There was room enough on the floor to make places to sleep, and he'd done a reasonable job.

Nicki had set aside the way she'd felt when she first saw Peter on the island. She was so happy that he was alive and seemingly unhurt that she had practically thrown herself at him. His distant response had hurt her. Rationally, she thought she understood why – he said he'd watched people die here, and now she was exposed to the plague. But it still hurt. She thought he would be as overjoyed as she was. She thought he would warmly embrace her, and kiss her, and tell her … what?

She looked over at him and he smiled wanly. He started to speak but it turned into a coughing fit instead.

"I need sleep," Melville announced, interrupting her thoughts. He looked completely shattered, worse even than Peter felt. He lay noisily in one of the nests of blankets Peter had made earlier and covered himself.

"Yes, me too," said Nicki. As Peter stood, Nicki started to settle herself in another.

Peter touched her gently on the shoulder. "I don't know what to say," he said, looking at her like a lost little boy.

"Then shut up and get in." She moved to one side and held up the blanket for him.

As Peter lay next to her he put his arm around her and held her tight, kissing the back of her neck. "You may be the most amazing woman I have ever met."

"You're delirious. Go to sleep." She snuggled in closer and went almost straight to sleep, still smiling.

45

Xeng's relief at seeing land had soured somewhat. It was not New Zealand, not Stewart Island. In fact it was not any island that he knew, and he had no idea whether he'd be able to land the plane without damaging it. Or even land it at all. He followed the northern coast to the west, now flying at an altitude of around five hundred metres. Dawn was still a little way off, but there was enough light to make out features on the ground. No sign of life and no airfield, but at least there were no large trees to be seen. Fuel was depressingly low. Another half hour and he'd be dead in the water. *Literally.*

Then to his left he spotted something he hoped could be an airstrip. He veered sharply ninety degrees to port and dropped down to a hundred and fifty metres. It *was*. He slowed to landing speed and very carefully brought the plane down toward the ground. He knew that it wouldn't take much, a large pothole, furrows or mud and he might not be able to take off again. Of course, that assumed he could find some aviation fuel, and if not repair the navigation systems, at least find a working compass.

The wheels hit the ground and the plane veered a little to starboard, just off the edge of the hard gravel strip and onto the grass. Xeng fought to maintain control. The ground was rough, but at least he hadn't crashed. Then, suddenly, he was thrown sideways. He heard a loud tearing sound as the starboard wing scraped across the ground, and he cursed viciously at Colles. As the plane came to an abrupt stop, Xeng's mind was racing to stay in control of the situation; he needed to be completely in control. Colles could not win.

He was armed, and he was a masterful tactician, and fearless. If there were any people on this rathole of an island he could kill them and take whatever he could use. Xeng Pang would not be stopped this close to victory. The plane was tilted awkwardly to one side. He hoped there was no serious damage.

Xeng killed the engines and surveyed the cockpit. No visible damage inside that he could see, other than the sabotaged instruments. He thought it likely that Colles had tracked him, at least some of the way, so he knew he didn't have a lot of time to lay his hands on what he needed and get off this island. He retrieved his handgun and knife, and climbed awkwardly out of the aircraft.

"Hey! There's another plane."

Melville's calling, Peter realised, slowly shaking off the brief slumber.

Nicki murmured softly as she woke, gently extricating herself from Peter's warm embrace. Neither had moved since falling asleep, and Peter's arm was numb from where Nicki had lain. It was not yet dawn, so they'd only slept a couple of hours.

Melville came back inside with a concerned look. "Another plane has just come in. I heard it approaching, and I'm certain it landed."

There had been no message out to Colles, nor could they receive any inward communication. But Melville was sure Colles would not have allowed anyone else to fly there.

Peter stood up, none too steadily, his ankle now less painful but more swollen. He looked at Melville, noticing the man still looked exhausted.

"I've been up for a while," Melville said, responding to Peter's quizzical look. "Working on the comms equipment. We still need to contact Colles."

"Any luck with it?" Peter asked.

"No. You look a little better, by the way. How do you feel?"

"Yes, a bit better I think," Peter replied. "You look like shit," he added with a grin.

Melville's eyes were bloodshot. "Think my arm is infected. Where that guy sliced me a couple of days ago," he said, unemotionally.

Nicki looked surprised. "You didn't say you'd been injured. Let me see," Nicki said.

"We need to see who just landed first, and warn them off," Melville said, as Masters joined them.

After a half-hearted argument, Melville agreed to stay with Nicki so she could deal with his wound, and Peter and Gary set off for the airstrip. The weather had improved a little, and behind them, through a faint mist, the sun would rise in a short while.

Melville took off his shirt, and Nicki was horrified to see a very red, swollen arm under a dark-crimson makeshift bandage. A red streak ran up his arm to the shoulder. A sure sign of blood poisoning from infection, they both knew. *He should be in a hospital, on IV antibiotics,* Nicki thought.

Melville laughed weakly. "I guess it would be ironic to cure a plague and then die from stupidity," he said.

"Well at least you agree how serious this is. Why are men so stupid? You all think you're superman."

Nicki gave Melville an intravenous antibiotic injection then removed the old bandage, cleaned the wound and applied a fresh dressing.

"Hennessy is right, you know. You're an amazing woman."

A kilometre away, Hennessy and Masters headed for the airstrip in the pale early light.

"Did you see the crash site?" Masters asked. He was clearly in a much better mental state than when they'd found him.

"No."

"That was when the trouble all started, just after that plane from Ross Island crashed, about ten days ago."

"I know," Peter replied. "We still don't know where the bacteria came from, though. I've been to Ross and there was no sign of it down there." Peter thought about the stone and the frozen grapevine they'd found. *Evidence of life from thousands of years ago suddenly turns up, then just as suddenly, people start dying of a previously unknown disease. Coincidence?*

"Did you search the wreckage?" Peter asked.

"Yes. Pretty thoroughly," Masters replied. "We brought the bodies back, and we tried to find out why the plane crashed. Nick Anakos has a pilot's licence. He went up there for a look, and the only odd thing he found was that the passengers weren't wearing seat belts. We couldn't think of any good reason for that. Must've happened very suddenly."

"I'd like to have a good look at it later, okay?"

"Okay."

Masters is in surprisingly good health, Peter thought. He seemed to have made a full recovery from the plague. Peter also felt he had a little more energy. Perhaps it was his imagination; or just having something to do that made them feel better. Perhaps there really *was* hope for them after all. They walked on in silence for another hundred metres or so.

"Do you think we should be careful?" Peter asked. Gary looked at him quizzically. "I mean, we know no one should be coming here. Maybe they're here by mistake. They could easily take this plague back to the mainland."

"Let's just keep our distance and warn them off," Gary said.

"Okay, but ..." Peter stopped mid-sentence as he heard a loud **crack!** He looked all around but could see nothing. He couldn't even tell where it had come from. "What the hell was ..." His words trailed off as he looked back at Gary, to see him lying motionless on the track. Peter jumped over, crouching down to help him.

Crack! There it was again. Someone was shooting at them. Gary's eyes were open and there was a small bloody hole in his right temple. He was dead.

Peter felt something whizz past his ear and realised he'd heard another gunshot. He panicked. Someone was trying to kill them. *Run!* his instinct said, but where? His mind was spinning – where were the shots coming from?

He half-ran, half-dived into the nearest shrubs, hearing another shot. He was fairly sure it was coming from behind him, from the other side of the track. He wished there were trees, or some thick bushes to run into. The pale pre-dawn light was both a blessing and a curse. He knew that standing here he was not much better off than a sitting duck. He moved back further into the low vegetation and found a small gap to squeeze through. There was a slight ridge, then the ground dropped a few metres into a long, narrow trench under the dense undergrowth.

He jumped the ridge, and heard more shots, feeling one stinging his arm. He almost fell into the bushes below and pushed his way through blindly, further and further from the track. *Who the hell's shooting at me? Someone from the plane?* One of the men they couldn't account for, in the same irrational state Gary had been in? But why would they want to *kill* him? Why kill Gary? In the madness, Peter thought fleetingly of when Nicki and Melville had brought Gary down to the base, the state he'd been in, how he'd provided the antibodies that might save them all. And now he was dead.

Crack! Another shot brought him back to reality.

Peter needed to think clearly. How many shots had he heard? Five, six? It didn't matter, he realised, he had no idea how many bullets his assailant had. Was it just one shooter, or were there more? And had Melville and Nicki heard the shots?

He had to get back to the base quickly, somehow. Even if there was only one attacker, Peter knew he was no match for an armed man. None of them were, not even Melville in his current state. Hopefully, together they had a chance, Peter reasoned.

There had been no more shots, no sound at all. Perhaps his attacker had moved on towards the base, or maybe he was just waiting for Peter to show himself. He knew he couldn't safely follow the track so got his bearings as best he could and decided to head roughly north to get back to Nicki and the others. It was a struggle to stay under the cover of the low bush.

The stunted, wet scrub provided just enough cover, and a little visibility, but he could not stand up fully so had to move more slowly than he wanted to. He kept moving as quietly and quickly as he could, trying to get away from the last place his attacker had seen him. There was no sign of the killer.

Peter could just make out the track to his right and the airfield behind him. There was only one track, so he assumed his attacker must have started to follow it. He skirted around nearer to the coast, staying at least a few hundred metres from the path. His ankle was very sore now, and despite the bitter cold, he'd broken out in a sweat. His clothing was soaked from brushing against the vegetation.

"Aghh!" Something caught his leg and tore his trousers. He realised he'd just cried out. He hit the ground, trying to keep his breathing quiet, listening for anything that might give away his assailant's location. Nothing. Had the other man stopped to listen too? He waited a few minutes, hearing nothing but birds and the ocean, which was now less than half a kilometre away. Still no sign of another person.

He looked down at his leg and saw a large rip in his trousers and a deep scratch above his right knee. The bullet graze on his arm was bleeding only slightly; he'd been very lucky. He was still breathing hard as he got up to move on. Half crouching, half running, he pressed on under the best cover he could find. He wondered what he'd do when he reached the base – he would have to cross a hundred metres of open ground to get to the others.

Xeng knew he didn't have time to waste chasing anyone. He had to find supplies and equipment. He had checked the plane and found to his dismay that a wheel strut was damaged. Not a major repair, but he would need tools. A farm would probably have what he needed, assuming there were farms in this place. There must be something, he surmised, and the track he was following must surely lead to it.

He'd fired five shots, which meant he still had four plus a spare clip. Plenty. And he'd already killed the big man. He ran along a shallow ditch between the track and the brush, all the time watching the horizon around him for signs of civilisation. He knew there was another man still alive in the bushes somewhere. The man had obviously been unarmed so Xeng had the advantage, as long as he got to a settlement before the man had a chance to warn them. He would take them by surprise, assume control, take what he needed and get out, leaving no witnesses.

Xeng thought he heard someone cry out, way off to his left. Perhaps it was an animal or a bird. It didn't matter anyway. This was the only track he could see, and he was going to get to the end of it first. He crossed a small rise and saw a compound of about twenty buildings. What was this? Not a farm. He moved into the cover of the bushes, as his mind turned over the possibilities. It wouldn't be military; the men he saw were not uniformed or armed. But what was it? How many people? Would the one who got away be in radio contact with this base?

He wished it was still completely dark. As he studied the complex, he saw that some of the buildings were no more than storage huts. One had been severely damaged by fire, recently. *Good.* A confused enemy always helped one who was determined and focused. Then, he saw a young woman emerge from one of the larger buildings. She quickly looked around, but saw nothing and, more importantly, Xeng thought, she obviously was not aware of any danger. *Perfect.*

Peter had come out of some thick scrub and was expecting to see the ocean, but instead he was back at the track. *Dammit. Have I gone around in a circle?* He looked to the horizon and could see where the sun would soon push its way through the distant mist. This time of year, the sun rose in the far north-east here, so he knew he hadn't gone the wrong way. Then he realised this wasn't the main track from the airfield. It must lead to the other hut. The ornithologist's hut, where they'd found Masters.

He ran down the track, as quietly as he could, knowing he couldn't be far from the main station. Knowing also that he'd be running towards the man with the gun. He slowed as he approached a bend, expecting to run into either a bullet, or the narrow neck of land that led to the station. Crouching low, he carefully made his way through the bushes, and just as he got a view of the base, he heard another shot. *Nicki! And the others!* They were probably inside, exhausted, *vulnerable.* He strained but couldn't make anything out. The place looked as peaceful as it ever had. Then he heard some muffled shouting before it went quiet again.

46

Detective Barker was mad as hell with Colles. The military man was obviously wrong, there was no doubt in Barker's mind. If there was anything here, they'd have found it yesterday. They'd searched right through the day, and on into the night at Colles's instruction. At one stage, Barker had contacted his chief to get Colles off his back, and get back to real police work, but to no avail. His chief had finally allowed Barker to reduce the team to three people – Barker and the two divers. Technically, this wasn't part of the murder investigation, so the chief was punishing him for something, Barker figured.

The dive team started again at first light, and by nine, Barker was already halfway through his first packet of cigarettes. Each time the divers came up for a break, and to warm up, they heard Barker muttering to himself. They were able to measure his mood by the number of expletives that punctuated each sentence. Currently the ratio was almost one to one.

"A lot of junk down there," one of the divers said. "We're looking for a cache of drugs, that might be wired to some kind of bomb – that right?"

Barker simply glared at the man.

The diver risked pressing on. "Sir, doesn't that strike you as odd?"

"The whole fuckin' thing is fuckin' odd." Barker's phone rang, saving the diver from another caustic comment. "Barker!" he grunted into it.

Barker had started to give an updated status to the caller, none too politely, when he was obviously cut off. The diver watched his face go redder and redder with anger. "Look, Colles, there's a lotta shit down there. We need more information if we're gonna keep looking." Barker was becoming more agitated. "How the fuck should I know? You talk to him."

"Hey. This is for you!" Barker yelled at the diver, handing him the phone.

"Hello," said the man, tentatively, quickly adding his name in a more confident voice. "Sergeant Kantarikis here, sir."

A clear, clipped voice addressed him. "Sergeant, Detective Barker has suggested that you're finding a lot of rubbish in the water. Describe some of this rubbish to me." The caller waited silently for an answer.

"Well, sir ... we've been told we're looking for drugs ... recently dropped, and that they may be, er, booby-trapped in some way." Kantarikis wished he had thought of a better term than *booby-trapped*. Still silence at the other end. "So we're ignoring stuff that's been there a long time, and stuff that's obviously just rubbish. Also we're ..."

"Tell me about the rubbish, sergeant," Colles interrupted bluntly.

"Takeaway food packaging and containers mostly, sir. Some magazines, bits of plastic. This morning I found a new-looking plastic container, but it was broken and there was nothing in it. Looked expensive..." Kantarikis heard Colles draw a breath, as if about to say something, but he had to wait for nearly five seconds.

"Thank you, sergeant. Give me Barker."

"Sir!" the diver called, waving Barker's phone. He heard Barker mutter something under his breath as he walked back over.

"Barker" he growled into the phone.

"Barker, I want you to make sure no one enters or leaves that park, including you and your team."

"What?" *What is this bastard up to?* "Why?"

"Has anyone been and gone this morning?" Colles asked, ignoring Barker's questions.

"No."

"Tell your diver to get the plastic container he told me about, along with all the rubbish within a couple of metres of it, and make damn sure *no one* enters or leaves the area. And have your men keep searching."

Barker heard the click as Colles put the phone down.

"Jesus Christ," Colles said to no one in particular. He picked up his phone and made four quick calls.

"Nothing but quality equipment here," Kevin said to Professor John Morton. Kevin was about to break the surface of the stone with a rather serious-looking electronically controlled drill. The drill bit was hollow and diamond tipped. Its purpose was to extract a core of material from whatever it entered. Morton had watched nervously as Kevin set it up, carefully clamping the stone into place under the drill head.

"I'm not sure about this any more, Kevin," he said.

But Kevin reassured him that the drill was the best way, and that it was designed to minimise any damage to the sample. They had already tried X-ray, but all that showed was that there was something less dense inside, possibly liquid. *Maybe this is the only way,* Morton rationalised.

Kevin brought the drill head down, delicately touching the stone's smooth surface. "Well, here goes," he said, quickly pressing a green button before Morton had a chance to say anything. But nothing happened. He checked the power lead, the power outlet and everything else he could think of. "We used this last week. It worked fine then." Kevin had the back cover off the drill's electronic panel. "The fuse is okay. Everything looks fine here." He unplugged the machine, picked up an old computer monitor's power lead and plugged it into the same point. The screen lit up obediently.

"I guess I'll have to do this the old-fashioned way," Kevin said, heading to a cabinet on the far side of the lab.

But Morton had got cold feet. Was this an omen? A warning of some kind? "Kevin, I think we'd better wait until the stone's owner has his say," he said, hoping desperately that Peter was still alive. He quickly starting unclamping the stone while Kevin noisily extracted an odd-looking hand drill, an awl and something that might have been a small ice pick.

"I'm sorry, professor, what was that you said?"

"I'm going to wait until I've asked Peter Hennessy about this."

Kevin looked very disappointed as he watched the professor put the stone into his coat pocket.

"Who?"

"He's an anthropologist. It's *his* stone," Morton explained.

"Okay." Kevin was clearly not okay with this, but he accepted it. "All right, I'll fix the drill, while you check with your friend." He put the hand tools down on the nearest bench. He was clearly still very keen to get on with it.

"No, thank you, Kevin, I do appreciate your efforts, but you must understand I should check with Peter first, and that's not going to be easy." Even if he *is* alive, it won't be easy. Surely Peter would want this stone thoroughly investigated and understood? He somehow felt in his heart that the stone shouldn't be defiled, but his head was telling him they should continue, in the interest of science.

"I'll tell you what, why don't we give Peter until the end of the day, and if I can't confirm with him by then, let's open it up first thing tomorrow," he said to Kevin.

"What about tonight?" Kevin was eager and perhaps a little anxious, Morton thought.

"All right then, tonight. Say, eight o'clock?"

Colles called Taylor at the Yea lab, but there was no more news. It looked like Hart was just an opportunist that Xeng's people had found. There were always people who would do anything for the right amount of money. *Weak and greedy people,* Colles thought. *Selfish and stupid people.*

People who didn't, or wouldn't, take responsibility for their actions. As long as the money was right, they didn't need to know what damage they might be doing.

Taylor also confirmed that they were no closer to a cure.

"More than anything else, the team here want information from Macquarie," Taylor had said.

"The situation might have changed, Taylor. Stay alert."

Taylor would have asked him what he meant if Colles had given him a chance.

Colles had arranged for collection of whatever the diver had found. A chopper was on its way to Cardinia with appropriate biohazard measures. It was a long shot and still might just turn out to be an old discarded plastic box, but Colles had learned to trust his instincts. The pilot had instruction to speak to Colles five minutes before arrival. That should be plenty of time for Barker to leave the container in a suitable place for collection and get the hell out of the way. The third phone call had been to the minister. Colles knew he couldn't isolate Cardinia from Melbourne's water supply without her approval.

Barker had called for another two men. He'd given one of them instructions to stay by the main road, to ensure that no one entered the area. Twenty minutes later it dawned on him that he now couldn't get any breakfast, and he was very hungry. He decided he hadn't been in the water so couldn't have been contaminated by whatever it was that Colles was obsessing about.

Barker got in his car and drove towards the gate. After all, a man's got to eat. As he approached, he saw two green SUVs that looked like army vehicles. Two uniformed men ran out onto the road. They were pointing machine pistols at his car.

"What the fuck ...?" His voice trailed off as the men pointed their weapons squarely at him.

"Stop the car, sir! Stop now!"

Barker did as he was told, cut the engine, jumped out and marched angrily over to the men.

"*Stop, sir!* Stay exactly where you are." The soldier's sharp command told Barker the man meant what he said.

"What's going on?" His voice betrayed his angry look. Whatever this was, it was *not* what Colles had told him. The soldiers didn't know either. "Can I get my phone?" Barker asked. The soldiers looked at each other.

"Yes, sir." Barker angrily dialled a number and waited, fuming, until the call was answered.

"Colles, what the fuck's going on?"

"I've had the area cordoned off. You're quarantined."

Barker was stunned. He recovered his wits after a few seconds.

"Quarantined from what, Colles?"

"I can't tell you." Colles sounded different, Barker thought. "What I can tell you is that a chopper is coming in a few minutes to collect that container your diver found. I'm going to have it tested, along with a sample of water from where it was found. Then I'll know when you can leave. Tell your diver to place the container, and everything else he found, in an open area, and then get everyone away from it." Barker did not respond. "Is that understood, Barker?"

"What? No. Tell me again." Barker was now much more subdued than he'd ever been with Colles.

Colles repeated the instructions impatiently, adding that Barker might have to signal the pilot as to where the container was. Barker got back in his car and drove back to the lake.

The divers had stopped for a short break. Kantarikis noticed Barker's changed manner and almost asked him why but decided against it. Barker had the divers gather all the pieces of the plastic container, put them into an evidence bag and leave it prominently on one of the picnic tables. Then, as the helicopter approached, the men stepped away. They stood and watched in awed silence, as someone in a bio suit climbed out of the chopper, collected the evidence bag very delicately and climbed back in.

The chopper had disappeared behind the hills to their north before anyone spoke.

"What's going on, sir?"

"We're in fucking quarantine, son. That's all I know."

All three men looked at each other. Suddenly, the place seemed terribly cold and lonely.

47

Xeng marched out of the scrub and onto the main track that led to the array of buildings before him. He'd decided a confident and direct approach was the best way. If anyone came out and saw him, he would wave in greeting, then, when they got close enough, he could take his pick, the knife or the gun. These people would be no match for a professional. He strode down to the main building where he'd seen the woman, casually looking from side to side, noting that the other buildings appeared to be unoccupied.

This was looking better and better. Storage huts with all kinds of useful equipment. They would certainly have tools to fix the damaged wheel. They might even have the parts he needed to fix the burnt-out electronics – and maybe even someone to do it for him!

He walked past two large buildings and noticed the home-made signs – Macquarie Hilton and Club Med Macquarie. A look of shock flashed across Xeng's face. He'd landed on Macquarie Island! The source of the plague! How could he possibly have ended up this far south? He knew he needed to get off this island quickly, and he decided he would kill anyone who got too close.

He stopped at the only building with any visible lighting inside. It was possible the other man he'd met near the airstrip had contacted these people and warned them, but very unlikely, Xeng thought. His instincts were *never* wrong. He opened the door with his left hand, holding his pistol in his right.

He looked around the room and saw four people. A man with a bandaged arm was asleep on a makeshift bed on the floor. The young woman he'd seen before was standing by a bench laden with plastic packs of a clear liquid – these he recognised as plasma packs he'd seen in hospitals before. A third man was awake but looking barely alive, in a stretcher bed on the floor. Another was lying still, a little further along.

The woman moved her hand. She was only steadying herself, but it was time to establish authority. Xeng fired a shot a few centimetres over her head. In that same five seconds he had contemplated killing them all right there, but he knew he might need them for a while longer.

The shot woke Melville who immediately tried to get up.

"Lie still!" Xeng commanded.

"What do you want?" Melville asked, groggy, but alert.

"Where are the others?" Xeng asked in a clear, measured tone.

"The airstrip," Nicki replied, a little vaguely. She didn't catch Melville's look until after she'd answered.

"How many?" This time Nicki did not volunteer an answer.

Xeng raised his pistol and pointed it between Nicki's eyes. "How many?" he repeated, glancing at Melville. He had caught Melville's look the first time.

"Two," Melville grunted.

"Good. Now I want to know who you all are and how you can help me," Xeng replied. "You first," he added, pointing the gun at Melville's head. Even injured, this man looked like the biggest threat.

"Melville. I'm a doctor."

Xeng smiled at him. "Of course. Put your hands behind your head and lie face down, Dr Melville."

Melville silently acquiesced, not without difficulty with his injured and infected arm.

Xeng then looked straight at Nicki, and she shivered involuntarily. *Had he already found Peter and Gary? What had he meant by 'good'? Were they okay?*

"Yes?" the man asked politely.

Nicki steeled herself to speak calmly to this evil-looking man.

"Dr Palmer, microbiologist."

"So many doctors. And you two are the patients?" Xeng asked, looking at Anakos and Micky.

Nick Anakos tried to speak but was unable to. He made a gurgling sound, then turned to his side and vomited some blood onto the floor.

Xeng raised his pistol and gently started to squeeze the trigger.

"*No!*" Nicki cried. "He's a pilot! He can help you!" It was the first thing that came to her mind.

"Thank you," Xeng said politely, "but I am a pilot also." He paused briefly. "Ah, perhaps you're right. This man may be able to help. Get up!" Nicki was aghast, but with a supreme effort, Anakos was able to sit up and lean against the wall. "Who are you?"

"Nick Anakos," he rasped painfully. "Pilot, meteorologist, engineer."

"Excellent. You're a lucky man, Mr Anakos. I have a use for an engineer."

Nicki relaxed visibly at Xeng's words.

"And him?" Xeng looked at Micky.

"Dead," Melville said.

"Hmm. Turn him to face this way." With some effort, Anakos managed to turn Micky's head towards the man. His skin was grey and there was dried blood around his mouth. His eyes were open and unseeing. There was no mistaking the face of death.

Xeng calmly turned back to Nicki. "Now, tell me exactly what you have there, Dr Palmer."

Nicki looked at Melville, but Xeng caught the glance. "Dr Melville will not help you."

"We are attempting to make antiserum for a disease we are all infected with," Nicki said, matter-of-factly.

"Ah, excellent," Xeng said, nodding. The man was not surprised. As he said it, she put two and two together. This man must be the maniac Colles is trying to stop. *But what the hell is he doing here?*

"You look troubled, my dear," Xeng observed, making her skin crawl.

Nicki looked across at Melville, but she could not see his eyes.

Anakos slumped back down onto the mattress.

48

Colles picked up the phone on the third ring.

"Taylor, sir. The plastic container has arrived and is being tested, but I thought you should know that the people here said it's not one of theirs."

"Shit. We're going around in circles. Any news on the dead man?" Colles demanded.

"Just a minute, sir," Taylor said and called to one of his team. "Yes, sir. The dead guy's name is Po. The police had his fingerprints on file from an assault charge ten years ago. Been clean ever since."

Or moved into a different league, Colles thought.

"They're checking his last-known address now," Taylor added.

"Keep me posted, Taylor." Colles hung up. Then he dialled another number. Ten minutes later, the search at Cardinia had resumed and a very angry Barker was able to go and buy his breakfast.

Three kilometres away from Colles's office, Jackson had just walked into a very tidy, sparsely furnished flat in Richmond, just outside Melbourne's central business district. The manager had let him in without any fuss; she didn't want any trouble with the police. Jackson had simply shown his police badge and asked. Unlike Barker, he found people responded well to a polite approach.

Jackson noted that this flat – well, more of a room really – was fit for a monk. There was no television or radio, there were no pictures on the wall. In fact, other than some clothing hanging in the small closet, there was little evidence that anyone lived in it at all.

"Odd," Jackson said to himself as he looked around. It was not at all what he'd expected.

He checked the drawers in the table beside the bed and the pockets of clothes but had turned up nothing. No notes, no receipts, no keys, no clues. The manager had opened the mailbox outside in the hall, but it contained nothing other than a hardware store catalogue and a flyer for a local restaurant. He went back into the man's room. *There has to be something here*, he thought. *Everyone has something personal.* And the dead man had been found with nothing on him. He must have credit cards, cash, maybe a passport, or *something*.

Jackson pulled the drawers out of the bedside table. He lifted the mattress off the bed, pulled the bed out from the wall, pulled the clothing out of the wardrobe. Still nothing, although he did notice the man had a strange mix of clothing – there was a variety of shirts ranging from 'working-class', shapeless cotton through to silk business shirts. There was a cheap blue coverall hanging next to an Italian suit that Jackson thought would be at least a month's pay for a cop. Next to that was a chef's tunic. *What line of work is this guy in?* There was nothing Barker or Colles would be interested in. The four pairs of shoes on the floor of the closet were also a strange combination of style and cost.

"This isn't helping," he muttered to himself. He rehung the clothing and started to put the shoes back in when he noticed a tiny gap all the way around the floor of the closet. At first glance it looked like any other cupboard with a fixed laminate floor, flush with the bottom of the door. But this floor did not look fixed. He tried to lift it but couldn't grip it sufficiently. Then he pressed each side, until, on the third attempt, as he pushed the back of the floor down, the front lifted about two centimetres. He grabbed it with his free hand a pulled it towards the front of the closet. It lifted out easily. The exposed space was about sixty centimetres square and ten centimetres deep.

Jackson took the clothing out again to get more light into the hiding place, and found what he thought he was looking for. There were two wallets, one worn, and made from cheap vinyl, containing a single credit card and three hundred dollars in cash. The other, a more-expensive leather wallet, contained several plastic cards, including a American Express Gold Card, and also three hundred dollars in cash. There were two different names on the cards in the two wallets.

Lying next to them was a set of keys. *These will need further investigation,* he thought.

The last item was baffling. A strange-looking Perspex container. It had no markings to identify it and was about the size of his baby girl's bottle warmer. He wondered why it was hidden amongst the other more interesting evidence, and picked it up for a closer look. But it was just an empty container.

"What the ...?"

49

Xeng assessed his captives and decided Nicki was the most expendable. The sick man was an engineer, so he might need him to fix the plane's undercarriage. Xeng would need the other man to refuel his plane and carry tools or spares. But perhaps the girl would have a use after all.

"You seem redundant, my dear," Xeng said calmly, aiming his pistol into her face. He started to squeeze the trigger, and Nicki involuntarily recoiled and closed her eyes.

"Stop!" shouted Melville, lifting his upper body off the floor with his good arm. "You've been infected, you'll need her to prepare antiserum for you, or you'll die!"

"Why?" Xeng asked calmly. "You said you're a doctor." He was enjoying this little game.

"I'm not a microbiologist. You need her alive!" Melville said, his voice rising. "If you kill her, you can kill me too," he added emphatically.

So I was right, Xeng thought, *the woman will have a use.* "Ah well, perhaps you're right. But if you disobey me, she dies," he said, still pointing the gun at Nicki's face. He looked over at the sick man, saw the grey pallor of the man's face and smelt the vomited blood and stomach acids. He decided Anakos was no threat.

"You ..." Xeng nodded toward Melville, "... get up and take me to your aviation fuel. You follow him," he added, looking at Nicki.

They left the hut, Nicki following Melville, feeling the gun still trained on the back of her head. No one had any doubts that this man would kill them in the blink of an eye.

"You need to be immunised, or you'll take this disease wherever you're going. If you make it alive ..." Melville said to Xeng, wondering whether he could inject an air bubble into a vein.

"Yes. You will prepare antiserum for me," Xeng said calmly. "But first, you will make my plane ready to fly," he added, as though he had all the time in the world.

Melville led them to the fuel supply hut. At least while they had this man's work to do they would stay alive, and there would be at least two trips back to the plane to refuel it. Melville walked in and managed to pick up two large, full fuel cans, struggling hard with his wounded arm.

Nicki could see fresh blood seeping through the dressing.

"You too," Xeng ordered, and Nicki picked up a jerry can, surprised at how heavy it was. "And another."

With more strength than she knew she had, Nicki picked up two cans and started to follow Melville up the track to the airstrip.

Xeng had counted four more jerry cans in the hut and had obviously decided he didn't need to get his own hands dirty. Nicki couldn't think of anything she could say or do that would help, in fact she really couldn't think of anything at all except Peter and Gary. *Where are they? Are they all right?*

The combination of the weight of the fuel cans and the biting cold was making Nicki's hands and arms ache; her fingers were going numb. As she struggled along behind Melville, she looked at the clearing sky and rising sun, thinking it was going to be a beautiful day. An odd thought, it occurred to her, for someone who was probably about to be killed. She glanced around as if to see what their captor was thinking and noticed that, as the man walked, he was surreptitiously scanning the brush on either side. *Gary and Peter must still be out there somewhere*, she thought hopefully.

The sun had started to rise now, but there was no warmth in it. Peter was crouched in bushes just outside the main base. He had to get closer to see what was happening and find some way to stop this maniac. But he needed some kind of weapon first. Could he make it into the supply hut? And would there be any guns there? What about the dormitory huts? He couldn't remember whether he had seen anything useful in them, but surely there would be something.

The man had killed Gary with a single shot from some distance, so Peter realised that he would not only need a weapon, he would need an element of surprise. And perhaps most of all, an element of luck, he thought grimly.

Peter saw the others in the distance, emerging from the hut. He quietly crouched further into the scrub, wincing as something scratched his bleeding arm. He strained his ears to listen to the voices, but they were too far away. He could only get a few words here and there. "... immunised ... make it alive."

Melville's voice.

"... first ... make my plane ready ... " Sharp, clear and emotionless.

The killer.

So, it seemed he was not here intentionally.

I need a gun, Peter thought again. The hut where Masters had holed up! *He would have had a gun*, Peter reasoned.

He watched as Melville disappeared into the hut where they kept fuel and other dangerous goods. Their assailant was watching Melville very closely, so Peter decided to take his chance now. He moved stealthily through the low scrub cover, skirting along the track to the birdwatcher's hut. He didn't think the wound on his arm was particularly deep, but it was still bleeding. He wondered how much blood he could lose before he would pass out. Up ahead, he saw the hut, hoping he was far enough ahead of the others, because he would need to break cover to get inside. If only it were still dark.

He ran through the door, looking back outside to see whether anyone was coming. The fact that he hadn't been shot was a good sign. There was a lot of blood on the floor. And broken glass. *That* might do, but he would need some way to hold it without slashing his hands. No, that wouldn't do after all; he would need to get very close to an armed man with two hostages. *Think man!*

He looked in the back room, and there it was. A flare pistol! *Now, how do these work? Just point and shoot,* he hoped. But would it be enough to stop a madman? He studied the pistol briefly and satisfied himself that the flare was properly loaded. He moved the safety clip to the 'ready' position, taking care not to hold the weapon by its trigger.

He peered through the door and saw no one approaching. He didn't know how long he had been in the hut, but it couldn't have been more than a few minutes, and he knew the others should be moving fairly slowly, carrying fuel and tools or whatever. He kept his head down and ran back towards the main track, turning to the airfield. He knew exactly where he was headed.

* * *

AUGUST 1 – ROSS ISLAND, ANTARCTICA

"Just somethin' for me 'ead, Doc," Bob said to Martin Brinksma. "Got a fearful sore throat, too," he added.

"Ven did you first notice dis?" Doc asked, and Bob Jacks told him about waking up during the night. Doc gave him a shot of the most powerful antibiotics he had, disregarding Bob's loud complaint, and some paracetamol. He then led Jacks into the sickbay, ignoring further protests.

"It's just a bloody cold," said Jacks a little defensively.

"I hef to find Ned, and you hef to stay here," Doc said forcefully, and

Bob reluctantly agreed.

Martin Brinksma ran off to find his friend John Kelly, with a tightening knot in the pit of his stomach.

50

Detective Constable Jackson quickly finished his rough notes on the search of the flat and phoned the NSO man, Taylor, as instructed. Jackson explained everything in detail, concluding with the find of the wallets with credit cards and cash. Taylor hadn't seemed overly interested in the unusual clothing and the fact that this man obviously lived a strange life, but when Jackson mentioned the plastic container Taylor had become quite agitated. Even more so when Jackson said it was empty.

Jackson was now driving back into the city, as Taylor had instructed, to a lane behind the Treasury Gardens. Taylor had not explained why and hadn't given Jackson the opportunity to ask. He'd just said 'don't get out of the car, don't open the window, don't stop for anyone, and don't take that container out of the evidence bag'.

As Jackson pulled off Jolimont Road onto Wellington Parade, he heard a helicopter close by. He was lucky it was Sunday; on any weekday, this trip would have taken him about an hour. He turned right into Lansdowne Street, and the chopper disappeared from view over to his left. He made a left turn into Treasury Place, as instructed, but he'd had no further instructions and there was nobody there to meet him. He continued slowly along the lane, following the road around to the right into Premier Lane, ignoring the No Public Access signs. There was a man up ahead, running towards his car, and the chopper had set down on the lawn just metres behind the running man.

He sprinted the two hundred metres to Jackson's car but wasn't out of breath. "You Jackson?" he asked.

"That's me," Jackson said, rolling down the window.

The man put a surgical face mask on. "What the ..."

"Come with me," the man in the mask said.

Jackson followed him to the chopper. "What's going on?" he asked, but the man didn't answer. "Come on, I have a right to know," he added, getting more than a little nervous now.

"Colles will explain," the man in the mask said unhelpfully. "Put this on." The man handed Jackson a surgical mask.

This isn't like any other murder case I've been involved in, Jackson thought. *Who the hell are these people?*

Colles had watched the helicopter land and then take off again from his window. He had just returned from another strained meeting with the Praying Mantis, in which she had threatened to blame 'this whole mess' on Colles and the NSO's bungling of the investigation.

"Minister, as you requested, my briefings have been verbal, but the fact that we've met numerous times this week *is* on the record. I would caution you against that course of action," Colles had said bluntly. He also informed her that she could not do anything without admitting that a significant risk of plague, potentially threatening the lives of every person in Melbourne and beyond, had been kept secret.

"You're in charge," he'd added, leaving her under no illusion.

If Colles's first point hadn't swayed her, his second point certainly had.

He walked briskly over to his desk and picked up the phone.

"Colles here. The container and the detective who found it are on their way to you now. I want to know, immediately they arrive, whether the lab people can identify the container. And I want the test results on both, the minute you have them. Are we any closer to a cure?" He listened for a few moments.

"Very well. Call me right away if anything changes," he said grimly.

Colles sat down heavily at his desk, exhaling loudly. He thought about Dr Palmer, wondering what she had found down on Macquarie. He had thought of Nicki Palmer earlier in the day, too, after he'd been informed that the tracking device on Xeng's plane had either failed, or he had strayed too far out of range. Radar was of no use either.

The last confirmed location they had was that Xeng was heading south-east of New Zealand, and that didn't make any sense to Colles. He was confident that Xeng's radio-controlled detonation device would now be out of range, but he couldn't be completely sure. They had to find that biohazard material! Why was the container in Xeng's man's flat? Had Xeng's man decided to change the plan and keep some insurance of his own?

In fact, a part of Colles hoped Xeng had crashed into the freezing ocean and drowned, but he wanted confirmation that the bacteria was neutralised first. He also knew it would get very difficult for him if he didn't get the Americans' money back. They were a bit touchy about people who lost twenty million dollars of their cash.

It seemed to Colles as though there was now a great deal riding on Dr Palmer's progress on the island.

51

Peter had found the trench he had fallen into when they first encountered the shooter. It wasn't so much a trench as a deep furrow, but it would provide enough cover, he thought. But *how* was he going to do this? He had to shoot the man with a flare gun and somehow not get Melville and Nicki killed in the process. He had no idea how accurate flare pistols were – what if he missed and shot a fuel can?

He assumed aviation fuel was even more volatile than regular fuel; it would no doubt explode on contact, possibly killing them all. Even if he successfully shot the man, would a flare kill him, or even knock him down? So many questions.

Surely it would at least surprise the man and throw him off balance, Peter reasoned. Enough time for Melville to grab him, maybe. But what if Nicki was between them? He had to try to focus.

In the end, Peter resolved that he would stand up in plain sight when the three of them were walking past, almost at right angles to them. That way the man would have to turn to fire at Peter, thereby taking his gun off Nicki and David. At the same moment, Peter would fire the flare directly at the man's chest, where it would stand the best chance of knocking him down at the same time as setting fire to his clothing.

He had to hope it would be enough of a distraction that he and Melville could charge the man and get his gun. If Nicki was angry enough, she would charge the man too, he knew. It should work, he decided, if they didn't get in each other's way.

If the flare pistol didn't fire, or Peter missed, he would probably be shot, Peter thought grimly, but that would at least give Melville and Nicki a chance to stop the man, and he knew they had to try. The man had shot Masters in cold blood and tried to kill Peter, without even knowing who they were, so he would obviously have no compunction about ensuring there were no survivors on the island to inform the authorities. He looked down at his arm to see his sleeve wet with blood, but there was no time to think about that; he could hear the others approaching.

Nicki's hands were numb, and both her arms were aching badly. Her legs, too. She was shattered before they started on the track to airfield, and was now beyond exhaustion, fuelled only by the pain in her limbs and the nervous energy that came from having a gun pointed at her. Melville was walking ahead in silence. All she could hear was his hard breathing as he slowly but tenaciously marched ahead. If Melville slowed too much, Xeng snapped at them menacingly to hurry up.

Nicki couldn't help but wonder what would happen to them when the plane was refuelled and they were of no further use to this man. There was little chance they could stop him; neither she nor Melville had the energy or strength to overpower him, and by the time they turned and dropped the jerry cans, he could probably easily shoot either or even both of them. But they had to find a way to stop him; he could not be allowed to take the plague with him.

Perhaps when they injected him with the antiserum, they could find a way to get the gun. But he seemed to have thought of everything. And where were Peter and Gary? Would they be up ahead, lying dead on the track? The man was still keeping an eye on the vegetation around them; surely that meant there was still a threat somewhere. Or perhaps he was just very cautious.

Then, as they made their way over a small ridge, she saw a man lying on the track ahead and her heart leapt into her mouth. She couldn't see who it was, but someone was either unconscious or dead. The evil man behind her was completely unconcerned.

"He won't be of any assistance today," Xeng said, smiling coldly at her. "Keep moving!" he barked.

Gary, she thought. She recognised his clothing. And a few metres closer she saw his eyes were open, staring at the sky. *Where's Peter? Did he get away?* She could picture him lying in a ditch, as cold and lifeless as Masters, and shivered involuntarily. *Maybe he's waiting at the plane, ready for an ambush,* she rationalised. *But surely Peter would realise this man would be prepared for that. And the man is armed, Peter isn't.* As they walked past Gary's body, she thought she heard a noise off to the left. Melville had heard it too, he was turning with her. Then she saw Peter, standing or kneeling, she couldn't tell, and he was pointing a strange-looking gun at them.

The cold-eyed man had whirled left with them, and had his pistol pointed at Peter.

"No!" she screamed, throwing herself half sideways, half forward at him. At the same instant, she thought she heard two shots fired, one a deafening crack near her ear, and the other a deeper a more muffled sound, more of a thud than gunfire. She felt a sharp, explosive pain in the temple and felt her legs buckle beneath her. As she fell to the ground, the world went dark and silent.

Peter had steeled himself as the moment approached. He hoped the murderer would be momentarily distracted as they walked past Gary's lifeless form. His stomach was clenched in a knot of fear and anger as they approached Masters. 'Keep moving,' he had heard the man growl at Nicki, who was just in front of him. A few more metres and this would be it. *This is the moment when one of us will probably die.* His stomach turned somersaults.

He would have to act very quickly, but needed enough time to aim the flare pistol carefully; Nicki was so close to his target. These thoughts seemed to be somehow outside of his body, and he recognised the rush of adrenaline taking hold of the primitive parts of his brain. He quickly stood up and aimed the flare pistol at the man with the gun. He squeezed the trigger, discovering that it required more pressure than he had imagined. The gunman turned suddenly and Peter was staring at the barrel of his pistol. Nicki and Melville both lurched towards their captor at the same instant the flare gun fired. Peter heard the other gunshot, but he was not hit. Then Nicki slumped to the ground.

"Oh God!" Peter cried out and leapt over to Nicki, without thinking. An inhuman scream drowned his ears, and he saw the gunman writhing on the ground. Melville must have knocked the man down, and was wrestling the pistol out of his hand. *Crack!* Another shot. There was an acrid smell of smoke and burning flesh in the air, and Peter saw the man clutching at his face. *The flare! I must have hit my target.*

Melville now had the man's pistol and was standing over him. Peter got to Nicki, lying motionless on the track. There had been no muzzle flash when the man had fired his gun at Peter. *Nicki must have thrown herself into the line of fire.* He saw Melville out of the corner of his eye, and something in the look of revulsion on his face made Peter look away from Nicki, and at their captor lying near her feet.

The man was still screaming and clawing at his face, from which a cloud of thick smoke was rising. Peter could barely make out what was happening, but as it came into focus, he felt physically sick. The flare had indeed hit its target. It had caught the man on the left side of his face as he had turned away from Nicki and Melville, piercing his cheek and embedding itself in the soft flesh of the man's throat. It was still burning. The torn flesh at the entry wound was now charred black, as were both of the man's hands as he tried to pull it out. He was being burnt alive.

Peter watched as Melville took aim and fired a bullet into the man's forehead. It wasn't so much from pity that Melville shot him, nor was it the sight and smell of the man's face and hair burning, but Melville knew that if the man managed to get the flare out, there were four cans of aviation fuel much too close for comfort.

The screaming stopped, and the man's hands fell to his sides. The flare was dying too, the red glow disappearing and the awful sound of sizzling flesh almost gone. Melville slumped to his knees and vomited; he had watched the man's face disintegrate. He had seen some terrible things before, but never anything like this.

Peter had scanned Nicki for a bullet wound and had cupped her face in his hands, gently rolling her to the side. She was breathing.

"Nicki! Nicki, no!" he implored her, and miraculously, she obliged. She moved her head to one side slightly and started to open her eyes. Slowly, she moved her hand to her head.

Peter could see the bullet graze just below her left temple. He felt the tears welling up in his eyes, as he looked into hers. "Are you okay?" he asked, immediately feeling rather foolish.

"Just wonderful," Nicki lied.

Just over an hour later, Melville had returned to the station. He, Peter and Nicki had walked back to the hut, supporting each other, and he left Nicki and Peter together. Nicki assured him that she was okay, it was just a graze and she'd fallen more from the shock of it than anything else. Melville was running, albeit awkwardly, back to the airfield.

Nicki and Peter found Nick Anakos lying where they had left him. They had feared the worst, but Anakos was still alive, his breathing still laboured and no better than before, but at least it was no worse. He looked very pale, but he opened his eyes when they walked in.

"What happened?" he rasped, and Nicki quietly explained. Peter marvelled at the way she calmly described almost being killed.

"Lovely morning out there," Melville said as he returned to the hut. "We have to get to work," he added. "I've contacted Colles, it took a while, but eventually I managed to get through with the plane's communications equipment. He's sending two planes, one will take you three, along with most of that," he was pointing to the antiserum, "back to Melbourne, where you'll be quarantined. They've got someone there who may also be infected."

Nicki and Peter both started asking questions when Melville held his hand up. "I don't know," he said. "Our work is here right now. The other plane is taking me and the rest of that stuff down to the Ross base. It seems they have a possible outbreak down there, too."

"But how ..." Peter started.

"I don't know that either, but Colles said they had found another one of your stones. He didn't see how, either, but he said your friend Kelly had been adamant that the stone you took back to Melbourne should be locked up safe somewhere."

"It is. Well sort of ..." Peter said, picturing it in his study at home.

"No, it isn't," said Nicki, becoming concerned. She explained how she had given it to Professor Morton to get the analysis under way. "He told me you two had discussed it," she added, now very worried.

"We've got to get a message to him. Now!" Peter exclaimed, dragging his weary frame off the stretcher bed.

Peter and Melville both set off back to the airstrip, leaving Nicki with the sleeping Anakos. Nicki checked his fever, which had clearly broken. At least they could be fairly sure they had an effective antiserum.

But another outbreak on Ross Island? Where had this disease come from? *Could* it be the stones? Sure, the stone she had seen certainly had some weird properties, of that she had no doubt, but could they somehow be carrying the bacteria? Who would seal a life-threatening plague in stone? And *how*, for that matter?

Melville managed to raise Colles on the radio again, and through bursts of static they had managed to get their message understood. Colles would track Morton down.

52

It was another cold, winter night. There had been snow in the nearby hills earlier, and the wind felt like it was coming straight up from the Antarctic. Peter longed to be back at his home, but it was not to be. Not just yet. He knew he was lucky to be alive. They were all lucky to be alive. Inevitably, he thought of those who were not so lucky. Gary Masters, who had been to hell and back, and who had provided the life-giving antibodies that had saved Nicki, Melville, Anakos, himself – only to be shot down in cold blood by a ruthless killer.

And the tragedy of the Macquarie base. Thirty-six people dead; their last days filled with dread as one after another had died from the mysterious plague of unknown origin, unable to contact their loved ones on the mainland to even say goodbye.

Taylor told him earlier that they had finally found Xeng's device in the Cardinia Reservoir. It was now safe and sound; in fact, it had always been safe and sound. There was a tiny explosive charge attached to the container, probably just enough to crack it open without vaporising the contents, but there was no radio receiver of any kind, just a simple timer.

Apparently Xeng's intention had been that the device would detonate and infect the city's water supply after a preset time. The transmitter was just a ruse. But the irony was that the timer had never been set; it wasn't even properly connected to the charge. Perhaps Xeng's man had a conscience. Or, more likely, perhaps he simply decided he wanted to stay in Melbourne.

The makeshift quarantine quarters – the smaller of the Yea labs – although spartan, was luxurious compared to the last few days. There was plenty of room for all of them. Peter hit the stretcher bed and was almost asleep within minutes, but Nicki had another idea.

She deftly pulled the frame away from the stretcher's padding and pushed it to one side, leaving a small mattress on the floor. She made Peter get up and she did the same to his, then pushed the padding together.

"That's more like it," she said, pulling Peter close as he lay down. "I used to be a girl guide."

"Really?"

"No. Hold me."

Peter pulled up the blanket and happily did as he was told.

He kissed Nicki and wished her 'sweet dreams', and the irony was not lost on her. He held her close, listening to the soft snoring of the three other men in the quarantine room, and they soon drifted into a deep sleep.

An hour earlier, one of Colles's men, a big man named Taylor, had confirmed they had got hold of John Morton and warned him. The stone was now in a sealed container on its way to Yea. Tomorrow morning, they would open it up in the lab and find out what the hell it really was.

Eleven hours later, a repeated knocking on the door woke them. Colles. He told them Morton had arrived and they were going to open up the stone. Nicki, Peter and the others could switch on the monitors in the room to view it. They were going to do it in the main lab's cell.

Nicki was now awake and sitting up. Peter looked at her. She had some superficial scratches on her face, her hair was messed up and her eyes were still sleepy and red. But Peter couldn't stop looking at her.

"I must be a sight," she said.

"A beautiful sight."

"Very funny."

But I mean it, Peter thought.

They turned on the screen and saw Professor Morton directing someone installing some heavy equipment in the little cell. They heard Morton say it would take a while, as they would have to set up to do the drilling by remote control.

Nicki found the intercom for the labs and surprised Morton when her voice came through the speakers.

"Hello, John," she said.

"Hi, John," Peter added. "Why remote control?"

"Because we don't know what's in it, old man," Morton replied, looking around the room for the source of the disembodied voices. "It could be the source of the bacteria."

"But Nicki and I have been exposed to the bacteria already, and we've been treated with antiserum. I can do it."

"Good point," Colles conceded, knowing it would save a lot of time. "Very well, but you'll have to do it in the cell. We're not taking any unnecessary risks."

A brief pause, then a female voice followed. "You'll find masks in the storage cupboard in your room. You'll need to put one on. Nicki can help you."

Chris Telford.

"Hi, Chris," Nicki said, opening the cupboard.

"I'm so glad you're back safely," Chris replied.

Peter put on the mask and Nicki double-checked it to make sure it was secure. Chris, wearing a mask herself, unlocked the quarantined lab to let Peter out.

As Peter walked through the main lab, Morton pointed out a tool that looked like a shiny and very hi-tech angle grinder.

"Bone-cutter," said Morton. "Seems appropriate, don't you think?"

Peter took the equipment into the cell along with the stone in its sealed container and began setting up. While he worked, he heard Nicki's voice through the intercom system.

"How are the people at Ross base?" she asked.

"One of the men was infected, but he's been treated and the prognosis is good," Colles said. "They're quarantined for a while, but we expect they're all going to be all right," he added, softening his voice a little, as he looked at the camera. "Thanks to you, Nicki. All of you."

As Peter finished his set-up, Colles explained that the last stone was on its way from Antarctica, so if they were the source of the infection, the 'problem will be contained'. They were all feeling anxious; nobody could see *how* these stones could be the source, but everyone believed the stones had something to do with it. And if they did, then *why*? Who would seal deadly bacteria into a vessel like this? Why not just destroy it? A chilling thought struck Nicki: what if these are the world's first biological weapons? As long as man has existed, we have been finding new and horrific ways of killing our fellow man.

"Ready!" Peter announced. He had secured the stone just above the bench with two clamps and was holding the bone saw in his hand. The stone was shielded behind a Perspex screen, and Peter had put on protective gloves. The cell was locked, and the nervous excitement in the room was now at a peak. Everyone was peering in, or at a screen, willing Peter to get on with it!

"Okay," he said. "Here we go." He switched on the bone saw and started to carefully cut an even line around the girth of the stone. Fine dust quickly coated the clear screen, and Peter had to find a cloth to wipe it off. After a couple of minutes, he switched off the device.

"I think it's overheating." He waited for a few interminably long minutes as the machine's blade cooled.

"Maybe if you wet the stone?" Morton suggested. But as he spoke Peter had started the saw again.

"I'm through," they heard him say. "There's some fluid leaking out."

They watched him look around the cell, eventually finding a small pan to put underneath the stone. He managed to wedge the plastic tray between the clamps and set back to work.

"Done! he soon exclaimed triumphantly.

The clear screen was coated with dust again, so he wiped it clean and the others watched as he separated the two halves of the stone.

"Oh my God," he said quietly.

They watched as he turned slowly to the window, holding the plastic pan so they could see it. There, sitting in a pool of yellowish liquid, was *a human eye.*

Nicki recoiled in horror. "Oh my God!" echoing Peter's words.

"Remarkable," said Morton.

"But why? Why would anyone do that? Safely preserving a deadly disease for millennia?" Nicki asked.

"I think the bacteria is just incidental. Probably what killed him. Or her. I'd say this looks like part of an ancient burial rite," said Morton. "This has been beautifully and painstakingly preserved. I don't know what tools existed thousands of years ago that could do this, but you must agree, these stones are beautiful. This is not a weapon."

"I think he's right," added Peter. "It makes sense. Many cultures believe eyes are the window to the soul. I think these stones could be something like vessels for the souls of the dead, perhaps of the elite or ruling class, or their equivalent."

"So you're suggesting Ross Station drilled into an ancient cemetery?" asked Melville, followed by voice and noise coming through the intercom.

"Nicki!" Melville's voice.

Peter instinctively leapt to the cell door to get out, finding it locked. "What's happened?" he called in alarm.

"She's fainted," Melville replied. She was lucky Melville had noticed her face suddenly go very pale, as soon as Peter had separated the stone. He caught her as her legs buckled under her.

"Is she all right?" Peter cried.

A moment's silence, and a shuffling sound through the intercom.

"She'll be all right," Melville said. Peter wished he could see her face. "I think she's coming around."

Peter's heart was racing, and he felt trapped in the small cell. He wished he could run to her. Then he thought he could hear her voice but didn't catch what she said.

"Saw who?" Melville asked her.

"I saw him again," Nicki repeated slowly. "Peter, the man from the vision. He was coming towards me again. I felt an overwhelming sadness. Like I couldn't breathe again."

The others were looking at each other, bewildered.

"I think John's right. This is some sort of ancient burial rite. There was darkness. I felt his *despair*. I could see him, and I could feel his pain and loss, but he couldn't see me or hear me. I think maybe it was me. *I* was the person that eye belonged to. Maybe the man's wife or child. I think he was *burying* me."

Epilogue

"I told you it was beautiful." Nicki was looking through the small window of the aircraft, down at green, tree-lined hills peppered with lovely old timber houses. They would be landing in a few minutes. The sun was shining and the water of the harbour looked inviting, though Peter was sure it would be very cold.

It does look beautiful.

Peter closed his eyes and thoughts of a distant place filled his mind. One day, he thought, the human race would unravel the mystery of Antarctica, of its civilisation that had apparently flourished thousands of years ago. What happened to those people? Were they decimated by a deadly plague? The existence of the ancient maps suggests there were survivors. People like Gary Masters, with an immunity. There must have been people who took the knowledge of their homeland to other parts of the world. A homeland that could not have been covered in kilometres of ice.

Thoughts raced through Peter's mind. *Was there some cataclysmic event that caused the continent to be 'snap-frozen'? An asteroid, or a comet, perhaps. But surely Antarctica couldn't have had a temperate climate, could it?* He knew there were theories about polar movement. *But wasn't that just the*

328

magnetic field moving; surely not the movement of the whole of the earth's crust?

Morton said he'd read of a theory of earth crust displacement and that the North Pole was once in Hudson Bay, Canada. If that were true, that would put parts of Antarctica (and the Ross Sea) roughly where southern New Zealand is today. *Could that be possible?* Half a world away, in the Arctic Circle, there have been prehistoric animals, including woolly mammoths, found buried in the permafrost in Siberia with undigested plants that come from much warmer climates.

Peter believed that today's accepted science couldn't explain these anomalies, but something like a displacement of the whole of the earth's crust probably could. If the North Pole had been near Hudson Bay, then Siberia would have been much further south. *Could an event like an asteroid impact cause this sort of displacement? A shift of the planet's orbital axis, or a dramatic tectonic movement? What sort of catastrophic event would that be?* It would probably trigger huge earthquakes, unimaginable tsunamis and extreme volcanic activity.

"Look at that," Nicki said, pointing to a small colony of seals on the deserted shore. They were just metres from the runway.

It had been a month since Peter, Nicki and the others were allowed to leave the Yea facility. Just enough time to fully recover from their injuries.

We've been to hell and back, Peter thought. He squeezed Nicki's hand as the plane touched down. They hadn't wanted to leave each other's side since getting back to Australia.

They had planned to stay in Wellington a few weeks, for Nicki to make the necessary arrangements to move her life back to Australia. Peter had been overjoyed when she said it was time to come home.

Author's Note

First of all, I would like to thank my family for their patience and support, and Louise Kendall for advice and encouragement.

Special thanks to Adrienne Charlton at AM Publishing for frank feedback, insightful advice and a sharp eye.

There are many others who have listened, advised and contributed in important ways, including Conor Occleshaw, Marie Occleshaw, and John and Anne Schofield.

Any residual mistakes are, of course, all mine.

Locations

The locations depicted in this story are real. However, the descriptions of the bases at Ross Island, Antarctica and on Macquarie Island, as well as the various government facilities depicted in this story, are my own invention.

Ross Island is a New Zealand dependency, and I am not aware of an Australian research station in that territory, but there is a long history of close collaboration between the two nations' governments.

Characters

All characters in this story are fictional. An author's quandary is to describe realistic protagonists and antagonists, for the latter often describing evil characteristics, without impugning any actual individuals or groups. In this story, the primary malefactor happens to be Chinese. I have never met a Chinese person with characteristics like his, and in my travels to China have only ever encountered warm, friendly and helpful people.

Over the past decade or so, I have worked with many cabinet ministers and senior officials, and in my experience these are generally good people working to make a positive difference. Some of the characters in this story are less savoury and are not based on any individuals.

Further reading and references

The theory of earth crust displacement was postulated by Professor

Charles Hapgood in his 1958 publication *Earth's Shifting Crust*.[1] He explored this theory further in *Maps of the Ancient Sea Kings*.[2] Hapgood's theory draws in part from the existence of ancient maps, specifically including the ones I've referred to throughout this book.

I first read *Maps of the Ancient Sea Kings* some years ago, after finding a reference to Einstein's foreword for Hapgood's book and correspondence between the two. Albert Einstein was quoted as saying he found the theory 'electrifying'. I found it very interesting too, and it was the germ of this idea. Pardon the pun.

The idea of an epidemic with influenza and pneumonia related symptoms is not a new one. There have been many similar events throughout recorded history, one of the more recent catastrophic incidents being the Spanish influenza pandemic of 1918–19. This was, of course, before the discovery of penicillin by Sir Alexander Fleming in 1928. The bacterial plague of this novel is entirely imaginary, although the threat is real, and antibiotic- resistant bacteria are on the rise.

A few years ago, I read Dr Geoffrey Rice's book on the effects of the Spanish flu pandemic in New Zealand.[3] His book gave me a good sense of the horrors of that global outbreak of a virulent influenza and, more particularly, the bacterial infections that followed it, killing millions.

A final word ...

I hope you've enjoyed reading *The Relic* as much as I enjoyed researching and writing it. My next novel, *The Doomsday Tablet*, will be released early next year.

William Henshaw, December 2019.

---

[1] Hapgood, Charles H, *Earth's Shifting Crust*. New York, 1958.
[2] Hapgood, Charles H, *Maps of the Ancient Sea Kings: Evidence of Advanced Civilization in the Ice Age*. Philadelphia, 1966.
[3] Rice, Geoffrey, *Black November: The 1918 Influenza Pandemic in New Zealand*. Christchurch, 1988.

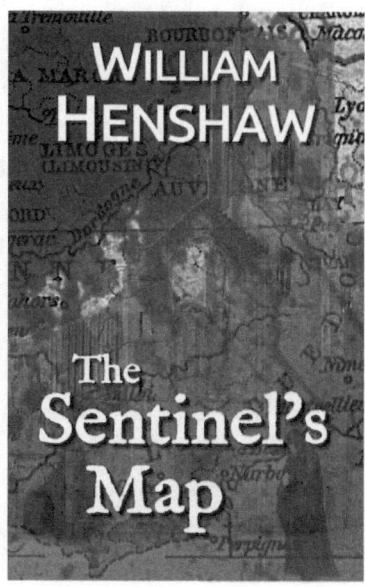

PROLOGUE

"Tell me, old man!"

The stricken man sat in his leather captain's chair, one of three antique chairs in the timber-panelled room.

It was warm; a small fire burned in the Victorian cast-iron fireplace. A black iron poker protruded from the red coals at an awkward angle, as if thrust drunkenly into the grate. Ash had spilled onto the flagstone hearth. A crystal tumbler of whisky sat on the leather-inset oak desk, a half-empty bottle resting just behind it.

The older man picked up the glass and drew a good measure of the liquor across his dry lips. His assailant, wearing a black robe over trousers and socks, towered over him; his shoes were presumably outside the house, a precaution that had enabled him to reach the room without being heard. He was dressed totally in black, including his strange and ominous headwear – a medieval executioner's mask.

The mask covered the man's head as far as his nose, where it split, allowing it to protrude. His mouth and chin were visible beneath. He had a broad nose and thick lips, and his neck was muscular. His face seemed to be expressionless, impassive. He was clean-shaven and spoke calmly, with an unexpected pitch of voice reminiscent of Peter Lorre. The older man reflected momentarily that this giant would be a generation too young to have heard of Peter Lorre.

The assailant suddenly struck out, knocking the tumbler and its contents across the room. It flew past the open safe and smashed against the wall.

"Tell me where it is," he repeated.

The man held the interloper's gaze unsteadily but remained silent as he attempted to place the accent. Eastern Europe, he decided.

He knew what he had to do. No matter his fear of what his attacker was about to do, he would not forget the words he'd repeated to himself over the years.

He had some idea what to expect from his assailant. Immediately after the man entered the room, he had silently picked up the poker and thrust it into the fire, then lifted him out of his chair by the throat and softly demanded that he open the safe. After some remonstration, he had agreed to comply.

The safe was set into the wall to the right of the desk, and the intruder had stepped politely out of the way to allow the man to reach it. Only when he pulled the door open did the intruder quickly approach to ensure there was no concealed weapon. He had slowly withdrawn a small bundle of banknotes and some papers and carefully placed them on the desk.

"Take whatever you want." He slumped back into his chair, his breathing shallow.

"I don't need this." He struck the man across the face, a brutally crunching blow with the back of his closed fist. "You know what I want," he went on quietly. "Tell me where it is and this will stop."

The man in the chair wished he still had his whisky. He knew this was not going to stop. Blood dripped from his nose onto his crisp white shirt.

"We've been hunting your kind for centuries. We know you have it."
The aggressor leaned in close, and the older man could smell mint on his
breath. It seemed incongruent. "Tell me now."

"I don't know what you're talking about," the man replied, with a
tremor in his voice. "Take the money. It's all I have."

"I don't want money." The huge figure in black loomed over the chair,
the upper part of his robe parting slightly to expose a tattoo of the
crucifixion on his chest. He crossed himself and struck the older man hard
under the chin. As his victim slumped groggily, he quickly retrieved the
poker from the fire. He crossed himself again, and with his left hand, he
gripped the man's throat with breathtaking force, driving his head into
the back of the captain's chair. At the same time, he placed his left knee
across the man's legs to further restrain him.

The older man could not move. Aside from the attacker's strength and
weight, he was frozen with an unexpected mixture of impotent fear and a
resolute determination. The intruder's impassive expression did not
change as the glowing poker pressed into the old man's left eye. He
screamed as he struggled desperately to turn his head away. He could
barely breathe, but as he did, he could smell the burnt flesh of his eyelid.
The pain seared through his body, and although his eyes were screwed
shut, he was sure he glimpsed a wisp of smoke rising from his left eye
socket.

He briefly lost consciousness, a blessing soon curtailed as the big man
threw whisky in his face straight from the bottle.

"Tell me where it is and this will stop."

He could not speak. The pain in his left eye was excruciating. An awful
smell of burnt flesh and liquor, tinged with the coppery scent of blood,
filled his nostrils. Whisky was in his eyes, and each time he blinked he
wanted to scream again.

The big man's face was just inches from his. He mustered all the
strength he had left. "I don't know what you're talking about." His voice
was weak and fearful; ethereal and unworldly. Nothing like the strong and
confident voice he had trained and perfected throughout his life.

"Dei gratia," said the big man softly. He crossed himself again and pressed the poker into the man's chest. There was a sizzling sound as the poker burned the whisky, blood and skin. He kept pushing. *He seems to have boundless strength*, thought the older man, by now unable to move, his good eye blinded by the pain. The poker seared the flesh as it slowly penetrated his rib cage, finding its way through the pulmonary artery and right ventricle, ultimately coming to rest in the plush padding of the chair's ageing leather upholstery.

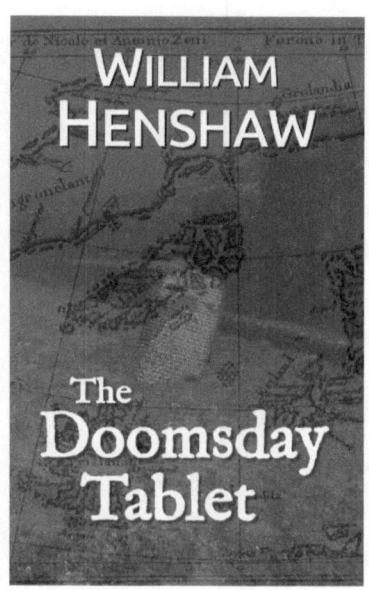

An ancient stone tablet is dredged up from the Mid-Atlantic. Generations later, archaeologist John Foxton begins to decipher the tablet's dark and mysterious omen.

Daniel Reade, historian, discovers notes his great-grandfather Foxton had concealed before his murder during World War II. Foxton believed the tablet was more than a doomsday prophecy. Something far more dangerous.

Archaeologist Elisa Mansfield is drawn into the mystery and soon unearths another tablet. The pair are thrown into a dangerous adventure involving an ancient civilisation destroyed by its own hand, a secret organisation born during the Nazi era, and a cataclysmic weapon based on the lost technology.

A fourteenth-century map and lost manuscript seem to hold the key to the destroyed civilisation, but how is this possible?

The stakes are high as Daniel and Elisa race to stay ahead of the organisation, and to understand what happened thousands of years earlier.

www.williamhenshaw.com